Praise for Gerald Seymour

'If le Carré had written at ...
Sey: ...   ial
    ...   . personnel. [A] masterly novel'
    The Sunday T ... on The Foot Soldiers

'There are strong echoes of George Smiley in Merrick's mild and unprepossessing manner, which disguises a razor-sharp brain and considerable courage when necessary'
Financial Times on The Foot Soldiers

'A cleverly nuanced climax in which tables are unexpectedly turned more than once . . . marks this as a novel of real quality. Top brass'
The Times on The Foot Soldiers

'Seymour's finger is always on the current socio-political pulse, and the new book is a welcome return for his curmudgeonly MI5 man Jonas Merrick'
i news on The Foot Soldiers

'This is multi-layered spy-fi at its best, with Seymour showing that even after thirty-seven novels he has lost none of his talent for thrilling plots and creating credible and sympathetic characters, nor his journalist's eye for modern espionage tradecraft and techniques'
Shots Magazine on The Foot Soldiers

'Ask aficionados who is Britain's finest thriller writer, and many would answer the veteran Gerald Seymour'
Guardian on Beyond Recall

Also by Gerald Seymour

THE
FOOT
SOLDIERS

Gerald Seymour

HODDER

First published in Great Britain in 2022 by Hodder & Stoughton
An Hachette UK company

This paperback edition published in 2022

1

A CIP catalogue record for this title is available from the British Library

Paperback ISBN 978 1 529 34044 0

Typeset in Plantin Light by Hewer Text UK Ltd, Edinburgh
Printed and bound in Great Britain by Clays Ltd, Elcograf S.p.A.

Hodder & Stoughton policy is to use papers that are natural, renewable
and recyclable products and made from wood grown in sustainable
forests. The logging and manufacturing processes are expected to
conform to the environmental regulations of the country of origin.

Hodder & Stoughton Ltd
Carmelite House
50 Victoria Embankment
London EC4Y 0DZ

www.hodder.co.uk

For Gillian

PROLOGUE

November

"What's the bet he's a dangle?"

"You reckon? A dangle?"

"Could be."

"It's a tasty one for them. Drop him in, lead us on a song and dance. Waved in front of us and we leap up like it's Christmas come early. Well briefed on what to look for, listen for. Learns what we know, then does a runner. That's what I call a dangle."

Wally said, "Looks cocky enough, doesn't he?"

Doug said, "Cat with a bowl of cream."

"And us running around after him like blue-arsed flies."

Neither were well humoured. Both had been roused out of their pits a little after three in the morning. It should have been Doug's youngest's birthday party later that day and should have been a visit to a store with his wife for Wally to look at a tumble dryer before the present one burned their home down. They were private military contractors: hired muscle. They were where the employment was. One was a former Royal Marine and the other had been a Protection Officer with the police up north. They had been at the airport at six, had been met by Frances, who'd seemed calm enough and clean and smart in a neutral way. In the departure lounge they'd shared the use of an electric razor and been on the first flight of the day to Copenhagen. Had been picked up at the airport by the team from the Denmark station – Griff and the Embassy security guy, Brian – and driven to the hotel, rather nice, decent view out over a bay. He'd shown up about an hour later.

The two of them, Wally and Doug, might have been at a county agricultural show, examining a bullock in the ring. It came from proven and tested land and should have been the proper business. If it were the proper business, then this bullock was doing a handsome job of confusing them.

He had introduced himself as Igor.

They'd spotted him when he had driven into the hotel parking area. He'd taken a grip bag out of the boot, then had slammed down the lid as if he were no longer the proud owner of that top-selling little Japanese car, not important to him any longer. He'd looked around him briefly, checking to see he was not tailed. Wally knew the Service jargon better than Doug did. Wally had suggested the guy could be a "dangle", but earlier had muttered something about competent "dry cleaning" ... It was the sort of talk that they enjoyed when having a quiet beer somewhere far from eavesdroppers, and both could take the piss out of their employers and the language that the staffer spies used which was thought to enhance elitism. Wally could handle any weapon from an anti-tank missile launcher through a heavy machine gun and down to a marksman's rifle. Doug was blessed with good eyes and fast hands and preferred a Glock 9mm pistol and an H&K short-range assault weapon. They were not armed. Had nothing between them other than competent unarmed combat drills. It would have been comforting to have had some sort of firearm tucked into a belt and out of sight below their heavy fleeces, if only because he was a Russian, bent – so he had said – on defection, and there must have been a chance that his brothers and sisters in their Embassy would come after him and not been coy as to what methods of force they'd employ to get him back. Two of the Danish PET boys, perimeter security they supposed, were lounging in chairs outside the room that had been arranged for them; they'd have had firepower, but it would have been a moot point if they'd use it. Right at the start, Wally had run an eye over the PET boy pair and had said from the side of his mouth, "Don't look much like Vikings to me ..." And had been answered, in a stage whisper, "They were Vikings a thousand years ago, a proper lot of water under that old bridge since then." Brian, the Embassy security chief, would have carried gas and pepper stuff in the shoulder bag that dangled off him, but not a shooter. And time was ticking and they'd not be on the move before the heavy mob came into town.

Truth was, and Griff had already said it: "He's brought next to nothing with him. I said to him last night that he should clear out every bloody file he could get his fingers into. The more the merrier. Paper and discs. Go for broke because he's not going back, emphasised it. Had to have a complete clear-out of their system . . . I mean, I knew of him, but he wasn't a target. We didn't rate him as an A-list celeb, only a bit of a gofer. There he was, and I'm on the beach walking the dog. Comes up to me . . . bold as brass . . . not furtive. 'You are Mr Griffin? Yes?' I must have looked blank, perplexed. 'Come on, Mr Griffin, it is not necessary to be shy. Where I work, we have a good file on you, a fat file, and you are respected.' I told him that he would need to excuse me as my dog needed walking. Did not faze him. 'Mr Griffin, I think you should be quite pleased, I am . . .' Gave his name, and his rank, said he was GRU, and that he intended to defect to us in the morning, and I gave him the usual splatter about coming to an arrangement and staying in place – which he ignored. 'No, Mr Griffin, it is tomorrow morning, and I am coming to you and no turning back and I will not look behind me. That is it, a decision made.' So, then it was all the stuff about clearing out every file he could lay his hands on last night, enough for a wheelbarrow load, or three."

That's what Griff had said. They had heard the first questions that the station chief had put to the Russian, and the answers were in good English, clear sentences but not vernacular. First up was the answer that very little had come with him. He was an officer in the Military Intelligence section attached to the Embassy. He had the rank of major in the Glavnoe razvedyvatel'noe upravlenie, and he should have been a treasure trove. Both Wally and Doug had heard the response to the question "And what have you managed to bring out with you?" GRU was top of the pile, the best quality intelligence-gathering organisation they had in their Federation, but he had shaken his head and had said with a dismissive waft of the hand – as if it were a trivial matter – that there had been colleagues in the inner sanctuary of the Embassy on Kristianiagade, white stucco and modern, and he had not thought it prudent to be seen downloading, printing, stacking material in a bag, nor hitting the keys and filling a memory stick. He had brought very little with him, and that he had detailed. They had seen the frown knit deeper on Griff's forehead. The man had shrugged and had said that he had plenty to say, that he would be most useful and had launched into a brief monologue of attitudes and policies emanating from the current Kremlin apparatchiks.

They were brought more coffee and a plate of biscuits.

Wally said, "Thank you, ma'am."

Doug said, "Grateful, miss, appreciated."

Not a hint of a smile in reaction, but she told them in a clean, clear, quiet voice, "Actually I'm not called Miss, Ma'am, or even Frances. Always known as Frank . . . Excuse me."

Griff came over to them – looked in poor humour.

"Talked my head off, haven't I? Need to know and all that crap, and I'm gossiping to a degree that would embarrass a good old-fashioned fishwife. Why am I spreading my supposed wisdom so far and wide? Talking too much because there's bits not making the best sense, so I'm trying to bounce it all at you. Breaking every rule in the book, but you would have heard his responses. Could have read that off the front page of any British broadsheet. Can I tell you something, boys?"

"Feel free."

"Unburden, usually the best way."

Both were looking past Griff across the room. The Russian was standing at the window, had opened it wide, his elbow on the ledge. Rain spattered the arm of his jacket. He had already tossed three fag ends out of the window into the jungle of bushes below. There was a No Smoking sign by the window. He had a good head of hair, thick, with a haphazard parting, and his eyes were darting and his gaze penetrating so that he seemed to strip into the thoughts of those who watched him, and a strong nose that was bent at the bridge as if it had been damaged, and when his glance traversed them he seemed to smile as if he were everyone's friend, except that these friends were now becoming boring and displaying indecision.

Griff said softly, "Just my fucking luck. Forgive the vulgarity, lads, but it's how I feel. Pretty much at the end of my stipend with the Service, only half a year to go, and right now that cannot come fast enough. I've been a Sixer for twenty-seven years. Russia oriented for the last fifteen of them. In that time, I've never had a sniff of one, not a proper full-blown defector. I have proposi tioned, done the first feeble chat-up lines with about as much success as trying to seduce a Mother Superior. Never been near to getting one. Then this joker pops his head up over the fence. Got really excited, know what I mean. The Mother Superior gives me a come-on, that excited. Hot flushes at home last night, put a bottle of bubbles in the fridge for tonight after I've dumped him into your tender hands and the cavalry coming from Vauxhall. Off home and I'm the hero of the hour. I don't think so. Think he's left us with rather a problem."

The woman who wished to be known as Frank served coffee to Brian who sat close to the Russian but who had made no comment on the quality of the preliminary debrief, nor on the violation of the no smoking edict. Both Wally and Doug would have appeared less than smart and the fast shave had done little to tidy them; they oozed the fact that they had been dragged out of their beds in answer to an emergency call. She looked tidy, showed no sign of lost sleep and her hand did not shake as she passed Brian the cup and saucers. The Russian, Igor, eyed her and held his glance in a way that might have embarrassed most other men and seemed to expect to make contact with her. He smiled at her. She ignored him.

Griff said, "Could be that he's just looking for a gravy train ride. Thinks we'll be a soft touch. Monty will sort him out."

He bit his lip. Wally wondered if he would start dribbling blood . . . Not that they were strangers to blood. After leaving the

Marines, Wally had gone into the short-term, well-paid world of PMC work. Not altogether glamorous ... taking convoys into Baghdad from the airport, Route Irish and seven and a half miles of arse-pucker journey, and had been shotgun-riding between Kabul and the Bagram base and on the bad run down to Kandahar – he was familiar with blood. Doug had done escort with a Secretary of State in Northern Ireland and high-risk prisoner escorts in Liverpool but had also spent time mentoring trainee police units in Iraq. They had similar personalities and a good understanding about keeping the lid on drama when crisis came calling. For both of them work in their field of Guns For Hire was diminishing and they would have been grateful to have been called in the night and packed off to Copenhagen. With a flick of an eyebrow the woman signalled to Griff that she had come off her phone and had more detail. He went to join her by the door. Not hard for them to understand his disappointment.

Wally said, "I'm not an expert."

Doug said, "Thank God for that."

Wally had a gallows grin. "A defection package does not come cheap."

Doug grimaced. "We had a guy in Iraq who used to come to the camp I worked at, been in Europe when the Soviet thing collapsed. He said they had busloads of old KGB, colonels and brigadiers and a few generals, offering themselves, hoping to be taken on by us so they didn't have to drive taxis or pick potatoes or protect gangsters,. Like it was 'Form an orderly queue, and here's a sheet of paper and a pencil so you can tell us what you know about the nuclear stuff, chemical warfare, germ weapons.' They were turning them away before Mr Putin showed up. Like a tap was turned off."

"The package costs plenty and the joker getting it has to have plenty to offer."

Griff was back with them.

Something about a hotel in Aarhus in the north and where the main assessment team for the Russian would gather. They were in the air now out of London's Heathrow. Chiswell and Barker and

Symonds and little Benedict were coming. Should have been Toni as well but she had babysitter problems and had cried off, and Monty was on the flight . . .

Another fag, half smoked, went out of the window and the sleeve was damper. The Russian had lifted his coffee cup and saucer and clipped them together, making a sharp little rattle to gesture that he'd like the cup refilled. Waggled the cup again, like Frank was a skivvy and should have come running. She did not hurry, showed no annoyance. When she reached out to take his cup and saucer he seemed, imperceptibly, to lower his hands so that she had to bend further forward to retrieve them. Wally understood. Doug murmured something about a "shitehawk". She took the cup and saucer from him and turned away, and Wally saw the guy's smirk. Doug muttered "arsehole". Might have thought that making her bend would give him a cleavage view or force her hand down closer to his groin. She glided away to the table with the coffee dispenser and Igor gazed at her ankles. It had all been noted.

Brian was up off his chair, dropping the magazine he had open but which would have gone unread. He crossed the room, stood close to her as she poured the coffee. Indicated, "I'll do that, Frank, if it's all the same to you," and managed a smile for her and she shrugged.

It might have been one of those moments as Wally would say when "a whole load of excrement is about to hit the fan". A moment of perfect calm before a storm broke. Doug had sensed it too like they were wired together. Brian was the Embassy security officer, had been a warrant officer in the Parachute Regiment, would never have taken a backward step and the cup of coffee was balanced on the saucer, and his hand was rock steady. One of those moments which prefaced total anti-climax, or one that precluded a few seconds of stress-laced tension: Brian could purposefully tip the scalding contents of the cup into the Russian's lap and let him howl – which did not happen. The coffee was handed over, Brian was thanked. He responded with civility, called the guy "sir", went back to his chair and resumed gazing vacantly at his magazine. The coffee was noisily drunk. Another cigarette was lit.

Wally had his mouth close to Doug's ear. "Did I imagine all that? Were we close to Armageddon? Real or not real?"

"Had me wondering. But then we're not minding a kindergarten. Table manners aren't the big issue."

Griff was back with them.

Griff said, "They're down. About five minutes, then we leave. If that's what's going to happen."

Griff turned away from them, crossed the room, stood in front of the Russian.

"I'm saying this, maybe it is the last time. We are about to get moving. Unlikely, once we do, that you can change tack, back down, reckon this never happened, and return to your Embassy and your office . . . Or you can pretend that it did happen and you want to make an arrangement with us, be well rewarded financially, and again go back and become a more permanent asset to us."

"I have no doubts, Mr Griffin."

"I want to hear you say it."

"I am defecting to you. I had a meeting with the Resident and my colonel in GRU, which was due to start fifteen minutes ago. I am not there. I would usually be punctual. They will wait perhaps another five minutes. They will send someone to my apartment. He will have a key, of course. He will see I have gone, he will also see that my car is gone. Where am I? First questions, then annoyance, then anxiety, then anger . . . and the bridge is burned. I want to piss before we go."

Brian escorted him.

Griff was back between Wally and Doug. Frank was tidying, piling the used cups, mugs and plates on the table and then she'd check around for anything dropped.

Wally asked, "Bit of a cheek, Mr Griffin, and you're entitled not to answer. Can you chuck a defector out?"

Doug quizzed, "Sorry, not today, maybe another day? Show him the door – thanks but no thanks?"

"Talking too much, breaking a lifetime's habits. Getting de-mob happy and this was going to be the final hurrah. Doesn't look to me as if he has what we'd want . . . but shut him out, shut the door on him? Not easy. And it sends a message. Getting our hands on a traitor, anyone prepared to snitch their country's secrets, is a shade harder, in the Russian theatre, than extracting blood from a stone. We give some Joe we've lined up, and worked bloody hard to get him on board, all that stuff about how much we value him. The Joe goes home from the contact, believing all the sugar we've ladled on him, and he switches on the TV. Who does he see? Sees our little friend, Igor, major in GRU, based in Copenhagen and defending the Motherland from there. What does he say? Says he was kidnapped. Says he was tortured. Says he escaped because of his excellent training and belief in the rule of Comrade Putin We are damaged and our prestige is screwed. I am not saying we have other agents in play, and I'm not saying we haven't. Just doesn't sound good, fourth rate . . . We're stuck with him, however useless, unless he has a bag of code books secreted deep up his back passage which he has so far omitted to tell us about."

Wally said, "Sounds a bit of a shambles."

Doug said, "Has us by the short and curlies."

Griff said, "Should have been weeks of planning, a job like this, and we're rushed into it. I really thought my podium moment had come. Doesn't seem likely. We have to stay with him even if he's fool's gold and a freebooter . . . Or, and I heard what you said early on. Might just be a dangle. But that's for Monty to sort out."

They went out into the rain. Reluctantly, the Russian carried his own grip bag, and the keys to his car were handed to a porter and a bank note was palmed him and the car would be "lost" somewhere. They went fast across the parking area and loaded up. Wally thought the guy was either a dangle or had made a life-changing move, stepped over a cliff and would not know how he would land, but seemed calm enough, chirpy, and had given the girls on Reception an eye as he passed them, and as they approached the car was watching the swing of Frank's backside. There was nothing to like about him, but neither Wally nor Doug was paid to like, enjoy the company of, be a best friend to, the principal they were tasked to protect. They scrambled into their seats and the rain came down hard. The PET boys would be in the lead vehicle with their own driver. In the second car would be Igor and Griff, and Frank. At the tail, with another Embassy driver, would be Brian and Doug and Wally . . . There seemed to be, as the storm blustered around them, a further delay. The Russian appeared to want Frank to sit in the back with him, but would have to do with Griff. Might have been told to "shut the fuck up" because tension was ratcheting.

Wally said to his friend, "What's the bet it all ends in tears? Chummy's tears. Has that feel. A time for tears, or he's planted and swung in front of us."

Doug said, "We'll know soon enough."

"Think I'm following your drift."

"They'll come after him, that's their style, if he's not a dangle. Always do. They get powerfully angry with a turncoat . . . Come after him hard."

"If they come knocking, hope I'm not around – expect I bloody will be."

I

The following March

A cutting wind caught them as they came ashore.

It was not an elegant landing. The tide was dropping and the ferry needed to moor low down on the jetty and the passengers had to step carefully on to soaked seaweed. On the jetty's far side was a metal rail but the surface was lethal and glistened in low wintry sunshine. Getting a grip on the jetty was made even more hazardous by the bluster that blew hard against them. Gulls made a mockery of their clumsiness and seemed able both to shriek in a fierce choral harmony and to balance with a dancer's grace, undisturbed by the gusts. It had hailed while the boat was at the pier at Orford but the clouds that had carried the splatter of the stones were now blown inland. Vera held tight to Jonas's hand.

A boatman called, "You all right, Mrs Merrick? Can you manage him?"

She answered, into the wind and over her shoulder that, yes, she could manage to get him up the slope of the jetty. She had booked their crossing with the company that ran the ferry service from the village of Orford on the mainland across the channel to Havergate Island, had done it over the phone, and had booked the berth at the caravan site on the headland above the cliff at Dunwich, had made all the arrangements within half an hour of Jonas telling her that it was possible for him to take some time from his desk at Thames House: they could manage an extended weekend away. Now, he gripped the rail and she supported him on his other side and they went up over the seaweed carpeting the concrete and towards firm ground. She had heard little titters of sneering laughter behind her but was not affected, did not try to move faster than she thought sensible. She wore waterproof over-trousers and a quilted coat and had a scarf at her throat and a beanie dragged over her ears, and she had on the boots that she wore out with her walking group in the Surrey hills. The other passengers, backed up and waiting for Vera and Jonas to get off the jetty, were equipped as for an Arctic expedition. Not her husband. Jonas had chosen to wear the shoes that took him to work and back home five days a week, or more if he could muster up the excuse, and his sports coat of heavy Harris tweed, a check shirt and a sober tie and, cloaking him, a heavy raincoat with a fastened belt. He had forsaken his usual trilby, replacing it with a flat cap that was well oiled and obviously rarely used.

Vera knew that everyone behind her, most of them with expensive cameras and binoculars draped around their necks, or shouldering tripods with scopes attached, and contemptuous of her husband's halting progress, would have been surprised that at their Raynes Park semi-detached home, hidden at the back of her knicker drawer, were the Queen's Gallantry Medal that had been pinned on Jonas's chest at a discreet investiture by a "senior Royal". And along with it, in a small plastic bag, was a silver bar with a decoration of laurel leaves, and a length of medal ribbon, blue at each end and then going inward with two sections of pearl white and with a red vertical band in the centre on which was fastened a silver rosette: he was QGM and Bar. The decorations were not spoken of in the house, none of the neighbours were aware of them and only a very few at his workplace would have known of them.

Slow progress but they made it and stepped off the jetty and on to a solid pathway. She thought it a piece of great good fortune that they could get away with the caravan for three full days. It happened so seldom. And she was excited and saw already that his interest was alerted by another island farther out across another channel and jutting into the North Sea, and by the ruined constructions on its skyline.

Their fellow passengers swept past them, as though the minute or two of delay was important. They turned to the right and began at route-march speed to head towards a distant wood-built hide. Jonas turned to her, might almost have beseeched her, and Vera grimaced and led him left along another path towards another hide, and was rewarded with a grin, almost sheepish . . . She knew little of the reasons for the awards except that the man Jonas had taken into custody, alone and without back-up, had been wearing a suicide vest and had the Houses of Parliament as his target and that had earned the first one. Knew also that when he had come home cut and bruised and exhausted, he had earlier that morning handcuffed himself to a committed and war-experienced Isis veteran who had been on his way to collect an horrendous weapon to launch at a military base: and this had won him the second, the Bar. She seldom had full ownership of Jonas. A rare chance, and she grinned and showed a touch of mischief.

"Hope that damn phone's switched off."

Later, as night followed day, his restlessness would grow and a moody frown settle on his forehead, but not yet. The wind slashed at his coat, flattening his grey flannel trousers against his shins and he had to reach up and steady his cap for fear of losing it. But it would have been the same for him on many mornings when he passed the Archbishop's Palace and came out on to the open expanse of Lambeth Bridge and walked, rain or sunshine, calm or gale-battered, towards his place of employment, the Security Service headquarters in Thames House. What did he do there? She did not ask and was not told, but had in her knicker drawer the evidence that some at least thought it important work.

They approached a deserted hide and, once inside, he would be able to sit and she would fish the small binoculars from her bag and would start to scan, and she would also take out a thermos flask. She thought herself a little blessed.

She said, against the whip of the wind, "I'm hoping Jonas, that we're going to see some dunlin and some red knot, and there should be avocets and sandwich terns. Also this is good for red and black-throated divers. If we are very lucky, there may be a short-eared owl. And you must watch for marsh harriers, very impressive, and the weather is holding up well."

And his answer, and his little grin, as they reached the hide. "Don't be too confident. I think it is merely the calm before the storm hits."

When Frank had lit her screen, and gone through the restrictive security schedule, Benedict's message was the first one up . . . no surprise that she was inside Vauxhall Cross, or Ceaucescu Towers as those Sixers contemptuous of the architecture called the SIS building on the south side of the Thames. Weekends meant little to nothing to her. He had been asked for his assessment prior to the Resettlement team's progress meeting on Sashcord later in the day. She downloaded, sipped her mug of tea, read what was in front of her. Went down the two pages, fast.

Conclusion: Am satisfied, after this length of time in his company, that he is not a "dangle". Questioning has gone on too long and in too great a detail for him to deceive in that area. Believe he is genuine, but short of pertinent information. If not a dangle, then we have to take great care of his security while he remains with us. Because of procedures in place for his debut presentation opportunity, I am confident we are not unnecessarily hazarding his safety. But, BUT, with his former employers' past exploits we should not lower the effectiveness of the protection screen. Also, see GRIFFIN addendum.

Ex Griff: RussiaFed Embassy locally continues to downplay Sashcord disappearance. Have only stated that a "junior official", has disappeared, and is believed to be suffering "mental stress" and may have had "suicidal tendencies" and his family remain "deeply anxious" for his welfare. Saw RussiaFed GRU bossman at Norwegian Embassy bash, Harald V birthday, was greeted correctly and without any indication of animosity: no sign of linking disappearance to defection into our care! Would have expected paranoid reaction, but that is not apparent. Also signs exist with Sashcord of advanced "cabin fever" and consider planned expedition acceptable.

She had not dressed down for a weekend day at the office, the MI6 centre of operations. A grey skirt and jacket and a white blouse that neither aged her beyond her thirty-seven years, nor loaned her further youth. Stud pearl earrings and a fine gold chain around her throat with a small precious stone as a pendant, but not obtrusive, and an understated brooch on her jacket made of small diamonds mounted on a silver ring and they rarely caught enough light to be noticed. Nothing on her fingers. She had cursorily smeared on lipstick, done a little work on her eyes. Her hair was up, and not one out of place . . . Those who were coming into the building later, grumbling about the disruption, would be in stages of down-dressing and likely as not none of them would notice Frank's smartness, let alone comment favourably on it.

He was careful with his preparation that Saturday morning.

It would be the first time that they had allowed him out, placed a minimum of trust in him.

They called him Sashcord. He had heard the code name used as they talked among themselves and when they were on secure phones. He did not understand the relevance of the word but did not think that it gave him sufficient importance.

It rained.

Always, over the city of Aarhus, the clouds were gunmetal grey and now the heavens had opened. Igor, or Sashcord, was in his room in the safe house. The house was in a clean, quiet street. No one shouted, no one dropped litter, no one came to spray-paint walls, no one drove by with a radio playing loud rock music. No one stood in front of the rented house and peered at the windows that had blinds drawn throughout the day. Igor only saw the low clouds and only felt the spatter of the rain on his face when he was taken outside and eased himself down into the rear seat of the car. He would then be driven to a museum, and another museum, every fucking museum that the city boasted of – or he would be driven to a park and allowed to jog. Occasionally, never more than once a week, he would be escorted to a restaurant . . . That had been his life for fifteen weeks, or maybe sixteen, and his temper was fraying.

If he went to a museum then Benedict was always with him and either Wally or Doug, pretty much body to body, against his

shoulder. Further back, ten or fifteen paces, would be Danish
security people. If he was allowed to run in a park then both Wally
and Doug, and the Danes . . . He enjoyed the trips and the chance
to stretch his stride because one of the Danes was almost always
the woman with the big chest and sometimes if he slowed then she
caught up with him and he liked that best because, when it rained,
her T-shirt clung to her body, and he could dream: had tried to
chat to her, had once gone as far as pretending to have a heel
blister that needed examination but she'd abruptly called her
colleague, a hairy and smelly guy, to come and examine the skin
and he'd been rewarded with a look of malice, as if he were nothing
more than a smear of dog turd on his shoe. He could have said
with certainty that he had not formed any kind of relationship
with Benedict, nor with Wally or Doug, nor with any of the Danes
who were down the street in a closed van. His temper was more
raw each day.

Igor could ask casually, or could shout, or scream at the top of
his voice. Same question, just minor variations.

"When are we out of this shit place? When do I go to Britain?
Why am I still here?"

The two minders would shrug as if it were not their business.
Benedict would pull a sad face and gesture with his hands that he
was helpless to make that level of decision. A multitude of excuses
had been offered: the disruption of the Christmas holiday, the
unit's reorganisation, he was still being evaluated. He just needed
a little more patience.

And whether he said it, shouted it, screamed it, there was only
one response. "Then I go back. Then you unlock the door and a
taxi arrives, and you pay my fare to the airport and there is a
connection at Copenhagen to Petersburg, and I go home. You
show me some fucking respect, or I go back . . ." Benedict would
respond, not the others, and always that self-same call for "a little
more patience".

Different when Montgomery came. About every two weeks,
the big man flew in. He was Denys Montgomery. They called him
Monty. They had exhaustive sessions which were taped, the

questions probing both his professional experience in GRU, and the motivation for his flight. Igor noted when Montgomery's lips narrowed and a little hiss of air came through them, and the cigarette perpetually between his fingers was dragged on harder, and he would know that he had *failed* to provide an answer that satisfied, that opened a further seam of questioning. It stood to reason that he would have failed, was still failing, and would continue to fail, because he had been only a middle-ranking officer in GRU, not a high-flyer, not pigeonholed for fast-track advancement. Was not told to his face that he had failed, nor that he disappointed. Sensed it, knew it. But that morning as they had eaten breakfast he had been told, without fanfare, that a diversion was in place for the following day. Like it was a throwaway . . . and the minimum of explanation.

They were to drive south. They would cross the frontier, leave Denmark, go into Germany. Would travel to Hamburg. Would go to a safe location, and Igor would lecture a hall filled with German police officials and officers of the security apparatus on the techniques and aims of his former unit, the GRU.

"Tell them what?"

Benedict had waved a hand expansively. "Training, tactics, techniques. All your spycraft. Authenticity is paramount . . . They spend their professional lives worrying about people like you, Igor, and what you can achieve – and you'll be there in front of them, breathing and alive. Four months you've been with us and you deserve a change of scenery. Entertain them. Should be a piece of cake."

"I do that, and then we go – at last – to Britain?"

No answer. Benedict had a lovely smile. Igor thought it was like a banker's smile when asked for an additional loan and not willing either to accede or refuse. Igor had gone off to his room: what clothes to wear and what to say.

In the wardrobe was a grey suit and a navy suit, and the jacket in which he had defected, gone to the Copenhagen hotel. Also in the wardrobe were four shirts, clean and folded but not ironed, underwear and a pile of socks, and an extra pair of lace-up shoes and trainers for jogging. He had only brought the grip with him and what was on his back. They had purchased the rest ... Benedict had supervised and Wally had measured and Doug had written down the sizes, and they had done the shopping. He reckoned this was going to be the chance for him to achieve status as a key player in the new chilly relationship between his old country and where he had assumed he would now be living, and living well. He had brought enough clothing for one night or two and then had expected that he would be taken – as a sort of celebrity – around the shops in the Piccadilly and Regent Street area of London, and Jermyn Street and Savile Row, be made to feel something special and valued ... The clothes in the wardrobe were inexpensive by Danish standards. He would dress carefully and would make the best impression that the opportunity offered ...

A lecture had been given to his year as they were about to pass out from the Military-Diplomatic Academy, the prestige training centre of GRU on Narodnogo Opolcheniya, and they had been told of the desperate lengths to which the Western agencies would go in an attempt to subvert them, what bribes would be offered, what money and promises would be showered in an officer's face. Igor had never been approached, neither in Moscow, nor in Lebanon, nor in Copenhagen. No proposition had ever been put to him ... The decision to defect had been his own. Unprompted. A string of reasons had caused him to go to that beach where it was common knowledge amongst the intelligence staff at his embassy that Griffin, the UK's station chief, exercised his dog most evenings.

At last, something to cling to. At last and about fucking time. He examined what clothes he might wear, and what he might say.

It was a huge and cavernous railway terminus. It dealt with journeys from Moscow to the east of the country and far away beyond the Urals and across Siberia and through a mass of time changes. The station's architectural appearance had barely changed since the days of the Tsars. Noise reverberated: announcements over loudspeakers, the scream of engine brakes, the gathering power of diesel turbines, and the cries and shouts of passengers and fast-food traders.

Alexei stepped off the train, his rucksack hitched over his right shoulder. His eyes swept around him.

Stiffness enveloped each joint of his body. He had been twelve and a half hours on the train. His ankles and knees ached. For all of those hours he had sat on a hard seat in a full compartment as the engine pulled the line of carriages over 798 kilometres of track. He had only once during the journey abandoned his seat and gone in search of a toilet. His elbows and shoulders hurt, and his neck.

He had left his home and his workplace, the city of Kirov, at twenty-five minutes past one in the morning. Cold wrapping around him, frost and a smothering of snow on the ground. He had sat upright because there was no chance to spread himself out on the thinly upholstered seat. The train was punctual.

The display wall ahead of him relayed the time, a few minutes after two o'clock in the afternoon. He had reached the crowded, noisy, bustle of the Yaroslavskiy station on the eastern side of the capital city. Most of those who had travelled on the same train, people who lived on the edge of the Siberian wasteland, would have gasped at the size and opulence of the rail terminus. His own pause was brief; he had no need to stare around him.

He did this journey every two weeks. Every other weekend he went down to the station at Kirov and bought the ticket and reserved the seat, and had a discount because of the nature of his work. He almost tripped because of the pain in his knees. He arched his back, tried to rotate his head.

The manoeuvres were not to get back greater suppleness in his body. He broke the rules of what was called tradecraft. Alexei, twenty-four years old, and with a clerk's job, was on a fast learning curve on the necessary disciplines. He tried to do as he was told, and could not. They specified that he must never show that he looked for a tail; worse still was to take obvious evasive action if he believed that he was under close surveillance. He was supposed to seem as natural and relaxed as any young man would be who came to central Moscow to spend the weekend with his mother:

was not supposed to twist his head, look around him, imagine that he saw confirmation. They might have been there, *might* was enough to make him gasp and a chill sweat to break out on the back of his neck, and his legs seemed to go numb.

Maggie had said he was not to worry.

Maggie had told him that she had kept a counter-surveillance position behind him when he had last taken the train to the capital. He had been certain of it, the tail, when he had come two weeks before to Yaroslavskiy station. Maggie had been cautious, had not confirmed, had not denied.

Maggie was the link . . . He looked around him again. Stopped, turned, twisted, let his eyes roam across the host of faces and looked in particular for anyone who was turning their glance away from him, or was engrossed in the day's edition of a sports news-paper, or who was examining each tired salad bread roll in a kiosk when all the fresher ones would have gone hours before . . . If they had decided to take him it would be brutal. He had seen it played out a host of times on the TV news. There was a special squad that worked only for FSB, the TV said, and their expertise was purely in the area of the lifting of traitors. Might be the lead story on the TV that night, or might be held over until the Sunday evening bulletin . . .

Maggie, pushing the buggy, had told him two weeks before that he let his imagination rip and that was not sensible; for a moment she had held his hand tightly, then had released it, and crossed the road, and then she and the buggy and her small son were gone.

The start would be a shot from a surveillance camera, a view of him walking across the station concourse, and there would be moments when he seemed to duck out of the camera's view. Then he would be picked out again, and for a few seconds the focus might go soft, but it would tighten. There might be a chance to recognise his guilt from the furtive way he looked around him and tried to persuade himself that the suspicion was not warranted – at that stage there would be almost a chuckle in the TV presenter's voice. They would let him leave the station and he would come out into the winter air, and it would blow hard on his face and his teeth might begin to chatter and the shiver start in his legs: not from the cold but from the guilt, and the guilt bred the fear. He would have walked out of the station, leave its grandiose architecture behind him, and he might have seen the van that pulled up slowly ahead of him, happy to double park, and in front of the van would be a saloon car with dark privacy windows. The back doors of the van opening and the side doors of the car, and men emerging, all masked and wearing black and all with weapons on webbing belts. People around him scattering because they wanted no part of it. Someone might have come from behind, the approach not anticipated, and there would be a crashing blow against the back of his legs, and Alexei going down and the paving stones – old, chipped, stained, there for forty years – rushing to greet him, and more of them diving on to him, and his arms twisted half out of their sockets, and his cheek and chin slapped down again on to the ground, and the breath gone from his lungs. Cuffs on his wrists and a gratuitous blow to the back of the neck, softening him – and he would be dragged to the van, and would be lifted, and thrown inside and his body would slither on the metal flooring and he would slide to the bulkhead. He might see the cameraman who filmed it, but might not. There was a memory stick in a cavity of the heel of his right shoe. It might take them ten minutes to find it, or it might take them less.

He had not seen the tail, could not confirm he was watched, followed. But he believed it was there.

On the pavement, waiting for a bus, he was sick. He heaved his guts up and dumped the vomit in the gutter and those near him gazed in disgust.

He went to see his mother.

Frank was at a side table, typing on her laptop.

If Frank had a family for whom she felt any degree of affection, then it was here. Not that she had chosen love or friendship with those streaming in each morning and having a wealth to say on hobbies, families, holidays or . . . it was the building and its labyrinths of corridors and work areas, the whole edifice. She did not have a family outside: her father had walked out when she was two years old, gone, done a runner. When Frank was nine, her mother had come off her bicycle and had been hit by oncoming traffic. She had been brought up by the childless Rex and Prudence, uncle and aunt . . . no fun, no naughtiness, no emotion. She had never cried, not at any time in her life, not tasted the wet salt of tears.

A decision needed to be reached. The question of Sashcord required resolution. The operation in Denmark, to house, guard, and humour the little beggar leached money. Pressure from an upper floor demanded progress.

Around the long table, none of those who had come in that Saturday morning acknowledged Frank's presence. She was not asked whether she had understood a muttered aside, or an interruption, nor was she expected to complain if a remark was curtailed, left incomplete. It was assumed she would make sense of what each of them said, and hack out the grammatical imperfections, attend to the punctuation, correct syntax and spelling, erase profanities and slanders. It was what she did.

The easiest targets were those across the sea.

Chiswell said, "I don't like to say this but it's not the time to pussyfoot around responsibility. It's down to Griff . . . he should have stalled him, put him off, allowed us to suck and taste what was on offer. Griff lumbered us."

Barker said, "I'm not getting any pleasure from pointing out the obvious. Look at Griff. Runs a minor station. Must have dreamed of one good day before that evening when the sherry decanter, or whatever it is these days, is handed over and retirement consumes him. Altogether too eager. The finances are a burden on our section and it has to be resolved."

Symonds said, "Call a spade a spade, we are getting less than clarity from little Benedict. God's sake, what do they do all day out there? Drink Pilsner? Do the football pools? We're getting nothing back . . . he seems to spend all his time sending interminable messages relaying Sashcord's moan about not being brought to the UK. Myself, I think it well past the time when Benedict should put a rod across our Russian friend's back."

Toni said, "Have to say, I would have thought it was pretty obvious to the lot of you – Griffin then, and Benedict now – that we have a pig in a poke. Took him on trust . . . I do have to say that had I been there – had that bloody au pair not walked out on me – then I'd have been breathing some common sense into it all. Griff is a complete tosser and way over-promoted. Frankly, people like Benedict, minimal degree of talent, should never be employed here. We need a clear-out, need the stables to have a good wash through . . . I'd say get a pin and a revolving globe, close the eyes and spin it hard, count up to three and shove the pin in – send Sashcord there. Funny if the pin landed in the middle of Siberia . . . Sorry, just my little joke. Anyway, ditch him."

Frank had been quite desperately correct as a child, a teenager, a student. No tantrums, no hysteria, laughed only when it was expected of her. Had overheard a tutor describe her as "nice enough, pretty enough, but sadly rather dull".

The only one amongst them that she thought worth listening to was Monty. Denys Montgomery, only mid-40s but the best of them in terms of conciseness, clarity – and always easy to transcribe. She knew from the documentation she recorded that he had twice turned away "dangles", knew also that the consuming interest of his life was the model train display, tracks and engines and stations, housed in the loft space of his home. Knew also that he had never looked at her, never absorbed her appearance from the ankles to the throat where a very small amount of eau de toilette was sprayed. She did not look up, just typed.

Monty said, "We have had defectors, in my time, who were platinum value. Penkovsky, Gordievsky, Polyakov and Popov. Long and distinguished list, all traitors to their people and all of use. And we have had those who failed to step up to the mark . . . I consider the problem from a differing angle. Defection, the programme we run, Resettlement, is pretty much the moment of failure. Start there."

"So we do nothing?"

"Let Griffin get his decanter or carriage clock or silver pencil, whatever, and keep shelling out the dosh into the sunset?"

"Has to be an end game, costs too much and all we're getting is blank paper in return."

"Fire him, what I did that week with the au pair, little bitch. Get rid of him, put a cheque in his pocket and wave him off."

Monty said, "We don't want defectors. Pain in the butt, all of them. Take them down to the Fort, put them in the flat, do the debrief, most of which we know already, and then they're spilling us old stuff. They're no longer at their desk, not reading de-coded and classified signals, not able to make assessments of new thinking, new strategies. They defect and immediately they're old hat. But we have a duty of care."

Not well disguised, Chiswell's yawn.

A glance at his wristwatch from Barker.

Symonds doing a drumbeat on the table with his pencil.

Toni picked at her teeth, then poured more water.

Monty said, "We have a duty of care. Not through any altruism, but self-interest. Not sentimentality . . . I don't want a defector over here whining that he should have met the monarch and had a medal pinned on his chest, and grumbling about the food, and that he's got no totty to shag. I want him where he is of most use to us. Where he works. Where he continues to work. In FSB, in SVR, in Vlad's private office, in GRU. Want him there, sending us back the nosebag of goodies, keeping the brush contacts going, and sending the dead letters . . . Best chance of that is if our boy – or our girl – believes in the utter honesty of what we tell him, her. Chuck this useless creature out and the word will escape that we have no belief in duty of care. Value drained, usefulness exhausted, and we are no longer interested. We have an asset in place, and half the days of the week he nearly messes his underpants if he believes he is vulnerable. What he clings to is our facile promise that we'll look after him if the going gets too rough . . . So he's sitting in some ghastly tower block, shivering in very justified fear, and the TV is on, and old Sashcord comes up – Igor who was a second-rate major in GRU – and he tells a stooge interviewer that he has just endured a shit few months from those lying bastards across in London. We are stuck with him . . ."

★　　　★　　　★

High in a building known as the Aquarium by those who worked there, a senior man sat at his desk and satisfied himself that the plans put in place by his subordinates were well thought through.

He carried the rank of brigadier but his authority ran into areas way beyond the parameters usually available to an individual of that level. Probably his mother had called him by his given name but she had been extirpated from his life thirty years before. The name he answered to was Volkov, and behind his back he was referred to, without a need for explanation, as the Wolf. His name was derived from the word for the common grey wolf of which thousands still lived in Russia. In modern Moscow, he was a throwback to long-ago times: he was not the senior official responsible for the running of the GRU complex, nor did he have the ear of the President of the Federation, nor did he control a budget overflowing from a slop bucket. He was a throwback because – most simply – he determined which condemned enemies of the state were next in line to be sent to meet their Maker, in what order and by what method of assassination. The Wolf, in the minds of those who gave him that name, was not an open personality, but a creature of subterfuge and cunning who stayed out of sight, who stalked, who could manufacture a terminal zone and leave negligible traces of his identity.

Few in the more palatial work suites above him cared to know the detail of what he set in motion. To know the least, to be able truthfully to profess ignorance, was preferable. The names went on to the Wolf's desk, barely large enough to be functional, and he devised the style of death: always in the hope that it would create maximum fear in opponents of the regime whether inside the Federation's territory, or far beyond Russia's boundaries. He had few of the physical attributes of the military and rather less of those possessed by the old Vympel boys whom he kept track of, on loosely drawn contracts. When he went into the Metro and began his journey to work, men and women in the city, old and young, smartly turned out and in the confused clothes of the student masses, did not pay him a second glance . . .

insignificant, with neither presence nor an aura of authority, short built, with rimless glasses on the bridge of his nose and a balding head.

Messages, incoming and outgoing, were kept to a minimum so that any evidence of a spike in traffic would be denied those who monitored his efforts. He thought the concept of the execution was good. He might have cursed the short time available to him, but could live with it. He liked the men who were now on station, thought them competent and determined. Most important, he reckoned that each of them could look into the face of the man they would kill, smile, see the fear spread. The President himself was never ambiguous in his demands of the programme overseen by the Wolf and his assessment of a target: "He's just a spy, a traitor to the Motherland. Think about it as a citizen would. What would your attitude be to someone who betrayed your own country? He's just a scumbag." He could assume his back was covered, but that protection might be short lived if the job were botched. He had been given his role following a chaotic failure to end the life of another "traitor", one living in the suburbs of a British cathedral city. Failure was not tolerated. The taint of failure could damage the health of a man with a rank as high as that of brigadier. He had men in the field, good men and well motivated, and with a history of reliability.

The consequences of failure did not concern him that Saturday morning. He was satisfied that pieces were slipping gently, inexorably, into place.

Normally Gunther would have worked out of the police station in north-west Hamburg that was designated as PolizeiKommissariat 27, on Koppelstrasse. He was twenty-three years old. He had passed out from the training programme four months ago. His current girlfriend was Ursula: Ursula worked in a city centre hair salon. She had sinewy fingers, fine, manicured nails. That she had been attracted to him, despite the pimple on his chin, astonished him. Fearful of losing her, he spent most of his off-duty time with her. She was away that Saturday with a family group up at the port city of Kiel but would be back on the Sunday and they planned to club and dance in the evening. Until his Polizeiobermeister had texted him.

He was required to do an extra duty on Sunday evening.

Perhaps, if Gunther had not been ambitious, anxious to progress in his chosen career, he might have pleaded influenza or a wrecked ligament in his knee. He did not, made no excuse that would have reeked of deceit. The Polizeiobermeister's message did not specify what duty would be required of him but stated that he should be at the police headquarters in the pleasant suburb of Alsterdorf and that he should expect to be involved until past ten o'clock. There was a Green demonstration scheduled in the Anhalt district that same evening and he assumed that the force was stretched, and assumed also that he would not be linking up with Ursula when he came off work.

He cursed, and called her.

The phone was answered. There was laughter, young men's and young women's. Then a shush for quiet, and a subdued giggle. Then a voice trilled, "Is it him, is it your little police boy?" And another shush, and more muffled laughter, and he thought it sounded wrong for the family group with which she was allegedly driving to Kiel for the birthday of a favourite aunt. He wondered if the relationship had run its course. He might have been a subject of fun, when she was with a different group of friends; she might have rolled her eyebrows and flexed her fingers and waggled those lovely nails that did so much damage to his resolve, might have . . . He cut the call.

He had been ironing creases out of his uniform. It would be right, if he were to work at the headquarters building, to look his best. Would he be noticed? Unlikely, but more chance of being marked out if his appearance seemed slovenly. Gunther liked the excitement of car chases and the pursuit of thieves, and was stimulated by the sirens and the flap of the heavy pistol on his hip. To be on duty at the central office of Hamburg's police gave only a small chance of an adrenaline rush. A small chance? He corrected himself . . . a minuscule chance.

He sent the confirmation text to his Polizeiobermeister. Correct and formal. He would be there. The weather forecast was grim for Sunday evening. He assumed that an officer as junior as himself would not be stationed inside the building in the warm and the dry. Reckoned he would be outside, peering into driving rain and probably uncertain why he was there and what he was looking for.

He thought it unlikely he would see Ursula again.

The car was top of the range.

They approached it warily, not that taking the vehicle would be a problem to them, but both feared an enhanced alarm system that they were unfamiliar with.

The street was dark, and traffic was occasional. This was the "bacon belt" of Hamburg where the houses were large and the gardens deep and wide and the properties were ringed by high walls and the gates electronically controlled. There were cameras in place that covered those gates but the regulations demanded that the lenses did not show the street, the kerbs or the pavements.

The saloon car had caught the eyes of the two men – dark-clothed, gloved, and now with balaclavas slipped down over their features – because it suited this purpose. They were Anatoly and Konstantin. Two kilometres away, further north and on the fringes of the city, was Leonid who would normally have worn the uniform of a full colonel, but on this evening, in the dusk, he too wore black overalls and a black face mask and he was sitting in an unmarked van. On his phone, he was shown the car. He authorised its taking.

It might have belonged to an unexpected visitor to that address, or there could have been a social gathering inside and the parking area of the driveway was already full. Irrelevant to them. The chosen vehicle was a Mercedes-Benz. The model was the C257 Mercedes-Benz CLS. Expensive. They had been told that "top of the range" was required . . . for a reason that both Anatoly and Konstantin knew well. Any vehicle in a price range close to 100,000 euros was vulnerable to the attention of any kid, fifteen or sixteen years old, intent on taking it. Anatoly and Konstantin were veterans of conflicts, and they knew how to take cars when they needed them – probably both were as proficient as the teenagers who lived off the trade. Konstantin had the pocketful of devices that would short-circuit the alarm system and Anatoly had the multiple purpose key that any respected auto dealer would have owned.

In silence, the doors of the vehicle were opened and the engine fired. A fast U turn in the street and they were gone. They would rendezvous with Leonid and the van and they would drive together to the rental garage on the east of Hamburg, out by the airport.

Later, when the night deadened the streets, they would be out looking to relieve another vehicle of its registration plates. Then they would go to collect the load that this quality Mercedes-Benz sedan would carry, military-grade stuff . . . A long night and a busy one. Each of them – the two hard men who had been in the ranks of the Special Forces, Vympel troops, and the elegant and educated high-flying colonel in the Intelligence division of the regular army – understood that the job entrusted to them had importance: it was about the sending of a message, the reaching out of an arm. The colonel, Leonid, had told them of a quotation attributed to a black boxer, American, about his next opponent. *He can run, but he cannot hide.* It would be a clear message and well worth a smile or a chuckle of cold laughter.

Alexei was with his mother.

Like any other couple, parent and adult child, making slow progress towards a shopping mall.

Little of the luxury that had engulfed inner Moscow had filtered this far out. They turned into the mall. The windows showed cheap jeans, cheap winter coats, cheap sweaters, cheap boots. There was a pharmacy that sold inexpensive drugs and low-cost cosmetics, a mini-market that stocked basic food, nearly fresh vegetables and packaged meat; and there was a shop that sold the opiate that so many needed – widescreen TVs. To reach the mall they passed decorative old lamp posts, from the days of the Stalin regime, or Kruschev's . . . Across the road, three lanes of traffic in each direction, Alexei had seen the girl with the buggy; she had paused, intent on looking at the second-hand Japanese cars that were close packed on a forecourt. He wondered, gulping down the images of her, that she seemed so calm. As his mother was ... showed no sign of the stress that was twisting in Alexei's mind and through his body.

He was justified in harbouring that level of stress; he was the principal in the conspiracy.

His mother was a convenience, a disguise. The girl with the buggy, who seemed intent on the Nissans, was a courier and without importance. The conspiracy relied on him. He was the source. Without him, and what he carried in his shoe, in the hollowed space in the heel, they were irrelevant. He was the centre point ... Because he occupied that ground, he knew how it would be for him if that imagined van had sprung its rear doors, and those of the saloon had burst open, if the men in black with masked faces had come out of their hiding places and had charged him. Blows to the face and kidneys, sharp steel handcuffs, the bruising from impacting on the metal floor of the van. Sirens howling. Motorists backing off. Such a van, at that speed, the noise, and with its blue lights rotating, would be carrying a prisoner of note.

A lawyer? Some goddamn chance. A reading of his rights? They did not exist so would not be read. Food? Disgusting. Sleep? No chance. They would question him through the whole of the day and the whole of the night and would shine lights in his face and make him stand for endless hours, or lie on the cell floor in his own shit. Would he be able to stay silent? Small hope. They might use drugs or they might rely on wooden batons, or slaps, kicks or punches. He did not think he would be able to hold out for long if they had him in the interrogation rooms of the Lubyanka. Might cry for them to stop, might scream names and dates and the details of the material he had passed on to memory sticks. His mother, if she had any sense left in her head after questioning, would be best off disowning him ... And the others? Those he worked for? The girl he knew as Maggie, with the buggy and the child, coming on nineteen months and named Hector, would be held no longer than overnight in a similar cell to his, then would be released into the custody of an Embassy security officer and would be driven back to the modern, grand building on Smolenskaya Naberezhnaya, would be given time to box up her possessions and little Hector's toys and then she would be put on a flight to London ... A day later, her boss – Lucinda – would follow her out. A diplomatic spat would break the surface, but would soon be forgotten. Not by Alexei. If he were still alive, if he had not succumbed to inflicted injuries, he would stay crippled in mind and body for years, or months, or might only be weeks, till death took him ... He had reason to nurture stress.

He should have stopped. Should have taken his mother's arm and eased her to stand still beside him. Should then have made a play of glancing behind him, just pausing, doing it with enforced calm. Done a swivel and looked for the men who he was sure were following him. He did not – but he did gaze across the street and follow the girl as she appeared, then disappeared, lost between the lorries and buses, cars and tradesmen's pick-ups. The girl was at the lights ... he thought her a miracle, and clever.

Maggie was a junior in an office at the Embassy. He knew that she had been given the job of meeting him because his fears that he was under surveillance had warned off the woman who had been his original contact point, his handler. Knew that it was a miracle he had been given a contact who was pretty, and had charm and confidence, and mischief. Knew that she was clever because her clothes came from street stalls, and the buggy had been taken from a rubbish-strewn area beside a playground and it must have been repaired inside the Embassy. She was good on detail and had called out a car to meet her and have the buggy loaded into its boot in a side street not covered by a camera. If he were close enough to her to see the detail of the skin of her cheeks and forehead, then he would notice the pale powder, cooking flour, she smacked on her face. The result was that she looked like any other pale, drab kid, with a baby, and probably without a job, having a justified place on this street, and in the shopping mall.

*　　*　　*

Did it well . . . He saw her blow her nose hard on a tissue, then use it to wipe the child's face, and she had a tired, wan smile as she waited at a crossing point for the lights to change. It was the signal that she *believed* he was not followed.

In the mall, Alexei stood outside the shop that sold limited fruit, but had good stocks of root vegetables and kale and cabbage. Maggie walked past him with the buggy, followed his mother inside. Close to his mother, she started to finger the produce, good food and at a healthy price.

A seeming chance remark from an older woman to a younger one, perhaps on the quality of a swede or a turnip, and then a slow tired smile on his mother's face and a glance into the buggy at the sleeping child. Alexei went inside and Maggie might have asked him which of the beets looked best, always a favourite for soup. He bent and crouched because a shoelace was loose and that gave him the opportunity to peel back the heel of his trainer and extract the stick. He straightened, realised his breathing came fast. Who went into a vegetable store, stood among the produce with a heaving chest and wide staring eyes . . .? Alexei reached into the buggy and his fingers touched little Hector's chin . . . that was the brush contact. A few words exchanged, strangers offering pleasantries, and they would go their different ways. His mother to the counter to pay for potatoes, pecking in her purse because money mattered. Money mattered because Alexei charged them nothing. He could, he assumed, have demanded thousands of American dollars for what the memory stick carried on each visit to Moscow. For a moment the stick had been against the child's face, but Maggie had bent down and had smoothed his blanket and rearranged the buggy's canvas cover that kept out the icy winter wind.

His mother joined him. He took her plastic bag. They walked away.

His mother said, "That was a pretty girl. You should have a girl like that."

He could not say, "She thinks there might be a tail and there might not. She does not know . . . she tells me to stay calm. She says that in her office they all admire and respect me." He said instead, "She was not sure which of the beetroot plants was the best. I said the one she had was good."

"I thought you might have known her, at least seen her before."

"Never – how would I have known her, where would I have seen her? Pretty? I didn't notice."

He lived so many lies now. Lied in the office where he worked, to his colleagues and his line manager, and now he lied to his mother who thought him only the dutiful boy who came to see her: sitting for twelve and a half hours on the train, each way, to be with his mother, and lied to her also about a girl, disowned her – and worshipped her. He hoped he would see Maggie the next day, had much to ask her – would ask, would demand . . . felt weak, frightened. They walked home, did not speak, had nothing to talk of, and the memory stick was deep under the bedding in the buggy and would be on its way to the huge glass-fronted Embassy complex in the wealthy and comfortable Arbat district. There they would read what he had stolen for them.

His wife made a pot of tea, and Jonas turned the pages of *Practical Caravan*, where he usually found articles to interest him.

It emerged almost from beneath her feet, would have found a small space where the kitchen units joined the floor. It looked around for a moment, its head raised, nose quivering. Only a moderate-sized mouse, nothing spectacular.

The kettle whistled, milk was in their mugs. The pot would be warmed first and then the boiled water poured on to the tea bags. Jonas's feet hurt.

The mouse's route took it along the edge of a rectangle of carpet and towards their lowered dining surface, where a plate of biscuits waited. Under the foldaway table was the tray of cat litter and the carrying basket, open, in which the cat lived, and where he was shut away when they travelled. The animal was a Norwegian Forest cat, as large as they came, with thick long hair. It was the family of Jonas and Vera, the children substitute. For many years it had not been given a name but eighteen months ago, for no particular reason, it had been awarded one: Olaf. The mouse scurried past the litter tray and seemed on course for the cat's wire-framed basket. Big amber eyes were fixed on it. For a cat of that size, a mouse was barely a meal. Olaf was motionless except for the tip of his tail, the size of a healthy fox's brush, which flicked left and right, an indication of irritation.

The tea was poured and a mug passed to him. He did not point out the mouse because Vera would have complained and demanded action from Jonas. He seemed to study his magazine but in fact kept the mouse and his cat under close observation. The mouse was now near to being within range of the cat's giant paw, where claws were buried, and a lurch forward would have put the little beast within range of its teeth.

They had walked further than he'd wanted. Had done the whole island, damn near frozen to death, had seen the birds she wanted to observe and been blessed with the short-eared owl on the wing, and a pair of harriers had raked over the reeds. They had exhausted the island, been ferried back to Orford, had not visited the castle, which was a relief, then he had driven, at her direction, to Staverton Thicket.

The cat was lazy. It was also supremely well fed. The cat never ran if it could walk. It showed no concern, contented itself merely with twitching its tail. The mouse advanced, then might have realised that further progression was unwise: about as equal a contest as an infantryman advancing on a main battle tank formation. Jonas grinned bleakly. The mouse showed such innocence. Jonas could have shifted on his bench seat, could have coughed lightly, any motion or sound would have been enough to frighten the mouse and send it back to the gap by Vera's feet. Jonas stayed still, silent, and watched . . . was not proud of himself but wanted to see how it would play out, the matter of death in the late afternoon, and dusk had settled around their caravan.

His feet hurt because she had walked him further than he'd enjoyed. She had found a reference to the thicket in a guide of the area. There were old oaks here, part of a diminished ancient woodland, and many would have been more than four centuries old, and up to 200 years before had been pollarded regularly. Their bark was gnarled and distorted and holly sprouted from the trees' rotted centres. Rare-breed cattle grazed among the trees, but Jonas was more interested when their path took them to the edge of the woodland and behind a single strip of electrified wire was a wide field for pigs and their half-moon shelters. He liked the image of their snouts in the troughs. Food must recently have been brought to them: the animals crowded around, some of them standing in the troughs. Jonas was a man who stood without ceremony, who disliked privilege intensely, and he could be disagreeable with little encouragement. Naked greed upset him.

He had enjoyed the sight of the pigs but it had been a long hike back to the car . . . at least, on Havergate Island, he had been able to look through the open door of the hide and observe the structures, long abandoned, on Orford Ness which leaked history and the research of warfare. It would have been, forty years before, a prime target for any Soviet intelligence office – whether a "legal" and attached to the Embassy, or an "illegal", in the country under bogus cover. He had agreed to come on this caravan jaunt when the opportunity to visit that strip of marsh and shingle was offered as bait; the location where radar had been developed before the Second World War, and where the Atomic Weapons Research Establishment had set up a Cold War base and learned the science of imploding explosives around a plutonium core, the trigger for the detonation of the atom, or hydrogen, bomb . . . It would be fascinating for him to walk where the boffins had worked, where the old enemy, still the enemy, had stalked. Jonas was on indefinite deferral of retirement. He had, a couple of years before, been switched from Counter-Terror and the hunting of the Isis boys to Russian penetration. Interesting work, and . . . he knew about "grey mice". The little creature froze. One of Olaf's eyes, had they been fully open, would have been larger than the mouse's head. Perhaps the little person, male or female – Jonas did not know, but presumed female – could see its own head reflected in those great malevolent eyes. It turned and ran. Olaf pretended that he had not noticed the intruder . . . Silly of Jonas to have thought of "grey mice" but there were too many times, as Vera said, that he seemed wrapped in the trade he followed, seldom able to escape it, or willing to make the effort.

He told Vera about the mouse. She looked at her feet, saw nothing on the floor, shrugged, went on with the preparations for their meal. He said it was a small mouse, harmless, and grey, and was about to explain the significance of a grey mouse, but did not finish the sentence.

The lights in the caravan flickered, seemed about to go out, then came alive again. Dipped once more, then regained their full power . . . as if giving a warning.

The rain had started again and the wind.

Jonas said, "I told you, didn't I? We've just enjoyed the calm before the storm."

2

They were out early on Dunwich Heath.

Neither Jonas nor Vera had slept well. They were on open ground, few trees to offer protection and the wind came hard on them, and the rain spat. Jonas had pulled a miserable face, one of his favourite expressions, and had used a familiar quote: "Things are going to get a lot worse before they get worse" and had suggested that they should take their exercise after a dawn break-fast, because the storm was chasing them.

A poor night for both of them in the pull-out, then stowaway, bed. Some time in the small hours, Jonas had been up and had switched off the refrigerator. He'd done it because of the electrical cuts. The power would go off, then the fridge would start to bleep a warning, then the power would come back on and the engine would crank up and have to work overtime in order to lower the inner temperature. Switch the damn thing off and pull out the plug had been his technical answer to the problem. That had not solved the difficulty of sleeping. The movement under the bed had bothered him, the sound of scurrying, of scratching. He blamed the "grey mouse", the "wee, sleekit, cowrin' tim'rous beastie", the little wretch that attracted no interest from Olaf.

Jonas was in sour humour . . . At the start of their walk, Vera had accosted a ranger taking a small party of enthusiasts for a hike on the Heath and the man had – with no good grace because they were obviously not fare-paying punters – said where they *might* see the Dartford warbler. Jonas was told it was rare, that it would be exceptional good fortune to see one, that it was the size of a sparrow, that a three-second sighting would be a triumph. Jonas humoured his wife, nodding with fraudulent enthusiasm, and his mind had slipped ... His work now encompassed another great rarity: the expanding numbers of Russian intelligence officers, attached to the Embassy, who claimed to be engaged in "legitimate diplomatic activity" and not in hostile spying.

They tramped into the wind that blew in hard from the North Sea and flattened his clothes against his body, and he clung to his cap.

He supposed a rest, a break from his work was to be appreciated. He had moved – not strictly accurate, had *been* moved – from Counter-Terror to Counter-Espionage after his single-handed arrest of Cameron Jilkes. Wearing a handcuff on his own wrist he had wormed himself close to the Isis veteran who had returned to the UK with a heart overflowing with hatred and with a target to take down. Jonas had then clipped the free cuff to Jilkes' wrist while sitting next to him in a park and appearing to be a boring, lonely old man in need of conversation: had damn near had his arm pulled from the shoulder socket before the backup had arrived. Jilkes, at Southwark Crown Court, had been sentenced to a minimum of twenty-seven years' maximum security imprisonment. And Jonas? There had been a bar to his Queen's Gallantry Medal, to go with the original awarded after he had disarmed, single-handed, a wannabe suicide, complete with a primed vest, close to the Houses of Parliament. And more for Jonas? A second disciplinary committee had convened and once more he had been warned that his conduct ran counter to all accepted practices of waiting on site for trained personnel to arrive, and again he had been reprimanded.

In the Thames House offices of the Security Service only a very few knew of the detail of his involvement in the two arrests. But it was recognised that he possessed, though not from specific training or a university education, a nose that was more than valuable. Actually, a rather unremarkable nose and with a nuisance mole on one side that probably should have been cut out years back, but a nose that gave him the ability to think outside conventional parameters. At Thames House, his champion was the current AssDepDG, on a floor above Jonas's own cubicle in a corner of a room on the south-facing side of the building, third floor, and with the number 13 on the door. He had, in S/3/13, the company of men and women of the A4 Branch, a surveillance team who had learned to tolerate his eccentricity, his rudeness, and to appreciate his brilliance. His nose, bloodied when Jilkes had failed to break free, was as good, a detective in the Flying Squad had remarked, as that of any of the "thief takers" in the classic days of Scotland Yard legends. To keep him clear of risking his life in further contravention of regulations, Jonas was transferred to the Russia Desk, had been there for two years. A bit slow, he would have said in confidence, except that there was nobody he talked to inside such strictures, not even Vera. He did not speak Russian, had never been to that vast country . . . He sat most working days in the small area with the partition that was his den, studying photographs and case histories and surveillance schedules of "legals" and "illegals" and their assets. Perhaps because it *was* all "a bit slow" Jonas had agreed to take owed days off and tow the caravan to the Suffolk coast for a long weekend. What he had been working on earlier that week . . .

But the memory nudge was tipped from his mind. The group with the ranger were a hundred yards ahead frozen on the path, except for those who were tugging at their cameras or elbowing for a better vantage point: all would be disappointed. There was a blur of movement. Rain on the lenses of Jonas's spectacles distorted his view. The bird came towards him and Vera had a hand on his arm to keep him motionless. Its chest was russet, its back dull brown and it had a high geek's forehead. It flew towards them, away from the enthusiasts, and perched on a sprig of winter gorse. He heard Vera gasp with pleasure. Just another bird as far as Jonas was concerned, but he was pleased for Vera. A full five seconds it was with them, a dozen feet away, and then it scooted. Jonas saw, the ornithologists gazing at him with naked envy. He shrugged, smiled, grimaced, as if it had all been just luck. He had seen the bird, they had not. *Luck*. Jonas liked luck. Luck was more important in his work than the famed quality of his nose . . . He wondered how the little grey mouse was, whether it stayed lucky, whether Olaf, in between extended bouts of sleeping, had put an end to the mouse's lucky streak. They trudged on. And he wondered about the electricity in the caravan, when Vera allowed him back there, and whether she would manage to produce a hot meal.

He liked the company of luck, had needed it in his life, never bad-mouthed it. And said, "I'm not complaining but a big storm is coming, believe me."

Alexei looked unremarkable. Just a young Russian lad. Wore the hood of his anorak high on his head, the buttons fastened to protect his chin and mouth, thick jeans and ordinary trainers. There were squalls of snow in the air, some of the flakes resting on the top of his rucksack, more on his hood. The pavement was a wet and dirty slush, and he felt the damp in the heel of his right trainer, in which he'd transported the memory stick. Was he given a second glance by those who flowed either side of him? Were they approaching him or passing him? He was certain he was watched.

Guilt gnawed. There was good reason for him to be tailed.

He had seen them after he had left the bus, crowded that Sunday lunchtime, and had started to walk the last few hundred metres to the station. He was now a bare hundred paces away from the extravagant main entrance. There was no doubt in his mind. Fear welled in him.

Two of them wore suits. Not the elegant suits favoured by those going to the fat-cat jobs in the centre of the capital, but the cheap crumpled suits that were the uniform of the bureaucrats, and over the suits they wore heavy bulging anoraks. They stood out, were telegraphed, and they moved at the same pace as he did. One ahead, occasionally ducking his head close to his collar so that he could speak, and at other moments seeming to scratch his ear with an irritation that indicated he had trouble with his earpiece. In another ear, level with him, he had seen a flicker of light; they had been passing a pizza outlet and garish neon blurted out from the interior and lit the drab grey of the street, and a fraction of the light had found the device buried in a hairy ear and Alexei was certain he had seen a loose coil of peach-coloured wire that led from the ear down into the anorak. Good enough? Certain proof. He had reason to be frightened.

He was only a clerk at his workplace in the city of Kirov. The workplace was an out station of an important part of one of the most secret and sensitive organisations in the Federation of Russia. A junior clerk. A junior clerk who found, every two weeks, enough cash, though the figure was reduced because of the discount he received, to come to Moscow to see his mother: a round trip of 1596 kilometres.

She was on the far side of the street. She would have seemed like any other young girl in Moscow, pushing her buggy and threading between the crowds. She was on the far side but she would have been able to see what he saw, and recognise it. He made a sign. They had, between them, a small library of them. He stopped. He pulled a handkerchief from his pocket, washed and ironed by his mother, and blew his nose: that was for her to come. He pulled a small folded street map from his anorak and studied it, his eyes misting so much he could barely identify the lines of the individual streets. That was their signal for her to approach him – immediately. He stood, seemed to have trouble with his map. Alexei looked up and saw her react.

Barely a glance at the traffic ... her arm raised as if she was confident the cars would brake or swerve around her. The briefest of pauses on the central reservation and then she launched herself again. She was shabby and pale, just as she had looked the previous afternoon. She was off again, with a tired smile that might have charmed the drivers who stamped on their brakes or swung a wheel. She made it across ... Alexei thought her wonderful, had no one else – in his deceit – to cling to. He was guilty. If he lived long enough, survived interrogation and came to trial in a court-room, he would face the full weight of the law of his country. It was a year and a half since Alexei had been recruited.

A warm evening. Work for the day finished. The officers he worked for had gone for a drink and a meal, and would not have concerned themselves with where the clerk went or what he did in the evenings. They were a GRU team. They had flown to the city of Limassol on the island of Cyprus. The officers and himself were in the GRU section of the Military Industrial Commission. They were tasked with ferreting out the most blatant acts of corruption and theft from the state by fellow officers serving abroad, where opportunities for grand larceny were as abundant as the oranges growing in the island's groves. Cyprus was, almost, a Russian fiefdom and they had the commercial banks there to prove it. It also had the British Sovereign Bases of Akrotiri, Episcopi and Dhekelia to justify Russian interest, and the volume of signal intelligence sucked down by the antennae on the Troodos mountains that could tell the UK's military analysts what was being said by individual Russian tank commanders serving in Syria, and Russian pilots on bombing runs, as well as the location of helicopters dropping barrel bombs loaded with lethal gas. The investigation, of which Alexei was the most junior cog in the wheel, was of a local team that had omitted to "create a roof" and had thought they could play the field without paying those who should have protected them.

He had spent four successive evenings in his hotel room; on the fifth he had gone out for a walk as evening fell, had had no map, had become lost and had realised that he was in an area of cheap bars. Gazing around him. A gay bar, and a boy with peroxide hair eyeing him. Music blasting. Alexei gawping. Knew all about a grim high-rise residential corner of Moscow, knew Kirov, a back-woods city on the edge of Siberia. Knew nothing of a gay bar in a Mediterranean sink town. Looking, watching, and the gang came behind him, unseen till he was bounced. Fellow Russians, merchant seamen, with their evening squeezes, already drunk but short of fun. Started with jeering and pushing. He'd stumbled and a leg had gone out, had flailed into the thigh of one of the tarts. Excuse for a pile-in. Beaten and punched and kicked, a football for enter-tainment, and a couple of the tarts pulled his trousers down to his knees, and he was fearful and shrivelled and that produced more raucous laughter, and one of the girls seeming to mount him and shrieking she could not find anything, could not even find a "cock-tail sausage". More laughter and a few more gratuitous kicks, and he had shouted out, shrill and nasal, that he was GRU. More punches and more kicks and then he was bleeding and bruised and his ribcage hurt, and they'd moved on, and not a backward glance, gave not a flying fuck for GRU ... But one passerby stopped. Someone cared. She had a boyfriend with her and she was kneeling beside him, cradling his head, and telling him that he was safe now. He didn't want police involved. She said they would not be called, but she had a colleague ... Her name was Daff Boult. She'd staunched the blood from his cut lip and was wiping dirt off his face, and her boyfriend had taken her phone and she'd given him a number to ring. The boy said he was calling on behalf of Daff Boult, said that Daff Boult was in SigInt at the Dhekelia listening post. Said that Daff Boult was in the company of a guy that the colleague might wish to meet ... how it started.

Might have been better if he had been left lying in the middle of the street, abandoned outside the gay bar. Was sure now that he had recognised the tail and it was keeping pace with him. Alexei was trembling and thought he might topple over. The buggy was beside him. Little Hector must already have learned a trick from her. He gurgled happily, then defiantly chucked a toy on to the pavement, some sort of soft bear that was cuddly and would have been a friend. Alexei bent to pick it up and she crouched beside him. All so natural. Their heads close, they grasped the bear as the snow came on thicker.

"Definite, they have me under surveillance. You saw?"

"Shit, yes. I saw."

"Not an error."

"Definite. I saw four goons."

"I want out."

"That's a big-time solution, Alexei."

"Maybe in two minutes I am in custody."

"Maybe in ten minutes you are on the train. Maybe it is just a routine check."

"I am about to piss myself. You know about fear. I want out."

She took a deep breath. "Go now, get on the train. I'll talk with people, do it tomorrow. When do you come back?"

"I come next week, and I want out. I want, if I am still free, safety. It was promised me, a way out. It was called 'exfiltration'. I was promised."

"I can't answer that . . . See you next week. Stay safe."

She had the bear in her hand, passed it to the child. Hector bawled, as if a good game had played its course. Alexei straightened. She smiled at him, a distant smile as if they were strangers, and then she was gone and the buggy wheels squealed and the last he saw of her face was when she bent at the waist and tightened the fastening over the buggy, hid her child. Then she was back into the traffic and not a backward glance.

He started to walk and waited for them to surround him. He was not stopped . . . he saw them for a last time when he approached a barrier, his ticket in his hand. They watched him, he was sure of it, thought he might be sick. Alexei walked to the train. Were they playing with him? Were they teasing, taunting, destroying him?

He sat in his seat and waited for the train to lurch out of the Yaroslavskiy main station – or for them to come for him.

Benedict, sitting at the back of the auditorium, watched.

"Whether we are in London, or Stockholm, or Berlin, the most sensitive section of the Embassy is that in which GRU operate, and we are alongside – I mean 'they' because my allegiance has changed – the elements of SVR and of FSB. But, among them, GRU is the elite. The elite because GRU has the best techniques in tradecraft."

Benedict listened, and thought it was crap. He was over six feet in height, solidly built, with an uncombed, unbrushed, mop of hair, a complexion as smooth as a child's, and was always given the marker of "little". Did not bother him. Nor was he bothered that the rest of the Resettlement crowd seemed to have damn near washed their hands of decision making in relation to Sashcord. Not for much longer; it had to be resolved.

"We – again my mistake – they operate at the highest level of training. We are the prime players when it comes to defeating your surveillance. The tactics are loitering, which throws a tail into confusion. Or, without warning, doubling back, which causes most of the show-outs from German agencies. And, if in a vehicle, the constant monitoring of following cars in traffic and always checking and remembering detail."

Sashcord was on a low stage. He had a hand in his pocket, wore a plastic face microphone which barely showed against his skin, and carried no notes. He was smart: collar and tie, a pressed suit and polished shoes. Benedict detested him.

"I tell you, if I were to be on foot in the centre of your city, you would need a team of at least twenty to follow me, at least that number. So, what if I send out two other colleagues, trained to the same level as myself, then do you have sixty personnel able to do the job? You do not. You will be overwhelmed. That is why we walk all over you, and we take the job with the greatest seriousness and your population worry how much it costs and how much tax they must pay to meet that cost."

Benedict murmured to Wally, sitting beside him, "If he was so goddamn marvellous and they were so goddamn clever, why the hell didn't he stay where he was, where he belonged? God, what a shit." Not for Wally to reply, just a flicker of a droll smile. They had driven down with two Danes ahead of them as far as the border, and then a German escort had taken over, and one of them was female, curt and cold, and Sashcord had said, loud in Benedict's ear, "Needs a good lay, that one, what I could give her, and wipe that scowl off her, gagging for it, she'd be." At least every week, the Russian asked him with feigned concern, "You worry me, friend, because you're not getting it ... and the worry is because you don't show signs of missing it," and always then a sneer and a laugh.

"Inside the GRU there is value in old methods. GRU thinks they are the best ways. New students regard them, at the start, as childish but learn to love them. You have to send a message, so you put a chalk mark on a telephone pole. We want to cancel that meeting so we put a banana skin or an apple core on a window sill. We always think the 'dead letter box' is the best way of exchanging information, and we think of the brush contact as difficult, dangerous. Juvenile, perhaps. Effective, yes. GRU runs rings around you because you do not take the security of your secrets with sufficient seriousness. I say, very frankly, you are a pushover. We want political or economic insights and you hang it on trees for us to take. Most important is your Research and Development and we save billions by taking a loan off your work."

Before Sashcord was brought into the auditorium he had been entertained at a select buffet gathering. Girls serving, and drink offered. Obvious to Benedict that their stooge regarded himself as of celebrity status. His hand had hovered close to the backside of a waitress and remarks were made and she'd blushed but had stood her ground, so he might have been on a promise. He'd said a few minutes later to Benedict that he hoped "when this circus is over that we won't dash away too fast. Have time for a coffee and . . ." And there had been more in the car coming down, Doug driving, Wally beside him, and Benedict with him in the back, about the impatience to get to the UK, to be accepted, and to leave the suffocating life in the Aarhus safe house. He thought the speech was poor, lacklustre, and doubted any of the Germans in his audience had learned anything that was new to them.

"You need to smarten your game. You have a wide open society. You were wide open, insecure, when there were two Germanys, when the East had their own people, and you have learned nothing . . . The chief aim of GRU is to recruit agents inside your society. You think that difficult? Believe me, friends, it is easy. I will take questions."

The pause was long, would have sent a message. The Russian, Igor or Sashcord, had done himself less than justice. The address was supposed to have been a dry run for him to be hawked around Europe, given benign employment, put to use before the final decision was made as to what to do with him. As for himself, Benedict reckoned he had exhausted his role, had extracted what little there was to be taken from the man but had failed to lock on to any intelligence of value. He eased back in his chair. No questions had yet been offered . . . An officer from Germany's BfS organisation had started on a ponderous vote of thanks, about as insincere as it could get . . . Benedict thought of his home, his garden in the London suburbs, all locked up. He was camped in Denmark, his wife was in Scotland, doing stand-in shifts at a GP practice . . . Benedict knew his reputation as a Sixer. He was the unflappable one, had not been known to lose his temper, to panic. This guy tested him, sorely. He was supposed to bleed information from a foul little reptile. No love there, and mutual. Eyes almost closed. The response droned on.

Anatoly and Konstantin would have considered themselves masters of the arts of concealment, and of the many other disciplines hammered into them during their days in Special Forces. Experience of working deep in the countryside, hills and forests and hostile villages in the Caucasus, and in the more lethal tower block estates of Grozny in the Chechen snake pit, had perfected those skills. Which perhaps was why they had survived those months, years, of close-quarters killing, perhaps why they were still in demand and work was easy to find. They had parked the Mercedes, now with new registration plates, had chosen a place less than 100 metres from the main gate, and the vehicle was half on the road and half on the pavement. They reckoned that a car of that quality could park anywhere and not arouse suspicion. It was equidistant between two street lights.

They had identified a house that seemed shuttered for the winter; leaves had collected on the step of the main door, and had been blown into scurrying heaps on the driveway.

Each of them would have said it was a crying shame to destroy a Mercedes, a saloon and a C257 model. It would be obliterated. Konstantin had done the wiring, and their officer, Leonid, had assembled the device. Simple. Explosives that were military grade, a detonator stick, electronics that came from any mass-produced system that warned of cop automatic cameras, and when the switch was thrown there was sufficient ordnance inside the car, hidden in the boot, below a rug on the leather rear seats and in the forward passenger well, for the vehicle to come free from the

chassis and the integral parts to be lifted and spattered sideways
– enough to make a crater, and very reasonable sized foxhole for
fighting men. What they had been, fighters and killers.

Crouched behind a low wall, with the rustle of windblown
leaves around them, with a gap in the hedge which gave a view of
the car and beyond it the compound's main gates, they settled
down to wait . . . and afterwards they would sprint down the side
of the deserted house to a gate at the bottom of the garden which
would have once been for the delivery of coal, and they would cut
into the path, keep running, and Leonid would be there to meet
them. Engine started, door slamming, accelerator, and high fives.

The target was a GRU traitor. The explosives were Russian,
manufactured for military use. They were on the territory of a
supposed prime member of the North Atlantic Treaty
Organisation, and they did not give a shit if a trail was left, nor
did their officer, and they could assume that the man who tasked
the operation was not concerned about a footfall on a discreet
Hamburg street. In recent months a rebel Chechen monster had
been shot dead in Berlin's Tiergarten, and another had been
stabbed to death across the border in a northern French city. The
reaction was nothing, just empty threats and finger pointing and
a jabber of protest.

They could see uniforms at the gate . . . had also seen the arrival
of the two cars as the evening was closing in and had noted the
lights on the lead car and the flash of the headlamps that had
caused the gates to be hurriedly opened. They knew the time of
the meeting that the traitor would address, knew what time it was
estimated to finish, and reckoned they knew at what time the
bastard's last breath would be drawn. They waited.

It did not seem important to Anatoly or Konstantin, not worthy
of anxiety, that a young and slender policeman, well wrapped
against the cold and the wet, stared down the road towards the
darkness where the Mercedes-Benz was parked. Other officers
had been there before him, had glanced into the car, shrugged,
gone on their way.

*   *   *

He knew the car had been checked, but not by him.

At a distance, and in the poor light at the edge of the street lamps' range, Gunther was intrigued to see this model for himself. With no tax or pension payments, no accommodation to be paid for, no utilities used, no outgoings, in three years he could possibly have afforded to buy such a vehicle. It was a diversion . . . he needed one. Required a distraction from thoughts of his girlfriend, or his former girlfriend, or some other guy's girlfriend, of Ursula.

It was a dream vehicle, sleekly black, a model that could have graced the front cover of any magazine specialising in top of the range cars. Gunther reckoned that – had he been on the autobahn, the Number 1 route from Hamburg to Bremen – he could have taken that vehicle up to 250 kilometres per hour, and felt no shake, no resistance, still with power to spare. Looked new, barely out of the factory, but then all those specifications were new, had hardly had time to bed down.

He stood beside it. He drove an old VW, seven years on the road and 175,000 klicks on the clock, and a tear in the back seat, and she was difficult to start in the winter mornings. It was all he could afford, but he could dream . . . He looked at the registration to see where the vehicle had come from. Most likely supplied by a garage in the Altona district of Hamburg because there they had the greatest concentration of wealth. He put his torch beam on the registration.

The radio in his ear said that the two-car convoy was ready to leave, would be exiting the gate in three minutes.

He had not felt it before, never. The cold clamped on the back of Gunther's neck. Might have been an icepack secured there. Hardly out of the recruits' college, hardly in receipt of his uniform and his issued weapon, hardly familiar with the weight of responsibility. He saw that lights blazed on the far side of the wire gates, and heard the rumble of high-powered engines, then the blue lights came on.

A vehicle that had been off the production line for only two years. A registration number for a vehicle issued four years before . . . He felt a trembling in his arms, his legs, blinked, shook his head, looked again, saw the vehicle model, saw the registration plate date – and saw that the boot of the Mercedes was low as if it carried substantial weight.

If he were right, he might be praised but only if he were listened to. If he were wrong he would be castigated, bollocked, condemned, laughed at. He started to run.

They were opening the double gates. He sprinted as best he could with his arms wide. The cars edged forward . . . He screamed at the top of his voice.

Who would listen to him? A grand evening inside and he had watched as the men and women arrived for a lecture and the whisper had it that they were political police and counter-espionage experts, some of the finest in the German state, and had watched as a two-car convoy had come fast up that approach road, not slowing. Though privacy glass had covered the rear windows he had seen the passengers behind the driver, noted them through the front windscreen, and one of them would have been the target.

Assuredly a target. Most definitely a bomb weighed down the rear seat.

He ran faster, screamed, frantically waved his arms and the cars would have had to run him down or stop. Might be ending a brief career. The cars stopped. His Polizeiobermeister strode towards him. Something like "What the fuck do you think you . . ." Lights shone full on his face, near blinding him, and he heard a chorus of abuse because he had delayed the cars' departure.

He stammered the words, told them.

The escape of Anatoly and Konstantin was confused. They blundered past the empty house, capsized rubbish bins, had to scale a high side gate; then one of them ran into a stone bird bath and the other stumbled on a hidden step into a sunken area of the garden. Their calls to each other, punctuated by obscenities, were quiet: they were not the fit young men they had been in the Chechnya days and their breath came in spasms and their grunts were more frequent. At the fence it was necessary for Konstantin to cup his hands for Anatoly's boot and then heave him upwards. And equally necessary for Anatoly, astride the fence, to reach down and heave Konstantin up. Together they rolled off, landed in the way that their first paratrooper instructor had shown them, and rolled and rolled and then ran. They passed another house and crossed another wall, through a trade entry and then were into the street they needed. No breath left in their lungs and no strength left in their legs, they reached the waiting car. Doors dragged open, the two of them sagging down. The interior light showed them Leonid's face.

"Where is the fucking explosion?"

Neither willing to be the messenger, to give the news of failure – then spilling it. The car powered away. They jerked back in their seats. They, old lads from the better days of Special Forces work, would have to give an explanation to Leonid who they answered to . . . both recognised that Leonid was then left with the harder job of explaining further up the chain of command that an order had not been executed. They headed off into the night and Leonid spat staccato questions at them.

A degree of collective pandemonium enveloped the car, Wally driving, Doug beside him, and Benedict and Sashcord sharing the back seat.

When they had stopped at the gate, the young policeman pounding towards them, Benedict had seen the shape of the Mercedes-Benz parked in the street ahead. The cop had waved at it. Had shouted that word, again and again, and yelled that the vehicle was armed to explode. Brave boy, big call. They had been held and two older policemen had run forward and the boy had gone back with them. A hard kick at a door and it had reluctantly opened. Only a brief glance needed . . . they had come back running, running fast. "Bomb" was the word.

The escort driver, the car that would have led them out and down the street, passing within a few feet of the Merc, would have caught a little less of the blast than themselves – but enough probably to kill – swung hard on a U turn, used the full lock. Wally followed him. Benedict was no expert in "close protection" but the basic necessity would have been, bloody obvious, to get the principal clear and away, "burn some rubber" as their American friends would have said, put in some distance. Wally drove well, followed where he was led. They crossed lawns around the head-quarters building and through freshly planted beds of shrubs where the frost was already settling. No snow now, and no sleet, but the temperature dropping and ice forming. Across an artificial sports surface, clipping a goal post, and seemed to be aiming for a hedge, but a gap materialised and they went through it and the branches scraped the sides of both cars and they came to the back gate. A goon stood there. A guard on the gate. The gate was closed. The guard had no authorisation to open it, had not been informed it would be used. Not just a good show, a great moment, Benedict thought, and the lad was out of the lead car and had the guard by the throat and lifted him clean off the ground and swore at him, mouth to mouth, then dropped him. The gate was opened.

They drove north. Soon would be on the main route that would take them via Flensberg to the frontier. Benedict understood. What he would have ordered after a Grade A shambles: get the unwanted and unwelcome visitors out of the city, away from the jurisdiction, cut responsibility like they were using a cleaver. The road number was 23, the one they had used to come south. Wally drove fast.

Benedict eased back, sucked in air. The Russian had been squealing complaint, had been ignored ... they would not have spoken on the journey anyway. Benedict had rated the speech as poor, the man's attitude insufferable, and worse ... Just before they had left he had seen that the "principal", Sashcord, was off down a corridor with a waitress skipping after him. Would have gone at it like a buck rabbit given the chance. He had ordered Doug to prise him off the girl and bring him back. Benedict had stayed polite, remained correct, had not told him to "shut the fuck up" when they had careered over the grounds of the headquarters complex and when they had burst through the hedge. The road ahead was open.

All the way out, Benedict had been draped over the Russian's body, covering him. Not a hero's action, but what he thought was necessary. Igor took out his fag pack and his lighter. The car's interior was festooned with *Rygning forbudt* signs. Not a time or an issue on which Benedict would mount a defence. If he had had a hip flask he would have swigged from it. The lighter flashed and smoke billowed.

Benedict took out his phone and texted Monty. Not a lily that should be gilded. Dear old Monty, the clever one. Sunday night, and Monty was likely crouched, in his attic with his beloved train layout with the miniaturised replicas of the great days of steam, the engines of empire and industrial power. They still played that game, didn't they, the Sixers? Getting harder by the day to punch above their weight. He imagined Monty – probably on his hands and knees and fixing some bloody signal that was playing up – and a little trace of a frown would plough into his forehead, and that would be the end of a gentle session going along the Up Line. About as welcome as a bucket of cold vomit.

The cigarette was stubbed out.

Sashcord said, "Tonight, for all your airs and graces, you covered yourselves with no glory. Perhaps you will be sacked. Sacked for incompetence."

"Not tonight please, Igor. Inquests in the morning."

A gentle sing-song voice, as if the moment was almost enjoyed, but still brutal. "Where I come from, from GRU, a failure like that would lead – not a doubt – to dismissal. You know, sent to Siberia, a boot in the arse and out."

Benedict did not say, "Well since you are no longer in GRU, Igor, since you walked away from that organisation and betrayed your friends, colleagues, fellow officers, played traitor, what would have happened inside GRU is not really for you to comment on, so, do us a favour and close your goddamn mouth." Instead Benedict said, "I think it best we use the good, well-worked, cold light of day. Then evaluate. That's best."

Igor said, "And not just you, my always best friend, who may face dismissal, for failure, in the morning. Think of the boys who carried out their orders and were supposed to kill me, and kill you also which would have been collateral, and our best friends in the front. Think of them. What was their mistake? Why did they not succeed? What was the level of their failure? I tell you, they will plead for a chance to make good that failure, pray they are given another opportunity. They do not go once, not succeed, then give up. I think I have the right to speak because it is my body, or bits of it, that should by now have been arriving in the Hamburg mortuary – and I would have had you for comfort, close by, the next bay, or parts of you. It was just incompetence and you know the implications. You know? I will tell you . . ."

He did, and Benedict could not disagree with him.

Frank was at her usual position. Her business was done the old-fashioned way: she had a lined note pad and took the minutes in shorthand.

"Up the creek, no paddle." From Chiswell who was considered the rising star, knew the billing and enjoyed that reputation, and when he wanted to grate with the others on the Resettlement team he would let his upbringing from a town west of Leeds run riot and give the accent full licence.

She had little light to work in and the shadows were thrown around her and most of them would have probably forgotten that she was with them. Denys Montgomery had phoned her and had started to negotiate whether she might – because it would be much appreciated if she could – interrupt her plans for the evening and come into Vauxhall Cross. She had said she would come as if it were not a problem and had not spoken of washing her hair, doing some ironing, settling with a small glass in front of the TV. Had discarded her jeans and T-shirt, and changed into a trouser suit and a blouse, starched and white. Had locked the door of her flat over the kebab shop, had taken the bus, the 36, from the stop outside the big Paddington hospital, left it in Pimlico and then had walked at a snappy pace over the bridge. She had been first in and had made sure that the table they would sit around was wiped clean, had turned up the heating, and made coffee.

"An absolute disaster, on a mega scale. And I think I'm already on the record as opposing giving houseroom to him," from

Symonds. Not a star, and not going anywhere in the stratosphere and he had made the point that it was a weekend and he had a life outside. He was still in his tennis-playing gear, a towel at his throat, and stank from his exertions. He had more talent for the game than for his work, and was a regular in the Six doubles squad. He was unlikely to contribute more but stared sharply at Frank as if to make sure that, in the shadows, she had heard his defence and would note it.

Had she been thanked for coming in? Why would she have been? Her face was impassive. If it had been inconvenient then none would know it. She had heard Barker say that she was indispensable: an aside to Toni a couple of months back, "When I go, it'll barely be noticed, and I'll be forgotten in a week. But, and I'll brook no argument, if Frank walked out, the whole section would collapse. I'm not exaggerating. The glue that holds us all together and I'm glad I won't see the day." And she would be in early again on the following day, the start of the conventional working week because it would be busy, busy and interesting, interesting and fraught.

"Don't understand why they would have gone after him. Low grade and bloody useless. Hardly worth the effort, shipping in a team and getting the hardware delivered, taking that sort of risk for a man so inadequate – except that they don't care. Have no scruples because there's no comeback. Won't be more than a sigh of exasperation from the Hun, they can be sure of that . . . Anyway, I never rated him." Barker shrugged as if that were all the contribution required from him. He was a stalwart in a pub darts team and had been called out in mid-game with a result in the balance, so did not think it necessary to hide his irritation.

"Cut him adrift and a one-way ticket to anywhere in the far distance. We were too welcoming and the sooner we're rid of him the better." Toni needed to be back home in Streatham. Husband abroad, nanny off for the evening, a neighbour with bad grace looking after the brats.

Monty had started the meeting with a résumé of what he knew, what had been fed him from Hamburg. Frank would include that in full, the others' remarks she would paraphrase. She had, a few years back, wondered if Monty were in fact steeling himself to make a pass at her, but nothing had happened. She had been left confused by what she might have done if he had . . . Time had passed and it was rumoured in their section that he had taken up with a hospital nurse and shared his life with her and with the layout of his trains. He was very bright, often came to work wearing odd socks, was thought to be pretty helpless in the domestic field.

A pencil rapped on the table, as if Monty thought they were drifting, and he seemed impatient with them. He said, "I don't want to preach about damnation, that sort of level of catastrophe. I think this evening's business is worse than you think. Much worse . . . Some facts are worth examining. First, the German hosts in Hamburg were not informed beforehand of who they would be listening to this evening. Could have been our own Director, could have been our esteemed leader of Russia Desk, P5, for all they knew. I am assuming the target was a defector, and I assume also that the German end is blameless. Not the Danes, our colleagues, because they knew only that their people were needed to provide a security escort to the border and were not told where – afterwards – the Joe was to be taken: they, too, are clean. The Russian attack could not have come from inside the safe house, from the Aarhus end, because all the major players were in the car and sitting within a metre of Sashcord. They would have died with the target had a rookie policeman not been rather clever: clear in outlook, not intimidated, prepared to speak up. Which leaves us. I think we all knew that Igor, the unwanted major, was to travel this afternoon to Hamburg, to address a room full of intelligence gatherers and security policemen. That is Chis, Simmo, Barky, and you, Toni, and me. And it was authorised at a higher level and the logistics put in place at a lower echelon. It's not nice, leaves a horrid taste to think about . . ."

Frank did her "worm writing" – what the others called it – briskly. Had it all down.

"I think this is where it's from. Cannot dress it up nicely. It is a leak. Could be done in innocence, could be a mistake, or it could have been done with malice, intended. Sorry and all that, but the conclusion is inescapable. This is about as bad as it gets – it is a leak."

Frank abandoned her shorthand and wrote the word in full. It had a stench of poison to it, contagious in any intelligence agency. She underlined it as if that one word was the most important to come from this Sunday evening meeting. Wally liked the gallows bit. Doug liked the humour bit. One of their favourites:

"Was he pushed or did he fall?"

"If you're the guy at the bottom of the stairs doesn't matter that much."

Wally said, "I was wrong, I admit it. Big time wrong. He wasn't a dangle."

Doug said, "I'll buy that. The genuine article, and they came after him once and knew where to look, and fucked up, but they'll come again, try to make a better job of it. And we're alongside."

They had done the changeover at the frontier and a Danish PET boys' car was ahead of them, their lights slicing the darkness on an empty road going north.

A candle was on the caravan's fold-down table.

Not enough light for Jonas to read from.

The power was still off and Vera had a battery radio playing Beethoven, but quietly.

After the expedition to the Heath, and the sighting of the Dartford warbler, he had driven to a parking area above the beach. They had eaten their picnic while rain had flecked the car's windscreen. Then they had walked. Had walked alone. Not another beachcomber, hiker, dog tramper, for company. Jonas could play bloody minded and stubborn, could make an art form of obstinacy. The mood he could manufacture had been sufficient, years back, to halt a suicide bomber at the political heart of his country, and to take down a lethal activist on his way to blast into a sensitive military camp. On both occasions, any man with a degree of common sense would have backed off and howled into a mobile for help to come, and soonest. He had relied that Sunday afternoon on the same pig-headedness, and similar reservoirs of the "started, so I will finish" ethic. He had walked the length of the open beach. Vera, dressed for the occasion and for the elements, had kept pace with him, rather pleased with his reaction. They walked where the shingle petered out and the tideline left clean sand. His cap kept the weather off his sparse hair and his coat protected his jacket and his upper legs. His shoes and good soles, seldom tested in his daily walk over Lambeth Bridge, and kept him steady while the wind blasted him. The point of the walk along this section of Suffolk coastline was moot. It was a degree of exercise, he was battered by fresh air, his cheeks ran with rain-water, and his spectacles needed frequent clearing and drying with his handkerchief. Vera could spot the different layers of soil and rock strata and kept up a commentary in his ear that gave him insight into various ages of composition from a million years back and further. Gulls stayed abreast of them and shrieked as if they were a pair of unwelcome intruders: Vera knew which species they were and the black-backed gulls were the most noisy and threatening and flew closest to them. Extraordinarily, the birds perched on the shingle seemed unconcerned by the wind or the rain, and would only take off when Jonas and Vera came too close, invaded their space. He had walked well and there had come a moment when they were almost at the point where once, a millennium before, a prosperous Saxon boat-building town, Dunwich, had started to collapse into the encroaching sea, and there Vera had decisively turned. They had retraced their steps, had followed their footprints in the sand and been safe in the knowledge that within the next hour the incoming tide would have erased them. She had remarked on that, had cupped her hand against his ear, had told him that their efforts were slight when set against the march of time . . . and Jonas accepted that meekly. Felt it each day he arrived at the side entrance to Thames House, showed his card and was admitted along with his coffee from the café near to the entrance of St John's Gardens. Often thought that his own efforts were puny, would barely stand the test of time. He thought humility was healthy, practised it.

They had come back to the car. Had discarded their soaked outer clothing. She was dry underneath her weatherproofs, and he was only wet below his trouser knees.

At the caravan – many spaces around it now because other weekenders had gone home early to avoid the growing weather depression – they had fed Olaf, had changed his litter tray, and Jonas had changed his trousers. She had started to prepare a hot meal, and Jonas had sipped a mug of cocoa. Then Vera had noticed it, and remarked on it, had required him to clear the mess.

There was a smear of blood on the floor. Beside it was a length of mouse tail.

The stain was the size of a 50 pence coin, the tail was the length of a household match. The cat was in a sleeping position but his eyes were slightly open. No triumphalism. No victory roll. No turning down his dried pellet food because he had already feasted on fresh-killed grey mouse. The cat's lack of conceit appealed to Jonas. He assumed the mouse had thought itself safe and had come out from its nest and had decided to go for another reconnaissance trip around the caravan's interior. A paw would have bashed it, then claws pinioned it, then a mighty jaw would have closed around its head. Would have been fast, rather merciful in fact. He took a piece of kitchen roll and wiped the dried blood as best he could – housework never his strong point – and then picked up the piece of mouse tail. He took it to the door and threw it out. The door slammed shut in his face, caught by the wind.

The wind had increased and the rain had come on harder and the light was fading, and the power went off . . . the soup not quite heated, and the rolls not warmed through, and the casserole not even bubbling. A foul evening in front of them. No suggestion from Vera that Jonas might check the fuse box. He listened to her music and she tidied away the soup bowls, and they drank a glass of wine each: they would probably be early to bed, and sometimes the caravan was buffeted in the wind, and the rain lashed. She seemed sympathetic about the mouse but would never criticise their cat.

He said, "Forget the mouse, it's a bad night, a fierce storm, a difficult time beckoning."

3

Vera had again spotted a wildlife tour group ahead of them and had hurried him along and they had scooted quickly around the edge of a flooded reed marsh and had reached a point where they could hear the group's guide. Some of them must have been deaf because the guide had raised his voice, which was convenient.

Jonas had just heard that this was the territory – a sandy bank beside the path and overlooking the lagoon – of the heather plasterer bee, then was told it was where the red-legged spider-hunting wasp might be found in summer. He admired the name and liked the legend that went with the creature. This breed of wasp settled on top of some helpless item of prey, injected it with a paralysis serum and, having immobilised it, the beast scoffed it . . . The guide moved on to describe the predatory habits of black wasps and their skills in trapping a spider, and then carting it off to an already burrowed hole, then laying eggs on it. Then, the hatched larvae, whenever they appeared, would find a ready meal and feast on the insect . . . tough stuff. Probably, the group in front of them were in a hurry to get to a hide where they would hope to see a heron or a kingfisher, but the stories of the heather plasterer bee and the killer wasps had intrigued Jonas. That was good because the weather had already set in for the day, and there was no power in the caravan.

He had not weakened. Nor Vera.

He had not suggested that they hitch up the stricken caravan and tow it home to Raynes Park. She had not demanded it.

For Jonas the next day was primary.

Irrespective of the weather, they had the booking on the ferry that would take them from the pier at Orford over the channel and land them on Orford Ness which was a place – as Jonas knew – of rare and unpolluted history. Rain ran down the lenses of his spectacles and caught the hems of his trousers, and when the wind came into his face the rain caught the knot of his tie and the collar of his shirt.

The wasps had interested him. Always a desk man, and sometimes known disrespectfully, before he had taken into custody the disarmed suicide, as the Eternal Flame, *"Never Goes Out"*, Jonas had for years pored over his computer screen, and read papers that might increase his knowledge of potential opponents. So . . . whether it was the killing technique of the black wasp's kids or of the red-legged spider hunter, they would have been admired by the activists in the South Armagh district of XMG or by the East Tyrone Brigade crowd on the hills overlooking Dungannon. Would also have gained approval among the Isis people who ran the internal security show in Mosul or Aleppo or at the shrinking oases of power along the banks of the Euphrates. It was said that the old KGB boys had taken spies down into the basements of the Lubyanka building in downtown Moscow, and tossed them through the opened hatch into roaring furnaces that provided the central heating for the office radiators. His retirement was on hold, he still had time to contemplate the potential for bestiality by those he pitted himself against: was not a shrinking violet.

The group in front of them had disappeared, and would have been aiming for a café that Vera said was now within reachable distance. They had enjoyed, moderately, a cold breakfast. No porridge, no toast, and cold water for him to shave in, and a hefty slice of fruit cake. The cat had refused to go out of the caravan . . . there was little to see of the place on the floor where the grey mouse had been gobbled, all but the lower length of its tail. But Jonas and Vera would not pack up and quit.

He would not have entertained Vera's suggestion of this discovery voyage if the promise of Orford Ness had not been thrown in. He could imagine how it would have been in the great days when the science of military defence, and offence, was on the design sheets, and security was the perpetual nightmare, the headache without relief. He knew about spies, turned men and women, those who were feted and those who were detested. He would be a happy man, however foul the weather, walking the tracks of Orford Ness: in the meantime he would humour Vera and would contemplate the horrors inflicted by the red-legged spider-hunting wasp. There would have been a security officer billeted in the village and going across on the boat every morning, and praying each day to his God, humbly and with sincerity, that a traitor did not leak secrets on his watch. He had already seen, from their first expedition to Havergate, the buildings that Atomic Weapons had erected on the Ness, those that were called the pagodas, and had been able at that distance to reflect on the scale of resources heaved on to the island. It interested him that also present on the island, and with secrets of the highest quality tucked in their brains, would have been the best and brightest of nuclear scientists. Unlikely that the security officer, who would have drawn the short straw in being awarded the posting, would have matched their intellect. He could dream . . . Jonas liked that, was happy to reflect on the problems that others had faced, were facing, would face as sure as night followed day when the tedious little matter arose of keeping the nation safe.

The rain pelted on him and Vera. Waiting for them at the end of their day was a cold and slightly damp caravan where a little grey mouse had been savaged, where the power had failed. Good that he had Orford Ness to cheer him the following day, and good too that he did not share the responsibilities of a hapless security officer, fearful of a leak, running merely to stand still. He walked well, felt a freedom.

The Brigadier, Volkov, should have been receiving a call from one of the *siloviki* who stayed close to the court of the President. should have been a message relayed to him from a crony adjacent to the big man. Not naming him . . . not mentioning news reports coming in late the evening before from Hamburg . . . not referring to an assassination and the identity of the victim nor congratulating the Brigadier on the work of his team. He had expected to hear before dawn that the team of Vympel veterans, who would have been trained in the complex run by Military Unit 35690 in the Balashika suburb of the capital, were well on their way home, job done, scumbag in bits, message sent loud and clear and other scrumbags shitting themselves, looking over their shoulders, fearful of shadows, and . . . no call yet.

But he had made one. The Brigadier was confident that the quality of the officer he had sent in a supervisory role, known as Leonid, was not in doubt. A good man and a dependable man, but still a man who would face sharp criticism. No punches pulled, kicks not restrained, and the verbal attack was sharp, pithy.

He had said, "This is a fucking disaster. This is a shit shambles. Is this the best you can achieve? The messages I have, what is available to me, are not from you, Leonid. They are from the fucking German press agency . . . it is reported that a mafia-type attack was blocked near to police HQ in Hamburg. The attack, the source adds, was believed to have been launched as a warning to investigators not to pursue evidence linking organised crime groups in the city. The device did not explode when intended, the agency states, because of the crass amateurishness of the criminals involved. A new model of car, an old registration plate. Not enough care taken to deceive even a recruit officer. That is pathetic . . . I could bust you, bring you home, and you would never work again in this building, Leonid, and the Vympels would never be employed again anywhere. I can do that. Or I can give you one further opportunity . . . Where? How the fuck do I know, but I will know . . . a further chance and that is lucky for you."

Not a word spoken with a raised voice. Long ago a lesson had been learned. In the communist days, when the satellite states had been under disciplined control, the leaders or General Secretaries, or Commissars, always greeted foreign politicians with a handshake, and made certain that his outstretched hand was always low, at the level of his genitals. To shake that lowered hand meant bending at the waist and ducking one's body as if in respect, which was the moment that the state photographer captured the meeting ... The Brigadier – not known lightly as the Wolf – had adopted a tactic of lowering his voice when administering verbal chastisement. A subordinate had to press the receiver hard against his ear, concentrate and listen. He was never interrupted and when rare failure ghosted around him then it would be known that his powers and patronage were considerable ... Leonid might face a transfer to some crap-hole city in eastern Siberia with small chance of a return to the capital, or of favour. The men with him – Anatoly and Konstantin, and he knew them both, and thought them loyal, efficient and trustworthy – could either face a tax investigation and the possibility of imprisonment or could have their public service pensions reworked and face a life in poverty on the streets. They should be grateful for the further opportunity.

Volkov smoked, drank coffee, and waited.

The call came.

A louder voice than the Brigadier would have used. No silk, no subtlety and no preamble, like he was just a fucking office boy.

"This is shit, incompetence at a high level. Do not believe that high rank shields an officer in the face of accusations of culpable inefficiency. People will have been irritated that success was not brought them. Am I understood ...?"

Very clearly understood. There was an officer who was responsible for the planning of the Polonium-210 poisoning of the scumbag, the traitor, Litvinenko. The operation had killed the target but he had lingered long enough for the dose put in his cup of tea to be identified and blame was beamed on the organisation carrying out the London attack; that officer, so Volkov had been told now, drove a Yandex taxi, on the airport run. Another officer had been the driving force behind the Novichok attack on the one-time spy, Skripal: the target had lived and the names of the attackers were known and the fallout was unwelcome: he also drove a taxi now, but from the Gett company. And himself? That was a problem.

"... Faith has been put in you, and that trust will not – hope-fully – be abused."

The call ended.

He had contempt of them, for those who soared close to the Sun Tsar, but they possessed the patronage without which he was emasculated. He did not have a portrait of the President on the wall behind his desk, nor did he have a bank of framed photographs of himself greeting the head of state, or the Defence Minister, and wearing full dress uniform with a chestload of medals and ribbons. Only a photograph of himself in Syria, a cheap frame from a street market, and he was dust-caked and filthy and on foot patrol with an airborne platoon. He hoped he sent a signal with that photograph, and also with the cold, quiet response to the bad news from Germany. But there would be a further opportunity, he believed, for the promised killing.

Benedict thought the man was entitled to react in that way.

"I did not sleep and that is a stupid fucking question . . ."

The Russian had not yet dressed nor shaved, and had not eaten breakfast. He stood at the door of his room and faced Benedict. Behind Benedict, nursing a mug of coffee, was Doug. Wally had done the night shift and was crashed out.

". . . You ask me 'Did you have a good night, Igor?' What sort of fucking question is that? What do you think? I tell you, I slept well, and I thought of heaven and of angels. I wondered if they would have found enough of me to know whether they were putting only me together or whether I might be mixed up with bits of you . . ."

There was a need for pretence, for pleasant conversation. And that is what Benedict attempted to do, with a bit of a shrug and a hint of a smile.

". . . You have no security . . . if you had security they would not have known where to look for me . . ."

They were blurted sentences. They came with a bucket of spittle, and Igor's face was contorted and the veins bulged on his forehead.

". . . You are a disgrace. You are failure. You lie and deceive . . ."

Benedict said something about the team working hard to create a new environment, attempted to soothe as if the problem were no

greater than a TV overheating and scorching the carpet. Not much
that was possible for Benedict to tell him because the problem was
now deep in London's court and he imagined that heavy guns were
lining up on the overnight "difficulty" and that meetings would be
convened. Thought also that the usual "pass the parcel" exercise
would be mounting in urgency. Would have been a pleasure to slap
him down, but that was excluded in his job description. He absorbed
the blows, a boxer on the ropes, stayed calm.

"... Why have I not been taken to London? Always that is put
off, delayed. Why? Why am I wheeled out, a performing flea in a
circus in front of those idiots last evening? Of all the European
agencies, the one we despise most is the German operation.
Toothless and bureaucratic and without imagination. That is the
Germans . . . But you do not rate me, do you? Like I am a fraud?
Enough is enough. What do I mean . . .?"

Benedict did his little smile again and there would have been a
trace of sympathy in his eyes and a little shake of the head to indicate that Sashcord's impatience was predictable. Stayed quiet . . .
did not say, "You have not been taken to London, Igor, because
– until last night's intervention by your former mates – we were
still a little uncertain as to whether you were a genuine article, or
what we call a dangle, a plant, and we felt it unwise at that stage to
parade you around our little hideaway at Fort Monckton, down
on the Solent, and put you in the top-grade defector hospitality
quarters, the apartment over the guard house, and let you see all
the faces that come and go there . . . Next point, Igor, was your
being shown to the Germans. They wanted a little bit of theatre, a
sort of cabaret at the end of a conference, like big companies do
for their sales teams. It was easy to offer you, not that you were
impressive. Your stuff was all pretty meaningless. But it had been
decided that we would see whether you were worth putting on
tour as a bit of a feather in the cap for the UK. But you did not
measure up and that is unlikely to be on offer again . . . What you
might have forgotten, Igor, is that we have invested a wheelbarrow
of cash in you and time and personnel, and so far the return is
minimal. That is where we are." Did not say it. Benedict reverted

to the shrug as if he were only a junior and did not have the rank to make decisions on anything other than requisitioning more toilet rolls or paper clips.

"I think I know what I should do."

"Well, Igor, the senior people in London will be most concerned about last night's events and will be seeking solutions to the dilemma we have. In the meantime, we have more than adequate security around this property, and I have no doubt that we are secure here, and also that we shall be moving on in the next few hours. Sort of slip off the radar, if you know what I mean."

"No faith and no trust, and I want . . ."

Obvious to Benedict what next would be wanted, so he interrupted. Behind him, Doug had drunk his coffee and had his arms hanging at his sides and might have appeared casual, relaxed and not paying particular attention: the wrong assessment. Benedict appreciated that a pressure cooker moment was coming, and he sought to diffuse it.

"A cup of tea, Igor? Tea is always the best solution in difficult moments."

". . . and I want a promise as to when I go to UK, or I will . . ."

Which was an inevitable foray into the argument, and to be deflected.

Benedict said, "A cup of tea is always a good answer when the going gets tough, Igor. Milk and two sugars. I think that Doug will be a good fellow and do the kettle for us, and maybe some biscuits. Let us not take this further – thank you."

". . . or I will quit."

He seemed not to hear the ultimatum. If there was a surprise it was that it had taken so long in gestation. Benedict had been on the Resettlement team for four years, and long before that he had been a young staffer in Iraq. Because of Iraq and because of the Iranian involvement there he had kept a keen and well-tutored eye on that festering corner, and a big story had been the Iranian nuclear programme and the efforts of the Yanks and the Mossad people to put sand in the petrol tank, stymie it. Mostly successful and the Iranian scientists had to deal with critical computer failures and had been suckered with the Stuxnet punch that had inserted a virus into the centrifuge programme. And always the big question, at what level was that door through which the information was coming? A big man? Unlikely. An ordinary joker? Probable . . . Might have been from Shahram Amiri, nuclear technician and middle rank, who defected to the Americans and stayed a year but bleeding for his wife and kid, and saying he wanted to go home. A Central Intelligence Agency staffer had said that they did not keep anyone against their will. He was put on a flight back to Tehran and been met by the wife and the kid and been given a hero's welcome, and had gone on local TV to talk about his "kidnapping" and the regime had smarmed smiles. Benedict remembered all that, and remembered thinking that it would end in tears. Amiri's arrest came two years later . . . Four years of imprisonment and a secret trial and then the return of the body to the family for washing and burial, and there were rope burns and strangulation marks on the guy's throat. It had seemed to be a good story to squirrel away if he were going into defectors and resettlement. It was a hand grenade story, but not one for today . . . hopefully.

And Benedict seemed not to hear the big statement of intent.

Did not say, "See if we care, Igor, see if it matters to us to be shot of you, and see if there's a wet eye in the house when we hear you're propping up a cell wall in the Lubyanka and wondering whether the next beating will be from an iron bar or a lead-tipped cosh. All we'll remember about you is that you were a pain in the arse, a carbuncle between the cheeks. Good riddance, most will say." He kept his peace.

Benedict marvelled at the way Doug could make the handing over of a mug, the tea bag still floating in it, and a splash of long-life milk, and two sugars, and might have stirred it with a ballpoint pen, quite such an event. Done with a smile, an ooze of sincerity . . . The tantrum, of course, was justifiable. Sashcord had been within a couple of minutes of death – and Wally and Doug and Benedict, too – and no one from London had been on the phone to offer sympathy and to assure that a root and branch inquiry was underway, or to tell Igor how important he was, how valued. And no one had rung Benedict and asked how *he* was, and if the minders were okay . . . There had been a text which told him that a new safe house was being organised and they would move in the morning, and that liaison with the *Politiets Efterretningsteienneste* was good and that more guns were around them.

"Did you not hear me?"

"Like I said, Igor, not the time and not the place."

"I quit."

Benedict smiled again, seemed to imply that the door in the hall was ajar and across the hall was the front door and that could be opened and then he could walk across the front driveway, and past the PET boys' cars and take a short bus ride into Aarhus, all possible . . . he did not argue. If it happened then it would be the end of his career, and he smiled once more and said it was a pity that they could not do another museum trip that afternoon. A career shot down in flames if the defector walked away on Benedict's watch.

"An internal inquiry will be messy," Chiswell said.

"I doubt very much that there's any appetite for bringing him back here," Denys Montgomery contributed.

"It'll be run by some ferret-faced little bastard, or bitch, who's only interested in career advancement and who'll be looking for bodies and not declaring our innocence," Symonds said.

"Always has been and always will be destructive for morale, will run like a virus through the building." Denys Montgomery had his fingers together as if in prayer and his elbows squarely on the table around which they sat. On the wall behind him was a decent image of the river and barges being towed upstream by a tugboat, only a print but pleasant, with shafts of sunlight coming down on to the dark water in front of the Westminster facade. Not right for that day because the cloud was low, seemed barely above their tinted window, blast-proof and missile-proof, and the rain distorted their view. The weather matched their mood.

"Anyway, out of our hands now and no longer a matter of 'bring him here or cut him loose'. Not acceptable to fly him in, like a time bomb ticking. They've had one go and will hardly back off . . . Even less acceptable to push him off the plank and lose a minimum of control," Barker said.

"Means that he becomes a totem. Like one of those French infantry Eagles so coveted in the Peninsular. We have to keep him and they want to knock him over, and we didn't see it coming. But, I don't care for hindsight," Denys Montgomery said.

"I'm told it will start tomorrow, the inquiry, and there will be crap about a 'rigorous examination of all areas of responsibility', whatever the fuck that means. Agreed, awful people and a presumption of guilt . . . Count me out because I won't tolerate it, won't be accused by innuendo . . ."

Toni looked across the room, had to twist in her chair, beaded her eyes on Frank at her usual table with her notepad resting on her thigh, and her pencil in motion. The pencil was lifted imperceptibly, but it was acknowledged.

"I think in these circumstances we follow that old and worthy adage 'Better to hang together than separately'. Nearly right, yes, Benjamin Franklin . . . I think a united front is called for. Difficult times beckon when they start examining us, but out of our hands . . . Frank, could you rustle up some more coffee for us? Thank you."

Denys Montgomery's prayer session was complete and he lowered his hands. His last words were almost lost to them, were spoken to himself, "To face an internal inquiry – looking for a source of either extreme stupidity or – worse – venal treachery in our midst, is as big a humiliation as I can comprehend." He stood, swayed, had to grip the table to steady himself.

Alexei, on the bus from the centre of the city of Kirov and going along the west side of the river, was not followed. Could have sworn that no tail was in place.

The driver knew that most of his passengers alighted here, and the seats would be close to empty when he pulled away. There was

Gerald Seymour

a wire perimeter and a main gate where the staff needed to show identification cards to be processed through. Alexei was certain that on the train and leaving the capital and travelling for nearly thirteen hours, he was not watched. He had left the Kirov station, gone out into a frozen night and the last public transport had not turned up, and there were no taxis, so he had walked to his apartment block, climbed three floors because the elevator was broken. Twice he had paused and tried to remember the details of tradecraft that had been dinned into him by Maggie and Maggie's boss, but he had seen no stamping watchers, slithering on the icy pavements, nor a cruising car with its headlights off . . . No matter, when he had left Moscow and walked the last metres towards the rail terminus, they had followed him, observed him – that was a certainty. Nothing here, but the fear stayed with him.

He stood in line, waited to be checked through. Another tiny part of a production line of junior civil servants who kept the apparatus of the regime functioning. He looked to see if he attracted attention. If he had, then he did not recognise it, except that the fear created paranoia . . . they might have been playing with him, hacking at his nerves by not having a tail hanging close to his shoulder. He had reached his one-bedroom studio apartment, as described by the landlord, and had gone to bed but had hardly slept. The central boiler of the block had kicked into action at just after five in the morning and its heaves and wheezing sounds had finally allowed him to drift away, but too soon his alarm had sounded.

At work, Alexei did not wear military uniform but instead had pressed trousers, a jacket, a clean shirt each day with the collar open, and his shoes were always clean but not always polished. He was nestled now inside a thick long coat with imitation fur at the collar and he wore an old-style hat, with ear flaps, that had the heritage of GRU. He worked for Military Intelligence, and they regarded themselves as elite. Very few of them – or the thousands who served in that organisation – had heard of this young man. From top to bottom of GRU, in their glasshouse building in Moscow, in their stations inside the Federation boundaries, those attached to embassies abroad and those living under cover in countries reckoned to be hostile, all would have agreed – had they known of him and his work – that the damage he could inflict was beyond considerable.

He had walked from the gate to the main door. The wind came off the wide Vyatka river that flowed south into the Volga, the longest in Europe. Always now, in winter and autumn, he shivered in that wind though his coat was thick and insulated and his gloves well padded, and he wore his hat far down on his head. The building had been constructed in the 1950s as an infantry training base for conscript recruits. They had moved away some fifteen years before, and the complex and its facilities had been snatched by a GRU general. Why had he wished to be so far from the fountain of power, from Moscow? The most commonly held rumour was that his mistress needed to be near her elderly mother. Who knew . . .? The town's sole importance geographically was as a hub on the route of the Trans-Siberian railway line. It had a population of half a million, endured a brutal winter when the river was iced over for five months, had a few fine Tsarist buildings, the familiar alcohol and substance abuse problems, acute unemployment, a football team, a small university, and the GRU complex.

He went up two flights of a wide staircase. There was additional security at an inner door. He was admitted. Alexei shrugged out of his coat, hung it inside the metal locker awarded him, and took off his hat and his gloves. He did not bring food or coffee because there was an adequate canteen in the basement: the servants of the GRU machine were well looked after. He went to his desk and switched on his computer, and then crossed to the window and looked out over the grotesquely uniform endless landscape, beyond the river, of plains covered by shades of grey and white, and pricked by carpets of pine trees. The officers, for whom he was the dogsbody, would not be in for another hour and they would then huddle in their cubicles and bitch to each other about the penance of living, working, here, not Moscow, of being overlooked for foreign travel, of being buried in this backwater where expenses and fraud were investigated, where monies were sent to legals and illegals in the field, where the covert financing of operations was housed. Had the unit been based in the Moscow glasshouse, then it would have been subject to acute and fastidious security . . . It was not, was 500 miles from the capital located somewhere that the majority of high-flyers in GRU had never heard of.

He was twenty-four years old. Father long dead from alcoholism, an uncle in GRU and opening a door: not as a potential officer but as a clerk, and fortunate to have that opportunity. Conscientious, hard working, and the work easy, and a little money left over to help his mother, and given the donkey work by that team of investigators and his work was satisfactory and they received the plaudits. They had taken him to Cyprus, where the fraud was on the scale of "taking the piss", cheating the system and not lining sufficient pockets in the process. The shy lad had been seconded to go with them, inhibited, nothing manly in his frame, hating football and never running if he could walk, and without a girl . . . All different now because he had paused on a warm evening outside a gay bar.

A sweet girl had cradled his head and dabbed his wounds. Her boyfriend had called a number she had given him. Taken to a hotel, a room on the first floor. Cast into the hand of the night porter. A wait of twenty minutes and the girl's hands soothing on his face and on his chest where he had been kicked and punched, and his trousers and pants rearranged after the whores had violated him, screaming in laughter at his "failure". She was Daphne, Daff – he never knew her boyfriend's name. Another couple had arrived. One might have come from a party, wore a floral shirt, his breath smelling of barbecue and whisky, and a brisk woman who was older. His rescuers had gone, not a backward glance, and he was recruited . . . All done quickly and with precision, and no emotion, but he was treated with the respect accorded a jewel. His English was good from school, but the woman's Russian was flawless, almost at interpreter level. "We could be very good and grateful friends, Alexei. We could help you to exact a very sweet level of revenge against those thugs who hurt you, and against those officers who left you outside their clique, and against that system that doesn't give a fuck about you. Easy enough, Alexei. We are experts, we will keep you safe, will always be there when you need us . . . Now, Alexei, a solemn guarantee, my promise, for your peace of mind, we offer you haven. Not saying that it will ever be necessary, but should you need to quit, come out, we provide that service and then a refuge where they cannot reach you. You owe them nothing, Alexei. What do you need to know, Alexei?" He had said, and he could recall the croak in his voice from a year and a half before, that he did not want any money . . . And they had nodded sagely, and had shaken his hand as if the deal was closed . . . All different now.

He had thought, could not be certain, and did not understand her meaning, that the woman muttered to the man, "This is just fucking incredible . . . and I believe in mermaids."

He started his day's work: where money was to go, into what accounts, what passwords were applicable. But his concentration was poor and several times he had to go back over his work and check it, and remove errors. He had told her, the girl whose face was always in his mind, Maggie, that he wanted out.

Had said it . . . *I come next week and I want out* . . . Most times, Maggie was kept at arm's length of the station chief.

She would slip away from the Military Attaché's office where she worked and would climb a flight of stairs and stand at the locked door of that part of the Embassy where the Sixers operated. Lucinda would come to the entrance. Always pleasant enough, and polite, but made it plain that Maggie – a lance corporal from the Logistics Corps – was a co-opted temporary member of a team monitoring the asset, codename Environ, useful in the short term, and her input was not required except as answers to direct questioning. The memory stick that had been secreted in a trainer heel had been handed over the previous evening.

Lucinda had said, "Thank you for the delivery, and thank you for the rundown. Where we are, more's the pity, I'm not there but that's how it plays out. I saw the surveillance once, you've seen it three times. Neither you nor the boy are trained in counter-surveillance so we have to assume he is watched more often than we know, which is depressing. Now, your message, about his requirements. Pull him out, put in place a major exfiltration job. Have you any idea what that involves? We might do that for a top man, but I am afraid that this lad hardly fits that bill. We appreciate what he brings to the table, and can do useful analysis with it, but the moment he leaves Russian territory then he becomes little more than a dried-out husk. Sorry, Maggie, but look at it realistically. The day after he is no longer in front of that computer down in Kirov, he has become deaf, blind, dumb. Nothing to offer. That's the business, Maggie, that we are in, and if it offends you then I am sorry and we can pull you off these weekend meetings. While he is operating from Kirov we are getting fresh material that is pertinent to us and our allies. Take him away from that desk and he is just one more drifting and rather dull young Russian boy with no great insights that we would wish to have. No, Maggie, he stays in place and we milk the udder until it runs dry. If he is picked up then we field the protest, take an expulsion or two and carry on as before. If it is you who is arrested then we raise Cain and we'll have you out of their cells within a few hours, and it will be something that little Hector can eventually tell his grandchildren about. As for Environ, well, it's a tough old life doing what he volunteered for. And he *was* a volunteer . . . He will probably have been given supposed guarantees by the recruiters. If they did, they should not have. We are not the social services, Maggie . . . What I do not want is him telling you next weekend, if he is not already in custody, that he is packing it in and refusing further meetings. Your job is to keep him going until that is no longer possible, jolly him along, keep him on side and always emphasise that we are a highly professional outfit, caring deeply and going the extra mile to keep him safe. But, pulling him out, going to all that trouble, no question of it . . . And thanks for your efforts, appreciated."

Maggie had turned away, had walked towards the lift, had said under her breath, "Fucking cow. Grade A bitch." And she'd thought of the boy and his fear through most of the night, and thought of his plea. Imagined the arrest team moving in, flattening him, and snatching at her arms and little Hector screaming.

No measures of fine sherry had been poured for them to sip and savour, no plates of biscuits offered. Not even tea or coffee. Two men and a woman had been led into a secure room in the Ministry of Defence in Whitehall, high on the fourth floor. This was neutral ground; there would be no written or recorded minutes, and the location determined that individual corners would not be defended. The group represented the key areas of intelligence gathering and faced a pressing problem: how should they respond to the allegation that a leak existed in the heart of the Secret Intelligence Service. A mandarin had put them together, and no politician would be allowed close to the decision. They were a *former* Director of SIS, and a *former* boss of the Security Service and, taking the chair was a *former* head of the Government Communications Headquarters. Their days of waging turf war with each other had slipped away as the virtues of retirement and private industry boardrooms had beckoned.

"They won't like it," was the conclusion of the dour man who had once ruled Vauxhall Cross, the MI6 place across the river.

"We'll do it, if that's what you want. But it will be delicate," said the woman who had run affairs at Thames House.

"Grand. I think it's for the best." He had taken charge a decade earlier of the doughnut complex in Cheltenham, GCHQ. He had gravitas, also a waspish humour, and he had led his two former colleagues towards a conclusion that would surprise, would make waves, certainly result in some shouting. He went to the door, opened it, beckoned into the anteroom and they were joined by the Permanent Under-Secretary. None of them had ever faced – God forbid – the vagaries of hustings and elections and being answerable to the rabble out there on the streets. But it was their job to keep that rabble safe, which was a task they took seriously.

GCHQ said, "So there are no misunderstandings, I shall recapitulate where we are. There will be an inquiry into the supposed leak at VX, but not an internal inquiry. We accept that the

equivalent of 'cousin dating' is not appropriate, and would likely
lead to delay, obfuscation, all that stuff, and dirt going under the
Axminster. We will invite their sister organisation at Thames
House, to manage the investigation, with all due sensitivities and
an understanding that dignities will not be trampled on. That is
the intention. We also agree on the importance of a swift conclusion to this exercise. Had the Hamburg attack succeeded, then
the Lubyanka crowd, or GRU, or whoever, would have notched
up a significant propaganda success. All over the broadcast
media, splashed in the papers, and the President scowling at a
favoured TV toadie and talking of dire deaths for the betrayers.
And the propaganda links easily to the effect this will have on the
morale of our agents inside the Federation frontiers. They have to
believe that we are efficient, that our word is our bond, all the
usual soothing speeches we offer. Who would work for us if our
security appears so pitiful? We have two aims. We should keep
this individual safe and offer appropriate protection. They will
come again – that is our reading of them in the past – and we
should humiliate their operatives – or hurt them – when the inevitable occurs, and they come back. All clear? Thank you. A good
outcome I think."

They would return to their respective retirement dens. To
Wiltshire and an evening of bridge. To the Hampshire coast and a
sailing lesson. To a Surrey home where a recent divorcee was
showing interest in cooking dinner for a widower of four months.
Not the Permanent Under-Secretary . . . He had already texted
the Director General at Thames House and had asked for,
demanded, a meeting within the hour. And had done the same with
VX within two hours . . . Interesting times, and he was left to
wonder what sort of man might be suitable for such a job. But the
Permanent Under-Secretary was merely the messenger and did
not have to decide.

Benedict called London. Said that Griff, one of his last duties
before retirement – lucky bastard – had given him a list of estate
agents offering short-term lets in the Jutland region on the Danish

west coast. He had lined up a property and they would move at first light. He would vet the property and its suitability – its defence capability – when they were there. And the PET boys had doubled the muscle around their current safe house. Denys Montgomery agreed with the plan. Not much else the poor beggar could have done.

Benedict said, "And the problem of Sashcord gets worse. Bloody-minded, short-tempered and constantly demanding to be brought to the UK. I'm stalling . . . but he's threatening to walk out, turn his back on us. There was a leak, Denys, and not at my end, and Sashcord and all our team, and the Danes, are potential targets. Getting to feel like we're the foot soldiers in a front-line foxhole and magnified in the crosshairs. You have to get a suture on that leak, Denys, and soonest – or is that just the bleeding obvious?"

The AssDepDG had been preparing to go home after an uneventful day, when he had been phoned from a floor above his in Thames House.

A name was mentioned; the response was a grin, then the raising of an eyebrow, then a chin scratched in pleasure.

The Deputy Director General, told him, "I like it. They won't . . . His very appearance will serve to tweak their arrogant goddamn precious noses. I ask you, very frankly, have you ever been over there and been greeted like a colleague? Ever been over the bridge and met any of them and felt from the reaction there's dog turd on your shoe? I like that name. Just the man for it, and an operator of proven quality."

The AssDepDG answered him. "I'd say he'll do all right . . . I'd back him to come up with a result . . . Better than all right."

The car's lights beamed across the caravan site.

Jonas saw them, and so did Vera. They lit up the caravan's interior. There had seemed no point in drawing the curtains because they only had the light of the one candle, already guttering. Vera had a tapestry frame on her lap but the candle was barely

sufficient for her work. Jonas was waiting for his trousers to dry
but with the power still off that would take time. Bad enough
having to endure sodden ankles during the walk and then their
cold clamminess in the hide where half the afternoon had been
spent. He had been drenched again getting back to the car – and
again when he had been sent to the caravan in the next bay with a
plastic jug of vegetable soup and a pair of pasties to beg use of
their microwave. The car came slowly and the headlights moved
on, and he heard the engine race as if it had hit a boggy section off
the hard core. Then it reversed. Came nearer. The engine was
killed.

A door opened. He heard low voices, recognised one of them.
Jonas pursed his lips. A car door slammed. Perhaps a town shoe
slithered on the mud and he heard a vernacular curse.

There was sharp knock on the caravan's door.

He stood.

Vera said, "Who on earth can that be?"

He did not have to answer her.

"Can't they ever leave you alone?"

He went to the door. Olaf was already in his cage, seeming to
sleep. Jonas would have said their hunter killer never slept. Jonas
often quoted to the cat, "The price of Liberty is eternal Vigilance"
but without a response. The knock came again.

"Shouldn't you put your trousers on?"

He did not reply, opened the door and let the dark night air
flood over them.

The rain sheeted down on the AssDepDG's head, and spattered on his jacket. "Are you going to allow me in?"

He stood aside.

"Sorry and all that, Vera. 'Fraid I need to steal him away. A
problem with the lights?"

Vera told him about the power failure. Told him that Jonas was
not very capable with a screwdriver, a hammer, pretty much
anything that was in the DIY line. The AssDepDG did a competent appearance of genuine concern then turned in the doorway,
gave a sharp whistle and beckoned for his driver.

The driver was Harry. From the car boot, he retrieved a tool box and with Vera to guide him, would investigate the outage and do the necessary.

Jonas and the AssDep DG sat in the car. A window was lowered, and the AssDepDG lit a cigarillo.

"It was thought, in the time allotted, that an outsider, one without the usual prejudices of loyalty to the Six self-indulgence, might perform better than something attempted from the inside. Don't suppose you know many of them, Jonas . . . correct? I spend a couple of days a week in their company. They have a low opinion of us, a high opinion of themselves. They reckon they are a hand-picked elite and we are the modern-day equivalent of the British officers in the colonial police forces before the great wind of change. They think they bring intellect to the table while we hide behind procedure . . . We may not have had, Jonas, a clear run at success in the last several years – Isis bombs, Irish bombs – but I would say that our Russia stuff has been outstanding and Litvinenko and Skripal are just two of the more catalogued investigations. When they, the Sixers, want to drawl their expertise at you, then you should not forget, might indeed remind them, of the hundreds of young lives lost in the South Atlantic because their Argentina station gave no warnings. Or you might see fit to recall certain dossiers and weapons of mass destruction and Saddam, that bullshit, another flawed judgement and another list of names carved into memorials . . . What I'm saying, Jonas, is that you don't take a yard of obstruction from them, not a foot, not an inch. We will be behind you and so also will people with authority. I said to the DeputyDG that I thought you'd be all right for this one . . . Now, just in case you have the impression that we may be exploiting a temporary advantage over a somewhat wounded colleague, I will disabuse you. This matters, Jonas. This is about national security and a breach in our defences. It is also about our ability to give certain promises to potential assets – Russian or Chinese or North Koreans, Islamists and Irish – who have a line into their current crowd of potato-faced activists. The promise is about keeping them safe, protecting them from retribution and letting them know they work for principled and honourable people. Like you and me, Jonas. Know what I mean? Don't laugh . . . That is what is at stake. Good luck."

"Thank you for that. Not altogether necessary, but my thanks."

The cigarillo, what remained of it, was flicked out. Jonas pondered. He was not hurried, was given time. He thought of those great buildings on the island of Orford Ness, the pagodas and the work that had been done there, and the men and women who had believed their role on that barren and gale-swept plateau of shingle had preserved, to a degree, the nation's freedom, liberty, all of those big things that people seemed to care about. And thought about the security officers who would have watched over the boffins and engineers and would have looked for weakness, or signs of the behaviour that laid an individual open to blackmail. Would have been concerned with who spent monies far beyond the Atomic Weapons wage, and who now seemed to hate the world around him, and who paraded himself with an ego that strayed far above his talent. Wanted to be there; it was the reason he had agreed to Vera's plan for the extended weekend.

Jonas said, "We were due to go to Orford Ness tomorrow, going to have a poke about there. Live a bit of history . . . You know, we actually saw an otter this afternoon, just a flash and a glimpse but we saw it, and we've seen representatives of most of the water bird life that exists in the UK and I now know about the way in which the red-legged spider-hunting wasp deals with its prey before munching on it. Tomorrow, where will I be?"

Lights suddenly blazed through the windows of the caravan, flooded the car.

"Back home tonight. Into London tomorrow, as early as usual. Pick up some bits and pieces, then off to VX . . . the Ness will have to wait, expect it will still be there."

Vera was in the doorway and Harry scurried to the car. Harry said he had done a lash-up job on the electric cables, enough to get the power back on, and that mice had done the damage – had suggested impishly that the "bloody great big cat" should have a sharp cut in its rations. Had said that Mrs Merrick had the kettle on.

The AssDepDG said, "I think, Jonas, that the opportunities for those episodes of fun and games that you enjoyed with the explosives vest and that Islamist fanatic, will be limited, very severely limited. I expect you to return to us with not a hair out of place, no adventures permitted . . . Good. So now we can get the show on the road."

4

A man was eyeing him closely, sitting opposite Jonas Merrick: a stranger. Jonas never talked to anyone on the train into London. It was the usual one, his routine had not been broken, and he had been in his familiar seat when it had pulled away from the station just before 7.30. He might have been examined closely because of his appearance, outwardly normal but his expression might have displayed the inner strains he felt . . .

Always caught the same train from Raynes Park, always used that particular carriage, always seemed to find that seat free, always had his briefcase across his lap and the fine chain from its handle attached to the locked ring on his wrist. He rarely read on the journey because most of the documents inside the case were classified and not supposed to leave Thames House, and he always sat with his eyes almost closed and his face seemingly at peace as if this quiet time was good for meditation . . . Not that morning. His breathing was irregular, and he blinked frequently, and his fingers twitched. He had not, before, known such stress, thought that was for other folk, was usually churlishly dismissive of such feelings. Was having a bit of a funk.

Down at the caravan site, at Dunwich, he had not actually been asked whether he fancied this mission. The AssDepDG had not said that he could take it or leave it, that nothing would be held against him if he turned his back on the offer and went on with his holiday, stayed the extra day so that he could walk around the nuclear warfare mausoleum that was Orford Ness. Not said, "Quite understand, Jonas, if you tell me to walk away and go back to London and rummage in the files and find someone else. I'll pop upstairs to the DeputyDG and mention to him that you declined – as you have every right to – the opportunity to sort out the problem." The bar was set high, and the medal and the ribbon in Vera's knicker drawer had raised it. He supposed, sitting on the train, that he feared failure. Might have blinked too often, might have gasped as if short of breath, and he had a cut on his neck where a new razor blade had done damage, and had had to hunt for another shirt which had almost made him late. He feared failure, was scared of it. He had not said as much to the in-house psychologist who had interviewed him after he had disarmed the device carried by Winston Gunn, nor when he had captured the dedicated activist Cameron Jilkes. Had given no reason why he had flaunted all the survival codes and done the job himself . . . He was nervous, and the man opposite him looked puzzled.

Jonas had hurried out of his home that morning, running a minute and a half late, had barely spoken to Vera as she had prepared his lunch box and his thermos, and had not commented on her promise to be in touch with an electrician for the caravan – and had not acknowledged Derbyshire, his next-door neighbour who sold conservatories, or his daughter who worked in a hair salon in Ewell. Both had offered him a polite greeting but he had stridden past them and not responded. He could remember the last time he had been seriously apprehensive about going to work, but that was four years before, his retirement due that evening, and a drinks party booked in the atrium, and a gift of a shopping voucher to be handed over. Thank the Good Lord that Winston Gunn had intervened in his life that evening while he had self-isolated out in the little park by the Burghers of Calais statue . . . He felt nervous, frightened even, and knew that he was relied upon to deliver.

Perhaps the stranger, sitting opposite, had seen his hand slip up involuntarily to scratch the mole on his nose or adjust his spectacles, and had seen the chain holding the briefcase to his wrist. And wondered what he did, where he was going. The train drew in at Waterloo, and Jonas pushed clear.

His usual route to Thames House took Jonas along the south side of the embankment and past the high wall of the Archbishop's Palace, then a brisk walk brought him over Lambeth Bridge, where his workplace awaited him . . . His friends were on duty on the pavement, Kevin and Leroy. Always had a greeting from the policemen, but they would have to be satisfied with only a curt nod of acknowledgement today. Both had assault rifles hanging from straps across their chests, wore bulletproof vests, and were weighed down with gas and the rest of the gear. He did not go inside the building, but turned down the street alongside and went to buy his morning *cappuccino*, served in a cardboard beaker, from the café. He took it with him into the dripping garden further down the Horseferry Road.

Three days a week, early in the morning – Tuesdays, Thursdays and Fridays – Jonas saw the gardener. He was raking debris from the paths that circled this former cemetery, brought down in the night from the wind and the rain. Jonas would never, God forbid, be called a gossip, but many Fivers sat on the garden benches for a fag during the working day. Several years before he had heard a pair of them talk about this gaunt middle-aged man: a former military sniper, a traumatic stress casualty, plucked from his recovery programme for a Five operation on the Costa del Sol, had – and their voices had dropped to barely audible whispers – taken down a bad guy, an organised crime baron believed responsible for the death of a rookie from their own family. Had been brought back, dumped in the garden, used and now forgotten.

Jonas drank his coffee. Breathed hard. Stood, then walked towards the gardener. The man went on with his work shovelling debris into his wheelbarrow.

Jonas said, very quietly, "I work in that building up the road. Forgive the intrusion, sir . . . I need advice. I may not be capable of delivering what I have been asked to do. May fall flat on my face. I've been chosen and didn't know how to decline. Sound familiar? I am rather dreading it. If I fail I am told there will be consequences that will affect many people, and I feel seriously burdened . . ."

The gardener smiled, his deep-set eyes showed nothing of past torments. "Head into it, whatever the storm. Face it, take no nonsense, no shit, from any bastard. Give it your best, can't do more . . ."

His shovel scraped the ground, was raised and tilted, and more rubbish went into the wheelbarrow.

Jonas thanked him. He reflected on his own work. By its nature he insinuated himself into others' lives. Might meet them, but rarely, might have them flicker up on his screen, more frequently. Might have a profound effect on those he became involved with and likely on many more than he would even know of. The rain had eased but there was more coming. To speak to the gardener could have been weakness and could have been strength, but he felt better for it. And wondered which lives he would now cross, and where those lives were lived. Wondered if his collision with those lives would be positive for them or negative, and if they would ever see him, know of him, or remain in ignorance. Some might thank him and some might curse him, and many would never comprehend the reach of his intervention . . . He checked his watch, then was on his way, and felt a little spring in his step.

They went in a swirl of vehicles.

The PET boys' car led. Keeping close to it was the Hertz job they used, driven that morning by Wally. Behind them were more of the Danish security guys in a high-performance BMW, then a vanload of police, all togged in combat gear, with rifles across their knees and wearing ski masks.

A kid, astride a tricycle watched them go, and the kid's mother held a taut lead as the family dog leaped and snarled at the convoy. It moved fast to the end of the street where a police motorcyclist was blocking oncoming traffic. Doug reckoned that the whole street knew that a man was guarded there. Too many deliveries of fast food, too few efforts to clear the back garden of winter leaves, whole days when the blinds were not raised. Doug thought that the neighbours would have assumed the police were holed up there with a state prosecution witness: not much chance that a little bit of a new Cold War was being enacted on the edge of the city.

The headlights made bright sparks on the wet road surface. The motorcyclist powered past, leading them out of the city towards the open road and the signposts for Silkeborg.

Doug would like to have stopped there, maybe lost a couple of hours in the town's museum. He had spent an excess of hours as a minder, with little to do but escort their guy on occasional walks and outings to places of culture. They had had Silkeborg on their list but had not made it. He had read the brochures for its museum: the centre point was the bog body, probably 2400 years old, and it had been dug up seventy years before. Exquisitely preserved, and with a bad story to tell, had been hanged and there was an intact leather noose around the throat as proof of how death had been achieved. Might have been an execution and might have been a human sacrifice . . . He'd had conversations with Wally on that score and they'd preferred the concept of ritual sacrifice rather than a felon left to swing in the wind from a branch, and had more sympathy with the corpse preserved so well in the peat that he warranted the greater part of the museum all to himself. Doug and Wally agreed they had an understanding of sacrifice. Hung out to dry, that sort of sacrifice, a rag torn by the Baltic gales and pinned to a washing line, and they'd spoken about it again that morning. Doug thought that Wally stayed daftly close to the PET boys' car in front and the motorcyclist set a hell of a pace.

After Silkeborg, and the preserved body that Doug would never get to see, they went on towards Herning, a town astride a major junction with five principal off-shoots. From there they could turn to the north and head for Viborg and ferry ports for boats to Norway or Sweden, or veer west for the northern coast and Thisted, or go directly west towards Ringkebing: there was also a road to the south-west and another due south, the back way to Germany, or east and Odense and ultimately Copenhagen where the whole bloody thing had started . . . The convoy would break. Their direction could not be predicted. The police motorbike would leave them, and the van of guns, and the car behind. Only the PET boys, ahead to ride shotgun, would stay with them. Doug and Wally accepted that trust had to rest in one lap, and the numbers who knew their direction and location of the new safe house were now diminished . . . The big matter was to keep together: Doug and Wally, Benedict and the guy they knew as Sashcord – sometimes called "that bloody knobhead" – and the two PET boys. If there was a further leak then they would all be hit.

The Russian was quiet. He smoked continuously, staring at the back of the car ahead, and did not speak . . . for most of the journey Benedict clicked at his phone . . .

The Russian would explode. Doug was certain of that, all the toys coming out of the pram. If there was another leak then there would be a second attack. There were some certainties in life which was reassuring to Doug. He would hate to have been bored, and thought Wally felt the same. He did a fair bit of thinking, sitting in the passenger front seat. He was not a man to spend time on complaint, and gave little indication that he was uncomfortable. The reason was that he sat with half his weight on a Glock 9mm pistol – with a full magazine loaded – that was stowed in his hip pocket. It was reasonable for him to carry gas and pepper spray grenades, packed in his bag in the boot of the car. It was not reasonable for him to carry a lethal weapon, armed and ready to go, with three more filled magazines in his bag. Against the regulations and terms of reference, against all the protocols agreed with their Danish hosts, against international law, against what was agreed in London. The shipment had been arranged by Brian, the security guy at the Embassy, who had delivered a heavy sports bag an hour before they had quit the house in Aarhus. Both Doug and Wally had spent too many days of their lives with the weight of a protection weapon close to their skin . . . not that it would have helped had push come to shove in Hamburg when neither of them had been armed. They were now.

The eruption, from the guy behind them, would be volcanic. He was a horrid little creature as Doug read him, but might have good cause to blow a fuse. He grinned to himself and shifted his backside.

Volkov had the rank that warranted the use of a full-time driver, and most of them who were at that level of rank in GRU would also have the services of a team of personal protection flunkeys. He used neither.

After a working breakfast, he had taken the Metro. He had sat unrecognised and unknown, surrounded by small-time businessmen and sales staff and students, housewives and pensioners. He thought the fripperies of escorts and chauffeurs were required only by those who needed to bolster a failing estimate of self-importance. For fuck's sake, nearly half the city was closed down and roads blocked when the new Tsar wanted to get to the Kremlin, or leave the Kremlin, go for his breakfast, or come back from his lunch, and all the shit-stirrers clung limpet tight to the presence of power. He did the job assigned to him with as much efficiency as he was able. He did not have a mistress installed in luxury, nor did he have sons who had been slipped into positions of financial comfort, nor daughters who were married off to the sons of the *siloviki*. He and his wife never visited the *dacha* forest homes of any of the 500 families in the Federation who had acquired the greatest wealth, the greatest influence. He had been awarded a job, and he did it. He took pleasure from that job, and from doing it well . . . If it ended badly – and he assumed that was the future of the regime, ending badly – he had planned to have already slipped away. Would have gone with his wife, and his daughter, who had expertise in applied mathematics and little else, on the train from St Petersburg to the Finnish capital of Helsinki, would have been over the frontier when the mob came calling. In the meantime, he worked at his job.

Breakfast had been with the leader of a surveillance team. The meal was brief and sparse. Warm sausage, a hunk of bread, a slab of cheese, a glass of orange juice. Taken in a public café. Heads close as they ate and drank. He was given details of a surveillance operation. The Brigadier had many irons, many fires. He had, the previous evening, received a computerised résumé of the seeming significance, or otherwise, of the actions of a suspect, a man believed to be guilty of treason, but it was his nature to seek out the leader of the team whose boots were on the ground. He enjoyed the minutiae of frontline work. He was told the route the suspect had taken, the tram, the pavements he had walked, and which station he had used. Enough information to warrant an arrest? Probably, but he would sleep on it. The difficult stage was deciding when a suspect had run enough or when he was to be dragged in.

He came out of the Metro and walked towards the glasshouse building.

A small man, with an unremarkable appearance, he slipped into his office barely noticed. A raft of overnight emails awaited him. One was from his faithful Leonid. Leonid and his Vympel boys had sped from Hamburg after the failure, had driven north and east, were now holed up in the old port city of Rostock on the Baltic, what had once been hardcore territory, loyal to the old Soviet system. He thought Leonid a good man to have at his disposal. A stupid man but loyal. He valued loyalty above the disadvantage of stupidity ... Leonid and his team awaited instructions.

He messaged back: *Gone from sight. Confident of soon receiving detail of new location – no indication that target is airborne.*

He *was* seriously confident of soon knowing where his target would be housed. Could imagine a hasty and fearful flight and a new location decided without time to evaluate. All of them lucky to have the possibility of a second chance ... He made coffee for himself and pondered the question of an arrest and its timing.

"Stand to the side please, sir."

He did as he was asked.

"Name again, sir?"

Jonas gave his name.

"Some ID, sir."

He showed the card, hanging from a ribbon around his neck.

"And who is supposed to be meeting you, sir?"

He had not the faintest idea.

"And at what time were you supposed to be met, sir?"

He was a bore, a blockage, nudged right and left by the workers arriving at the Vauxhall Cross building. He stood at the gates where armed police gazed past him into the traffic lanes and the roundabout and the distant station entrance, and cyclists in lycra and joggers in sweaty vests flashed plastic at the machines and were admitted. He was supposed to be met at nine o'clock.

"Then you are a couple of minutes early, sir ... Please, a bit more to the side."

He edged a few inches to the right. A bicycle's front wheel went over the cap of one of his brogue shoes, and a shoulder barged into him, and a knee caught his upper thigh and a shopping bag rapped into the small of his back. Jonas stood his ground and let the mob arriving for their day's work edge around him, and ignored the sour glances of both the police and the gatekeepers.

"Thank you, sir. So you'll just have to wait, and we'll see if anyone comes."

He would wait, and would *take no nonsense, no shit, from any bastard*, and thought the gardener's advice was sound. Jonas had not expected that the Director General of the Service, the top Sixer, would have come down to greet him, but had anticipated that a covey of minions would welcome him, scant sincerity, then escort him inside. The armed police at the gate wore full waterproof clothing as well as the vests and the canvas belts from which their gear was slung, might have intimidated. Jonas felt good ... insults and humiliations strengthened him. If he had to wait much longer his dislike for the place and for the people who worked there might have sharpened.

She was threading her way against the flow. She had a phone against one ear and held one of those tiny foldaway umbrellas that could barely withstand a mild breeze let alone the rain. He thought her middle thirties. She wore a grey skirt and a grey jacket over a white blouse. Her hair was tucked up at the back of her head. A thin smear of lipstick and a pair of stud earrings, pearl, and a gold chain was around her throat with a pendant bouncing below. Only rarely did Jonas Merrick make a judgement on a woman's appearance: did not find it within his remit to judge whether she was attractive, pretty, ugly or beautiful, but it crossed his mind she appeared "plain", a word Vera might have used, which was deliberate. He noticed that the fingers holding the phone were bare – no wedding ring, nor one to mark an engagement and no ring that might have been an heirloom. Obvious to Jonas that she would be the one to greet him. She spoke briefly to a gatekeeper and a barrier was opened. Another word to one of the armed police. The man had his right thumb alongside the upper casing of a Heckler & Koch assault rifle. The thumb twitched, a minimal gesture, in Jonas's direction. He stood in the rain and waited, let her come over to him. Their eyes met. He thought that she instinctively shifted the umbrella towards him, the better to shield him. His gesture was clear, firm; he took the stem of it and held it over her.

She said, "Sorry for leaving you here on a foul morning. I don't suppose they offered you somewhere dry to wait? No, they wouldn't have . . . anyway, it *is* Mr Merrick, Jonas Merrick?"

He handed back her umbrella, opened his coat again and showed her the card on the end of the ribbon. She studied it, nodded, and headed back to the gatekeeper. There was a piece of paper on the desk. It had been covered up by a newspaper. Purposefully? Jonas was impassive. No apologies made. He had been expected, a number was supposed to have been rung. He shrugged, smiled in a rather helpless way. His details were taken and he was ushered into a booth where he stood on large painted footsteps and stared at a lens, kept his spectacles on but removed his trilby hat. Then inside . . . He used a small key to unfasten the chain to his briefcase and placed it on the scanner belt. They wanted his raincoat and his jacket . . . *take no nonsense, no shit, from any bastard* . . . would probably want his belt and his small change. He heard her snort with impatience. She turned away from him and hissed, that this was a guest, a visitor, deserving of respect. Jonas stood, gave no sign that his patience was near to breaking point. He opened his briefcase, empty except for his lunch box and flask. And they were through, and a badge was pinned to his jacket lapel and he thought the photograph made him look like an imbecile, with silly staring eyes behind his spectacles, and he would value that image.

"Sorry about that, Mr Merrick."

He shrugged as if the delay was predictable.

"We have a room set aside for you."

He nodded, repeated the limp smile that gave, he believed, an impression of a small man, small in stature and small of intellect.

"Please follow me."

It was one of Jonas Merrick's several skills that he did not allow himself to be burdened by the weight of a knapsack of preconceptions. He had not considered what sort of space they would offer him, what facilities he would be given. He followed her, across an inner hallway, and cutting across to the left side where the flow of workers was surging towards the banks of elevators. He had not bothered to wonder whether he would be put in an upper-floor room, with picture-window views of the Thames, of the Houses of Parliament, and perhaps even of distant Thames House on the far bank. He might even have been able to glimpse the window of his cubicle on the south side, third floor, Room 13. Through a doorway, along a corridor, artificially lit, then down a flight of stairs. A line of doors faced him ... one was a bathroom. She unlocked a door. Opened it and switched on the ceiling striplight. The room was about twenty feet by sixteen feet, had composite floor cover and no carpet. A pair of VisitBritain posters were the sole wall decorations, Edinburgh Castle and Stonehenge, and an iron-legged table had been placed in the centre of the room with a hard chair on either side of it and cabling to a wall socket. A phone was on the table, one without a keypad. Two more hard-backed chairs were against the wall that displayed the posters. Near to the door was another table, half the size of the first, and sitting on the chair was a closed laptop on top of a cushion. Close to the side table was a floor safe, open.

He was asked what agenda he had for the day.

Jonas said what he wanted to read through.

She said, "I'll get that paperwork sorted for you as best I can. Your own phone won't work in here and anyway should be put in the safe. It will be paperwork because you are not permitted to use your own laptop in the building, nor permitted to use one of ours. Apologies if that sounds difficult but it is a standard ruling for visitors. I'll put together what I can and print it out ... Not all entirely straightforward as you'll appreciate, Mr Merrick."

He thanked her.

"Oh, and I'm Frank. Well, Frances really, but everyone here calls me Frank."

Benedict's text was for the line manager from Russia Desk who oversaw the Resettlement team. He read it back, tidied the syntax and punctuation. Read it again because there would be inquiries, inquests, and electronic and paper trails would be hunted down.

At new location. Not bad, not perfect. You have the address. Could have been better. Budget was a constraining factor, also letting agencies are wary about offloading furnished property to vaguely defined parties, and for only a month. We will be cramped but will manage.

Have a PET pair with us. Firepower. Difficult to assess under what circumstances they would use the force at their disposal. More important, understand we face growing resentment from PET seniors concerning the length of stay of Sashcord on their territory. Outstaying our welcome. Decisions needed. Seems their political hierarchy is unaware of Danish involvement in the housing of Sashcord, while Danish PET's briefing on the Hamburg incident is between sketchy and economical.

And the man himself? I await an explosion. I continue to stall on his demand for a move to UK. Threatens to quit, return home and claim he was kidnapped and has escaped and do a media circus clobbering us. Increasingly fraught atmosphere.

We also are frontline now and expect future Federation action if our new address becomes known.

Please, decisions required.

★   ★   ★

On the third floor, the Resettlement team gathered in the work area of their line manager. Frank had arranged the chairs, made the tea and opened a new packet of biscuits. She was not wanted to sit in and would wait outside, beyond earshot. No note of the meeting was required. It was the line manager's moment – young and flying high – to demonstrate his seniority.

"To kick off, I want to explain the role of our visitor. He's down below, reading what we have given him ... You could call this a political sell-out by the Service, but I think that interpretation would be unfair. He was foisted on us. There are occasions when a deflection is better than a roadblock approach and I believe our God Almighty rated this as not an occasion for argument. He's here, and he will see what we consider suitable for him to see. He will be with us for the day and he is permitted to speak to any of you late this afternoon so we would appreciate that you stay around, make yourselves available. Should he demand face-to-face questioning I would ask you to accept that nothing will be permitted along the lines of a Salem witch trial, and Frank will do a transcription of any interview granted. The assumption is that he will be out of the building some time this evening – not, of course not, with a boot in the bum – and no doubt he will write a perfunctory, anodyne, report for local consumption.

"First, the Hamburg bomb ... Our position, and I have the Deputy Director's support here, is that the leak of intelligence on the visit of Sashcord to their police HQ would not have come from here. We have, sparing your blushes and sparing the blushes of many thousands of colleagues, an excellent record of internal security. This is not the bad old days. They are for historians, not writers concerned with the contemporary. In those days – Blake, Philby, that gang, and all operating before most of you were a gleam in a parent's eye – the Service reached near self-destruction and morale was tumbling. That inner suspicion was, I am told, corrosive ... You have all been subjected to Positive Vetting, you have all passed those rigours. I am prepared to hold my hand up, to commit myself. The leak would not have come from here, not from our end. I know this section, know its sense of duty, its discipline and its belief in the ethics of our work, know it well. The leak originated elsewhere.

"It is accepted that Sashcord has proved an expensive disappointment. Accepted also that it is in our own interests to keep him alive, in rude health and on our side. To lose him would be an unsustainable loss of face for our Service. Accepted that we seek, the longer the better, to keep the miserable, useless little beggar on Danish soil. Accepted that we will endeavour to hold expenditure at a minimum . . . Very few inside the PET ranks know the location of our current safe house, and I believe that we have excellent prospects of keeping him there, out of sight and, in an ideal world, out of mind.

"I have a very mild criticism and it is directed at one of you, your internal team leader, Denys. I do not want, Denys, for this to become a running sore. You stated, Denys, that you believed the leak must be internal because neither the Danish end nor the German participation had the necessary information that was needed to launch such an attack. It may not be clear as of today, but I am very confident that the necessary names and timings and locations *were* passed to our friends, to Copenhagen or Hamburg, and that the 'hostiles' were able to join dots or whatever, make a line. Something very small and something easily forgotten, but that is an answer I would bet on. No way will I be putting my shirt on a wager that we have a turncoat among us . . . Such a contamination will not exist here. So, Denys, I am prepared to contradict you, and that is why I remain happy for the current information supplied us by Benedict to continue to cross your desks.

"Now, to our friend from Thames House . . . We expected them to send over an attack-dog, one of their sour-faced Rottweilers, but they have surprised us. He looks as though he might have been dragged out of their post room. Rather humble, out of his depth and not seeming to know why he was thrown this far into the deep end. I popped in to see him before coming to this session. Seemed happy with the crumbs offered him. Anyway, you'll have your chance later this afternoon to run the rule over him. Thank you. And let's hope this unsavoury awkwardness is soon behind us."

He let them file out, all but Denys Montgomery. A little additional massage of feelings was applied. An easy error for him to have made but he probably should have given greater consideration to the calibre of his colleagues. And a personal opinion: the line manager reckoned that the damage had been done at the German end. Wouldn't there have been sufficient gossip in Copenhagen circles that the Russians had lost a GRU man, gone walkabout? Wouldn't that have filtered down to the German team there, and been passed on to BND, swallowed up in Berlin, and then gossiped about . . . and wouldn't the Hamburg people have heard a very likely identity for their mystery guest?

"You know better than me, Denys, that the Germans are colanders where intelligence is concerned . . . You've a fine team working alongside you and I'll not hear otherwise. And the fellow from over the river, rather fourth rate. No idea what they were thinking of."

At the door of his apartment, Alexei stopped, hesitated, looked around and listened. Heard nothing and saw nothing, and put the key in the lock and crouched.

It had taken him, before he had left for work that morning, a contortion to put in place the single hair. The hair came from Ludmilla's head. It had lain on her shoulder and he had been the polite young man who had removed it from her pullover. Ludmilla had auburn hair. The single strand was more than ten centimetres long and he had carefully brought it home, had laid it on his bedroom chest, and in the morning had cut two narrow widths of transparent adhesive tape. Leaving for work, he had crouched to close the door almost shut, not quite, and had used clumsy fingers to stick the hair between the two fastenings, the door and the jamb, then had closed and locked the door.

He opened the door, gradually, and with caution. He saw Ludmilla's single hair become taut. Was satisfied. He opened the door fully. The hair snapped. He peeled the tape off the woodwork and went inside. He sat on his easy chair, his head in his hands. Silence in his apartment, one bedroom, a living area with a kitchenette in a corner, one bathroom and a short, narrow hallway. The apartment was spacious by the standards enjoyed by most of the kids with whom he had been at High School. He would have been accused by them of enjoying privilege . . . The apartment, he was sure of it, had not been entered while he was at work. He had not seen a tail when he had gone to the complex at the start of the day, nor when he had emerged into the frost-laden evening, near darkness. But no tail and a strand of unbroken hair in no way calmed Alexei. He thought they played with him. Better never to have started? He shrugged. Light from the street fell on him. He had come back to Russia, had explained to the officers with him in Limassol that he had fallen in the street, had tried to laugh it off, had claimed he had tripped on the kerb: not that they had cared.

On the first trip from Kirov to Moscow after his return, the woman had been outside the entrance to his mother's block, built in the Brezhnev era, the concrete stained, the metal window frames rusting and the walkways criss-crossed with cracks from which weeds grew. He had skirted around two drunks, insensible, in the ground-floor hallway, and had gone out into the light. And his name had been called, a soft piano-note voice. They had walked among the trees in the park area on the far side of the road from the block. He could have spoken to her in rudimentary English, but she had good Russian. He had not been propositioned, not asked if he wanted to cooperate . . . it was assumed that the deal had been closed in the Limassol hotel room. She had pestered questions at him about the nature of his work, what he did, what crossed his desk, what sums of cash were transferred, and he had seen her face light with a sort of excitement. Her eyes would glow, and they would widen as if in real pleasure and then she would seem to want to control her enthusiasm and she would revert to the blunt and the brusque. She had told him what she wanted, had told him about the method of delivery which was the "dead letter box" system at the start a gap between concrete blocks at the rear area of the building, where the communal rubbish bins were. He had told her of his mother's life and procedures for contact had been agreed in addition to the regular visit he would make to this block every fortnight.

She was pleased with him. Occasionally she had even said so. She would have been, he thought, about forty years old. Dark hair, cut short and hugging her scalp, and a warm mouth and she had the power to enthuse him. And there had been meetings that had always lifted him. She only needed to touch his arm and indicate that his last shipment, the contents of a stick, were useful and he would walk away, almost stamping with pride. It was her talent. And they did brush contacts and also – as weeks passed into months and there was no sign of surveillance – she would meet him, would walk with him, always in the deprived corners of the city, never in the downtown areas of the city's central luxury.

And, of course, she made him a promise . . . almost a promise. "We look after our people, Alexei, look after them well. Every decision we make is governed by the prime factor: is this in the interests of our friend? We would never put a friend at risk. We really value the courage you have shown by coming to us. We will protect you, always remember that. In London, very few people know of you, Alexei, but those who do are senior, in positions of great influence, and they would want me to pass to you their warmest wishes. We acknowledge you as a friend, not only as an asset, a true friend."

A voice of syrup smoothness. There were days when she would come to the entrance of the block where his mother lived, and others when they would meet in the park when the trees and bushes were in leaf and there was cover . . . On a high summer day, the previous August, they had been together on a path and it had woven between bushes and they had needed to step over a couple, a boy's bare arse in the air, and she had taken his arm and had grinned and he had blushed scarlet. He had no girl. She had said, "What? A good-looking kid like you, Alexei? No girl?" Other times she would materialise alongside him as he walked from the Yaroslavskiy station, and they would do a brush contact.

Until a day nine weeks before. She had stiffened. Her nose had seemed to twitch. Her eyes had swept the street ahead of her and around her. She had dropped a handkerchief and had abruptly positioned herself to pick it up to give her the opportunity to look behind her, rake the pavement and the traffic. He had seen what she had seen . . . Two men on the far side of the street, loitering when it was the depths of winter, snow on the ground and slush under their feet from the spread salt, and sleet in the air, and two men who kept pace with them as they approached the station. He had heard her hiss, "Fuck and derision", and then again had dropped the handkerchief, and was down and close to it, and had said, "Has the look of a tail. Keep calm, little boy. Two weeks and there will be someone else for the pick-up . . . You'll like her. Good luck, and keep very calm." She had ducked away, handkerchief in her coat pocket. There one moment and gone the next. He had stopped in front of a shop window and had seen two more men behind him. He had gone to catch his train and spent a dozen hours of knife-sharp worry on the journey to Kirov. That had been the start of the growing anxiety. Two weeks later, coming back to Moscow, fear in his guts, he had met the girl who called herself Maggie, who had a husky bear's voice, and had a buggy and had Hector, and he was smitten . . . Was also, that evening, frightened.

Burning in his pocket, seeming to scorch the material, was a memory stick. Forbidden under pain of dismissal to remove state-owned items of equipment from the building where Alexei worked. It had been, as he believed it, a supreme act of courage that day, to download to his stick from his machine. Cash transfers had been made in the past two days to bank deposit accounts in Brazil's Sao Paolo, and in Washington State on the west coast of USA, and to Bologna and Lyon and Piraeus in Europe . . . Late in the day, and it had meant that he was later than usual returning home, he had been required to move 25,000 euros from the holding account to one newly opened in a branch of the Hanseatic Bank in the city of Rostock which he knew to be a small German town on the Baltic coast. Monies had not been sent there before. It was the work of a few seconds, copying the instructions to the memory stick. It was work that could have justified the surveillance, justified his arrest, justified the pain of a beating and lying blood-stained, shit-stained, on a cell floor . . . He had told them he was finished, wanted out, demanded an end . . . He sat in the darkness and shivered and the block's heating did not warm him.

She was different from the rest of them. Lance Corporal May, Logistics Corps, on attachment to Moscow, no husband or partner in tow but a child who was little more than a baby. Had more on her mind than any of the others, had responsibilities, was front-line . . . Known to all as Maggie, she worked alongside the Air Force girl and the Navy girl. A shortage of space determined that they were pressed together while the attachés, Army, RAF and RN, had cubicles to themselves. The girls were at the bottom of the food chain and between them and the officers were a layer of warrant officers and flight sergeants and chief petty officers. The other two were always smart in their non-uniform dress code, but with Maggie standards seemed to have slipped. As if an iron had not been deemed necessary, nor hair carefully brushed, and the barest smear of lipstick, perhaps, but often askew, but there was never complaint and she was not taken to task. Would have been something to do with her usual expression that could have been described as feisty, no nonsense, and a chin that jutted determination. She was without doubt attractive and able to turn heads, and was the chosen plaything of the spook lady in the building, the station chief, and was used for "special duties". In fact, her time was shared, and an uneasiness existed in the mind of her principal employer, the Military Attaché.

He called her into his work area.

She was late with a report she was supposed to have prepared for him . . . his assessment of the capabilities, qualities, deficiencies, of the new Armata T-14 main battle tank. His notes, a mess that she had to rustle into order and give shape to, concerned the crew survivability, the effectiveness of the laminated armour, its sensors that were supposed to deflect incoming fire . . . and suggestions as to how it would stand up to attack from

Tube-launched Optical-tracked Wire-guided missiles – it would be TOW-carried HEAT warheads that the US army would fire at them and there would be a wargame scenario of the T-14 in combat with the American tank, the Abrams M1A2. Should have worked on it on Sunday but had been out with her son and on the road to the Yaroslavskiy station, should have finished it on Monday but had been debriefing Lucinda for the Six report back to London . . . had fallen behind.

"Just a couple of minutes of your time, Maggie."

The colonel could have called her by her surname, May. Might have addressed her as Lance Corporal which was the rank she held in the Corps. She was not in uniform, neither was he: military dress was not obligatory in the attachés' unit. But, his shirt was fresh on and his mess tie neatly knotted, and her blouse carried the stain of a coughed-up mouthful of Hector's supper the previous evening. His hair was combed carefully, and hers was a golden mess. And . . .

"Just feel there's something to be discussed – where lines are drawn."

All officers, to Maggie, were "Ruperts" – useless, needed to be humoured but never bowed to. The attitude was in the family make-up. Her father was a company sergeant major, also in Logistics, and had one year to retirement and had done time in both Gulf wars and in Afghan and Bosnia. Her grandfather, eighty last birthday, had been in the Royal Corps of Transport and had a Military Medal for Gallantry, when he had driven alone, Aden 1967, with only a rifle to defend himself between the fire bases of the Parachute Regiment and the Lancashires in a tanker that sucked out the contents of the latrine pits, had been the wizard handling what the squaddies called the "shit gobbler". Herself, she could drive heavy army trucks, do most things to an engine to get it running after a failure, and she had ambitions – one day – to get into 11th Regiment of the Logistics and do Explosive Ordnance Disposal and Search, which was hard to crack, and a good recommendation from the Moscow posting might seal that for her. She followed the colonel into his cubicle.

"I really rather needed that tank stuff, and it seems to come down to priorities."

"Will be done tomorrow, sir."

"Good, and my suggestion would be not to allow further sidetracking."

"It will get done, sir."

"And you'll work around little Hector's needs, I hope so."

"He's fine, sir."

"Quite the little star, I hear, in the cloak and dagger."

"Don't know what you mean, sir."

"We'll try a little lecture, then. You spend time with the spook crowd, who I wouldn't touch with a bargepole. You dress up and go out – yes, we see you – looking like a scarecrow and with white make-up on your face and you take the child with you. You're running errands for those people. I suppose they have decided that it is not practical for them to carry out legwork on whatever caper they're involved with, and so they have chosen you as the useful item of cannon fodder. Frankly, you are much better than 'useful' and you should not be rated as expendable."

"Thank you, sir. Can I go now, sir?"

"When I have finished. I have spoken to Lucinda, our very charming station chief, and suggested that she leaves you free to do your day job, not involve you in her business, for which you are not trained, not qualified. With a turn of phrase that I'd expect from Lucinda I was told to 'Fuck off and keep your bloody nose out of matters that don't concern you'. Put mildly, I would urge that you show caution."

Straight-faced, no impertinence but certainly no gratitude. "Thank you, sir, for your advice."

"They use people. Use them while it suits them and then ditch them, and not prettily . . . I think you did a brief tour in the Province and drove for Mil Int. The ethics of Military Intelligence and this grade of spooks are quite separate. There will be an asset out there and he will be clinging to the belief that a great power is going to see him right, protect him, and you are the messenger. I expect they have rehearsed you so that you give him the talk and convince him to do their job for them . . . You may be asking why I care about your involvement with the spooks. I have every right to. I've done the Province – did XMG, the South Armagh fun-park where the police still can't manage the heavy lifting – and twice my platoon were called out to body-bag cadavers, informers. Hooded, nutted, and the refined touch was to remove their shoes and that seemed a further humiliation. Never had the handlers there when we were retrieving their stiffs and the families were left in the lurch . . . That is not a pretty world and one, in my opinion, you should avoid. Only advice."

"Thank you, sir, and I'll get back to your paper."

"The pleasure is all mine. It is a rather formidable weapon, the Armata Universal Combat Platform. High quality. The Russians possess more than ten thousand tanks, and we have 227 at the last count. Finland has more tanks than the UK. They rather enjoy the power that tanks bring to the table . . . Stalin once used the Pope to sneer about Rome's paucity of tanks and armoured divisions: 'How many has he got?' More advice, go carefully when you are on Lucinda's business because I would hate – I mean it – to see you go under the tracks of a local tank. Figurative speech . . . it would be unwise to play the crusader, righting the world's ills, because crusaders are rarely around at the victory parade."

"I'll get on."

"Last question . . . is he a boy, a lad, young . . .?"

She might have freshened in the cheeks. "I don't think I should discuss detail."

"There must be pressure building on him, or they wouldn't have wanted to enrol a pretty girl to stiffen his backbone."

"And I have to collect Hector from the crèche in an hour."

"Don't get fond of him, the boy . . . That paper by the morning, please."

She left the cubicle. She sat at her desk and gazed at her screen, and cared not a toss for an assessment of the prowess of main battle tanks, ours or theirs or anyone's, then had to blink hard because a tear had dripped on to her keyboard . . . Bit bloody late, wasn't it, not to get fond of him.

★   ★   ★

Her name was called. A shrill, elderly voice yelling for her to come.

Her fire was laid, her table tidied, dishes washed and dried, purse and shopping bags ready. It was a duty performed each week. In the near derelict hamlet in which she lived, by far the youngest resident and her in her fifties, she had the only car. She had acquired the duty of taking her neighbours, in turn, for the drive to the nearest town and the nearest supermarket – bread, milk, vegetables, fruit if possible, cigarettes, even an occasional bottle of cheap vodka, and sometimes meat from the scrag ends of the butcher's bench. She lived off the main highway that linked the city of St Petersburg with the Finnish capital, Helsinki. The track to her community was well used because it was the route used by the troops of that element of FSB who had responsibility for the security of the border. They oversaw the Closed Zone that was ten klicks deep, with a ploughed strip to be examined each day for footprints – and hoof prints of deer and the paw prints of occasional bears – of fugitives from modern Russia, and they checked the fence and the tumbler wires that would alert their Control if they bounced, tightened, sagged, as an illegal attempted to scramble over the barrier. She slept poorly because every night she listened for the staccato burst of gunfire. The troops were well armed. She knew that. Knew also that they patrolled in all weathers, and knew that they would use their automatic rifles to protect against violation of the border.

Her name was called again. She swept up what she needed from her table. She closed the door behind her. Rain and sleet slashed at her face. A bowed and irritated woman waited beside the car: it was old and battered but reliable, and was a link with the world that was beyond their track – shops and a dentist and a doctor, and a church if a priest was needed. For her there was also an opportunity to buy books or visit a library – once she had been a scholar.

"Come on, Galina. Hurry please. I am so cold. You are late, Galina."

They took her for granted, used her, burdened her. It was her choice, her decision, that she lived here, close to the fence and the guns that went with it.

She said that he could not. Was Frank sure he could not? She was certain he could not.

He accepted. One of the rules governing the professional life of Jonas Merrick, Counter-Terror and Counter-Intelligence officer, was only to pick fights that were worth winning, and that he would win. The woman, Frank – what she seemed to want to be called – insisted that he could not put the thin file of paper printouts in his briefcase and take it out of the building. He had read its contents, gone over the detail a second time, had taken notes with a sharpened pencil on a lined pad.

"But you're not going, are you?"

"I think I am, have a train to catch."

"The team are upstairs and waiting to be called down."

"I only work late if it's an important matter, otherwise I catch my train. I'll see them in the morning, or the afternoon, but tomorrow."

Which confused her . . . the paper she had prepared for him, and no doubt sanctioned from on high, gave him an interesting insight. He now knew of a defector, *Sashcord*. Knew also of a team in the Danish capital who had been alerted when the Russian GRU major was looking to bolt and offer himself up, and had the names of Griffin and Brian in Copenhagen. Included were transcripts of the early to-and-fro messages, and he could imagine Frank and the two muscle men being kicked out of their pits for a red-eye flight to Copenhagen, and that first assessment: hardly precious, more the stuff of fool's gold. He had pecked at the information provided for him, was a sparrow under a bird food tray . . . She had an unsightly frown on her forehead and he imagined she was rarely confused.

"I am afraid, Mr Merrick, that I do not know what plans are in place for tomorrow, but the team was on standby for you today, and . . ."

"They'll keep for tomorrow, I'm sure they will. If you think it necessary then please apologise to them on my behalf for any waste of their time."

And he rewarded her with a pleasant smile. There would have been a few of them back in Thames House on the north side of the river who would have claimed that the sight of a Jonas Merrick smile was hardly an indication of genuine warmth. Might have said, "If the old beggar smiles – worse if he apologises – then it's high time to be filling sandbags and hunkering down". He had the identities of the team, the impatient ones now awaiting his call, those who had come on the second wave and had then overseen the protracted debrief of Sashcord. More paper listed in vaguer terms, with blacked-out redactions, the assessments of intelligence provided by the young Russian. And, what to do with him? A paper from one of them – which Jonas thought poorly written and without the main points properly listed – on the value of keeping out of harm's way those who had come across and who relied on the team to protect them from the fruits – or just rewards? – of their treachery.

"And I'm not sure, Mr Merrick, about tomorrow and what access is possible. It was hoped, I believe, that the team and yourself would work late tonight, and . . ."

"I always catch a train at the same time, and I am hopeful tomorrow will prove convenient to everybody."

He had eaten his lunch. A sandwich and an apple: he had peeled the apple with care and used a sharp little knife that had been wrapped in tinfoil and secreted in his lunch box and had made it through the ground-floor scanners – which counted among his victories of the day. The art in apple peeling was to take off the peel in one strip, no breaks. He had noticed she had watched him doing it with a degree of astonishment that any man could be so "bloody pathetic" as to think that had been a good use of time on a supposedly busy day. He had drunk coffee, with a slight splash of milk and no sugar as he'd requested, and twice had been escorted to the door of the toilet. After lunch he had immersed himself in the report provided by the Hamburg police, and a further intelligence assessment by their internal security division.

Had read Benedict's detailed statement and his description of the escape from the Hamburg complex. She had worked on her laptop, the screen hidden from him by the angle at which she sat. They had made no small talk . . . When he had broken to eat the contents of his box, and the chocolate bar, she had locked her laptop in the safe and had set a code in the bank of numbers but her hand had hidden it and he was not able to see the numbers she'd used later to open it. When she had gone out, he had not tested whether she had in fact locked him in or had merely closed the door. He stood, stretched, then straightened his tie's knot. He slipped on his raincoat and put on his trilby. He secured the briefcase, containing only his lunch box and empty thermos, to his wrist.

"Well, I think that's enough for one day . . . We have a problem with our caravan and my wife may need a spot of help tonight sorting out the difficulty. What time do you finish?"

"I finish when nobody has any more need for me. I don't have fixed hours."

"I'm most grateful for the help and I'll see you tomorrow. It has been a good day."

She escorted him to the main doors. He had a glimpse of a group looking down at him from an upper floor, like it was a cattle market and they needed an evaluation, and he hoped he appeared suitable only for the knacker's yard – which would be, on their part, a serious mistake. He thanked her again for her attention and went out into the gathering dusk. He thought he dealt with a matter of life and of death, and he walked briskly. Not game playing but real, and it usually was in his experience when death came on to the playground.

5

"Nothing listed for you, Mr Merrick."

"Then the mistake is at your end."

"I can only deal, Mr Merrick, with the information I am given."

Same place, same time. Rain a little heavier than the previous day, and the surge behind him rather stronger. Jonas stood his ground.

"Then, please, get on the phone and sort it."

The gatekeeper wore a uniform. Did not have officer's pips on his epaulettes nor a couple of layers of medal ribbons on his chest, but he would have believed he had the authority granted him by right of his presence at the front gate of the Vauxhall Cross building, home of the Secret Intelligence Service. Also, wary and watching behind him, were two armed policemen with automatic weapons to back up their status in the necessary pecking order. Worldwide there were in excess of 4000 men and women working full-time as Sixers staffers, and there could have been as many as 1000 who were attempting entry into the building at around that hour of the working day. A good proportion of them were blocked by a diminutive and elderly man, brogues and trilby and raincoat, with a briefcase in his hand and spectacles on his nose, who seemed to be short of an entry pass, and short also of a greeter.

"If you would not mind, Mr Merrick, please, moving to the side, not obstructing . . ."

"And if you would not mind getting on the phone and doing the sorting – thank you."

It would have been a deliberate slight. Could have been their response to him not staying half the evening and doing perfunctory interviews and missing his train back to Raynes Park . . .

Had he not been there, with bodies bumping into him, and shopping bags and handlebars, Jonas would have been at his desk, S/3/13, in Thames House on the other side of the river. On his screen, split with identifying photographs and brief biographies, would be the details of two men, part of the delegation with the grandiose title of Federal Agency for the Commonwealth of Independent States Affairs, Compatriots Living Abroad, and International Humanitarian Cooperation. A mouthful for the Russian staff working in a block off Kensington High Street comprising, the estimate of Jonas and others, a fifty-fifty ratio of intelligence officers to administrative dogsbodies; they specialised in watching the scores of ex-patriates who had made London their home, and recruiting them or threatening and intimidating them if their politics strayed into hostility towards the regime. The two men were working hard, attempting to earn whatever corn they fed off, burrowing for worthwhile contacts, and would also look to turn those London-based Russians who mixed freely with, and were trusted by, those who denounced the Kremlin's person- alities. Jonas had a free rein. Took his time and was allowed to wallow in his research . . . that much faith was put in his work by the AssDepDG. The pictures showed one of them taking his chil- dren to the Embassy-based school on his way to work, and the other pushing a trolley out of a supermarket. He would be back with them soon, not more than a week away from them, he assessed. But first he required entry to VX.

He was ridiculed, sworn at, cajoled, but stood his ground. The rain dripped off his hat. He felt his socks dampening.

"Would you please, Mr Merrick, move to the side and later on, after the rush, we may be able to work it out."

"Thank you, but very comfortable right where I am."

"Not wanting to be difficult, Mr Merrick, but there is no noti- fication today of your visit. So, aside, please."

He supposed it was why the AssDepDG had nominated him to come to the home of the self-proclaimed senior service and see off their predictable attempts to unsettle him. Little unnerved Jonas Merrick, other than fear of failure.

A police officer had stepped forward. "You have been asked, sir, and very civilly, to shift yourself, and have so far not done so. I would be loath to take action, sir, but am prepared to. Would you, please, move to the side."

Jonas took out his phone. Hit the keys, sent the message . . . where he was, what was happening . . . thought it would go from AssDepDG to DepDG and might go on to the chief of staff of the DG. Then would make a fast crossing of the river, scooting above tugs and barges and river ferries, into the ghastly heap of architecture in front of him.

"Move." A gloved hand came off the stock of the Heckler & Koch and reached out for the front of his raincoat.

He did his smile. Just an elderly throwback to a past age, and likely as not incapable of harming anything more threatening than a household fly. He turned his phone on the policeman, and his gear and his sagging rifle and his vest and weatherproof kit would have filled the lens. Quite a gentle smile but the policeman would have seen the eyes behind the spectacles and would have known that his pleasantries were bogus. He might have wondered who the daft old bastard was, and who that text had been sent to, and who was now watching the scene – and he backed off.

Jonas addressed the gatekeeper. "As I requested before, please, just get my entry authorised."

He sat down. He made himself small. The tails of his raincoat were under his flannels, kept the seat moderately dry. He tucked his briefcase, held to his wrist by the chain, under his armpits. A woman tripped over him and had to grab at a man's coat to prevent herself from falling, another man kicked him in the small of the back. He was an impediment, a bloody nuisance, and surprise was voiced that neither the policeman nor the gatekeeper shoved him out of the way, pitched him clear. He liked the thought of that – an impediment, a bloody nuisance, awkward and stubborn and obstinate, which in the world of Jonas Merrick were all quality virtues.

He sat on the pavement and waited.

⋆   ⋆   ⋆

As he stood among the gravestones, light rain pattered on to Benedict's shoulders.

He had needed to get out of the house. Had the door not been unlocked and opened for him by Wally, he might have smashed at it with his fists and taken it off the hinges, and chucked the bloody thing across the parking area and over the lawn and the pavement and into the street so that it cannoned into the PET boys' car. He had needed to get outside, had predicted a volcano close to eruption and had realised that its source would be him. Benedict had been subject to dripping criticism from Sashcord: incompetence with security, hesitation with decision taking on the UK transfer, cabin fever in the new safe house ... Not Benedict's bloody fault that they were corralled together in a three-bed bungalow, with a garden behind that was barely big enough to swing a cat in. Inside was a TV without a bank of DVDs, and a fridge that was less than half full, and houses overlooking them from the front – and behind was a wooded area, overgrown, boggy, about as unsuitable for a safe house as it was possible to get. Whose fault? Probably down to Benedict, but it was where they were and what they had. Sashcord was looking for a fight, seemed bent on finding it ... He had gone out into the rain, had left Wally and Doug to field him, and decided to give up on attempting any more debriefing. No more questions about GRU's policy aims, its targets, its agents: the well had run dry and the bucket just clattered on the stone at the bottom of the shaft. And he was still wound tight, like a drawn bowstring, near to losing his self-control.

The PET car was at changeover time. Two guys pulling away, a guy and a woman replacing them. There would have been a brief exchange, probably a sardonic grin and a titter as the household in the bungalow was discussed. The window had been wound down for him. Where could he walk? The PET woman, plain and blonde and with a shoulder holster visible under an open anorak, dismissively pointed up the street and across the main road, mentioned a cemetery having space.

They were not ordinary headstones. Rows of graves were marked with fine white stone quarried in Dorset, from the Portland peninsula. The dead lying here came from a long-concluded war. The anger was filtering out of Benedict. He started to walk along the lines. Read the names and read the ages, and read the carved inscriptions.

Known unto God. To live in our hearts Is not to die. Peace came to him Early in the dawn Away heavenwards His soul was borne. I have fought a good fight, I have finished my course, I have kept the Faith.

RAF flyers and Polish crew, Canadians and Australians, and New Zealanders. Many in their early twenties, some not yet out of their teenage years. A pilot of twenty, and already awarded the Distinguished Flying Cross . . .

He called London and asked for backup, more resources – some "bloody support would be welcome" – was told that Simon was coming with a box of tricks and would be there later that afternoon . . . And he thought of the courage of these kids who had been in the big Wellingtons and the bigger Lancasters and on a northern route, over Denmark, towards Berlin or Hamburg, and had to negotiate ferocious flak batteries. Mused that it might have been easier for them because they knew their enemy, could touch it and feel it, as their aircraft jolted from the explosions. Reflected that in this new age of Cold War, as intelligence guys, he and his people fought in a fog and their viewpoint was into mirrors. Behind a trimmed beech hedge was a line of different stones, darker and squatter, and he read the German names, and their units and their ranks, and their ages. Had a silly thought . . . wondered if, late at night, when the lights were switched off and the gates locked, there were games of football in here, and gatherings and the swapping of girlfriends' photos, and songs sung, fags shared. And felt himself calmer.

He turned, wiped the rainwater off his face, felt the weight of his sodden jacket on his chest. The next crisis would soon be on them, that he could guarantee. Benedict was glad to have walked in the company of the young men at rest in the Fourfelt cemetery of Esbjerg, felt better for it. It would be good to see Simon that evening and have his gear rigged, but would have been better if a platoon of the Parachute Regiment would drop from a lead-dark sky.

"I like that name, Mercader, it is a good name," said Anatoly, once of the Vympel unit.

Whenever they were away, the two men took magazines with them. Would read and reread them until they were dog-eared and about to fall apart. Mostly the magazines advertised brands of surplus military kit, which was a principal area of conversation between the pair of them.

"It is a good name, Ramon Mercader. A name to be proud of – and what a weapon." A chuckle from Konstantin.

But also there were magazines, popular with veterans, that dealt with former glories of the old Red Army and the successes of NKVD and its successor KGB, and on into the modern-day exploits of FSB which both of them thought were shit. Kit and killing were the two subjects they most liked to chew on. They talked about Mercader regularly.

"An amazing weapon, an ice pick. You are in Central America. Where in Mexico City in August does a man find an ice pick? Incredible, so original."

"A clever man to be able to infiltrate Trotsky's guards, the most security-conscious guy in the country. He is sentenced to death, and Stalin is annoyed because his enemy is still alive, and already attempts have failed, but Mercader deceives all the guards, tricks Trotsky and wins his trust."

"That is supreme. Artistry."

Konstantin said, "Hits Trotsky who will die the next day. Hit in the skull with an ice pick you are lucky to last twenty-four hours, but he is captured by the other guards."

Anatoly asked, "What is the dispute, Stalin and Trotsky? I forget but you have told me, my memory . . ."

"Two big men and the head of a nail to sit on, and not room there for two big arses."

"You are good because you understand politics. He did twenty years in a Mexican gaol. That is devotion to the trade."

"Awarded the medal of Hero of the Soviet Union, came to Moscow after his release. A great honour . . . He spent more than seven thousand nights in the prison in Mexico and he would have been comforted in the knowledge that one day he would receive that medal."

They laughed, caps coming off beer bottles drinking from the neck. German piss but they could not get Baltika Number 7 Premium in Rostock.

"You have an ability, Konstantin, to see the positive. The medal would have been important. You know what he said at the end of his life? You remember?"

"He said, 'I hear it always, the scream, and I know he is waiting for me on the other side.' "

"'Hear it always, the scream'. I like that. See their fear."

"See their fear, hear their breath. And not all the clever shit, the nuclear stuff or the nerve gas, and the fuck-up . . . Old-fashioned, a bullet – or an ice pick."

"You think we have another chance?"

"I think so. I hope we get to see that bastard again – and we can do a Mercader."

They fell silent. Anatoly went back to his magazine with the special offers on webbing and combat boots, and Konstantin started to strip his AK, and he would clean each part before reassembly . . . they wanted to see the fear, hear the scream, which was their trade.

A short text had appeared on Jonas's phone.

Backsides will be burned. On the case.

Quite unnecessary for him to have sat in the wet on the pavement outside the check-in gate, and he had intimidated a gatekeeper and a policeman who were going about their daily duties, but he thought that his stubborn tactic would have caused a minor degree of panic. So simple for them, the Resettlement team, to have kept him hanging about for fifteen minutes. But Jonas Merrick was adept at rattling cages and the AssDepDG would have enjoyed the chance to go upstairs with a complaint.

Perhaps, by now, a senior figure was being hauled out of a meeting and told to "Sort this bloody mess out" and asked "What sort of fucking message are we supposed to be trying to send?" Jonas thrived on contrariness and felt well.

As if displaying tactical wisdom, the policeman and the gate-keeper now ignored him. The crush had thinned at the checkpoint. If he had been at his own desk and not sitting in a puddle, he would have been concerning himself with the personalities working from that address in Kensington, their efforts to suborn and threaten . . . The previous week, Jonas had been studying the personalities of the trade delegation up in north London, in Highgate. Interesting people operated from there, and had done so for more than nine decades, but the feeling was that their efforts were now ramped, intensive and extended. He had been examining their movements, usually managed it with credit card details and logging the places where they used the cards, buying fuel or light lunches, or running up bills at wine bars. He had never, of course, actually seen the people that he tracked and they would not have known of his existence, but he felt he knew them. He thought about them when going home, eating his supper, sitting in his chair with Olaf on his lap, and coming back to work in the morning and walking over the bridge; pretty much swamped by them. The day on Orford Ness among the buildings where atomic weapons had been developed and where previous generations of Russian intelligence, no doubt from Kensington and Highgate, would have probed . . . The gatekeeper hovered close to him.

"The problem is sorted, Mr Merrick."

He nodded, not graciously.

"Actually, not my problem, Mr Merrick. No slip-up at my end." And nodded again.

"No one had informed us that you were attending today, no one was here to meet you . . . but hardly necessary, Mr Merrick, for you to sit on the pavement and get wet."

No answer required. Another of Jonas Merrick's talents was to hold his silence and let others around him babble. He would have said, if he had wished to, that it was *very* necessary for him to sit down, make an exhibition of himself, end up with a damp seat. He stood, straightened his back and heard his joints creak. Saw that the policeman who nursed the assault rifle eyed him with dislike, but was wary. He saw her come out of the main building and walk fast towards the security area.

He thought his point had been well made as a response to a minor degree of rudeness. He could look forward now to the rest of his day, reckoned it would be a good one.

Probably her fault.

Not directly, but probably.

She had been in the building since six. Had gone through the overnight messages, had had them ready for the team when they had drifted in, clutching coffee and cold bacon sandwiches. Had not been thanked, never was.

Probably Frank's fault because she should have remembered that there was no authorisation for the Five man, funny little creature, to be escorted into the visitor reception annex where he could have been left with a beaker of water from the machine and a newspaper or a magazine a week old. Denys Montgomery – Denys to her and Monty to his colleagues – had not given her a visitor slip. Their line manager had not. None of them had – not Chiswell, not Symonds, not Barker, not Toni. Probably Frank's fault because they all relied on her to remember *everything*.

The work that morning concerned a new safe house that Sashcord had been moved to, out on the north side of the city of Esbjerg. Had never heard of it, had never had cause to hear of it. There was now a photo of a bungalow on the file. It was the sort of bungalow that the aunt and uncle who had brought her up had lived in, south Oxfordshire. Rex and Prudence had taken her in, and had been well rewarded from her mother's legacy. An unremarkable bungalow, as was this one. Benedict was complaining and Benedict had cause to. Not for Frank to comment on the quality of the bungalow or its suitability or the budget that controlled what sort of property was within reach. Not for her to give an opinion, and she had not, and time had gone by. Reasonable to assume that a message had catapulted from Thames House, had gone to a high-flyer in her building, up there on the top floors to which she did not get invited. She imagined that the buck-passing, parcel-shifting exercise had gained intensity with each floor it had descended. So, from line manager to Denys, "and the smug pint-sized bastard is actually sitting on the pavement, making a bloody exhibition of himself – sort it out". And from Denys to Toni, "Really pisses me off when we demonstrate our failings to the wide world, especially to that gang of paper clip counters across Lambeth Bridge". From Toni to Frank, and she was always the dumping ground for criticism: "For fuck's sake, get down there and bring that horrid nobody in here, and give me an answer by the end of today as to why you hadn't taken it all in hand". Why? Had not been asked to. She collected the ID card for the day, and came out of the building.

"Very sorry, Mr Merrick, but I am afraid there was a misunderstanding."

Strange and a little disconcerting, but she won a pleasant smile from him, as water dripped from his coat and his hat, and she thought his briefcase might be wet inside, and his shirt collar was dark from damp. It still rained . . . looking out from the security area she could see, clearly marked out, a square that was drier than the pavement around it and that would have been where he had sat as messages had flown with increasing acrimony over the Thames and down through the floors of Vauxhall Cross. She would have expected biting anger. Any of the crowd she worked for would have been chucking insults at the skies and stacking complaints, and would have – Frank's opinion – shoved in the ball-breaker, as Barker would have put it, of "Do you know who I am?" The smile died, replaced by an expression which she read as "all part of life's rich tapestry". But that was for her. For the team, for the officers, he would have sent a message: Not to be trifled with.

"Please follow me, Mr Merrick."

He did. No fuss and nothing snide said to the policeman nor to the gatekeeper. They would have watched him go, trailing dutifully after her, and would have wondered what he had sought to achieve. Frank thought he might have achieved plenty, and had raised the temperature.

She was told when he wished to see the team. And he said what he wanted from the overnight file. Not for her to refuse him, and she doubted anyone else would. What he had achieved was the attention of the mandarins on the upper floors and showing off the battalions he had behind him. The overnight file on Sashcord and the messages from Esbjerg which normally would have been so closely guarded. Clever, she thought, and not the work of a man who could be dismissed. She took him downstairs and opened up the room, and she made coffee, remembered how he had liked it the day before: Frank had a reliable memory for things that mattered. He took off his shoes, and socks and she left him for a minute and went in search of a newspaper that she could shove into his shoes. He barely seemed to notice . . . She used the printer in the corridor to make him copies of the signals, and the photograph of the bungalow.

He went to work. She supposed that his whole life involved the study of traitors, of treachery, of turn-coats. Frank would not short-change his intelligence, others might, not her. She supposed it dominated him, a study of the spirit of betrayal.

From his supervisor's office came Ludmilla, with her shoulder-length auburn hair.

She walked directly to Alexei's desk, her heels sounding unusually loud.

In her hand was a folded slip of paper. Heads pivoted as she approached him; everyone had stopped working. He was in the back row and she had to pass everyone else who worked in that part of the organisation that monitored and controlled the expenditure of GRU personnel. She did not smile when their eyes met. She had not minded when he had removed the single hair from her pullover the day before. This morning he could see at least half a dozen strands on her shoulders, caught in the weave. He would need a minimum of three more hairs if he were to repeat the security procedure on his front door each day for the rest of the week . . . if proof of entry were needed. Ludmilla was not attractive and it would have caused amusement among his colleagues if he, little Alexei, who was not thought to have a girl-friend, had the courage to touch her. But he needed the hairs.

She came to his desk. "For you," and Alexei was handed the folded piece of paper.

He reached up to her. His lips moved. Perhaps she did not understand what he intended. His hand was on her shoulder and at least three hairs were between his fingers. He blushed. She would have felt the movement of his fingertips and looked down at him with curiosity, and there were titters of suppressed laughter from their audience. She gazed hard at him, then turned away and Alexei ducked his head and read the note, and his breath came faster and his head slumped.

He was informed by the supervisor that he should attend, in the next five minutes, the office of the Programme Manager. The number of the room was given him. The Programme Manager worked on the floor below and Alexei had never before been summoned there. His screen was a blur and tears welled, and his fingers seemed leaden on his mouse and his keyboard as he tried to complete his current assignment, flagged "immediate". It involved payments to be made to a bank in the city of Kaliningrad, to a branch of Gazprombank, on Mira Avenue. The recipient of the cash order was not listed as having a shore-based address, but his *poste restante* was given. The contact was on a beam trawler, the *Katerina*, working the Baltic Sea. He completed the task. It was a new order and if he had had the opportunity he would have recorded it on his memory stick – the last one he would use. He closed his screen.

He started to walk from his desk to the main double doors of the work area; in front of him would be the staircase and he would go one flight down, and then on into an area of privilege, of carpeted floors, of recent decoration, where artwork hung on the walls. His mind ran riot . . . It was how they would do it. A reason-able summons to a meeting with the Programme Manager. He had been on the trip to Limassol, had never bothered to exchange a greeting with Alexei, had never complimented him on his thorough work, had not queried the facial injuries he had displayed after his beating . . . How they would do it. Down the stairs, along the corridor to a desk where a receptionist would be sitting, who might look at him with vague interest, or might study him as if anticipating entertainment, leading him to a closed door, and knocking on it. A sharp voice permitting him to enter. Going inside. The door closing behind him. Seeing his Programme Manager at the far end of a spacious and light-filled room, then seeing the two men against the wall in which the door was set. Suits, tight shirts and loose ties, cropped heads, malice or indifference on their faces. They might make the accusation immediately. Might question him then and there. Might punch him, kick him. Might take him out on to a fire escape and drop him down to the parking area where a van would be waiting, the tail doors already opened.

He walked down the corridor. His legs were weak, and his knees shook, and cold gripped the back of his neck. He told the woman at the desk who he was to see and held out the note and the paper shook in his hand.

He had told her, Maggie, to get him out. To free him, get him away. Did not know how it would happen but had believed in her . . . and now too late. He stood in front of the Programme Manager's door . . . like a bullock or a lamb that had been herded down the corridor between the narrowing rails, towards the heavy plastic flaps masking the killing zone in a slaughter house . . . and remembered the men who had matched his stride as he walked towards the Yaroslavskiy station, and thought . . . Knocked. Heard the voice on the far side of the door.

Opened the door, went inside. The officer behind the desk was scanning a close-typed sheet of paper. Alexei fidgeted, then dared, from the corners of his vision, to check the wall either side of the door. No one there. No goons in suits and dulled shoes, with scars on their scalps. So, they played another game with him, and the men would come when they were summoned and perhaps by now they had came up the stairs and were outside the door . . . The officer did not hurry. A game that was being played out. Why else summon him, immediate, and then ignore him? The paper was put on one aside. The cap was replaced on the pen. He drank from a glass of water. Alexei waited for the denunciation.

"You were dealing with the Kaliningrad transfer?"

He might have murmured that he was but could not hear his own voice.

"I don't hear you – did you or did you not deal with the Kaliningrad transfer?"

"I did," Alexei stammered.

"Well, fucking speak up . . . Your behaviour gives me a problem. You know what you are here for?"

He did not, shook his head and his body quivered and he thought his bladder fit to burst, and saw Maggie's face and tried to cling to it.

"My complaint, young man, is that your work has become less than satisfactory. We are GRU, we are the best. We require work levels well beyond the level of satisfactory. Last week, I am told you were twice late checking in for work, and on one of those days, having been late, you were found asleep in a rest area. Asleep when you should have been at your desk . . . I am told you go frequently to Moscow, and you see your mother, thirteen hours or more each way on the train. Of course you are tired, exhausted. You have, young man, responsible work, trusted work, and I will not tolerate that work being treated as incidental. You are fucking lucky to have that work, and you are abusing it. Fall short again and you will be out on your arse. Go."

He went out into the corridor. It ran hot, steaming down inside his trouser leg. He stumbled the length of the corridor and out of the officers' area and towards the toilet . . . Had to trust in Maggie, had no one else.

Galina fed her chickens and her ducks.

In the middle of the day, regardless of the weather, she brought out grain and vegetables that she had chopped up and mixed with fine gravel, and the fowl would come, clucking and screeching, from their two shelters. It could have been snowing or it could have been mid-summer when the sun was hot and the mosquitoes swarmed but they were always fed at that same time. She had fine chickens and they gave her good eggs, but those from the ducks were better. Today she was outside between sleet showers. She was well wrapped in an old blue coat of a heavy material, and wore rubber boots. In the far distance to the north was the soft but steady rumble of traffic on the E-18. The heavy lorries used the two-lane highway from very early in the morning, long before it was light, until far into the evening when darkness enveloped the road. But, scattering the food, she hardly heard the traffic because of the raucous noise from her birds. And where she lived, on the edge of an almost deserted village, the community was surrounded by dense walls of natural pine that were broken only by the near stagnant waters of large and small lakes. Her village was between the main road towards the frontier out of Vyborg, and the gulf of the Baltic Sea that lay to the north of St Petersburg. Galina had no interest in that great city, had only minimal interest in the old town of Vyborg. Apart from the weekly shopping trips, she barely left this small cluster of houses that had once been home to a vibrant community. A dozen or so single women lived there, all widows bar three, and two older men who had lost their wives long ago. They were almost self-sufficient. In the summer it was easier because they grew vegetables and once every two weeks there would be a killing, almost ritual, like that of a primitive society, of a goat or a pig or a sheep. In more remote cabins lived men who had skills that were blunted by their age and infirmity but whose expertise at plumbing or carpentry had lasted. Women made and repaired clothing, cooked and preserved their food. Almost, they were a forgotten community. They were mostly pleased and grateful to have slipped off the state's records.

Galina was not only younger than most in the village, she was also an incomer ... Some of the women in the village laughed at her, with her, called her a stranger, said that to belong in their community it was necessary to have a grandmother buried in the graveyard. The church no longer had a roof. The graveyard was mostly a tangle of bushes and bramble except for the newer section where the most recent burials had taken place – those of the last ten years. The graveyard was why Galina, now fifty-three, lived in this crumbling village. There were many such villages inside the boundaries of modern Russia, beyond the range of the wealth and power of St Petersburg and the fine highway leading to the checkpoints and the border. She had a Masters degree in Social Sciences from the Sholokhov Moscow State University for Humanities, had been rated an exceptional student by her tutors. The university was acknowledged as excellent both in regards to drug abuse by its students and the corruption of its staff, but job placement was considered a "problem" and following athletics and arts was a "major problem". A short marriage, a husband gone in a litany of complaint about her passion for argument leaving a son for her to rear and to indoctrinate. Ten years before, her boy then aged twenty-two, and filled with the anger of youth and rebellion, and already a leader of protests against the perpetual Putin rule, had fled. He had attended a demonstration that had veered into violence outside the St Petersburg headquarters of the regional FSB. Astride a Ural motorcycle, his pride and joy, he had been chased towards the Finnish border by a convoy of FSB cars . . . Some said he had been driven off the road, others that he had been shot and wounded and had swerved into the forest, some said that he had been hunted down and shot on the ground, an already injured life snatched, and left to rot and be found by hungry foxes. Some said that loggers from the village had found him and had taken him home, carried him on a makeshift litter. His grave in the cemetery was not marked by a stone or wooden cross but by a growth of wild flowers that erupted each spring, camomile and orchid and daisies. That was when his mother had arrived at the village: had been at the roadside with flowers where the motorcycle had crashed, had been approached by a villager had been told of the burial. The loathing her boy had felt for the regime leader, safe inside the Kremlin walls, had been returned by his mother. She thought that a good reason to feel endless, soulless guilt. The cemetery where he lay was two kilometres from the Closed Zone, and a further ten kilometres to the west was the frontier with its armed patrols and a high fence, and beyond a sort of freedom which her boy had not reached.

The road north from Moscow, the M-11, was wide and fast, and the toll charges in difficult financial times meant that the traffic was thin.

She had made good time. Maggie was a trained driver, probably better at the wheel of a three-ton military truck than a Fiat 500. She knew how to nurse the engine, get the maximum performance from it, and she had now reached the first of the service stations where she could fill up the tank, premium quality gasoline, the most expensive and best performing. She was past Novgorod, and Hector slept soundly.

She could have assumed that the colonel for whom she worked entertained, as others did, a certain tolerance of her demands. She did not think herself pretty, but she accepted – rather liked it – that there was something a little wild about her features. "You're quite a feral little thing," Hector's father had said to her in the back of the car. "Delightful and hopefully a trifle dangerous."

Late the previous night she had gone to the apartment inside the Embassy's complex where her attaché lived. A dinner party, a table of friendly diplomats and their wives, and the port about to be passed. She was the conversation stopper . . . a pale-faced waif of a creature, with tangled hair and her jeans torn at the knees and a T-shirt that proclaimed allegiance to an Irish rock band, and she'd had her child hooked up on one arm. She had asked if she might borrow the Fiat. He would have thought the request was ludicrous, would have been certain that whatever idea she entertained was risky, would have marvelled at his own stupidity, but had gone to the bedroom that doubled as a private office, retrieved the keys and given them to her. Would have believed that this was about the boy, and would be hazardous. Would also have been able to recite, word-perfect, the exact words of warning he had given her. The Fiat 500 was kept in a garage within a mile of the

Embassy. Several of the friendly diplomatic missions used that particular garage, and paid over the odds for its discreet service. The Fiat looked ancient, had dents and scrapes in the bodywork, was perpetually dirty from the winter salt dumped on the roads, but the engine was kept at a high state of performance. The benefit of keeping the car there, nondescript by the standards of modern Moscow, was that a trusted member of the attaché's staff could go inside unnoticed and emerge at the wheel of the little runaround, then slip away below the radar of FSB surveillance. He would have had an idea of where she might head and thought the possibility strong that he might be, having facilitated her journey, damned in hell's fires. She had stopped once to change Hector, and fill the tank again and was now beginning to watch for the signs of the ring road route around the east side of St Petersburg.

She had left at four that morning. Had walked out of the main gate and past the Embassy's security people and had smiled sweetly at the Russian police who shivered and stamped and punched their gloved hands together. She had pushed the buggy and they would have seen Hector peering up at them, and on cue he had howled. She had pointed to her teeth and there was a good chance that the Russian cop would have been a parent and knew about the pain of teething, understood the therapy of a night-time walk, had even smiled at her. She had driven out of the garage as the great clocks in the city chimed the hour in unison. Had driven north, towards the second city, and the dawn was late, almost five hours after she had set out.

There had been a dinner at the School of Infantry. Maggie was back from her Ireland stint. The Warminster camp in Wiltshire was dull but better things were hinted at. Military Intelligence had almost promised they'd get her back with them, get authority for her to return to the Province. Patience was required. That evening she was driving a senior civil servant who had spent a day at the School: a live firing exhibition in the morning, with the excitement of an air strike and a Milan anti-tank bombardment and machine gun fire and a platoon assault, then lectures, then the obligatory dinner. She had sat in the car, waiting for him, and was due to drive him to a hotel out on the Shepton Mallet road. A late summer evening, warm with a big moon. He had placed his hand on her camouflage combat trousers, and he'd said, "No offence if you decline, but I'm rather in the mood for a quickie." Would have been fiftyish, might have been older than her father, had silver hair and plenty of it, a good chest and a flat stomach, and she had not really thought of a good enough reason to give him the cold shoulder. Because he was important, MOD procurement, a Jaguar had been allocated to ferry him. Quite comfortable on the back seat. They'd spent rather longer than anticipated, and he'd seemed happy enough and she had not complained . . . Afterwards, he had sat in the front passenger seat, had lit a cigarette, and had complimented her. She had driven him to the hotel. "Thank you very much," he had said. "Thank you, sir," she had answered with all the formality of a lance corporal driving a senior official at the end of a busy day. A couple of months later, the consequences became apparent.

So, she had Hector for company.

She had the map on her phone, and a book map too – 3 miles to 1 inch – of European Russia. Had Hector to talk to and to keep her awake, and remembered the story of an exfiltration some thirty-five years before when Lucinda's predecessors had spirited an intelligence colonel out of the country in the hours before his arrest. The target had been a prized asset, ranking far above Alexei: to get him clear there had been a complex operation involving the best and the brightest of Six and a plan that might work and might not. Wrapped in tinfoil, he had been driven, diplomatic plates, across the border beyond Vyborg and into Finland, and the silver stuff had minimised the smell of his body when the guards checked the vehicle. All far beyond her reach.

She thought they would go across country, blundering through bogs, trying to navigate along firebreak paths in pine forests, then charging at the wire, then . . . So she was driving for twelve hours there and twelve hours back, and hoping to have spied the land, known where to go when the dogs of Hades would come after them. She was approaching the St Petersburg ring road. Big lorries spat sludge at her windscreen and the wipers strained to clear her view. She started to sing. Liked to sing, and Hector enjoyed it too. It was a tiny car, pale blue, and the mechanics in the garage had done a great job on the engine and it sang with them, a humming drone accompanying the two bright, sharp voices.

She did it for Alexei. Thought she loved him. Loved him because he was frightened and vulnerable, and brave.

Had never slept with him, nor had the chance or might have. Had not kissed him, would have done but they were strangers. Not even held hands, but had no doubt of the hold of love. Loved him and drove north in the hope she might find an escape route, for the two of them and for Hector. What a wild girl would have done, a feral kid. The small car was hemmed in now by huge lorries, many of them dragging trailers. She followed the signs, and the weather was slipping and sleet mixed with the muck thrown up by the tyres.

Past noon and the middle of her day and time running out on her, and still going north.

Benedict had sanctioned it, had hoped to build bridges, reduce tensions.

Sashcord could go and run in the woodland behind the bungalow. Two or three kilometres was enough, and there were tracks among the trees. Of course, not alone. Benedict understood the volcanic effect that acute stress could produce, what they knew as cabin fever, and mixed in was the adrenaline rush from the failed bomb attempt. Benedict didn't run himself – avoided unnecessary exercise like it was a plague bearer – but there were plenty at work in London who came to VX in the morning in their athletes' gear, headed for the shower rooms, and arrived at their desks, feeling virtuous.

Benedict had said, soft-voiced, "Tempting as it might be, don't lose the bastard."

When the proposed route from Aarhus had been talked about, Benedict had noticed it went close to the town's university. He had done some research, little else to do, and had learned of a Royal Air Force raid, with Mosquitoes, on a building in the campus then occupied by Gestapo interrogators. October 1944. He had driven there on his own one morning and had stood in front of the target building. He was not a war groupie but thought lessons could be learned, as when he had stood in the cemetery. Scores of SS men had been killed and Danish civilians, "collateral". Explosives to damage the structure and then incendiaries to burn the heavy paper files, and the Resistance given breathing space and a chance to regroup after a betrayal. He had stood there and had rolled the single word on his tongue, silently. "Collateral". The cost of war. There were always unsung victims caught up in the vortex . . .

Doug was going and the PET woman, and she wore a heavy tracksuit and trainers, also had a shoulder holster that would stay hidden under her top.

He watched them scramble over the garden fence, and heard them blundering off, Sashcord in tow.

Benedict went to do the expenses, check receipts. They were demanded by the ferret-faced people in VX. Benedict could have escaped with a caution if an Afghan prisoner had suffered coronary failure while under severe questioning, his corpse showing signs of persistent bruising. Might have survived as an officer in the Service if he had bashed an Isis boy's skull against a wall, and turned him to a vegetable state. But not an expenses error. Could be greed, could be a mistake, but fiddling expenses was a dismissal offence. Had not done them for three weeks. Had put them off, always did. Wally was snoring softly in his shared bedroom. Benedict had receipts in pretty much every pocket, and the PET boys' timesheets. Time drifted.

Was just starting to make order of the paper chaos when Wally's mobile rang. The sound of a dawn chorus. The snoring stopped.

Then, a voice laden with exasperation. "I do not believe it. What is the matter with that fucking guy? Doug, I'll kill you if you've woken me and are just pulling my pisser. No, of course you're not. All right . . . all ears, just spill it out."

Benedict reckoned that a new crisis had broken around them. He put away the receipts and the notepad he was using, crumpled them all together and did not care what order they now found themselves in: food, fuel, clothing, toiletries, newspapers and magazines, DVDs, Russian beer (finally located after raking through most of the town's supermarkets) and . . . He heard stockinged feet slithering towards him.

"You'll not guess, Benedict, what the reptile's done."

"Try me."

"They are out running and . . ."

"Cut to the quick, please, Wally."

"They are out running. It's a winding track and there are pools, puddles and Doug's not a spring chicken."

"Doug is at the back and up front they've dropped him. Keep it rolling."

"And Doug loses his bloody shoe, and he's further back, and he hears this almighty yell. Doesn't recognise it, not the language, except that it's Danish and the woman, and up ahead and out of sight, and can't find his shoe and he trundles on one-legged up the track . . . It gets worse, Benedict. There's a squeal and that's the reptile and all manner of choice language out of him. Doug keeps going. Turns a corner. In front of him, this is how he tells it, it's not pretty. Start with her, the PET women – what's her name? Jette, yes. She has the front of her tracksuit open and there's a T-shirt underneath all rucked up, and her holster's half off her shoulder, and I'm thinking that our little friend might have made a small mistake. Or a big mistake, because there's a welt on her forehead, like an impact point . . . And him? Not getting any better, Benedict, not the way Doug's telling it. His shorts are near down to his knees. His face seems rearranged. He's been done a headbutt, what Doug says. Except that he called it a Glasgow kiss. If it had been against his nose then that would be broken. She's not the height for that, but it's his upper lip, and the claret's flowing. That's about it."

Benedict felt uncertain of what he had done to deserve it. He turned away. Looked through the windows at the back, and his eyes covered the garden – where Simon would be working that evening – and he could see the stark branches of the trees and rain falling gently and everything was distorted.

He imagined the scale of the disaster . . .

Jette would put in a formal complaint. The complaint would be dealt with by Human Resources. They would be an army of busy people, likely more than they had on the Russia Desk. Would go from HR to a sub-committee, and would be deliberated on . . . would get to the intestines of the Danish civil service, and on to the desks of politicians. The first big question. *This fucker, this Russian, what is he doing on our territory? Why have the Brits, arrogant as always, dumped him on us, like we are some fucking holiday camp for them to use as a lodging house for their trash? So when are the Brits taking him out?*

And Wally, true to form, said, "But the good news, Benedict, is that Doug found his shoe in the mud. Went back to get it. Sort of 'all's well that ends well'."

He thought charm would be needed, a shedload of it, didn't know whether he had enough.

Sailings from the Baltic port of Kaliningrad and the military harbour at Baltiysk had been authorised. That afternoon, a trawler would leave the quayside where it had, officially, been undergoing repairs to the engines. A frigate would sail under cover of darkness from the naval docks at the entry of the Vistula Lagoon. The trawler, the *Katerina*, would be in position in little more than fifty hours to collect fugitives from a North Sea beach, on the Danish coast, and transfer them at speed to the frigate which would then make for the open seas. The authorisations had been coordinated from a GRU office in the glasshouse.

Jonas stood as they filed in.

He thought it useful to have them brought down the stairs and along that dimly lit corridor and on to unfamiliar ground. There was little that he did without planning.

He had studied their photographs and knew them. Had their names listed on a single sheet of paper, and his pencil hovered. At her small table sat Frank – silly name, he believed it unwise for a woman to allow herself to be treated as a token male. He would have liked to call her Frances, and assumed that the time would come when it was appropriate to follow his instinct.

Chiswell was first in, allowing his annoyance to be noticed, and his sense of superiority to run free. His eyes checked out Jonas and his sneer was poorly disguised. By his name Jonas wrote the capital letter "E".

His hips hurt and the chair given him was unforgiving, and the damp must have seeped into his joints when he had made his gesture and lowered himself inelegantly to the pavement. He wished his performance to be regarded as "pathetic", that he be seen as a pompous little man, not to be taken seriously . . . The leak came from one of them.

Next was Symonds. The photograph in the file flattered him. He looked tired, strained. Struggling to maintain his place in a team that would have seen themselves as an elite – overused word, Jonas thought. This was a man living in suburbia, teetering on middle age, and still at home with his mother. Again the movement of the pencil a "C".

He had read the digest given him of the defection, of the time in the Aarhus safe house. Had studied the reports of the German police and their agencies, also of the experience of the team accompanying Sashcord. Had the files on the team, and the three still in Jutland, protecting the Russian. It was not much, but the benefit of complaint, he reckoned was slight. "Make do and mend" as Vera sometimes said.

Then Barker. A cuckoo in their nest. Old-style, old-fashioned and plucked from a previous age of recruitment, and now about to pack it in, get the present, have a glass of warm fizz and go home to polish up whatever piece of cut glass was given as a parting gift. A bluff figure, obviously everybody's friend. Might have tapped the side of his nose when asked in the saloon bar what work he had done before retirement. The file, of course, contained family details — wives, children, dependants, relatives in care homes, all the financial commitments. Would be in the ranks of the Just About Managing brigade. Was given "M".

Much was hidden from him and yet the file provided gave him insights into those who were responsible for the censoring and the redactions, insights they might not have anticipated. He was not unhappy. Quite buoyant actually, not that he cared to show it. He played nervous, and twice fiddled with his tie as if anxious that it was out of place and might have left him feeling inferior to them. Rubbed at the mole on his nose as if he were self-conscious.

He thought the photograph of Toni did her little justice: maybe it had been taken on a bad hair day, or maybe she made a point of looking indifferent when pushed into something as tedious as a file photograph. She was bored with him, insulted at being there. Her letter was "I".

They had formed a line. He could not see the table and chair, nor Frank. He smiled limply. He assumed that by now he was becoming an irritation to them and that his interference in the smooth running of their organisation created annoyance, and worse, he hoped. They waited.

Last in, and ducking his head because of his height, was Denys Montgomery. The file said he had the best brain among the team members. Fluent Russian speaker, an ability to make a defector feel wanted, prized. A bachelor – once a rumoured association with a nurse but nothing coming to a head – and whatever was missing romantically in his life was said to be made up for by the ambitious model train layout in his attic. There seemed no malice in the man, more confusion, as if he failed to comprehend why an individual such as Jonas Merrick should have been imposed on the team. But, if what he had heard of Monty was even half correct then he would be the first of them to see through the image that Jonas portrayed. He stood, feet tapping and fingers fidgeting, but Jonas never hurried. No letter beside this man's name, because all might have been appropriate, or none. He looked down, as if casually, at the column of names and the letters awarded. An E, a C, an M and an I, and jumbled together they formed that familiar four-letter word – MICE – so beloved in Jonas Merrick's trade. In his experience it never failed to provide answers.

He smiled again, his humble smile.

"I am very sorry to have been inflicted on you, to be a distraction in your busy lives. Why they chose me for this sort of work remains a mystery. Still, needs must ... I am charged with producing a report concerning a *possible* leak of information concerning the location visited on Sunday evening last by the defector, codeword Sashcord. I do not say *probable* ... my experience of foreign agencies is less than yours but I would accept that levels of German special agency security would often be found wanting. With your co-operation I am certain we can come to a satisfactory conclusion. Now, not far off lunchtime, and I like to eat early, and I have to go out of the building for forty minutes. So, I suggest that we start the limited, very limited, conversations with you individually at two o'clock. I would be most grateful, Mr Montgomery, if I could lead off with you. My thanks and my apologies for the intrusion."

He thought he had set out his stall, and wondered which if any of them were inside the tracks left by the MICE, wondered also if any of them were fooled. Surprised him, how often clever people were fooled by him.

6

Jonas supposed, shuffling papers and requesting printouts of maps, that the team would by now have made assessments of him and his capabilities. Assumed them not to be idiots, also assumed them capable of believing what they wanted to believe . . . a wry and private smile that she, Frank, might have seen and might not.

She brought him two maps, as requested, of the Danish town of Esbjerg. One showed the extent of the conurbation and one highlighted the area inland from a fast road north, passing an industrial complex and showing open spaces, a cemetery, woodlands and a latticework of suburban streets, detached houses. When he worked it was usual for him to slip off his jacket and hang it on the back of his chair. She had walked behind him and had been about to lift the jacket from the chair and take it to the hook on the door, where his raincoat hung, and his trilby, but he had waved her away. That had been his indication that he needed no help from her other than specific pieces of information and the gathering up of the paperwork and the maps and bringing them to him. She would learn . . . He thought her typical of the women in both his organisation and likely of the Sixers' service. The stereotype would be that their devotion to the job made up for their lack of advancement, their meagre pay, their role of skivvy at the hands of officers. They were abused, but on that day such an affront was low on Jonas's list of priorities. He worked quietly, and occasionally she shifted in her chair as she dealt with her emails. When he did speak it was abruptly.

"What's at Esbjerg?"

"What do you need to know?"

"What's there?"

"Have not been there myself, Mr Merrick. Only ever went once to Denmark, on the Sashcord business . . ."

"What you do have will be appreciated." No warmth . . . they were not his friends here and there were no friends at Thames House. They were people he dealt with, who strayed – willingly, more often unwillingly – into his orbit, had a small window of usefulness and then were pushed aside. Could have been targets, could have been helpers. He was loath to display anything that could be described as charm or chumminess. "I'd appreciate a picture painted, what happens there."

He thought she would have been an encyclopaedia of the information that could any time, any subject, be required by the officers in the team. She might, quite gently, have laughed at him.

"I said that I have not been there. My impressions are purely from what I have read. Should I print out the guidebook material?"

"In your own words, please."

The room was a small oasis of calm, not even the disturbance of a buzzing fly to distract, and the ventilation was quiet and the heating subdued. His feeling was that, beyond any oasis, would be a hostile desert where enemies drove pickups, where scorpions lurked, where dust and dirt choked in the throat – all that sort of nonsense. A gentle mood for him but he did not doubt that beyond the room a struggle for supremacy was being fought, and there would be blood spilled and time was not to be frittered.

She said, "A conventional and relatively prosperous small European city. Used to be a fishing place, but that went out of fashion. They managed to hold the place together by attracting oil and gas industries, the offshore wells. And they have done well with turbine construction for the wind farms out at sea. Plenty of technically qualified foreigners and the population can support them easily enough. Was an important base in World War Two for the German defences, the Atlantic Wall, and it's a jump-off point in the summer for an island, where they have camps and holiday homes, big tourism. Good parks, good amenities, an ordinary sort of place. About it."

She might have thought his mood changed, that he had become conversational, and might not have noticed that the snake was on the move. "And your Danish experience, just the once was it? At the start? You had the job of setting things up, working from scratch? Couldn't that idle mob in the Embassy have done it? But, they relied on you?"

"Yes, I was there just the once, a day and a night and back to London . . . I think Esbjerg would be a pleasant enough place. Not much to do there but off the beaten track: suitable for what's wanted. We do our own stuff, don't leave it to an embassy."

"Very helpful, my thanks. And get me something on that island – be grateful for it . . . and Mr Montgomery in an hour, yes?"

"You're kicking off with him, yes and I think they are all hanging around waiting."

"Tough times," and that small grin, but the humour was not intended to be shared. The mood had swung.

"And me, will I be interviewed?"

"Of course you will. Just as soon as I can dig up a lead-tipped cosh," and he laughed. She did not respond to his apparent joke, but people rarely laughed with him. "But I'll see the island stuff first, then get myself in shape for Mr Montgomery."

"What are you saying to me?" The girl, Jette, challenged him.

"I am saying that it would be useful if . . ." Benedict thought he was walking among anti-personnel mines. Had done that, remembered the feeling.

"If, what is *if*? Do you believe me, do you not believe me?"

"I believe you, do not doubt you. But it would be useful *if* . . ."

"*If* I binned it?"

He thought her a pleasant looking woman. Might have been thirty years old, could have been older. Was in the armed division of the PET team and that was a job that women with ambition in the services of the country would have hankered after. Part of the strong arm of one element of the nation's defence. Would have had a formal briefing in her Copenhagen office, been given bare bones to chew on, and not much about the politics of looking after the safety of a British-inspired defector whom nobody seemed to want. And throw in that a serious attempt had been made on his life just last weekend, and that it had not succeeded had been down to a rookie's keen eye and sharp nose, no other safety net in place. And . . . if they came back for a second bite then she might be in the crosshairs, might be trying to remember what the training manual said. Would have had a second briefing from the guys who she and her mate had taken over from. Something like "They're doing it on a shoestring. They have been hung out on a washing line by their office, and it's blowing a gale. Biding their time until someone makes a decision. Decent people, Doug and Wally, and their boss is okay but bending. Might just have a breakdown which would further fuck it up, and the target is a Russian with the manners of a wolverine. A vicious little bastard and you don't trust him further than you can kick him. Happy days, Jette." That sort of briefing.

"You must do whatever you think is right. I cannot influence you. It was unfortunate that . . ."

"*Unfortunate*? You know what he did to me? Want me to tell you?"

There were times in Benedict's life when things had been worse. This moment ramped up and was climbing as the man himself appeared behind her and stood in the doorway, leaning casually against the jamb. A cigarette, unlit, in his mouth. A smirk on his face . . . Words echoed in his mind that Benedict would have said if the Russian had not materialised.

"Perhaps 'unfortunate' was not the most suitable description of what happened to you, Jette, and I most sincerely regret the experience you've been subject to."

"You want me to clam on it? You know what he did, that fucking animal? Know? Want to know? What he did?"

Benedict was tall, well built but without the appearance of a fighting man. He had floppy dark hair that was forever in his face. His glasses were rimless, made him look younger than he was, and more innocent. Had been in minefields, literally, and had managed to hold his nerve when a poor bastard behind him had been blown up – not bad enough to kill but what bulletins called "life changing", a leg shredded. Benedict, then a youngster and new in M16, had been pushed off to Baghdad to cut his teeth, had ended up supposedly running a province down near the marsh people in the south-east. The Iraqi mob was baying outside the compound. The so-called "friendly forces" who were meant to supply close protection support had found excuses to stay distant. He was three years out of Oxford. The crowd was ugly in humour and thirsty for a mouthful of blood, principally Benedict's. He had two Italian nurses with him, a Nepalese doctor, half a dozen local staff who were looking at a lynching. They had, on Benedict's shout, gone out through the back, where scrub and weed and undergrowth had hidden a door in the wall. Had run, blundering in darkness – and he had known they were in a minefield when his Iraqi cook had lost his right leg, one of those horrid anti-personnel types of mine. That had been a bad moment. This looked to match it.

"I intend to write a full report and I will send it to my supervisor. He will pass it to my manager. It will be copied to Welfare and Gender Discrimination. It will go all the way. You know what he did to me?"

On Benedict's watch. Would go on his record. No blame attached to Wally or Doug. None dumped on the PET woman's lap . . . God, he loathed the little bastard who stood in silence behind her and made no move and she was ignorant of his presence. Benedict could see the mark on her forehead, could see where the blood had staunched on his lip. If he said what he thought, how he felt – told it as his wife would have expected him to – then it was all bridges burned and the likelihood of Sashcord grimacing, going into his room and shoving his stuff into his grip and coming back out, and no one to stop him walking out through the front door. Gone back home, spilling it on state TV, and that too would go on Benedict's CV. He would be out on his neck.

"He caught up with me. He stopped, I thought he was about to complain of a blister, a stitch, need for water. He was trying to get my trousers down, lifting my T-shirt. His fingers were in my bra, were on my tits – isn't that what you British call them, or boobs?

– I feel him all over me and trying to get his groin against me. Is that an adequate description?"

"I am very sorry."

"Very sorry, but you are asking me *if* – what is *if?*"

"*If* is whether you would consider that the matter of this 'incident' is not allowed to progress further. *If* is whether you could see your way to . . ."

There was a barrel laugh. Benedict stopped talking. He had summoned himself to deliver the plea, in spite of the audience in the doorway. He felt humiliated . . . and the laughter bayed from behind her and she was spinning around. Sashcord was grinning, then his lighter flashed and his cigarette was lit.

"What you call, you English, the 'boob' or the 'tit' . . . what I think, Benedict, is that they are flat, have little flesh in them, sag a bit. Just what I think."

Another crack of laughter, and he went back inside, a whiff of smoke in the house that had No Smoking signs in each room. His bedroom door slammed.

Benedict saw the anger climbing in her face. He said, "It would be useful if . . ."

"*If*, again, *if* . . ."

"He is an unconscionable shit – but it could be that lives depend on him. Depend on our continuing to protect him. I'll only say it once more. It would be, Jette, useful if . . ."

Maggie had come off the main highway, had turned down a track.

As the wheels of the little Fiat bounced in the ruts, and the undercarriage scraped on rich red compacted soil, Hector woke up and screamed.

Lights showed through the trees to the right and a rougher track, but she ignored it. Maggie went past the old sign, broken, that gave only part of the name of a village, and past the newer sign in bright paint on metal that warned a Closed Zone was near and permits were required to go further. The sleet, near freezing, clogged under her wipers. She turned a corner and braked.

As did the driver of the jeep confronting her.

It had a long wheel base and was open behind the driver's cab. Two in the front, their windows steamed up from the heater going at full power, and four more in the back, exposed to the weather with a fine layer of sleet settled on their forage caps and on the shoulders of their heavy-duty tunics, and on the backs of their gloves. But no sleet had settled, grey and soggy, on their rifles. Maggie had blundered into a Border Force patrol, and she could have sung out the details of the duties assigned to this arm of the FSB security apparatus. Hector was in full voice.

Headlights were flashed at her. She reversed the Fiat. Maggie had enough knowledge of military affairs, the mindset of men in uniform, to know they would not back off. Impossible to see the faces in the closed cab, but the senior NCO would be in there, warm and likely with a fag in his mouth. She knew about non-commissioned officers: her father was one and her grandfather had been one and she knew more about them than she knew about "Ruperts". The wheels of the Fiat had trouble gaining traction, then did, and she surged . . . too fast. A thud underneath and scraping and the car was sinking on her side and dawdling over a ditch. She swore. She blocked the track, and the guys spilled off the back of the jeep and the driver was belting his horn, and the NCO beside him was waving his arms like a bloody lunatic. Maggie was in a ditch and not going anywhere.

It was all beginning to seem stupid to her. The intention had been to get into the Closed Zone, park off a patrol track, get Hector wrapped up in thermal layers and hook him up into the carrying harness on her back, and get out her pole stick. Do some walking. Might have had two hours of light, a chance to spy the land this side of the fence, and leave short lengths of ribbon tied to branches, and keep on going until she had an idea of the ground they'd have to cross . . . her holding tight to his hand and propelling him forward. She had seen enough times in library photographs in the attaché's office the scale of the fence. There would not be mines or automatic guns, but there would be alarms, sirens, and cameras. Lights would flash in command posts, and they would need to move fast into Finnish territory . . . Once there they'd need to lie up because on that side of the border there was still a better than fair chance that the Finn authorities would put Alexei in handcuffs and drive him to the official border crossing point and leave him on the white line across the road for FSB to collect and take away. Lie up, let the chaos subside and then think through the next stage of escape. Stupid, but it was for the love of the boy.

The men advanced towards her.

Not by chance or error had Maggie been chosen for work in the Military Attaché's office. Not by chance or error had she been used as a driver by undercover goons and the boys in jeans and fleeces and balaclavas in the Province when out hunting "hostiles". Trouble was that the love of the boy had damaged her and she was now in a ditch and 600 klicks too bloody far from her office and her bed, and Hector was shrieking fit to burst, and the car might roll . . . She had difficulty opening her door. Clambered out and sank to her knees in the muddy ditch. Reached inside and freed Hector from his seat.

Smart kid, everyone said that about her.

Had only been stupid, an idiot, when the big man had done his stuff on the Jaguar's back seat and she had been without precautions and there had been no love. Was stupid and an idiot again, but this time love had trapped her. It was hard for her all the days of the week before she saw him coming off the train at Yaroslavskiy station. And worse as she escorted him back to the station when he went east on the long train journey to Kirov, and the surveillance tracked him . . .

Had not been love, but had been quite good, in the car. Consequences. Her mother had tracked the guy down, had made demands. Good maternity leave programmes had infiltrated the military, but from his bank account had come a private room at a Thames Valley clinic, good food and fresh flowers. He had come to see her two days after the birth. Had brought his wife. Quite a smart woman, seeming unfazed, and looking fondly at the baby, and she'd said that she'd two of her own, both at university. Hector was their suggested name and she had bought it. A famous fighter in mythical Troy with a massive kill rate in combat with the Greeks, before Achilles took him down. It was the name they wanted and paid for. The wife had said, "I suppose he told you about his needs, be surprised if he didn't. I think he usually likes to tell girls about his needs." She had been rude back, and had won a cheerful smile from the wife and the husband had not spoken, but had allowed his little finger to be gripped in Hector's fist. They had left an envelope on the bedside table, along with some fruit, and a healthy cheque had been inside it.

Not love, but it was with Alexei, which was why she was here, in a ditch, and was thinking, and had four Russian Border Force guards sniping orders at her, and headlights on her, and a horn, and everything was chaos.

She knew NCOs and knew squaddies.

The first of them to reach her, breath spilling from his mouth in the cold, had to drop his weapon and let it hang from the lanyard around his neck as she passed him Hector. She rolled her eyes at the NCO in the front of the jeep, like life was difficult and she was just a pretty slip of a girl. Hector had gone quiet as big arms wrapped around him. She and the other three had enough muscle between them to lift the Fiat out of the ditch, and turn it around to face the other direction. She called out the name of the village, had seen it on her phone, and all of them were pointing and gesticulating, and treating her as if she were an idiot. Good guys and kind guys . . . She thought that if she and Alexei had been on the wire, caught in the barbs, and the sirens loud then the guards would have fired. Would have died on the wire, and maybe Hector too.

Hector had been taken to the jeep and the NCO's window was down and his cheek was being rubbed by a gloved fist.

And Maggie played the game, and she thanked the guys in her pigeon Russian, and they might have thought her a Finn, or a Swede, and sure as hell she did not want to be there when one of them had the sensible idea of checking her ID. Hector was brought her. She strapped him in and blew them all kisses, and the bloody Fiat wouldn't start. The last she saw of them was through her rear window when they'd pushed her, four of them, and the engine caught, and she'd accelerated and had left them wreathed in a cloud of fumes and coughing up their guts, and one more wave and she was gone, and her breath came fast, furious, and she was shaking fit to crash the car.

Maggie drove towards the village, praying the jeep was not following her, and that it was a bad enough afternoon, cold and wet, for them to want to be back in their barracks and in front of a stove drinking warm soup – and she headed for the lights.

Pretty stupid, but she was Maggie and had not before fallen for a boy like him, like Alexei, who was both vulnerable and brave.

When they had a problem in the village, something that needed an answer they could not give, they came for Galina.

Came for her because she had a degree, had books that she could read, and wrote letters for them to the Town Hall in Vyborg. Could drive them to the shops, to the doctor. Could get a priest when death beckoned one of their diminishing number.

She had heard a car at the far end of the village.

And she was called by a knock at her door and a shout for her attention from her neighbour. Her coat was already on and she had kicked off her slippers and was about to take her boots from beside the fire.

She opened the door.

A young woman stood there. Wet and covered in mud. And she had a child balanced on her hip.

Might have been Scandinavian, certainly not Russian. Might have been from Germany, did not have Slav or Central European features. And she did not need her degree to make her judgement. Obvious to her. Was the young woman cold? Yes, she was. And hungry? Yes, hungry. And the baby needed cleaning and feeding? Yes. She stood aside and gestured for the young woman to come into her living-room, and the fire was smoking and made a fog in the room. She lit the main ring on her cooker, supplied from a gas bombola outside. She said that she was Galina. Was told the baby was named Hector, and then the young woman bit her lip as if a deeply entrenched rule book had been remembered and she seemed reluctant to identify herself, which further confirmed the obvious.

On the table close to the fire was a single portrait photograph. The youth wore his graduation gown and smiled and held in his hand a scroll of paper, its proof. The picture showed the smile, and also the stubborn rebellion that Galina had admired and had nurtured, that had killed him. The young woman stared at the picture, might have read the character of it. The answers she had been given were in English, and Galina assumed she was British. Why? A fair question but not asked. She sat her close to the fire and went to heat soup and make tea. A fair question would have been why this British mother, so young, was out in the middle of the day, off the main road from Vyborg to the frontier crossing, up a track that led only to a tiny community of the elderly that happened to be situated close to the guarded border. Was, almost, inside the Closed Zone where entry was forbidden except to the very few with the necessary permit. Galina lived two kilometres from the outer edge of the Zone and had no permit, nor did anyone else living there. Obvious that the young woman – without a name – had business at the fence. A fugitive . . . as her son had been.

The child had been cleaned and fed, was now asleep. Together they drank her soup, and chewed on her bread. Galina stacked the plates and the bowls, knives and spoons.

She said, matter of fact, "It is that time each day that I go to a cemetery, a graveyard, where my son rests. I speak a little English, from my university time. He was trying to reach the border defences, to cross them, but was intercepted, and he died. I go each day at this time to his grave. Perhaps you will come with me, and I can tell you about the border area. You would like that?"

"Thank you, I would . . ."

"Where is the fucking girl?"

"You could say, Lucinda, that she is just running errands."

"Who for?"

"Sorry, Lucinda, but perhaps it escaped your notice. Lance Corporal May, Logistics Corps, works in this office. Not in your office."

"I need her."

"Very sorry, Lucinda, but needing her and getting her are different matters."

For the Military Attaché to have the station chief in his office was a rarity. To have her with arms folded across her chest and her feet a little apart and to have her voice barking across his work area was unknown. Others within earshot ducked their heads towards their screens . . . Hear nothing, see nothing, know nothing . . .

"Will she be back in the next half-hour?"

"Could not say, could not possibly say."

Which was a lie, a brazen one. Her phone served as a beacon. It did not send continuous signals but one an hour and they registered as a blip and as coordinates. The signal came, then the numbers. Not difficult for him, or for his senior NCO, to find her location . . . "The fucking girl", Lucinda's description and apt, was thirteen and a half kilometres from the Russian-Finnish border, a high security zone, and was 860 kilometres from the Moscow Embassy, an estimated minimum nine hours and forty minutes driving, in a Fiat 500, with only a small child for company. So, that Wednesday afternoon, with the first of the dusk gloom settling on the city, he could be near to certain that he would not see her that day. He was a calm man by nature, had seen combat in the Middle East, had had a company of fusiliers in the Province, had a soft spot for this "fucking girl", what his wife called a "marshmallow place", but he struggled to contain his temper . . . It was a story of what happened when small people, the bloody foot soldiers, were involved in full-scale combat, the poor bloody infantry, thrown out of the trenches and into No Man's Land and on to the wire where the machine guns traversed. Not the training and not the backup, and would have exploded – gone personal at the Six woman – had it not been for his own sense of shame. Had allowed her the use of the car, had not quizzed her, had turned the other cheek as if it were not his bailiwick . . . It was what happened to the foot soldiers when their emotions ran riot. He did not know when he would see the "fucking girl" again.

"You'll tell me when she's back, from errand running?"

"Of course, Lucinda, will do."

Heard her shoes clatter away ... Secrets were hard to keep in that building. The station chief would not have let slip a headache, a problem, a worry, would have kept it bottled and sealed. And himself, a soul of discretion ... Technicians talked to each other, word could seep to the security unit. Gossip could spread. Word had it that a leak might have been sprung. Likely from London. Word was an asset might be compromised. Further word was that, a long tradition in this godawful country, "assets", if betrayed, faced hard times, might cry out in a cell for death to relieve them from suffering ... A word never spoken indicated that the "fucking girl" might have taken a fancy to an asset whom she was required to contact: too dangerous for the lovely Lucinda, the bitch ... And he still did not have his paper on the Armata T-14 main battle tank. A nightmare if the rumoured word, *leak*, were true, because there would be casualties.

He made his own tea that afternoon.

A slight cough from Frank.

Jonas reached, pushed away a mess of papers on his desk, cleared space for his notebook, the pencil beside it.

"Yes, thank you, yes – let's have him in."

She did not say that Denys Montgomery, the Resettlement team leader, his reputation in the building one of a supremely effective and loyal manager, had been kept waiting, kicking his heels, which was an act of bad manners. An intended act. If the swamp were to be drained, the stables scrubbed clean, then courtesies were low on the list. She scurried to the door, opened it, probably grimaced or raised an eyebrow, and he followed her inside. He had been an hour on a hard chair, a useful test of attitude, and had not complained, not gone back to his own area. Had sat and had waited – which told Jonas a fair amount concerning character.

"Grateful to you, Mr Montgomery, and apologies for running late."

"You are on a steep learning curve, Mr Merrick. Need time to read in."

"Still on the curve, feeling my way. Sorry, but I am not able to offer you fresh coffee, fresh tea, only water from one of those wretched fountains . . . I have very little experience in these situations and it was a considerable surprise to me when I was asked to look at this matter, a bit of a bolt from the blue . . ." He had that way, deceptive, of implying his limitations, selling himself short, and the expression across the table was cool, calm, and utterly unbelieving. And that would make matters easier. No requirement for sparring or personal chatter.

"I believe, Mr Montgomery, that you let it be known to associates that – in your opinion – the leak of information regarding the visit of your man, Sashcord, to the police premises in Hamburg came not from the Danish end, and not from German sources. Yes?"

"It is what I said, my opinion."

"But there *was* a leak?"

"Yes."

"And that leak gave an opportunity for an improvised explosive device to be installed in a stolen car, driven to the location?"

"Yes."

"And IEDs are not freely available at whatever chain of supermarkets they have in Hamburg, and preparation time would have been necessary?"

"Yes."

"And the Danes were not informed where Sashcord was travelling to?"

"No, they were not."

"And the German police and the people to whom invitations were sent were unaware of the identity of the speaker, a sort of cabaret turn at the end of a conference?"

"Correct, yes."

"I pick my words with care, Mr Montgomery, your team changed its viewpoint. Blame for the leak was laid at the Germans' door, or with the Danes."

"Not my view, but the view of a superior."

"Am most grateful for your insights, Mr Montgomery."

"Then you would seem easily pleased, Mr Merrick – which I doubt."

"Two questions and both answers will help me on the steepness of my curve."

"Try me."

"In your trade, what is the value of a defector?" A blunt question, and Jonas Merrick's tone indicated that a fulsome answer was required, an insight from an expert.

The man across the table seemed to exhale as if a tension was lifted, and a real world was again enjoyed. Montgomery leaned forward, his elbows on the table . . . A moment's silence in the room only broken by the rustle of Frank's fingers on her keyboard.

"Please, Mr Merrick, I do not think a charade is necessary. If you come from across the river you have experience of Islamists, Irish, or Russian intelligence officials roaming our streets. You will not have been chosen at random – and your sitting down on the pavement was good knockabout fun. You may well have dealt with defectors from the island of Ireland and from those communities where the radical *jihadis* are bred. My view, I am sure, is very similar to your own . . . a defector is very soon a failure. It is an operational non-event. They are useless. From the day we offer them hospitality, safety, their value starts to decline. Sometimes the arrival of a defector is trumpeted, as if we show our moral superiority over our opponent. Rubbish. Unless they bring suitcases of documents with them, or a pocketful of memory sticks, they are quickly empty vessels. The morning after they have arrived they are out of date. Within a year they are merely a drain on resources. They are tedious and embittered. Sometimes wheeled out at rookies' gatherings by way of entertainment. We very much regret a defector coming to us, would prefer him to stay in place and keep dropping fresh information in our laps. We want the rolls coming that morning from the bakery, still warm, not what was baked last week . . . The problem is that Sashcord was a 'walk-in', and the bridges were burned before we had assessed his worth. But you know all that, Mr Merrick, about the worth and value diminishing at pace. What we try to do, where possible, is keep them at it."

"Thank you."

"You need more of my time?"

"A few minutes, please."

There was a glance down at a wristwatch, a strong enough signal that Denys Montgomery had other places to be.

Jonas reverted to the humble. "You were all, your team, in Aarhus? In Aarhus, you learned of the limitations brought to you by Sashcord?"

A flicker of eyebrows, a scratch at the side of the nose, and a shake of the head, as if this were an unwelcome area . . . "He was not easy, not from the start. At Aarhus we started to learn that we had a freebooter on our hands. Always a disappointment when that happens, but it does. As I am sure, Mr Merrick, you well know."

"Do not overrate me, Mr Montgomery. I have not enjoyed an exciting, frontline career . . . Sort of chap, in another age and another place, who would be good at keeping the trains on time . . . But that is as maybe . . ."

In his notebook, the only word he had written was the name of the Danish town, Aarhus.

". . . always that little final point. Could have given him a new identity, packed him off somewhere. Lost him and forgotten him. Why hang on to him?"

"First, an identity package does not come cheap, and to work satisfactorily it requires the defector to have a work ethic along with an ability to slide unnoticed into a new society. A few can, most cannot . . . They are lonely. They miss old friendships, miss their kids, don't like the food, don't have the humour they enjoyed, are short of the glamour of being feted as a modern-day celebrity of the cloak and dagger society . . . We are no longer interested, and the phone numbers have changed and the contacts inside our crowd have retired or moved on and calls are not returned. They want to reforge the link with the Motherland. Two results. Firstly they travel back and tell FSB or GRU or SVR that they were kidnapped, tortured, and are plastered all over the TV. Second, their people get a line on them, locate them, and the hit team travels. Something clever, or something as basic as a couple of rounds in the back of the head when out jogging in a park . . . I recapitulate. We are trying to keep agents in place and at their work, and we feed them all the soft custard stuff about – at the end of the day – the little cottage in the Cotswolds with roses around the front door, and frequent visits from their old handler, and perhaps a minor medal from the sovereign. We do that, do it well, but it is always for tomorrow . . . If the agent sees pictures on the TV of a corpse in Berlin or Paris, in Belgium or down in the Gulf, feet sticking out from under a blanket, then he is less likely to believe in our power to keep him safe, in our promise to exfiltrate him when the going gets hard . . . It will get hard, it always does. I don't suppose you know the story, Mr Merrick, of General Dmitri Polyakov? That hard. We are always trying to promise – if we were honest, God forbid – what we cannot deliver. It is a sales pitch, 'You're all right with us, chummie', and a body in the street busts the lie."

He left. One backward glance, a minimum of respect, and he was gone. Frank said she would go to the machine and get coffee, and Jonas stared at the ceiling . . . and wondered if the fear for an agent's survival was general or specific, whether there was an agent at the moment whose morale would not be well served by the sight of shoes protruding from under the cover as the mortuary team waited for permission to move it. He knew about agents, had little love for them, but knew their lives.

Alexei stared at his screen. His incoming email file grew, but he sent few messages. He thought it further evidence of the pressure they put on him.

There was an administrative query concerning the department that issued funds and the Rostock bank: the bank could make transfers direct into accounts but could not pay out a cash sum of the size ordered. He needed to answer because the matter was flagged "Immediate". It stayed on his screen. The main doors into the work area squealed when they were pushed open. Squealed as loudly as pigs in the market when the farmers poked them with sharp sticks to better show off their weight before sale to the butchers. Each time he stiffened, imagined the entry of at least four men and them coming toward him, putting their hands on his shoulders and his chair being spun. Imagined being hustled out, fast down the principal staircase of the building. Word would soon spread a traitor had been identified. The doors had squealed when the old woman had barged through them with her trolley of soft drinks and hot tea and bread rolls and apples and chocolate . . . Had squealed again when a porter had come in with his trolley loaded down with packs of printing paper and folders and . . . Alexei assumed they sought to break him: thought they knew their craft. He would be dragged through the door, feet barely touching the floor, and later the detail would seep into the work area, would travel fast. He would be spoken of. No one would stand in his corner, claim to have liked him. Had no friends, was a loner, did not mix, no humour to him, could have been a pervert, and he would be most vociferously denounced by Ludmilla, plain cow, from whom he had taken hairs off her shoulder.

He slumped over his screen. He had the whole afternoon to endure, and then the whole of the following day, and then half a day, and they might come to take him at any time, any hour – or while he waited for the bus, or while he sat in his apartment and had the music on loud . . . then it was the train station and the long journey to Yaroslavskiy station, and they might be waiting there on the Saturday morning.

Then, if he were still free, he would meet Maggie, give her the memory sticks he had used that week, and the one that dealt with the Rostock payments. Then, he believed it, he would be saved, safe.

Beside him, a girl's voice. "You all right, Alexei? Don't look well."

Did not answer, "Of course I am not fucking all right. I'm a fucking traitor and waiting to be arrested." Answered, "I'm fine, maybe just some 'flu." Could have said that he was all right if they did not move on him before the weekend, and then he would be free of danger ... Had been told that he was safe in their hands, protected – had been told it in Cyprus and had been told it in Moscow, believed it.

As a senior officer of GRU, the man known as the Wolf followed the basic rules of advancement.

In front of him on his desk his computer screen showed a satellite photograph of a street of modest detached homes.

He was not a bribe taker. Brigadier Volkov and his wife were not corrupt in the sense that they might at any time be bought by consideration of a gift, preferably paid into a Swiss or Cypriot account, or into the City of London. But any squeamishness for criminality stopped short of declining the tasks given him by the regime. That regime, and GRU and the ethics of his work, counterintelligence and the punishment of those stepping outside its code of honour, demanded a visible response to treachery.

The accommodation, in his opinion, was poorly chosen.

He would have said, as would his President, "*Nothing is Forgotten, Nothing is Forgiven.*" He shielded his family from what he did, allowed his daughter to study and his wife to teach. "*The Less you Know, the Better you Sleep.*" Most evenings he ate with them, regretted it when he could not, and his work was never spoken of ... Most certainly would not be that evening when for a second time a proposal to execute rough justice on a traitor was on the table.

There was woodland and scrub behind the fence at the back of the property ... The report he received from an adjacent section in the glasshouse building indicated a shortage of rental accommodation available for immediate tenancy at the specified price range for the specified period ... He had never met this officer, had never heard of him before his defection. It was reported that the officer possessed few talents, which would have been the reason he had not strayed into Volkov's view.

His message had gone to Rostock ... No instruction, of course, came direct from the new Tsar. An intimation by an associate was the method of transmission of a "desire" that a matter be concluded. It would be done when his boys were in place, when reconnaissance had been done, when they were able to be close and then . . . the report of a death would come to him, and he would not need to confirm a killing to those close to the Court, who swaggered under the ceilings of gold leaf and along corridors flanked with portraits of majesty. They would learn from radio and television and from foreign news agencies, and would hear that a diplomatic dwarf, the Danish ambassador, had lodged formal protest. Pissing against the wind, all deniable, and all a provocation of misinformation.

A busy end of week faced the Brigadier. He oversaw a matter on the western coast of the Danish region of Jutland and also – closer to his workplace – had authorised the preparations for the arrest of a second traitor. He had no qualms about his work; had he done so, he would not have achieved his rank, been a man who was trusted by those who advanced him.

Benedict said, "I am supposed to make decisions. But I am asking for help . . ."

Sashcord in his room in the bungalow, a radio playing loud. Jette, the PET girl and Nils, the PET boy, in their car at the front of the driveway, the tinted windows closed and misted from condensation.

Benedict had summoned Wally and Doug. He had faced his own crisis in the Iraqi compound and taken the decision about the risk of flight and of open ground to cross and the mob spotting them while they were on breakout, and said how it would be and had been followed. He looked now for help – had no shoulder to lean on. Almost certainly, his colleagues back in VX would have grimaced or sneered at his need to share the load of decision taking. He would have said that it would have been hard to find, damned hard, better men than these two if the need was for common sense: rank, salary, education had no part in it. They lived together in the claustrophobia of the safe house; of course he would listen to them, value their input.

". . . Horny bastard, what he is. Tell it him straight. Unacceptable. Tell her what you're doing. Got history, hasn't he? Level with her. All you can do," Wally said.

Doug said, "Rip him down as many pegs as you can, and demonstrate you've done it. Might buy her off. Sure as hell, if a complaint goes into the system then it stays there, can't get pulled. Give him stick – but also bung a carrot in, and dress it up, about resettlement and a new life where the sun doesn't set. Be good to have an apology out of him . . . But it's your shout, sorry. Get her to stall, then hit him this evening when we're all a bit calmer. May work, may not. Benedict, we're just the hired help and it's your responsibility. But, my last word, it's his survival that's on the line."

Not an intellectual exercise, but an equation where a life was at stake. Jonas ignored her, sat at his table, his chin in his hands, pondered.

The leak would kill. The leaker, no doubt of it, meant it to.

He considered his session with Denys Montgomery, and applied the MICE formula. Had rather liked the man, which was unimportant, and had rather respected him. Had access to his bank details, and the size of his mortgage, and the gossip in the Positive Vetting about his university days and political affiliations, and his contemporary social life – and had the references to the model train layout in his attic. There were some who automatically ticked the boxes. Could be for shortage of Money, or greed; could be for Ideology and a hankering after the old views supporting pure and unadulterated communism; could be for Compromise and openness to blackmail, usually in areas of financial corruption or sexual deviancy; could be for Ego and a man who either rejoiced in his skill at living the lie or who had felt deflated at being passed over for promotion or humiliation at work. MICE was the foundation of Jonas's work on men who could be turned to advantage.

One down, but several more to play. Had always valued the benefit of MICE, and the memory came to him, the little grey blighter who had made a nest in his caravan, and who had run past him and Olaf had him, or her, with a single swipe of the paw, and only a length of tail remaining as a headstone. He chuckled . . . He sensed that Frank stiffened because he laughed out loud.

He picked up his phone. Could not make calls from inside the building, but could use the storage space to jog him along. He had spoken to a chosen few as he had walked along the embankment from Waterloo station. Jonas Merrick had never done interviewing of suspects, or interrogation, but had often enough supplied data for those who did. He had phoned an elderly warrior of the Province's era of the Troubles, Detective Sergeant (retired) Perry McKeag, almost housebound, and said to have been the best at interviewing activists.

The growl of the voice, and the coughing fits, had accompanied him from Lambeth Palace almost to the approach to the Sixers' place. "Good to hear you, Jonas. Fine to hear you . . . Still at it are you, Jonas? . . . I'm not well but not complaining. There's tactics and techniques, what they call the Reid system, and then there's the PEACE method that starts with Preparation and Planning and you Engage and Explain. Then it's Account and on to Clarify and Challenge before Closure, then Evaluation . . . You don't want that shit, Jonas. You don't have to follow the rules and have some feckin' judge beading down at you from his bench and checking your procedures line by line . . . Not that I am suggesting rough stuff – don't like it because it seldom works. You want to know, Jonas, where the guilt lies, and you'll go through the MICE ticks, and move on, and you get the laddie talking. When they're talking is when you see the guilt. Can't help themselves. Won't be in the language so the transcript doesn't show it, but look into the eyes. Always in the eyes, a bit in the hands and the posture, but the eyes are what sell them down the river. Eyes, never lose them. Soon as they lie then the eyes will show it. No good for a court of law, but good enough for you, Jonas. You still working then? And have the caravan, lucky beggar? And have the ear of people that matter? That is bigger than lucky, because I didn't. I'm taking it, Jonas, that you would not have hung around, kept at the grindstone if what they gave didn't matter. Does matter, yes? Lives at risk? Yes? You are more than lucky, Jonas . . . When you find who lies to you, getting it from the eyes, then best stamp on their throat. Stamp hard with your heel down on to the windpipe. Happy to have spoken to you, Jonas."

Good to have talked to the old boy. By now, his friend would be slumped in a cane chair in a conservatory, dribble running on to his collar. Still the best in the business on the techniques that produced results, a nose and the ability to watch the eyes ... He had a list of the rest of them in the team, and confirmed the order that he would speak with them. Was told that Chiswell had gone for a run and that Symonds complained of a headache and was threatening to go home, and that Barker was bitching and that Toni was due on an interview board.

Jonas blinked momentarily, cleared his mind, cut out the fog and looked to examine the throat of each of them, seemed to see the tread of a brogue on the clean skin of each. He said it would be Chiswell next, and if he were out running then he should turn around and get back and get showered, and meet the schedule. He said that he would leave the building for an hour, not more. Then, when he was back he would see Chiswell and did not expect to wait for him ... He thought that Frank might be the only one among them who evaluated him seriously. It would be one of them but did not yet know which, nor how the question would be answered, nor whether he had the time to prevent collateral. Never enough time, in Jonas's experience, and if there were not enough time he did not know the names of those whose blood was for spilling. Always came late on a crime scene, the nature of his work.

7

Would Frank, please, use her phone and ring his wife, explain to her that he would be late home for supper. How late? Only half an hour . . . And he had smiled as if the missing of his usual train would cause him grief, then had explained that his season ticket was not valid for the later journey and he would have to pay for an extra fare. She would have thought him ridiculous. Few of his actions were ill thought through, and he imagined that she might find the moment to inform the team of this latest request as they waited for him to call them forward. Tempers would be fraying, as he wished them to be. She said she would do that, and he wrote down his wife's number at the gallery where she worked. Not her mobile although without doubt they could have rustled that up within minutes, but it was a gesture . . . She said she would do that straightaway.

The safe was open. It had two shelves. In the safe were the maps he had requested, the timetable of events and messages after the defection of Sashcord, and the biographies of the personnel involved in London and in Denmark. Also in a separate folder, were the details of the new safe house, located in the Fourfelt district of Esbjerg, on the west Jutland coast of Denmark. The safe was placed next to her table, and he had become used to slipping off his chair, going to it, removing or replacing papers. Then he was close, as he bent, to Frank's ankles. Not that Jonas Merrick was a connoisseur of female legs, but they seemed to have – his opinion – the elegance of many of the women displayed in the magazines Vera leafed through. He watched, out of the side of his eye, the procedure.

She had the number he had written for her on his pad, then torn off the page. She bent low over the safe, closed its heavy door and then would have flicked the combination numbers. Jonas thought that was what she did but could not be certain because her back blocked his view of the four-digit rolling pad.

Would he like more coffee when she returned?

Another smile, and shrug of almost helpless gratitude.

The afternoon was wearing on. Down in his basement bunker, he did not know whether it still rained on Vauxhall Bridge, or whether the street lights along the embankment had started to shine against the coming gloom. As intended, he had all of the team kicking their heels upstairs, and the shedding of hours, even minutes, in the work timetable would make it easier for the A Branch people better to organise themselves, have a deeper briefing of the targets they were assigned to, the Tangos – not that Jonas ever used the insider language of the Fivers: vulgar vocabulary.

He had gained a considerable resource. The people who worked for that branch of the Fivers were not lemons easily harvested; they were precious, effective, as good as any in the trade. Jonas had dismissed a thought that Denys Montgomery needed the attention of the surveillance squads, but they were assigned that evening – mob-handed – to follow and track the remaining members of the team when he, Jonas, finally allowed them to go home . . . He hoped he would by then have created a necessary meld of fear and annoyance and from that mixture came impetu-osity, mistakes . . . Jonas was big on creating an environment where mistakes were made. The A Branch people needed a supreme versatility. They would come to work in the morning, would be tasked, then would need to evaluate where they would be oper-ating, in what socio-economic area: were they to be among City workers, in deprived sink estates, were they headed for the affluent suburbs at the upper end of the Central or Metropolitan under-ground lines? Some would be on foot, pavement pounding, and a few on motorcycles, and there would be cars in reserve if the Tangos went for taxis.

Jonas had been asked how long he envisaged he would need the A Branch committment. He studied the layout of a hotel . . . How long? A reasonable question because of cost and because of the finite nature of the quality. If Jonas Merrick had been granted the use of a minimum of twenty-four persons for a minimum of five days, then they were off the rosters for use in tailing and observing the potential battalions of *jihadis* in the capital city, and of Irish dissidents and Russian intelligence officers. He might have supposed it a true compliment to the trust placed in him that he had not needed to get in a queue and then lobby, barter, plead to be given what he thought he needed ... and he had asked for more. Had mobile phone numbers that had been given up reluctantly by senior managers. Had those numbers monitored.

Frank brought him coffee and he thanked her. A mental note was made. He had asked for inadequate resources. He should have thirty watchers, not twenty-four. Silly of him. He would need to rectify his error at the end of the day.

She did not acknowledge his smile, maintained that exterior chill, and crouched again in front of the safe and hid the flick of her fingers and the door came open and she would then have randomly spun the numbers again. Pretty ankles, a pretty face, and an understated scent that he noted when the coffee was put in front of him, that she must have squirted on her throat while she was out of the room. He started to look again at the file on Chiswell, Adam Chiswell, but did not hurry and thought there was good scope for anger to be poorly controlled, and he sipped the coffee.

Frank looked up from her laptop and apologised for not saying so earlier, but his wife was grateful for the warning that he would be home half an hour late. He pushed away the Chiswell file and picked up the brochure for a hotel with photographs of its public rooms, and the reports that had indicated a slackening of interest in the defector, in Sashcord, even that first night, and turned the pages of the brochure and saw gardens and conservatories and bars and bedrooms.

She glanced twice down at her wristwatch. He was indeed running late for the interview, and he ignored the message she sent him: would let the little bastard stew, and Adam Chiswell had already been awarded an Ego in the MICE box . . . and wondered how it would have been inside the team on that first night in Denmark. Confidence draining and expectation sagging and a long evening to learn what a turncoat had brought with him, and the end of a long, long day for them all.

"It was shit behaviour. Unacceptable. A disgrace."

Not that Benedict often argued, seldom with colleagues, rarely with his wife. Usually walked away and faced whatever view he could find, and dragged down fresh air. Trapped his breath, held it, then let it spill.

"That woman is here to protect you. Should be ashamed of what you did."

Both the PET girl and the PET boy were outside in their car. Doug was in the living-room doorway and Wally in the kitchen, washing the last meal's plates. The Russian was in an easy chair and Benedict stood or paced.

"Your action was both unpleasant and bullying. You may have thought that you are immune to sanctions because of who, what you are . . . I do not yet know, believe me, whether a complaint will be lodged with the Danish police, gone into the system and you will be charged with assault."

His voice was low, his words were hissed. God forbid that he should shout. He had an aim, what he wanted to win from the confrontation, and so far was miles from achieving it. Benedict attempted to be both disapproving and also chillingly cold and reckoned he was failing.

"Can I not get it into your head that your actions were just foul? Groping that officer, feeling her bosom, absolutely out of order. Might be acceptable in GRU, but you are no longer in GRU. You are with us, but that does not mean you behave in that ill-mannered, even criminal way. I tell you what I want, I want . . ."

And below him, lounging in his chair, Sashcord rolled his eyes. Had a fag, unlit, and moved it from one side of his mouth to the other. It was the humiliation of Benedict that he had aroused no answering irritation, anger, from the Russian. Water off a dog's back, that reaction, and likely he was about to shake himself and spatter the furniture, as any self-respecting spaniel would do after a swim, then wonder what the fuss was about.

"What I want is . . ."

Might want it, but no sign yet it was about to be given him. All that rested in Benedict's corner of the ring was that – as far as he knew – the PET girl, Jette, had not yet gone formal. Still had not sent a text to the HR team in Copenhagen that described the insult, injury, assault, visited on her. And all true, as Benedict knew, because he had the description from an eyewitness, from Doug. He must not lose his temper. Tried to stay calm and introduce a chill to his voice and ought to have been rewarded with at the least a dropped head, a mumble of regret. Like the reptile did not give a damn. Benedict was losing cool, and a relationship of sorts needed preserving. Likely the Russian knew that, why he was so deep in his chair, why he gave not a damn, why he thought it no big deal that he had enjoyed attempting to grope the Danish woman.

And he launched again, "After this impossible behaviour, I am left with picking up the bloody pieces. What I want is an apology. Best I can hope for is an apology, and a smoothing over – God knows you do not deserve it – of this loutish action of yours. An apology."

And Benedict was rewarded, had won a reaction. Taken its time coming, but had it. A broad smile and a flash of the teeth that were stained yellow by nicotine, and a kid's grin, and a chuckle. And seemed to know what he was about to be told, and turned away and accepted failure, and his head dipped, and . . .

"You get no apology from me. I tell you this. Maybe I charge *her* with assault. You know what? I make a complaint. I stumble. I do not have correct shoes. The rain pisses on us. Trying to run on wet mud. I slip. I reach out for support and am about to fall on my stomach. What does that bitch do? She hits me with her forehead. You tell her that I will lay a charge against her . . . How do you like that, Benedict? You like it?"

Sashcord did not raise his voice and Benedict had to strain to hear him.

"An apology from you would help."

"Can I speak?"

"A decent apology would probably clear the air."

"I tell you . . ."

"You have an apology in mind, Igor. Just get it over, have it done. Do not defend what is bloody indefensible. Groping her was poor behaviour and you know it."

Sashcord pushed himself up from the chair, stood close to Benedict. The fingers of one hand had caught Benedict's jacket and the cigarette was still moving across his mouth.

"I speak, I tell . . .?"

"Go out from here, go to the car and apologise. Then we can draw a curtain on your behaviour." Benedict's last throw and their mouths were inches apart, and then the sneer broke.

"I will speak, will tell you. That policewoman, she is a cold cow, and she has no large tits. I was looking for them and I could not find them. Usually I can find them, not with her . . . What I want to tell you, I would like again to see the woman you brought across. What a woman. She was brought to Denmark . . . All fire and all blood. That is a woman worth going after. Her room was opposite mine in that annex part of the hotel, no other guests there, only the party that had come from London. She had been attentive to me through the whole evening, and I understood. You wanted me to feel welcome. You call it 'creature comforts'. She was there, a gift to make me feel I was welcomed. Some went to bed because they were tired and others because they were bored and we had talked too much, and she was one of the last. She went to Reception while I had my last drink of the evening with your man, who you called Monty. She came back and she had her key and his key, and also had my key. All services provided and I did not have to go, myself, to Reception to get the key. You want to hear it? Whether you want or not, you will. And she was fantastic, not like the Dane who has no tits that I could find. She was an animal, incredible. The hotel is quiet, and I go from my room, just have the robe from the bath, and I tap the door. There is a query, and I answer, say who it is, and she is at the door and the chain is moved. Did she expect me? Why not? She wears pyjamas, you know that? Did you know she wears pyjamas in bed? Have you never been in her bedroom, Mr Benedict? Wears thick pyjamas and the top is buttoned at the neck. She has given me enough encouragement and what I have done that day is huge in my life, and I have the need to celebrate, and you have provided her. Can I tell you, very frankly, she is a tigress. I think you have to be quite a lover, quite a good lover, to ride a tigress. No foreplay, nothing at first. I need to get it done. She fights, she claws. I am bitten. It is magnificent, is the best fuck I ever had in all of my life. And I am raked. She has nails, incredible passion. And she belts me, no woman I ever had was as alive as that one . . . and I am gone. The next morning is breakfast, and I wear a scarf so that a part of my face is hidden, and she has used make-up and you cannot see the marks on her neck . . . I may have hit her, and her eye might have been a little coloured. She was a wonderful lay, Benedict . . . If you ever, ever, have a ride like I had with the tigress then you are a lucky man. What was her name, Benedict? I don't remember her name . . . you know I had the scratches on my back from her nails for many days. You know her, Benedict? Many in your office would want to take her to bed . . . and she had good tits, easy to find when she stopped hiding them in the pyjama. I do not apologise."

Benedict needed to hold his hands behind his back to hide them. They were clenched. Probably would first have removed his spectacles, pocketed them. Then thrown the punch. Would likely have been put down on the floor with a bleeding nose and a cut lip, and near unconscious from the force of the retaliatory blow that Sashcord would have struck him.

The Russian sat again, made himself comfortable. Benedict saw that Doug's face had tightened. Wally had abandoned the dishes and was behind Doug. Wally showed pure loathing, like he was looking for RPG-7 boys beside Route Irish or going down to the Baghdad secure area, the Green Zone. If he had let them slip, these hard men, they would likely have pulped the defector. And Benedict was supposed to protect him, and London dithered about a future life and a new identity, and an attempt had failed and another would follow. He heard a car approach, and then voices. Simon had arrived, dragging behind him two large suitcases.

Would get no apology, and now must try to soft-soap, sweet-talk a Danish woman who could land a useful head butt. He supposed that, in London at VX, there were some who were envious of him, reckoned he had an undemanding number, a cushy posting ... Supposed to guarantee Sashcord's safety in order to bolster the morale of others, and keep the noses of agents firmly on the spinning grindstone.

"Forget it because you have no chance of achieving it," Galina said.

There were the remains of a church building, would have been of wood and brick and with a sharply sloping roof to help the winter snow slide off, and a squat tower. The side of the tower that faced the oncoming easterly weather had collapsed decades ago. The roof sagged in the centre and most of the beams had now come down and it seemed only a matter of time before the whole building was reduced to ground level. Extraordinary to Maggie, the main door had survived. Hanging open and swinging slightly because the wind had strengthened with the steadier fall of sleet: a door of heavy wood and it might have been a century old, and been made by a carpenter in the village before the spread of the communist power had closed the churches, kicked out the priests. There would have been a bell in the tower, no longer, and ivy grew on the walls, the bricks, still bright red because there was no industrial pollution here, and never had been.

"It is where you would die, and your child, and for nothing."

She had told her story while they had walked from the village, past allotments now covered in a fragile layer of sleet, and weeds they were blasted flat by the wind and the weight of the winter's earlier snowfall, and followed a path that was trodden down.

"You and your child, both dead – and your boy."

The footprints on the path were of small feet, and Maggie knew they would have come from the shuffled tread of the old women living out the last years of their lives in the community. Not coming to the ruined church but to the cemetery behind it. There the forest encroached and old stones were hidden by the trunks of wild saplings and tangles of bramble. The cemetery had once been surrounded by a low wall, also of brick, but that had crumpled. The gate posts were upright, but they had to step over the bars of the rusty gate. The nearest part of the cemetery had been roughly cleared. The graves here had no stones but were marked by wooden posts with the lateral bar nailed in place to make the sign of the cross. Some had faded photographs, encased in supposedly weatherproof plastic, pinned to them. But water had penetrated and the pictures were curled and the colours had faded and all of them showed younger men wearing jackets and ties. Some were marked with plastic flowers that had once been in glass vases, but they had toppled. She was led to one particular grave, and it was tended.

"They are grateful if you flee their reach. It is what they want. Can clap their hands together as if they clean them and the problem is gone. They would like you to come to the border and try to cross, and they would shoot you."

Wild flowers grew on this grave. Some she recognised from home, most she did not. There must have been a small window in the climate that had brought the last dregs of the Gulf Stream far up the Baltic Sea, loitered for a few days, enough to have warmed the earth, ushered up the blooms with their bold colours. The photograph here was better preserved than those on the other graves, and Galina had taken her arm and led her closer, and Maggie carried the weight of Hector on her back. Tiredness welled in her. She thought him a good-looking boy and he seemed to have carried his confidence, his defiance, into the studio and the camera had captured them.

She said, "For them it was a good outcome. He is no longer a problem to them. Not a stone in their shoe, not a boil on their cheeks, not a thorn in their thumb. And the guards on the border enjoy it when they can shoot, it fulfils their ambition, and they will be told good things."

Maggie stood but the woman was crouched, flicking with her gloved fingers at the settled sleet to uncover more fragile flowers.

She thought they must have amazing powers of survival to last in this cold, with the drive of the wind shaking them and the weight of the sleet on the petals. Maggie had unburdened herself in the woman's home. She had huddled close to the fire and the shadows had flickered over Hector as he had slept. Had found a stranger to confide in and had talked of her status at the Embassy, and about a boy who came off a train from Kirov on a Saturday morning, and brought a memory stick, then went back to the station at midday on the Sunday to make the return journey. Had described fear, had listed the sightings of the surveillance and their brazen confidence ... Had spoken of a sort of love that was not sealed with a kiss, not even with held hands. Had listened to the story of the death of a son with a more striking face than Alexei's.

"You know what is at the fence ... Do you even know which is the real fence and which is the scam fence? Did you know there was a pretend fence? No? Two years back there was a trickster. He built a length of fence in the woods. There are migrant people who have travelled from the south of Russia, brought by criminals, and they get to Vyborg and there they meet men who say they have the knowledge to take them over the frontier, through the border. They come to this length of fence. And they get down on their hands and knees. That is after they have paid their money. And they go through a hole that is under the barbed wire, and they seem to avoid the tumble wires that activate the sirens, the alarms that alert the patrols. They think they are through, and into Finland and are safe, have reached Europe. And the troops of FSB pick them up at the actual fence, and they go to the gulag. It was a scam, did you not know?"

She had thought, when they had left the woman's home, that she would be taken to the cemetery, and then on into the forest, and she would be shown secret paths that would lead through the close-packed wild pines and would skirt lakes and bogs, and would come to a knoll or a hillock and she would be pointed in the direction she should go. Where she would take Alexei, and he might have Hector on his back, and they would be running, stumbling, and would challenge the fence and the barbed wire. Saw herself caught there. Saw Alexei trying to free her. Saw the contorted face of Hector, and heard his screams. Saw aimed rifles . . .

"In military speak, the death of my son was a 'good result' for them. Maybe vodka in the barracks. And the problem is gone . . . a voice of protest is silenced. Do they remember my son's name? Of course they do not, why might they? Put it from your mind."

So tired, and the light failing.

"They build the fence to keep people inside. They have the patrols to prevent people going outside. To keep people in and to stop them going out, they give the soldiers rifles and bullets. They will shoot and they will kill you, and your child, and the boy. The best, the heroes, they stay."

The sleet on the grave was cleared, but the ground would soon be covered again. It was a gesture. The woman used her glove to wipe the plastic that covered the photograph, and dried the surface. A bold boy, courage rich on his face, and a whole life beckoning, and . . . the woman's voice was calm.

"I knew nothing. I assumed he would escape. What existence then? In a colony of dreamers, of fantasists, men and women searching for patronage. No one cares for them . . . and they are the very few, who have succeeded. You want to try with your boy, and with your baby, and you think you will succeed. And you think you will find anyone then who cares about you, what you did? The heroes stay, they fight."

Maggie started to walk away and sensed that Hector was waking. The woman came behind her. Maggie had talked too long, painted her story too brightly.

"You know about Politkovskaya? She could have fled, did not. They killed her, used a grubby assassin and would have paid him a pittance. Anna Politkovskaya lives, a problem they cannot shed. Nemtsov could have gone, did not, was killed, and in his memory there is a beacon of hope. Rather than escape to exile, Khodorkovsky went to the gulag camps. Galina Starovoitova was another who they believed threatened them, so was killed. All of their names live . . . They are the heroes because they stayed. But if you die on the fence then it will do nothing, and if your baby dies on the fence then *they* will merely shrug, talk again about provocation. Not your quarrel. Go home. Your boy's quarrel and he should stay. That is what you tell him."

They walked briskly, Galina leading, Maggie staying close, difficult to keep her footing on the slithery path. They came again to the sparse lights of the village.

"Not what you wanted to be told? I have no apologies. I beseech you, do as I tell you . . . I do not want to hear the sounds of their rifles and I do not want to see, going slowly on the track, the ambulance. No klaxons and no lights because there will be no hurry when life is already finished . . . I will heat soup for you. You understand me? I never want to see or know of you again."

She would drive away into the growing gloom. Did not yet know how she would tell Alexei but would spell it out. Would drive fast through the night.

"Please sit down, Mr Chiswell."

The degree of dislike was mutual.

"I apologise that nothing more comfortable is provided, and apologise also for keeping you hanging about."

A curt nod that went with a curled lip, and Chiswell sat. Jonas had put the files away in the safe. Frank would be a witness of sorts and was at her table. He had noted that Chiswell had already speared a glance at Frank as if expressing distaste that she was present. The difference in their dislike, immediate, of each other was that Jonas masked his prejudice behind a smile, Chiswell hid nothing.

"To deal with my terms of reference, Mr Chiswell. I am asked to prepare a report on possible leaks from this section. No idea how I am supposed to achieve that, not a clue. I am not a policeman, am not gathering evidence for a court of law and so you are not in any way under caution. Nor is our conversation – that is what it is, I hope – being recorded. Frank is not here to take a full shorthand note or to load our words on to her computer, but more to mind me, make sure I do not stray in your fine building. So, we'll begin as best as I know how."

From across the table, Chiswell would have seen an old man, seeming to flounder, given work far beyond his competence. An outsider who had made a stupid but flamboyant gesture of sitting on a wet pavement that morning, and who had had the rudeness to keep him waiting, wasting time ... Jonas would have seen an individual who had a high opinion of his own qualities and an overstretched view of his abilities or would not have been dumped away out of sight in the Resettlement team. Jonas knew the school Chiswell had attended, the narrow terraced street where he had lived, the excellence of his university degree, his aptitude for the Sixers' entry examination and assessment. Had read also of a slip-back in achievement ... awarded him an E, for Ego. Had that in wheelbarrow loads. He probed, asked questions that were laced with humility. Seemed embarrassed that he posed questions that bordered on the impertinent.

Financial troubles, did he have overdrafts? Jonas already knew he did not. The suggestion was rejected sharply.

An approach, had one ever been made to him by an intelligence officer of the Federation? Nothing on the file, and the idea of it was dismissed out of hand, an expressive slap of the thigh.

Promotion, blocked or deflected? A difficulty with the personalities of his managers? Absolutely not.

Hobbies and relaxations, areas of interest? Already drifting off the usual course of interview, Jonas seemed to have run short of bullet points and was filling in time. A sharp rejoinder from Chiswell along the lines of ... things are no doubt different at Thames House but the workload at VX determined that the job was pretty much seven days a week, and again the satisfied grin ... and Jonas had then thrown in the little nugget that he and his wife, whenever possible, tried to get away with the caravan and the cat, find a site with a view of the sea, and Chiswell's lip had curled further and the man had fidgeted and recognised that they were almost done.

Jonas asked, "Just to recapitulate – and again I am sorry to have held you up, and am sincerely grateful for your time – You were in the party that flew to Copenhagen on the morning that the defector came over."

"Yes."

"And travelled to Aarhus, where you met him?"

"Yes."

"And were present at the preliminary debrief."

"Yes – and I think this is all well-trodden ground."

"And stayed the night at a hotel, all of you?"

"Yes. Are we almost done?"

"And the following morning there was a further group session, aimed at assessing Sashcord's value, then some of you went back to London and others stayed to move on towards the newly acquired safe house."

"Yes."

"On what terms did you part?"

A moment of hesitation. "Good terms, decent terms. Why not?"

Jonas acknowledged the lie. The old Ulster detective, Perry McKeag, would have grinned in his conservatory, such a damned obvious lie. The flicker of the eyes. "I think you rather liked him, liked Sashcord?"

"Did not like him nor dislike him. It was all professional. Bond with an agent? Hardly. That's not the way we do things . . . I am only going to say this once, Merrick, and you can take it any way you wish. We are professionals, know what we're doing. We have cutting-edge science and training behind us. We are the frontline of the modern defence of our country. We move in difficult, challenging environments . . . I don't think the less of you, Merrick, because you do not. We are sharp-end people and it won't be your fault that you are not within that range of operative."

"Give him a hug, did you? Tell him what a good guy he was before you flew off home?"

"Perhaps, might have . . ." Another hesitation and another flick of the eyes and they roved over the width of the table between them, and over the notebook Jonas had on the table and the blank page and the unused pencil. Another lie. ". . . Can't say I remember. If that is all, I have a full desk to clear."

Jonas wrote the single letter E on the pad, gazed at it for a moment, then put a line through it, dismissed ego and guilt, but registered the lies.

He said, "Well, I suppose you, your team, get Russian Federation defectors coming to you, breezing in, most days of the week. A dozen a month? Dropping off the trees like apples in a cider orchard. How would you remember whether you hugged him or not? . . . So grateful for your time, Mr Chiswell, really appreciated."

Perhaps then, perhaps later on, young Chiswell, the rising star or so he believed, might have registered the change of tone in Jonas Merrick's voice. Not a defector in the two years before the hasty journey to the Danish capital, and not one since. A little tempered steel in his voice. Frank opened the door. Chiswell had waited for her to perform that task, another little gesture that put a subordinate in their place. No backward glance, and out into the corridor, and she closed the door after him.

Frank asked, "Who would you like to see next, Mr Merrick?"

"I'll do a bit more reading, I think. Put Mr Symonds and the rest off until tomorrow . . . It's been quite a long day already."

And quite a worthwhile day, and not yet finished.

The wind whipped Thames House, and the river flowed dark, threatening and without charity under Lambeth Bridge.

That time in the afternoon when the AssDepDG, force of habit, stopped work and went to the window and gazed at the pedestrians, little ant-sized men and women, scurrying over the bridge. A bit early for Merrick . . . but there were occasions, an hour or so on, when he would see his man on the pavement, the river far beneath him, walking at the same speed regardless of sun or snow, calm or gale, and pretty much the same clothes every day, and gripping the old briefcase and holding it close to his thigh. Perhaps too much was asked of him. He had a good view across the river and up stream, towards the ghastly edifice of the Sixers' place . . . a lot was asked of Jonas Merrick. He recognised the footsteps behind him. The shoes probably had steel toe-caps and metal reinforcement of the heels.

"You all right?" the DepDG asked. "Looking a bit peaky."

"Fine."

"Any news from our friend, after his exhibition this morning?"

"Nothing. But where he is it would always be sensible to get the retaliation in first. Actually, I have rather high hopes. Might not be a happy ending for our Kremlin friends."

"Meaning?"

"Not going on the record, and no supporting evidence, but the high hopes talk to me of a bad outcome for those good friends – payback time. Can but hope. No one I'd rather have pulling the strings than Jonas Merrick, the miserable old beggar. Be very pleasant, wouldn't it, payback time? Can but hope."

"Be drinking fizz from the neck if he gets us there."

A chuckle, and the clatter of the shoes disappearing into a distant corridor. The AssDepDG could not have given a coherent answer as to why he allowed the course of optimism. And the man himself was probably still peeling his bloody lunchtime apple, achieving self-imposed perfection.

Alexei had worked late.

Had been convinced they were still playing with him. Had been given a series of cash movements to make, and banks in Luanda and Asuncion were involved, and it was necessary to dig out regulations for foreign transfers in Portuguese-speaking Angola and Spanish-speaking Paraguay. They would have arranged for him to be given further duties beyond his normal time of finishing the day's work. To what purpose? Obvious. To have longer to search the apartment. He had used another of the hairs taken from the woman's shoulder on his door when he had left home that morning.

An important football match was to be played in the city that evening. The first of the season after the winter break and many who worked around him were going. If he had been asked if he wanted to go with them he would have declined, but he had not been asked. In fact, had not been spoken to . . . it was already widely known that he had been reprimanded for poor work. The work area had emptied and in a few minutes the night skeleton staff would clock in. Two cleaners were working close to him, one wiping down desks and the other piloting a floor cleaner among the chairs, and bins were being emptied. One of them looked up and they caught eyes. Would have been about the same age as his mother. Likely that fate had treated this woman as badly as it had his mother . . . an alcoholic husband, a need to earn a living or starve. Perhaps this woman had a son of whom she was excessively proud and who she would suffer for: thought to be hard-working, conscientious, good and loving – then gone, denounced as a traitor. He fixed the cleaning woman in his glance and imagined how she would be if transferred to his mother's apartment, stifling hot in summer and damp with cold in winter. Sitting on a hard chair in the kitchenette, surrounded by the FSB search team, questions barked at her, cupboards emptied and drawers tipped out, and the contents of the wardrobe scattered. The only books that his mother cared for were religious tracts, and the various editions of the bible collected over half a century, and they would be taken off the shelves and the bindings would be slashed with penknives as evidence of further treachery was hunted down. His mother would lose her job. She cleaned hotel rooms and corridors, and the money was a pittance. He had thought himself too holy a figure to be paid for the espionage he performed. Only offered once, not repeated. Twice, recently, he had steeled himself to ask Lucinda for payment, but had not managed to cough up the words. He gave his mother a little, but most of his spare cash went on the train fares from Kirov to Moscow, and back. When he went out of Russia with Maggie, with Hector, he would be turning his back on his mother, abandoning her . . . He looked into the face of this old woman cleaning the office and she seemed too exhausted to respond and he saw crow's feet at her eyes and sagging skin at her throat. Could be his own mother. She worked around him, then moved on . . . And thought – could not be "out" by plane or on the train, or by road: would be over a fence that was guarded, regarded as escape proof, and patrolled with guns. He shivered.

The job was done, the transfers confirmed. Their data went on to his memory stick, joined the details of cash movements into Rostock and into a bank close to the harbour of Kaliningrad. He had no reason to stay any longer but was slow shifting himself up from his chair. He had no idea how it would be, going to the border, only knew that his faith lay with Maggie. And saw the small face of Hector, felt the weight of love . . . and they would be together and the pain of the stress would be finished. Knew that, believed that.

Konstantin drove, Anatoly beside him. Leonid was sprawled across the back seat, the hardware beneath him wrapped in greaseproof paper and with a further layer of tinfoil around the package. Their route took them west towards Lubeck, then north to Flensburg, and after that the road bridge over the canal and on towards the Danish border, and at the crossroads at Kolding they would choose the road that would lead them into Esbjerg. Minimal traffic on the A20 and they had a full tank and a four-hour drive. It was good gear hidden under the back seat . . . They would have a night to sleep, and a day to reconnoitre, then an evening to make final preparations, then would hit, and be on their way . . .

It was confirmed that already a trawler was ploughing through a mild swell and that the lights of Kaliningrad's inner harbour were far behind it and it would be nudging the best speed it could make across the Gulf of Gdansk, Polish territorial waters. And at a naval mooring, on the coast near Kaliningrad, a frigate prepared to sail and would make passage out of the Baltic and into the North Sea, and then would loiter in international waters until it made a rendezvous to take on three passengers from a fishing boat. All planned and all in place. And the car was quiet except for soft jazz music from a Lubeck station. Trained men, practised men, hard men, had little need for bravado talk when travelling towards a target.

Doug was at the front window. Wally stood behind him.

"Do you think she's called in yet?"

Doug had a view of the PET car, window down and could see the two faces and the guy was smoking.

"I think, the little I've seen of her, she'd have spat it to us if she had."

Behind them, Sashcord lounged in his chair, pretended to read a magazine but would have tried to listen to each word they said. Voices were dropped, and they spoke in side of mouth mutters.

"Has Benedict called in with it, passed the gory little moment upstairs?"

"Not that I know," Wally whispered. "In his room, head down. Best place for him."

The room was a mess. And cold. The back windows leading on to the patio and the garden were ajar. The boffin was outside. Cables and two screens and a console were on the low table. Sometimes the screens showed pictures, just tests, and sometimes the console's light buttons flashed: blue, red, green. Wally had Simon registered as a guy who rarely spent a night away from home; Wally and Doug rarely spent a night in theirs. He seemed anxious that he might not be finished in time to get the last flight out. Cameras and sensors were going into the back garden and there was the whine of a power drill that fixed gear to the fence posts. The PET boy had gone next door, said something to the householder about security needs, but it was just routine.

Doug said, "We're fucked if she does, goes upstairs and into the system. And Benedict's playing it right. On what he said, that low-life bastard, about the Six girl, keeping it close and private. Tell London nothing."

"Buttoned lips. What happens on tour stays on tour . . . You reckon it worth me talking to her, that girl out front? Do a bit of a warts and all chat? Worth it?"

"You got the charm, Wally, turn the tap on with it. Might even say that it's better to have a boob groped for than not have it noticed and so not groped for. Sort of compliment, wasn't it, that she had the shite's fingers all over her . . . Or, you could tell her we're deep in a cesspit, in a bad place and she's the power to make it worse, and . . ."

Simon was back inside. He closed the windows drew down the blinds.

Plugs went into sockets. Lights played on the console, and a movement on a screen. A shape moved on the grass, brilliant white against the grey background: a rat progressing across the garden. Simon beamed, his closework spectacles high on a shaven scalp, and expected compliments, deserved them – did not get them. Doug and Wally seldom paid compliments although the system in place looked quality, and an intruder into the garden, hitting from there, would show up well. What then . . .?

Simon said, cheerfully, "Just asking. What sort of idiot chose this place? I mean . . . traffic able to come up past the front door, and neighbours either side and close, and a back garden that has a fence a cat can get over and then woodland. I mean . . . it's a walking disaster area. Why I'm fucking off, and why I'm wishing you luck."

A taxi was called. Together with Benedict they were shown the console and told how the beams worked, and the rat came back and traversed the grass again and worked its way across a pile of leaves and twigs. Simon went off into the night. Wally said he'd go outside, fancied a fag, which meant he was going to talk to the PET girl, appeal a bit, joke a bit, and hope plenty. Doug reckoned Wally had a good nose for the scent of the significant.

Wally had not remarked on what the Russian had described, the business with the Sixer woman, had thought it more important to soft-soap the Danish woman. Had Frank been raped? Was Frank part of the room service on offer? Had she gone the extra yard to show how welcome he was? Keeping the show on the road depended on how great was the outrage of the PET woman for having her boobs groped. They were wrecked if Wally failed and that, Doug reflected, was the sort of responsibility that always rested on the shoulders of the little guys.

Jonas was escorted to the front gate by Frank, and he thought she stayed with him for fear of further hiccups with security. He needed his coat and hat in the sharp wind that circled the VX building and smacked into them as they emerged.

Jonas checked that the handcuff holding the chain to his brief-case was in place, yanked it to be certain.

She said quietly, "Wise of you, Mr Merrick. Can never be too careful."

Jonas said, "Too right. I'll see you in the morning. A quarter to eight here. Never can be too careful."

"Have a good journey home, Mr Merrick."

He thought she had an attractive voice. In fact, much about her was attractive. Neither of them could be too careful ... All the paperwork that he had pored over was locked away in the safe. In his briefcase were only his empty lunch box and his empty thermos. He passed a policeman and a gatekeeper. His antics of the morning would have been well circulated and he was greeted with hostile stares, as if he were trouble, best avoided: probably correct assumptions. He imagined, as he took the river walk past Lambeth Palace, that she would by now have reached the third floor and would be informing the rest of the team – other than the arrogant Chiswell and the pliant but clever Montgomery – that they were to be available from 07.50 in the morning. And they would mouth a chorus of dissent. "Who does the little bastard think he is?"

He did not look around him as he walked. Might have recog-nised some of his A Branch colleagues. They would be out, mob-handed. Would have been pulled off conventional work, mostly Islamists, and the scale of the deployment gave Jonas irrefutable proof of the trust placed in him. He could, and some-times did, cringe at such responsibility. They would have noticed him. Many pairs of eyes would have been on him as he came out into the wind, holding tight to his trilby hat, and then they would look away because he was not one of the targets assigned them. Could have been runners, could have been cyclists, could have been lingering by the bus stops, and could have been cab drivers, and all watching the door from which Jonas had emerged. They were good at their work, and Jonas had no doubt they would provide proof of a leaker's identity where as yet only his instinct led him.

The wind pressed his coat against his back, tried to tear the briefcase from his hand, and he set out with his regular chopping stride and ahead of him was the grey edifice of Thames House, and over to his right was the scaffold cloaked mass of the Houses of Parliament. He took out his mobile phone, returned to him from the safe, and punched an international number, and was answered by a hotel switchboard. It would have seemed to the operator, perfect English spoken, that she was dealing with a silly-sounding old person who had made an arrangement with the porters' desk . . . back in November of last year. Who would have been on duty that morning? Had he rung a hotel in Aberdeen or Altrincham or Appledore, he would have received the local equivalent of "How the hell would I know?", but he called Aarhus in Denmark. He was answered quickly and was given a name, and pleaded forgetfulness and was rewarded with a mobile number and would call it in the morning, and was so grateful.

He spotted. On the fourth floor of Thames House was a window where sometimes he was spotted by the AssDepDG. Could not see him, but the AssDepDG would look for him, then come down a floor and beard him in his cubbyhole and both of them early birds and the chance for quiet talk.

He crossed the bridge, went down Horseferry Road and into the café. Both were already there, nursing hot coffees, each with a bacon roll.

"Evening, Mr Merrick," they said together.

"Thank you Kevin and thank you Leroy, and hope this is not too inconvenient."

Would have been severely inconvenient, and they had their weaponry with them and another shift would have taken charge of the building's back vehicle entrance while they enjoyed the coffee and the bacon rolls.

"How can we help?" Kevin asked.

"Not asking for anything legal, Mr Merrick, I hope," Leroy said.

He gave them two names, wanted a rule run over two men. Done on the silent networks that existed among old fighting men.

Wanted an answer in the morning when he came off the train from Raynes Park. Where there was history there was, generally, co-operation. No coffee for Jonas, as he had a train to catch and his dinner would already have been delayed, and he hurried out into the evening, and the cold slapped him. It had been a good day, a long day, but a most worthwhile day. And, he did not know how much time was left him, nor how well he could rely on his judgement to see him through. He went back over the bridge and into the teeth of it.

8

Clouds scudded and lifted the gulls over Jonas as he crossed Lambeth Bridge. He was not in a good humour, had been rude, and it would have surprised those who knew him moderately, and he regretted it.

A sharp remark, a rejoinder that he wished he had stifled. It had been a rare intrusion of his domestic life into his professional world of counter-espionage. From the moment that he had his briefcase hooked to his wrist, lunch box and thermos stowed, and with more maps inside it that had been copied and printed at home, his concentration was on his work. He had been far away, had camped his mind in the city of Esbjerg, and Vera had spoken, anxiety brimming in her voice.

He had been sharp. She was due to get the estimate for the cost of the caravan's electrical repair. She would not have texted him at work with the sum and the query as to whether to go ahead, or whether to shop around for a better offer, or put off any decision until the evening and his return . . . He had snapped, "For heaven's sake, Vera, just do what you think right and don't burden me with . . ." He had left, the front door shutting noisily behind him.

He reached Thames House and went down Horseferry Road and might have been noticed by the AssDepDG but Jonas did not look up to see if his master, his protector, might be at his fourth-floor window. He had the support and patronage he required and did not need to check its validity.

They were there, both of them. He had timed his arrival well. Probably five minutes until their shift started.

Kevin said, "Checked on them, Mr Merrick."

Leroy said, "As good as you could find, Mr Merrick."

"Hoping you're not going off again into harm's way, Mr Merrick, but if you are, then they will be good for watching your back."

"Don't go there, harm's way, Mr Merrick, but should you have to then they would be right to have with you."

"Nearly as useful as us, Mr Merrick."

"Well, nearly . . . They're well spoken of."

"Experienced."

"Top of the range."

He thanked them, and they were gathering up their kit and taking a last gulp of their coffee, tea, whatever .. . . He was confident that there would be a network of older men who had once been on a frontline, now veterans, and they would have the ability to pluck out references that would not have appeared on a private military contractor company's website. He knew their photographs and knew their names. He had started to insinuate a route into the lives of Douglas and Walter, temporary muscle on hire to the Sixers . . . They would have been blown to their God, had the Hamburg bomb detonated and he had no doubts as to their loyalties, but wanted confirmation of their quality.

On the move again. He would have been cursed by the feisty and sometimes foul-mouthed Aggie Burns who worked in an office next to Jonas's. She did the allocation of that most precious commodity, the A Branch surveillance people. Her team, all of them and stretched thin, would be in place for the early hike to work of the Resettlement team, or would already have followed them out of their homes and watched as they took a bus or a bicycle, or ran, or a train and a cab, or walked, and there would have been chatter into hidden microphones and the crackle of communications into earpieces. He would have the facility, grudgingly given by Aggie Burns, for that day and the next, no longer.

Once on Lambeth Bridge, he rang the number that had been given him. The man spoke fine English. A date given and a morning departure. "You are the man I need, the man I am relying on . . . The British party that stayed one night with you – how were they?" A very simple question and he gilded it with a chuckle as if awaiting gossip, and was rewarded, and the initial flattery had paid well. Stony faces, embarrassed quiet, a barely cauterised scratch on a cheek, a bruised eye. He absorbed.

Jonas was eyed at the Sixers' entrance. A different armed policeman but the same gatekeeper. His reputation enhanced: a "miserable old bastard and stubborn, and he'll drop you in shit as soon as look at you". He thought he also recognised grudging respect. Frank was waiting. He was escorted through and his briefcase went on to the roller and through the X-ray, with his coat and his belt, his small change, his wristwatch and his pen and spectacles.

On his table, laid where he would put his notepad and pencil, was a bright-coloured gift bag. He opened it, showed delight, saw that she had brought him a portion of cake, walnut and coffee. He smiled with warmth and thanked her . . . and said he would see Barker first, not Symonds as he had indicated the previous evening. The switch in interview order was designed to create a greater degree of irritation, to spoil whatever schedule the two men had prepared. He said that the cake looked delicious and said how grateful he was, and that he appreciated the generosity. She shrugged as if it were a small matter and already had the safe door opened and was busy at her laptop.

And the matter of Vera was forgotten.

He awaited Barker. His coffee was made as he liked it. A good start to the day, and a useful contribution from the head porter's desk in a hotel, Aarhus, and a most useful recommendation concerning the qualities and loyalties of the two minders. He thought their photographs showed hard men, reliable men.

Doug washed up, big hands dripping suds and clutching small plates.

"So it's carrot and stick?" he called over his shoulder.

Wally was down the hall, had mastered the vacuum cleaner.

"What Benedict said – but more carrot and not much stick," Wally answered.

They heard a car arrive. Change of shift, and the PET woman back.

"You reckon this is sorted? Or will it go nuclear?"

"Good vibes. Would have stayed away if she had knifed us."

In the living area, Benedict was leaning forward on a chair and had a map out across a low table and was trying to interest Sashcord in it.

"Where is it we're going?" Doug cleared the sink, could see the sensors that Simon had put in place in the garden and could see the trees swaying in the wind, and the rain running down the window.

"A town down the road, ancient streets, postcard place. Be bloody good in the rain – but that's carrot." Wally had killed the vacuum cleaner and was winding in the cable.

"Don't think there's any stick left. Ran out of options, and our boy knows it."

"I laid it on a bit thick, with Jette, trouble it would cause, and told her he'd be gone from the country at the start of next week. Well, something like that . . . It'll be good to get out, walk somewhere. Can't spend a life cooped in this hole."

"Carrot and stick, right way to go." Doug dried his hands.

"This can't last. Has to have a resolution. Yes, be good to walk." Wally put away the vacuum cleaner, admired what he had achieved with it and could see the woman in the car. She had her window down, was smoking, and their eyes met. She grinned and tapped her head, had a finger on the impact point where she had split the lip of her abuser. Would be a grand day because the rain was steady, and like as not, pre-season, every bloody place would be closed to visitors.

A blast on the klaxon, and another, which was a sort of code and inside they would have seen the Fiat 500 in the forecourt and the garage doors were heaved open. Maggie drove inside.

Felt lousy and would have looked a wreck.

Could have been that the guys inside fancied her, or there was something in her personality that excited them, but three of them gathered around the car and all were grinning, and she smiled back at them and told them to piss off. She could be certain that the car would be hosed down within half an hour, and the smell of her body and little Hector's hoovered out. Bad weather all the way, more snow than sleet, and the temperature below freezing. She heaved Hector out of his seat.

The mechanics would have loved the mystery that she made, and would have been as discreet as was possible for local employees of the UK's diplomatic mission. Well paid and had better than decent bonuses, but would still cough up details if the FSB came calling and twisted an arm . . . Not much to report other than the vehicle had been off road, and that she looked to have driven through a blanket of tiredness, and that the kid was fractious. She had Hector on her hip and the bag with his gear hitched on a shoulder, and she headed for the bathroom. Changed him there, washed him, splashed water on her own face, emerged to face the world. Another rueful smile for the guys and she was on her way.

Facing the world would take an effort. She remembered men and women she had worked with, driven for, in the Province. Remembered how they'd seemed to bond with their touts, then had washed their hands of a supposed friendship and been transferred to another headquarters or taken the freedom bird out of Aldergrove and back to the mainland.

Remembered what she had wanted. Remembered that she had thought of him as her love. Remembered Galina and a cold grave below spring blooms, and the story of a fence. Remembered what she had been told by her father: "If life were easy then everyone would be doing it." A betrayal? Or facing the world?

She had her head up and the snow freckled her face and she hitched up the scarf around Hector's mouth and she strode the pavements and crossed roads and headed for the Embassy. She met the cops by the gate, and let them have a few seconds of pulling faces at Hector and gave them her best smile and was inside the compound. She had managed three hours of restless sleep in the Fiat at an all-night fuel stop with Hector deep down inside her coat. She had food for him and bought a sandwich for herself and had topped up the tank, and had paid cash. Felt rotten, but without that big burden: what to do about Alexei, *Environ*, who was of value, who was afraid. With cause. She took Hector to the crèche. There were other mothers there, dropping off their kids, and the nursery assistants, and they'd eyed her; and she ignored them.

She went to a locker in the corridor outside a line of toilet cubicles and shower stalls. Washed herself, and dried herself hard until her body was reddened and almost sore, and thought she was purged. Went to the office of her colonel. She would have looked awful, mud on her shoes, and mud on her trousers and mud on her top from when the Fiat had been heaved out of the ditch, and flecks of mud in her hair. Everyone else was pristine: but they knew that she lived a part of her life outside any of the loops they existed in. She switched on her computer, unlocked the drawer by her knee and tugged out the file. Her colonel could have done the work himself but seemed to rely on her to give it credence and a sense of published importance.

Maggie was good at that part of her work and the document would have gravitas; would carry graphs, charts, photographic evidence. She started to type the details of her man's evaluation of the Armata T-14 main battle tank and planned the sections that would deal with crew survivability and the quality of laminated armour, and comparisons with the M-1 Abrams and the German Leopard 2. Pushed a hand through her hair and felt the tangles unravel. Her vision was impaired as much by exhaustion as by the tears that now flowed fast down her cheeks. She pulled up the picture showing the tank on manoeuvres. The colonel brought her coffee from the dispenser machine, set it down beside her screen, looked over her shoulder to see how she constructed that page.

And asked, "That bad, Maggie, where you were, what you learned?"

Maggie did not look up at him. "Yes, that bad. As bad as breaking a promise is. Just did not want to get shot. Seemed to come down to that. A boy getting shot, and me and Hector getting shot, and us hanging on the wire, and dead. That bad, which is enough to ditch a promise."

The colonel said, "I doubt it will be consolation, but I think that sounds a sensible conclusion."

He stood between the Kristall business centre and the Yamoyka car wash.

Away to Alexei's right was the Old Bridge over the Vyatka river. He had looked up at it and had seen how high it towered over the river, but mostly he watched the dark flow of the water. The previous week small icebergs had been swept downstream by the current. He stood on the walkway, where the overnight snow still lay, and shivered. The wind always came from the north and he could imagine how cold the water would be. There were idiots who swam in the river throughout the year unless ice had spread across the river's width. Most of them had heavy, almost obese, bodies. Alexei was thin and the cold of the river would enter his body within moments. Close to where he stood was the rubble left by the collapse of a kerb of the promenade. When the thaw came and the weather warmed, a gang of men would turn up with shovels and barrows and would clear the mess of broken concrete pieces . . . They would be the right size, would fit easily into the wide pockets of his anorak. He tested himself that morning, and he was already late for work.

He could have gone up on to the bridge and stood on the rail, which was what most suicides did, and then wavered, looked down, and then jumped, or toppled, into the void before the impact of the water . . . Or, he could have put broken concrete into his pockets and scrambled down the slope, thrust out his right foot and stepped into the water, paddled a few metres and then been swept clear of safety . . . He could have done either.

Two women were in his mind, and a child. Do either and he would not see them again. If he jumped then he'd be reaching out, flailing, trying to find a girder or a stone ledge in the bridge's supports to snatch at, but would be falling, and screaming, death by impact ... If he walked into the water he would feel the ice crawl up his shins, then his thighs, and shrivel his groin, and he would slip on weed and go under, and of course his resolution would fail, but he would be held down, his fingers too numb to unfasten his anorak and he would choke, death by drowning. And, would not see his mother again. He had a crumpled sweet paper in his pocket. Would not see Maggie again, nor Hector. He flicked the sweet paper and the wind caught it and it landed on the water and was swept away by the current. So powerful, offering no second chance.

Late for work but a price worth paying. His mind cleared. Would go with Maggie to the border, had her promise, and they would cross the fence, the only possible escape route on offer. And imagined how it would be when they sank down into snow or sheltered beneath pine trees, her and him and holding each other.

Almost a jaunty step to the bus stop. And the same into his workplace, jogging up the flights of stairs because the elevator was already in use, and walking inside ... they would go on the Saturday. She would see him off the train and would take the stick from him, extracted from his trainer, and leave it in the dead letter box. They might have time to go to his mother for him to take her flowers, and then they would head north, would scale a fence and face freedom. He did not need to jump or wade into the river. Felt good, walked tall, and went to his desk and would apologise to his supervisor for his late arrival ... And the next Monday morning let all the little bastards around him, with their ferret faces, wonder where he was, what he had done.

"I tell you what we feel, Merrick, tell it you straight."

"That would be helpful, Mr Barker, always best to be out in the open."

"What we feel is that your crowd are really just glorified coppers. We are the cream of the diplomatic service. We are top division and you are second rate ... That is why we regard it as insulting that your agency should have been permitted to put an individual – you – into our back garden and let you poke about in our affairs."

"Extraordinary, Mr Barker, and none more surprised than me."

He thought the man opposite him had prepared each word of the salvo, had probably gone into the toilets, stood in front of a mirror and practised spitting out his denunciation. Jonas imagined he had taken on the role because of his imminent departure and that his reputation would be enhanced when news of his defiance, his rudeness – "putting that little nerd in his place" – became common knowledge. Jonas nodded agreement at each burst of the rehearsed accusation, seemed to imply that he could not have put it better himself, and in doing so encouraged further attack.

"There isn't a leak, not at this end. The bloody Germans need looking at, or the Danes. Not us. This is a very dedicated team. Well-fitted to handling difficult defectors. We work hard to drain out of them each last drop of information, and are good at our work. Your crowd – don't take this personally, Merrick – have a piss-poor reputation at duty of care with Irish and *jihad* turncoats. We hear that half of them top themselves after being put on the scrapheap. Abandoned and isolated. We look after our people, put a big effort in, take that obligation very seriously. And the idea that one of us is working against our defectors' safety, and our own people's security, is preposterous, damn near a criminal slander."

"Very powerfully put, Mr Barker, and I've no reason to doubt what you say about your team – all of them being first-rate professionals."

"I am speaking out, Merrick, and this is for the record and I am surprised that neither you nor Frank is taking a comprehensive – seems to be only precise – note of what I say, because my time has pretty much run its course. I'm about to go into what is laughingly called the Third Age, retirement duty. Nothing you can put on my record matters a damn. Your presence here is an insult to us. I'll tell you something else . . . this individual, this Sashcord, is bloody useless, a pain in the arse, but that in no way diminishes the effort we are putting in place to safeguard him, and the bloody expense of it . . . Is this filtering through, entering your skull? Got it, have you?"

"Think I am getting the drift, and not complaining, and your attitude is far from unreasonable. And I am grateful for your time and patience."

He knew that Barker had been thirty-seven years with the Service – that elite organisation that had not warned of an imminent invasion of the Falkland Isles, that had dismissed speculation that Saddam Hussein did not possess weapons of mass destruction. Would have been a natural cheerleader, and would be quitting to patrol a local golf course and to do his share of the driving when the pub darts team was on an away fixture, and was married to a woman who no doubt would dread the day when she too had to pack in her job and humour him all day and every day. Knew that his mortgage was paid off, that his bank statements showed moderate investments, that his children were well-paid City workers. Barker was what they liked to call a "safe pair of hands", and his pomposity quota was well filled. Would have been greeted with a Christian name if his path crossed that of the Director General in the atrium. He had given the letter "M" to Barker, which was Money, and thought the man had enough, was more interested in status than wealth. He wrote that letter on the blank page then decisively drew a line through it, and turned the page. Jonas smiled again, his weak one, and shrugged as if he had nothing further to ask . . . He made those little gestures with his hands that indicated that he was only a "messenger" and therefore should not be shot, a minion – a bottle-washer – and had no status. The politics of his appointment, sending him into the holiest of holies, the VX building, would have been taken at a level far above his own rank, would have been the work of a bureaucrat looking to create offence. He waited for the last, and inevitable, salvo.

"I tell you something, Merrick, and it's beyond your remit but . . . the safe house for Sashcord has been moved. A very few in the PET camp, Danish security, know of the new location. Different people to those we liaised with before. He is safe, the chain is decoupled. Because we have sliced through the information pathway there will be no further attacks. Bet my shirt on it. They may look, but they will assuredly fail. Frankly, this team – our people – are owed a big apology for the suspicion dumped on us. I don't hold you personally responsible, Merrick, and no doubt you want to get back to your desk soonest and I expect the work is pretty mundane, what goes across you each day, but someone has to do it . . . we are frontline and should be treated with regard. If that is all . . .?"

He stood. One more smile from Jonas, the self-deprecating one, but his eyes narrowed.

"You are very fortunate, Mr Barker, to have served on that frontline at times of personal danger and stress. Sadly, some of us have not had such an opportunity – which is why I hold you in such regard."

Behind him, Frank seemed to snort, like a laugh was stifled in her throat, could not help herself . . . She opened the door for Barker who swept out and no doubt would go upstairs immediately to regale them all with how he had stood his corner and told that "fucking little idiot" how things were. She closed the door. Their eyes met. An impassive face now and a pretty one, and a depth in her eyes that made them hard to read.

Jonas said. "Time for a bit more reading, please, then we'll break for lunch, and we'll do Symonds in the afternoon. I'm very much looking forward to the cake you so kindly brought me. All going along quite well, I think."

A quiet drive and fast, no music and little talk. Doug and Wally in the front and a firearm hidden. Sashcord and Benedict behind them, and all dutifully belted. It was a straight road from Esbjerg to the town of Ribe, with wide fields on either side, flanked by isolated farm buildings, and the fields were empty because surface water from the rains still lay there and it was too early for cattle to have been put out.

When they had left the Fourfelt suburb, the PET team – Jette, driving, and Nils – had come behind them on to the main drag then had slowed, allowing them to pull clear, and would have blocked a tail. Next, the escort had come behind them at speed and had passed them before dropping back to act as lookout and block. When they reached the new factories north of the small city, Jette had flashed her lights and Wally had powered away . . .

They had tried to read her that morning but a directed question, *Are you likely, my dear, to drop us in the manure?* had not been posed, nor the more serious one, *Have you already, my dear, dropped us in the manure?* They could have done some guide book talk but that had petered out before they were clear of Esbjerg, driving past docks for rigs and offshore supply boats, and a ferry struggling through spray and rain towards a misted strip of land across open water. Benedict had recited something that he had learned off his screen but neither Wally nor Doug had shown interest and Sashcord had seemed indifferent . . . Typical, showing fuck all gratitude and the whole thing arranged for his benefit.

Had he been asked, Doug would have said, "Waste of space and best place for him would be face down in a ditch."

And Wally would have said, "Unpleasant, needs a hoof in the arse into the great blue yonder."

Neither had been asked, and both were now paid – not handsomely but adequately – to protect him. They had, of course, noted an "atmosphere" on that morning after the first night, seen a scratched face and a puffed eye and him showing defiance, and her, Frank, purposefully looking through the guy like he didn't exist. Never discussed, left to lie, not their business. It was the way they were and both able to keep their mouths shut . . . When they approached the town, Ribe, Benedict made a further attempt to wind up interest.

"It is eleven centuries old. A Viking town. Prettiest place in the country. Was a big trading port and boats would have gone all the way up the Baltic and as far as Russian trading stations, and crossed the North Sea and landed on the English east coast and more likely rampaged there. It was home to a famous religious leader, Ansgar and he . . ."

"Not necessary, Benedict, we don't care," Sashcord yawned. "Do not care at all."

Not difficult to get a parking space in front of a supermarket. Coats zipped up and hoods unfurled, and umbrellas would have been useless because of the wind. Easy to assume that Benedict had children and was familiar with damp holidays, ghastly days when effort and enthusiasm were needed to get youngsters away from their phones and games and the inside of a holiday chalet. They reached a bridge and looked down on to the spattered surface of the river.

Benedict said, "This is where Viking longboats would have been moored and they would have kept their families here when they were away, and loot and profit came back with them, so this was a prosperous place in the tenth century."

Wally thought Benedict was earning his corn, putting on a good show, and rain dribbled off the little glasses perched on his nose. They walked along a main street with quaint buildings on either side and cobbles under their feet, and expensive little shops had their shutters up. Benedict said there were museums in the town but was unsure if they were open this early in the year.

Wally muttered, "You reckon they've a cat house here, where we could drop him off?"

Benedict led. Hands deep in his coat pocket, his head ducked, Sashcord followed and Doug and Wally were at the back, and Wally had the firearm tucked into his belt, and that was all he had to feel cheerful about. A church loomed in front of them, but was not yet open to trade, and Wally said something about wanting to buy a fridge magnet, something personal for them and it was hard to keep straight faces . . . Benedict had started to talk about the church, and the first foundations having been put down in the ninth century, and the big man doing the Christian conversions and Ansgar, the bishop, had started the building and Benedict had a statue to help with the story. A gaunt man high on a plinth, seemingly wrapped in ropes, and larger than he would have been in life, and around a corner were statues of two more bishops, and Benedict checked on his phone and said they were Hans Tavsen and Hans Adolph Brorson and both had been dead for 400 years. The rain was relentless and they had reached that state, recognised by holidaymakers, when taking shelter seemed pointless, and so they moved on.

"Do we make extra for this?"

"Bad weather allowance, should do."

And Doug saw nothing that disturbed him, nor did any shafts of anxiety strike Wally, and they kept the empty pavements under constant watch and had Sashcord in sight . . . and Doug might have thought about how the Danish woman was going to close down the uncertainty – "Piss or get off the pot, which?" Wally might have considered what the reptile had said of the woman who had come from England, who had made the arrangements for the hotel stay in Aarhus and who was described as screwing like a tigress, and nothing had been said the morning after. Just embarrassment and some hustling for the first safe house and the extended debrief – Wally and Doug among them – and some had gone for the airport and the flight home. And all of them embarrassed, and looking away, and she had a bruise on an upper cheek and he had a scratch on his face, and nothing was said. A big, bad dose of shame because the issue was not confronted, not as it had been with Jette.

Doug elbowed his colleague's rib.

"And what was that for?"

Doug said, "The first night and the morning after, and what we didn't do and didn't say."

Wally said, "What were we supposed to say, do? We're just the bloody boots on the ground. Wasn't for us to chip in."

"What do you reckon happened to her?"

"Not paid to reckon. Officers reckon. Crap like us don't do reckoning. Don't get medals for reckoning, and for fuck's sake, Doug, cheer up . . . we're having a day out, and might get an ice cream. What happened yesterday, or days ago, is not today."

They left the square and went back to the first bridge, and fast-food outlets were winding up their roller shutters, and pizza was going to be the top meal of the day, and the boutiques were filling their windows and the jewellery shops ... Not that either had a wife who needed softening up with gemstones or necklaces from Denmark, not that either had a wife who cared about them more than they cared for each other.

Walked on more cobbles and went past a line of old homes that faced the river and kept on going. Benedict, up ahead, still doing his tour guide bit. Not another human being in sight and they passed a deserted yacht club and a great mound surrounded by a sunken moat where a couple of cormorants were fishing. Benedict did the talking, and Sashcord followed almost meekly. The mound had been a Viking fortress. Its stone walls had been stripped out two or three hundred years back and used to build the town. There was another statue, and the town seemed packed with them, a sardine tin of statues, and this one stood on top of the mound, facing out.

Benedict did his bit, eleven out of ten for effort. He had raised his voice against the weather. "It's not much of a statue from the artistic viewpoint, but it's good history. That is Princess Dagmar. She was the first queen of Valdemar the Second who was also called the Victorious. She produced one stillborn son and another male child, Valdemar the Young, but he was killed in a hunting accident. The queen is commemorated because she died in Ribe. That was in the thirteenth century and this would have been a prominent fortification at that time. The whole place was wrecked in the seventeenth century when they had a great flood here and a rise in the water level of at least six metres that came right up-river from the sea, and caused massive loss of life and general destruction, and ... Where is he ...?"

The shout reached Doug and Wally.

"Where has he gone? With you, is he? Where the hell has he gone?"

Neither could see him. Could see Benedict, beside the wife of Valdemar the Second, the Victorious, could see the town beyond the moat and could see the cormorants still fishing, could not see him.

"Where in God's name is he?"

"He is with you, isn't he?" Benedict yelled into the rain and the wind.

Was swivelling, almost toppling, and yelling all the time at Doug and Wally in the central sunken area of the fortress.

Benedict could not see another human being. Not a dog walker, not an old man on sticks doing his constitutional, not a mother with a buggy, not a long-distance cyclist on the riverside path. The only movement was from the long grass at the side of the moat that bucked in the wind and the waves which rocked the cormorants each time they surfaced. His men raked the ground around them and he sensed panic.

They stood, buffeted in confusion, and looked around, and still did not see him. Benedict felt the cold on the back of his neck, and the weight of his stomach seeming to sink inside his belly.

"Have you seen him? Did he come past you?"

Both of them shook their heads.

"Well, bloody find him then."

Complete emptiness confronted Benedict. The three of them split. He did a sector and Doug had run, ungainly, and Wally lumbered but fast. They quartered the ground, and Doug peered into the holes level with the grass that had once been entries to the lower floors of the buildings, and Wally hurried around the entire circumference of the fortified hill, and Benedict looked again and again at the same places his eyes had gone over before. He could not believe his failure.

He yelled again, "Did you not see him? Did he not have to pass you to get back over the causeway?"

Only once before had he felt such fear for an outcome. Could assume most people never had a crisis of such gravity as this, other than perhaps a car accident or a bad medical prognosis. In his grandfather's day there would have been military service and convoy escort or the loneliness of RAF flights, or the sickening terror of waiting through the night for dawn and an infantry attack . . . Not today, not applicable. Doug would have known about fear, and Wally too. Benedict knew about fear because he had led a group of men and women out of a building in a small town south-east of Baghdad. A mob at the gate, howling and chucking rocks, and petrol bombs starting, and very soon the hardware would arrive. Could have sat around and waited for the backup, but the troops supposed to be on immediate ready to rescue his mission were not answering the call. He had led his people out, and they might all have been slaughtered, and he had felt fear when they had broken cover and run. A time of fear, but this was more acute.

They gathered. Benedict took the deep breaths that were supposed to calm. "What do we do?"

"You have to make a call, Benedict."

"Has he wandered off looking for a packet of fags and we didn't notice his going *or* did he take the opportunity to quit on us? As Doug says, sorry and all that, but your call."

"Planned or spontaneous?"

"Unplanned."

"Looking for the big exit route right now. Could be a bus station or a railway station. Can't be a hire car as he has no documents or credit cards. Could be on foot. Going where? Going home to face the music."

"What degree of force, Benedict, if we get to him?"

"Half bloody throttle him for all I care."

They hurried, loping, stumbling back along the river to the bridge, and then into the town, dividing responsibility for the stations. He would be hanged, in professional speak, left to spin in the wind if he had lost his defector. Would face suspension, be called before an inquest committee, would have to justify his self-appointed role of carrot donor and stick flogger, and would face interrogation on the matter of a PET woman and an unreported abuse allegation . . . And had always felt so damn proud to have spent his young adult years as an officer in the ranks of the VX crowd, a Sixer. All finished on a wet winter day, in the chocolate-box town, pretentious and sanitised and fake, of Ribe . . . He hated the bloody place. He ran along the main shopping street. The first tourist buses of the day had arrived and there were huddles of people under umbrellas. He heard Germans and Americans and Chinese, and barged through them. His breath came faster and his feet hurt on the cobblestones. Doug and Wally reported in. Nothing at the taxi rank, and questions about a Russian wanting a ride were met with shaken heads, and no sign of him at the bus station, no passengers waiting at the train station, and no staff to ask the question: "Don't suppose you saw a Russian trying to go north to Esbjerg or south towards Germany?" Did not know what to do, and felt alone with the weight of responsibility. He doubted any colleague would stand beside him and offer genuine support, and the guys on the panel of investigation would be correct and calm and would eviscerate him. Afterwards there might be a civil service reference that could get him into B grade management at Agriculture and Fisheries.

"I don't know what to do."

"Can't really help," Doug answered him.

"Needles and haystacks," Wally told him. "We're wasting our time. Pass it up the line, have to."

He had come up behind a man who seemed to have the right build and wore a bobble hat and a blue anorak with a sales tag still attached and thought that Sashcord might, could have, bought it or stolen it off a rack and was changing his appearance. He had grabbed the collar and yanked the man around and had seen the shock in a stranger's features.

Benedict told them to meet him at the car.

He went through each exchange with Sashcord recalling the growing irritation and the last words spat, and the rejoicing at the bedding of Frank, and the failure to provide a future, and everything said after the bomb scrape and the bog-standard security that went with it . . . and examined the talk of a traitor inside the Sixer building. Tossed around each phrase, and exchange, and strode the streets of a Danish tourist Mecca and had no source of comfort.

He met Doug and Wally on the bridge. They went together along the Nederdammen, around a couple of corners and could see the roof and the bright signs of the supermarket behind the parking area.

Doug said, "We'll take our share of the blame for this, Benedict. We lost him."

Wally said, "You're not alone, Benedict, not in fucking up. You have company."

They were not colleagues. The rain was steady. Dark clouds and heavy grey skies matched his mood. They crossed and a lorry roared past them, spray hit them as high as their waists. And were into the carpark and Benedict hated Denmark and a soft drink can had been dropped on the ground and he kicked it. His kids would have been impressed and his wife might have clapped, and the tin spun and bounced and rolled and he followed it, until it came to rest at their car.

Sashcord was sitting on the bonnet. He was smoking despite the rain and his face was expressionless. Benedict was not sure whether to kiss him or hit him. Doug used his zapper and unlocked the car, and Sashcord slid down off the bonnet and ducked inside.

Nothing was said, and probably nothing was worth saying.

Konstantin remained in the car. They were parked in the cemetery, close to the war graves. Many Germans were buried there and the car they had driven from Rostock had German plates.

Leonid used the map on his phone and led Anatoly. They were of that age when it was reasonable, that men should come to visit the grave of a grandfather or a great-uncle. They were able to slip away from the headstones and crossed through a hedge behind the chapel and were in a maze of wood-built summer chalets, locked and shuttered, dark and anonymous, without security cameras. They went through sodden leaves that had been blown into heaps and down paths that had not yet been cleared of weeds and on to a road.

An approaching bus started to slow, the driver thinking they were fares, but Leonid shook his head and it gathered speed and threw up spray. Neither Leonid nor Anatoly – never promoted beyond sergeant – were dressed for the weather. Jeans soaked, shoes carrying water, hair plastered down, and their short leather jackets inadequate in the downpour. They crossed the empty road and ducked into a belt of bare trees. Splashed their way along a path that was a sheen of slicked mud.

Anatoly's shoes were already wet and filthy from a tramp into a small forest to the south east of Flensburg, almost on the Danish border. There were many such places in Germany. Woodland heathland, scrub undergrowth, but with a hardcore all-weather track giving access. It had been one of the last actions of the old Soviet system's security apparatus. Weapons were buried in protected caches and it was the intention of those directing the programme that they might, eventually, be dug up if in the future there was further deterioration of the already fractured relations between the new Russia and the NATO bloc. The communications equipment was out of date, ready for the scrapheap, but the firearms would have lasted well. From the depths of a large domestic rubbish container, a single AK-47 rifle had been extracted, and a Makharov pistol, and a plastic sack, weeping moisture, had yielded 200 bullets and they had taken fifty. The rifle, the darling of all Soviet-era infantrymen, was cased in layers of water-repellent material. Konstantin had sat on the back seat of the car and had stripped the weapon, reassembled it, using his old skills. Anatoly could have done the same, and probably Leonid. It was said of the AK-47 that a ten-year-old child could master it within half an hour and that it never suffered from blockages, was not known to fail. Konstantin would shoot. Leonid would be at the wheel of the car, would wait, would hear the crack of the gunfire, would drive. Anatoly would be their eyes and ears. The fence was in front of them, without even the basic protection of a strand of barbed wire on the top or between the posts.

They could see the crown of the roof. It was the third house in the row. They recognised the chimney from the satnav image, and it had a streetlight high on a post in the front. Anatoly would have said that it was right to get away from what Leonid had called the "theatre of killing". Did not need a showboat occasion with poisons or gases or chemicals. Needed a magazine full of 7.62mm, muzzle velocity of 710 metres a second over the 25 metres of the back garden, needed the lever set to single shots, not on automatic where they kicked and flew, needed the reliability of the weapon credited to a design team led by old Sergeant Kalashnikov. The President had said that "a dog dies a dog's death" and where Anatoly had been raised, that part of cold Arctic Russia, a dog that went rogue was shot. They had fought together in Chechnya, Anatoly and Konstantin, and neither had ever considered their actions to be wrong. They killed, and afterward went for a beer, tortured in a makeshift cell, and went for another beer.

They went back to the road, ran easily across it, through the hedge and were back in the cemetery. They were intelligent men, and well led, and it was natural that they should continue play-acting. They walked along a line of German graves, and did what any distantly related mourner of a separate generation would have done and studied one stone, hugged each other, and did not doubt they would be picked up on a remote camera, or would have been seen by one of the few who ventured out into this place of quiet . . . Leonid thought it a sobering place but his sergeant was unmoved by the atmosphere of death.

The layout of the estate roads was on the phone map. They would drive once past the house, a bungalow, the third on the right side of the road, and would keep going and would leave without again passing the house. One chance. A vehicle with Copenhagen plates was parked outside, not on the forecourt but on the street, and they saw the glows of cigarettes. Enough. Did not need more. The intelligence was good and they would come again after darkness, and the failure of the Hamburg attack would be wiped clean.

More immediate was the need to find a place to change their clothes, keep warm and maybe eat.

The Brigadier was preoccupied. He was sharp with the security desk, hurried through the checks and into the atrium and took the elevator. He made a point of ignoring those he rode with. Had the right to be silent and even morose . . . He was a man bowed under the weight of the pressure on his bony shoulders. He supported the state, was its servant. He carried out instructions to the best of his considerable ability. Inside his office, a small mountain of work and a queue of meetings awaited him. Yet his thoughts would not register here, central Moscow, but on a small city on the western coast of Denmark, a country he had never visited. Unimportant, uninteresting, and yet it held the power on its territory either to thrust him higher in influence and prestige or to cast him into the gutter. He was supposed to facilitate killings on behalf of the regime, had men sidle up to him at receptions and offer a name, whisper an address . . . He was not involved in the major overseas operations, those which had backfired and brought only inconvenience. His speciality was in the recruitment of men who would stalk a prey, locate it, follow it, hit it, then withdraw and be well clear before the response. He organised, he employed. The Brigadier's own talents in marksmanship were low on any league ladder. He had never stabbed a man. Doubted that he had the strength in his fists to strangle another human being. But he was responsible. In the court of the new Tsar that night, men would seem distracted and less likely to engage in small talk at whatever function they attended and would be waiting for a short text message from him, from the Wolf, on whom they relied for sanitised murder. It could change. Could send him and his family and a minimum of suitcases scurrying to the station for a train north and then the further journey on towards Finland. Regimes buckled. He had been, many years before, when he was young and courting his wife, on a hiking and camping holiday, and they had stopped – could not have said why – at the city of Ykaterinberg and they had gone to the bulldozed site where the true Tsar and the Tsarina and their children had been shot to death. Nothing to see, but only months before the family would have believed that no harm could reach them. It could all change if the power of the mob were let loose: in Ukraine a president had been deposed and had fled for his life, and his wife's, with only her jewel box to replace the pomp and majesty of former privilege, and had scuttled for asylum and protection. And Mubarak, and Gadaffi had failed to get clear and been butchered as if on an abattoir bench, and the South African President and Mugabe had been thrown out of office, Saddam dying on the end of a rope. All had shared a look of astonishment that such ill fortune had befallen them . . . He relied on success. Relied on the quality of the intelligence passed to him. Everything about Hamburg had proved correct, and now there was a new location and a picture on his screen showed a modest home, and no doubt whoever owned it was on foreign work and needed it rented out to help his mortgage. When he sent the text, late that night, he would be rewarded with praise, or . . .

"The cake's very good," Jonas told her.

"Pleased you like it."

She was typing. Spent an inordinate amount of her day typing. He thought her the sort who needed to be busy, would be anxious if left idle. Might have been organising the team's last expenses sheet. She did not look up when he spoke but kept her eyes on the screen. Interesting to Jonas that she had bought him cake. Jonas seldom believed in the simple basics. Kindness and courtesy were foreign to him when he worked.

A question posed with a mouth half filled with the cake, and a bit of a splutter. "Do you do much of that sort of thing, cake making?"

"When I can, not often, finding the time . . ."

"Always the problem. So elusive, time. Do you make time for hobbies, Frank? . . . sorry and all that, if I may call you by that name?"

She looked up sharply, seemed to weigh him, make a judgement, then back to her keyboard.

"Hardly."

"I tinker with our caravan. Rather fond of it. We go away, my wife and I, when we can. Gets us out of London, away from work.

Not that at my level I get bothered with weekend calls. We like the south coast."

"I'm sure that's very pleasant." Polite but distant, someone who was used to speaking when spoken to.

"And take the cat with us. It's a Norwegian Forest, big and rather grumpy, but travels well."

"I'm afraid it's not possible for me to have pets, not with the hours."

"I asked you, do you have hobbies, Frank, or are they also casualties?"

Just conversation, bobbing his handkerchief at his lips in case crumbs were lodged there.

"Can't be relied on, never know when I'm going to be working late, don't get warning."

"Where I'm lucky . . . I can rely on getting my train home. We always have supper at the same time – well, except for last night. We spend many evenings checking out our next little break, usually Dorset . . . What hobby of yours might be a casualty?"

"Last thing I did was amateur dramatics. Well, stage managing really. A bit of that at Kent – did Ancient History so as much spare time as I wanted. Only getting costumes ready for the actors. There was a society in London that I was with, didn't last, but that was a few years ago."

"I have a nephew, was with an 'amdram' group in Highgate, said they were very picky, not very welcoming. Not your one, I hope."

Both Jonas and Vera were only children. Neither had a brother or sister; neither had a nephew or niece. There was no one that Jonas could call his nephew, but it was a ploy that he used and it came up well for him.

"Mine was Golders Green. Pretty much on their last legs when I joined. Happy to have anybody – but a long time ago."

And taken no further . . . He used the heel of his hand to steer the crumbs on the table into his lunch box.

"Will you promise me something, Frank?"

"If I can . . ."

"Tomorrow morning, on your way to work, whatever that God-awful hour is, would you kindly pop into that bakery, elbow your way to the front of the queue and compliment them on the quality of their cake. Quite exceptionally good . . ."

He packed away the box and the flask, removed his spectacles, pushed aside the papers on his table, and let his head drop. Might be able to doze for the remainder of the lunch break, might be able to think and plan. He imagined the matter winging towards a climax, but not yet. Thankfully, Patience was one of Jonas's virtues.

9

"An apology, Mr Symonds, is what you deserve and what you'll get." Jonas had bent his shoulders, taken on a craven pose.

Back in her place, Frank seemed intent on her laptop.

Symonds was predictably petulant. "Very deserved. I have hung around for the best part of two days waiting for you, Merrick, to sort yourself out. Anyway, good to hear that you weren't clowning at the main entrance this morning."

It had crossed Jonas's mind that Frank might be playing a card game on her screen, or doing a puzzle, and that she must have run out of expenses and holiday rosters.

"Please sit down and we'll get through this, not much more than a formality, as quickly as we can."

He waited until Symonds had sat before sitting himself. Just the notebook with a fresh page exposed and the pencil on his desk.

"I understood that it had been explained in words of one syllable to you, Merrick, that the fault is German. They screwed up, and this intrusion – you being put into our building – is an utter waste of my time and my colleagues' time, quite disrupting."

He seemed to draw in his lips then hiss through his teeth, an old trick and fancied by Jonas – as passed to him by Detective Sergeant McKeag – to show his acute sympathy with the position taken by a hostile witness, or suspect. He had in his mind the possibility that Symonds could have fitted into the Compromised box, someone who had been caught in the wrong bed, or had protected a felon and had made himself vulnerable. There was a lengthy list of opportunities for a constructive intelligence officer to utilise Compromise if the subject had shown valid weakness. He would be frightened and would see his career tumbling into dust around his ankles; usually happened when the underpants were in the same place, around the ankles.

"Well, let's get on and do some business. The sooner we start the sooner we finish, and I appreciate your courtesy."

"Agreed, because I do have other pressing items on my desk."

· He asked some boring questions, and won a little respite from the blazed annoyance. Was a bachelor, why not? Lived with his mother, and also why not? In his late thirties but had been in Resettlement for the last three of them which might be excessive – why not? A good billet to have . . . and jumbled the subject matter, and dealt with his good understanding of the Russian vernacular and in St Petersburg could have passed as coming from Irkutsk, and in Irkutsk might have been thought of as living in Volgograd, and dropped in a respectful mention of his tennis prowess. And again a defiant response, why not?

"I tell you very frankly, Mr Symonds, where I have a difficulty."

"I would have thought your difficulty, Merrick, was being inside this building, without reason, and . . ."

"If you will excuse me Mr Symonds, but what I cannot get my head around is the assumption that a member of this team, your team, would have been prepared to see colleagues – Benedict, and the two minders – blown into small pieces along with your unwanted defector. Cannot square it."

"The Germans. Look there. Do I have to put it up on a black-board so that you can comprehend the truth of it? The Germans, of course. Not deliberately, just out of carelessness. They leaked worse than sieves all through the Cold War and why should anything have changed? You want me to give you a short lecture on contemporary European security issues? Don't suppose that figures in whatever section of Thames House they dragged you out from. Would most likely have been very poor practice, but could have been deliberate. They are cosy with the Russians as an administration. Need to keep warm in winter and the Russians have the gas to heat their boilers. Is that it?"

Jonas wrote a C on the virgin page.

The man across the table from him was no longer reckoned to be a star in the firmament. His influence was declining. He was idle, coasting and had arrived in the backwater of Resettlement. Jonas doubted his opinion was asked for, and most likely ignored if it were given. It was the smugness of Symonds that convinced Jonas he was not a snout ... Probably the darling only of his mother and maybe of the rest of his tennis gang, and seemed to Jonas to harbour neither enough fear or wit to be subject to a sting operation.

"I think so, yes."

"I doubt we'll meet again, Merrick. The experience of this occasion has not been rewarding."

He was heading for the door, and Frank was up, hoping to get there first to open it for him. And a pencil stroke crossed out the letter C, and the page was torn off and thrown accurately into the bin.

Jonas said, clarity back in his voice and humility shed, "What I have learned in my work, Mr Symonds, is that the Russian agencies have talent spotters. They expect to be presented with men and women of calibre, ability. Free-thinking individuals. They are in the game for the long term, are not interested in journeymen – want only the best and the brightest ... Which means that many fail the high hurdle that would have been set. I hope the rest of your day goes well, and your own loyalty is not in any way impugned."

The door was slammed shut after him. Frank offered no indication of how she felt about the encounter but went back to her desk. He said that he thought that was enough for one day, and seemed to imply that age was now, rather rapidly, snapping at his heels. She asked if he would be working at the weekend, and he shrugged as if suggesting he did not know yet, but hoped not. He would do a bit more reading before he left to catch his train, but going a little early as he needed to fit in some shopping before getting to the station.

"Is it my turn tomorrow?"

"Well, I hadn't thought of that, but I suppose it will be, and Miss Toni."

"Then we'll have some more cake to sweeten the occasion."

Jonas nodded. "A very praiseworthy thought. But we'll not share. We'll keep the cake for ourselves."

Benedict sat in the living-room, leafing through the same magazine for the fourth time.

"Would you say I have fucked up?"

He had not been aware that the Russian stood at his open bedroom door. He jerked up, almost startled . . . Wally was on his bed and Doug was in the kitchen. It was a fair question and deserved a fair answer.

"You could say that, Igor, and I doubt you would be contradicted."

The atmosphere in the house after the return from Ribe was poisonous. Clothes that had been drenched in the rain were still going through the utility room dryer, and shoes were stuffed with old newspaper and had been placed beside a blow heater. Benedict loathed inquests while emotions were still raw; the disappearance and the panic hunt and the discovery of him waiting at the car had not yet been talked through.

"Fucked up bad?"

"And has hurt me – which is not important – and I have tried to . . ."

"Am I allowed to speak?"

"Actually, I am not in the mood for a monologue, any more self-justification – can do without your whining. I have a simple job, Igor, which is to keep you safe while my esteemed colleagues in London decide on your future. To cut you adrift or to go the whole hog and do a new identity, the full resettlement. Can we please leave it at that? And the good news is that our friend outside has been persuaded not to drag you up in front of a local magistrate. Actually, I am tired, Igor and my nerves are a bit shredded."

Benedict flipped the pages of his magazine, unable to read the words or recognise the photographs. The Russian came into the room, his wallet in his hand, showed his ID. Rather a boyish photograph. Benedict had heard the story with dull frequency, could have told it himself, but understood that he would have it inflicted on him again, except that Igor's voice was different; this time he hesitated, almost stammered.

"I told you I was destined for work with GRU. Said it was my ambition. In me from childhood, that desire . . . Crap. Not true."

Benedict's eyes jerked up from his magazine.

"I told you that my father died. True. Not from illness, from shame. Died on the end of a rope because he could not provide for his family. Did I say that before? A minor civil servant, a nobody person, in the agriculture ministry. What kept my mother and myself and him in food and clothing was not the ministry wage but bribes. Like the great majority, corruption fed and clothed us. The regime collapsed, communism seemed rejected. There was economic anarchy and the government paid him no wage, and no one needed his stamp on a permit and so the bribes dried up. We were starving almost and he was ashamed and so he hanged himself. That was my father, and I was aged six years . . . It is a story of modern Russia but they do not like to tell it often."

Doug brought in mugs of tea.

"My mother obtained work in a bank and she did not need me so I was offloaded. She had the job, I think, because she slept with a manager. That is good to know, your mother has found employment because she knew when to open her legs, but a child is a responsibility and can be dumped. Where to? To my grandparents . . . A village outside the ring road, the A-108, close to the M4 intersection. And my grandfather died, a victim of the struggle to retain self-respect. I was above average at the High School because I had realised that to survive I could depend only on myself. Did you have love around you, Benedict? If you did, you were fortunate. I did not. My youth is a story of survival. Fuck other people. Did I say this before?"

He had not said it before. That would have been the fault of the debrief agenda. Most of it had been set by Monty. If Benedict now took a handwritten note of what he was hearing, painted over the old papers he had submitted, then it would be an open door of admission that he had screwed up, and he would be in line for the brickbats. Benedict shook his head: no, he had not said it before.

"I said to you, my mother had gained a junior place in a bank. I think the bank did a scam to clean money for GRU officers. They like dynasties, continuity, so good to bring family in. I am at High School, am alone, perhaps lonely. I am called to Moscow. I meet a man in the bank, could have been the guy sharing my mother's bed. So, he is my new 'father' and the future is decided. I am told I have a place at the GRU's own Military-Diplomatic Academy, but after a guaranteed position at the Army Engineering School . . . Do I argue? Of course I do not. Do I say I want time to think about it? I do not. I am on a conveyor belt. You are disappointed with me because I have little information . . . I don't have information because I am a bad fit in the organisation and I have no ability to rise and to pretend. You want to hear more?"

The bombast gone, the arrogance binned. Each drank from his mug. Doug stood in the doorway and listened, and Wally, half-dressed, had come out of the bedroom and both recognised the sea change. Benedict in the failing light saw an uncertain man and the pillars that had kept him erect seemed to collapse.

"Keep it going, Igor."

"I do that and again am on secondment from GRU – but that place stays open – and I am with marines, near to Special Forces. I do not want that. I am not a thug, I do not enjoy the prospect of killing. You know, Benedict that we have Afghan vets now begging on the street. That is how a grateful regime rewards those who have fought for their country. Tells them to get lost and not moan about their traumas and stress disorders. Me, I now have the chance to milk the system, am on the inside, and . . ."

Too late, the truth of the Sashcord history would be told. Benedict settled for the long haul and as the light slipped away so the screen showing the garden beyond the drawn blinds behind him seemed to lighten and gain greater clarity. He listened.

Time for a last reconnaissance. Konstantin and Anatoly would be in the woodland at the back, Leonid taking the street and the front of the house for himself.

His vehicle was in a short cul-de-sac around a corner of the street and out of sight of the front of the bungalow where a vehicle was parked. He had passed it, heading for the main road, and it had been simple for him to evaluate the car. The address had come from the HQ where normally he worked, the glass-house. The vehicle had heavily tinted windows and it was not possible for him to see the faces inside. Two cigarette ends glowed even through the coloured glass, and the rain was heavy enough to require the wipers to be used regularly. He had walked up the street and past the car, carrying two shopping bags, both empty. He wore a beanie and had the collar of his heavy-duty waterproof anorak turned up, and his jeans and his lightweight walking boots were soaked. He had not gazed at the car, had not exposed his face to those inside. The firearms would be in the car. Might be more weaponry in the house but the interior was darkened and no lights burned. The car that had been parked up on the forecourt was no longer there. It would be back, with the target, or the protection vehicle would not still have been in place.

Leonid approached the car from the far pavement, and was rewarded when a window came down and a fag end was thrown out, and then the window was closed. A female hand, and he thought he noticed the shoulder of a bullet-resistant vest. Retracing his journey, in the dripping rain, his shopping bags were now weighed down. They would have thought he had been to the shops on the main road. The bags bulged, one with two half bricks from a collapsing garden wall and the other with three plant pots. He had gained confirmation that the intelligence given him was of the best standard. He carried on walking and disappeared around the corner, satisfied.

The mistake the boys had made with the registration plate for the Mercedes in Hamburg was a detail he might well have missed himself. Not that he carried blame, which had been passed down the ladder and Konstantin and Anatoly had fielded it. It would not be spoken of again because a second opportunity had been presented ... Leonid thought it remarkable that this quality of intelligence was available. He would be rewarded. By the end of the night, a select few would have been told his name and the degree of success he had achieved, and he would prosper. It was the way of the regime. Success brought status . . . Failure could dump a career. It would be an important evening, and night down into the small hours. Leonid had faith in the boys. The "boys" were both well past fifty years of age. Good men and loyal. Leonid had commanded an infantry company in Syria and had been near the front line twice when the black flag people had attacked under cover of darkness. But only *near* the front line and there would always have been a screen of at least platoon strength between himself and the forward bunkers of the position. Had heard the explosions, when the enemy had used armoured vehicles loaded with gelignite and driven by suicide kids and had seen the tracer rounds, red tips flying in straight low lines. The difference between himself and Konstantin and Anatoly was that they would have been inside the bunkers, first line of defence, first among the units to take casualties. They both had a knowledge of death: meting it out, seeing it drop the guy standing or crouching next to them. They too would now be on a final reconnaissance and would be slurping along the footpath between the trees, tying knotted bright plastic strips on branches to guide them when the light had gone.

Leonid, a full colonel, felt good, confident. He reckoned the strike would be surgical, fast, and praise would shower on him. He had not been in the actual team, the night that Nemtsov was hit, six years back. Just the reserve group. His people were not needed. A dissident, a scumbag, walking with his woman, and the joke was that the killing took place right outside the Kremlin walls, which had as high security as any part of the capital. The target's phone had been hacked and the direction he would walk was known. Excellent intelligence. Nemtsov had been shot and the fire brigade were out within an hour of the corpse being shifted, hosing the street, cleaning away the blood. Crowds had gathered and left flowers, but a helicopter had flown low the next morning, had hovered, scattering the flowers. Leonid had thought that was a class gesture. This would be a good strike and he would enjoy the praise . . . Failure was for losers, for others.

It was the end of Maggie's working day. She had asked no favours, had done the statutory hours, and a couple more because of her late start. And the paper for her boss, his assessment of the Armata T-14 main battle tank, was completed, had been forwarded to him.

"Grand, was hoping to catch you. Just a few minutes of your time, please."

Maggie doubted that the meeting was by chance, and doubted also that Lucinda relied on accidents for a contact. Might have been waiting twenty minutes outside the work area used by the attachés.

"Actually, I'm on my way to rescue the crèche minders from Hector. Overdue."

"Then we'll walk together."

Down corridors, past offices that were shutting down as the evening wore on, and out into the gardens where the chill was settling, and Lucinda talked.

"Heard about your drive north. Extraordinary feat of stamina. Heard what you found up there. Of course that sort of caper, getting through the border defences, was possible, with a rather large pinch of luck when the full resources of the Service were involved, and a multi-headed planning group. You are thinking that alone you might recreate the mission that lifted Gordievsky out – Pimlico, it was called – but it was huge and our little chap is nowhere near that league. What I heard was that you were now being *sensible*. Excellent word and so patronising, and you might be justified in administering a sharp kick to my ankle for using it. Which I might do again. You are being sensible and that works well for us all. I also heard that you had expressed interest in a particular military unit . . . Disposal of ordnance, making IEDs safe, clearing old minefields. Don't think I'd fancy that, but for you I'll make damn sure it happens . . . This weekend you'll do the meet, you'll have a brush and pick up what he brings, and you'll tell him the way the real world works, and see him back on the train to wherever it is the poor little beggar lives, and we'll be watching your back. Not entirely nice for you but it's better than a magazine of Kalashnikov's finest up your bum, and the wire gripping you. Everything will be taken care of because you have been a valuable colleague, and a sensible one. As I say not entirely nice but a rather better option."

They were at the door of the crèche portacabin. Brightly lit inside, heaters burning overtime and some of the windows misted. A couple of the minders had stayed behind and were playing with Hector on a rug.

"You are good at using me."

"Of course I am, and that is how the big world – mine and yours – works. Not much point kicking against the pricks, best to accept it."

"That's a promise?"

"My recommendation went off at lunchtime. It will happen . . . I understand where you want to be, Maggie. My first overseas jaunt was Sarajevo. Miserable, and rather a sad little place, but we were looking at a link between organised crime and the rip-off monies for reconstruction grants in the city of Mostar. I went down there three or four times, and there was a boy I rather fancied . . . Trouble was he was more interested in leading a team digging up mines than in paying attention to me. His idea of a picnic was a couple of bottles of water, sandwiches, yesterday's bread, and to sit on a hillside – well back and safe – and watch the guys working on mine clearance. Spooky stuff because neither of the goons trying to slaughter each other had bothered to map where they had laid mines, mostly anti-personnel, horrible maiming things, and also the devices can shift when the rain or snow makes the ground sodden. They go walkabout. I used to watch the men on their hands and knees and working in corridors marked out by strips of tape. One had a dog with him, and they were both veterans – Angola, Mozambique, Rwanda, then Croatia, and the last posting was Bosnia. He had total faith in his dog which sniffed ahead of him and was on a guide rope. Very tense, and watching it was rather addictive. What was important was the good quality of the field as grazing land, and all over the place the farmers needed to get back to work, know their ground was safe. They'd have a celebration, food and too much *slivovicz* when the guy finishcd, and would fctc him. The sort of work one should be proud of achieving. It *will* happen for you, the transfer."

"Sounds a bit of a bribe."

"Sounds, I think, like a sensible solution. One question. What'll happen to Hector when you're off training and deploying?"

Maggie said, "I thought his father might look after him occasionally, would treat him as if he had a new spaniel to train."

In fact she was pretty damn certain that her mother would welcome having Hector to fuss around, and her father. It hurt to be called sensible but she would survive.

Alexei cleared his room of everything that was personal, important, to him. A photograph of his mother in a cheap wood frame went into the bag and his two best shirts which she had given him. His favourite jacket and best trainers and two most read books, Pasternak's *Dr Zhivago* and Chekhov's *The Cherry Orchard*, his laptop and his best spectacles and a spare. And his better socks and underwear. Much more than he would need for two nights on the train and one at his mother's home.

Coming back to his apartment, kneeling to check the single strand of auburn hair, he had realised this was the last time he would do that routine. The next day he'd go direct from work to the station in Kirov and take the train west . . . and on the Sunday night when he would normally be back here and getting ready for the coming week he would be . . . He paused. Where? In the arms of the girl, in freedom, and without a witness other than, perhaps, little Hector. Would be with Maggie. Or on the concrete floor of a cell, three metres by two metres. Which? His hands were clumsy as he packed and nerves made him sweat . . . There would be no farewells in the block. None of those with whom he exchanged greetings in the mornings, or where he might go to beg milk if he had run out, or to warn of an expected parcel delivery, would know of his going until the FSB men came and used sledgehammers on his door. Then, they would all have a story to tell of him, and none would praise him. His bag was only two-thirds filled, and Alexei realised how empty was his life, and that all he would leave behind – success or failure – was his mother. He pulled the zip. Later he would go to a cashpoint and draw out most of his account, and would go drinking. Would have no need for roubles whatever happened.

Jonas was sitting on a bench in the gardens, the AssDepDG beside him. The senior man's new aide, a pleasant girl, was with them, holding over them a wide umbrella, one that carried a soft drink manufacturer's name and logo. Once the garden had been a cemetery but now lawns and flowerbeds covered the plots. It was where, most mornings, Jonas took his *cappuccino* and his Danish, and drank, ate, pondered, before going up to the third floor.

Jonas said, speaking through the cigarette smoke blown into his face, "They are a really quite unpleasant group of people, the Resettlement team, and arrogant, but I am not yet convinced whether any of them are guilty of betraying the defector. My assessment is that we'll know in the next twenty-four hours. I am not a fighting man, and God forbid ever will be, but I'd assume the opposition will hit again as soon as is possible for them. They will have the people close to theatre and if the leak came from here then they will want to utilise such intelligence as is available. If there is no strike then an assumption may be made that the team's innocence is almost proven. It's the critical time, the coming hours . . . They would be peeved at the Hamburg fiasco, would want to regain their laurels as quickly as feasible. Don't know what scale of victory parade they stage on Kuznetsky Most for top-level patriots but they'll be looking to be there. If they have a location then they will hit, go in hard and go in fast."

"Our people there, forget the little toad, aren't they light on the ground?"

"Are and are not. Don't wish to be pedantic, but depends what we want. Put the Household Cavalry around this bungalow and no attack will materialise and the bad boys will float away and we will have achieved, temporarily, the safety of the defector, and we will not know the source of the leak. Keep the level of security where it is, current numbers, and they will come – if they have the address."

"Our terms of reference requires that we keep this man safe."

"I am almost confident we can do that."

The AssDepDG flicked away his cigarette. Was rewarded with a soaking. The girl ducked away with the umbrella, went to the smouldering fag end, picked it up with blatant distaste and binned it.

"It's what they do with a goat, isn't it? They tether it out, and a big beast – even bigger than that cat of yours, Jonas – is attracted to come and do the necessary."

"Something like that."

"And the people we have there? Team leader and the boys, and the laddie they are charged to keep beyond harm's reach. What about them?"

"Probably they'll be fine. Something like that."

The rain made rivers of the paths around the muddied lawn area and the beds. It was a dark place, had never been a friendly garden, and the stones accentuated its morbid gloom. Jonas knew the history: Parishioners had paid for armed guards so that the recently buried were not exhumed and carted off to the hospitals' anatomy classes. The gardener worked at raking paths and collecting rubbish. Jonas thought about what the soldier, the gardner had given him and reminded himself: *If they didn't want the job done then they would not have asked me to come on board.* But the burden seemed to weigh more heavily on him.

"If the hit happens, Jonas, then what?"

"Dependent on a further failure. Little scope for us if their mission is successful. If it fails, and they must come one more time then I am confident, because it will be on our terms. And we narrow the field, have only a few players, and squeeze out the identity of the one that matters. I'll go beyond that and . . ."

"Was hoping that you'd go the extra mile, Jonas."

"I'd want authority, quite an amount of it. All communication from Denmark comes to me, not the Resettlement people."

"And another goat to tether?"

"Same goat, but a considerable amount of authority, and the communication monopoly – that's what I would want."

He had a train to catch and was up off the bench. The veteran leaned on his rake, the rain dribbling on his forehead, and would have assumed, rightly, that Jonas and the AssDepDG were at the old game of acting God and playing with the lives of others, and he might have spat in disgust into a puddle.

"I'll have an answer for you in the morning."

"Thank you. It'll be time enough. Early morning."

He would need to hurry if he were to catch the 17.49 and be back in time for his supper. Usually on Thursday evenings Vera did a meat pie which Jonas always enjoyed . . . If his prognosis was correct and his demand for authority justified, and communications, then early the next morning would be time enough. He headed on to the bridge, and would use the time as he walked to the station to consider which of them was his premier suspect.

The watchers fanned out.

The Secret Intelligence Service was little different to any Whitehall ministry as the afternoon was chased down by evening. The workers came out in a surge and it was one of the many skills of the A Branch people that they could recognise even in the swarm of movement those who they were tasked to follow. They had all sorts on duty, but none over 5 feet and 9 inches in height because then they might be noticed. The targets were identified and the tracking began. They scattered, and radios reported that each Tango was accounted for. The size of the commitment would have told each of them that a crisis approached. Came rushing.

Dark in the living-room and only the kitchen light on and the tea gone cold and the supper not cooked, and the only sound was Igor's voice and the only movement was the image of the rat crossing the width of the screen.

"I was married. Not for love . . . marriage was a necessary part of advancement in GRU. I am twenty-seven years old and she is the daughter of a colonel. It is a pretence. They think it makes men more reliable, more dependable, if they are married. At the time she was chosen for me, I was shagging the daughter of a brigadier, but she was not for marrying, out of my league. We had one daughter . . . You want to see the picture of my daughter? Perhaps not, perhaps already I showed it you. Ten times, twenty times. I show the picture of her wearing a party dress, but do not show you the picture of her wearing the hospital smock. She is sick, and . . ."

They moved as quietly as they were able along the narrow path, slid several times on the mud, but kept upright and had the street lights above the roots to guide them.

Had they been footballers, coming out of the home dressing-room in the Otkrytie arena, used by Spartak Moscow, Konstantin and Anatoly would have punched fists with Leonid, then hugged each other. Nothing like that, only a growl of encouragement from their colonel, only a mutter about the "shit awful rain", only a query as to whether the assault rifle had the safety applied, only a curse when they stepped out of the car, and chucked away the last fag end. They had disappeared into the trees. Leonid would keep the engine ticking over, just the hazard lights on, and would be able to speed away even as the doors closed on them. They would be running when they came back, and would have left all hell behind them . . . and what else to know? As good to know as anything was that a trawler from the fishing port in Kaliningrad was now inside Danish territorial waters and was making slow progress and their radio, surprisingly sophisticated for an ordinary fishing vessel, would be closely monitored. But that was for after the hit. It was hard to avoid debris as they went in the dark through the woodland and scrub. Impossible to avoid little fallen branches, damp or rotten, and Konstantin had the rifle under his anorak to shield it from the weather, and Anatoly stumbled and cursed and the stink, immediate, told both men that they had trodden on prime dog shit.

It should not have been a requirement for Konstantin to keep
the old AK-47 dry and clean. It had a reputation of being fit for
purpose whether it had been dumped in a lake for a week or
buried in mud for a month. But, on matters that were important
to him – using a rifle, killing, earning his bread – Konstantin was
a careful man. In the car, he had emptied the loaded magazine,
wiped the inside and then had placed each bullet, 7.62 calibre,
back in its place, armed it, checked the safety. He was more
comfortable with the weapon staying dry, but that was a mark of
the man.

Anatoly led, his arms in front of him, trying to ward off low
branches, and came close to the fence, close enough to recognise
the outline of the chimney stack.

He would have preferred to have been on a Moscow pavement.
Would have wanted to have communications in his ear, warning
him of the approach of the target, readying himself and seeing
traffic on the roads and pedestrians hurrying by, and knowing that
no impediment – least of all an alien legal system – would stand on
the pavement and block him. Would have wanted to know that –
on a Moscow street – he was free from the risk of prosecution or
imprisonment or of being brought to the ground, life ebbing,
through law-enforcement gunfire. He could hear behind him
Konstantin's breath wheezing in his throat, audible despite the
balaclava across his face . . . No hugging and no punched fists
when they had left the car . . . just two old guys, pretending they
still had youth on their side.

They had reached the fence. Two metres high, good-quality
creosoted wood panels. Anatoly had a view of the upper part of
the big plate-glass window and next door, on the right, a small dog
yapped as if it had identified them and the outdoor light gave
them a better sight of the window, covered but with movement
beyond it, like a shadow passing. Konstantin wriggled the weapon
out from under his anorak, his fingers tracing the metalwork. Had
already done the noisy action of cocking it, metal scraping on
metal, but needed to be satisfied that the safety was still in place,
and the magazine firm, and the selector lever at the position for

aimed single shots. They were not as good as they had been, not as cold and as calculated and as merciless as they had once been.

Anatoly whispered, "You all right, you good?"

Konstantin hissed back, "All right, good. What the fuck else would I be?"

"You know the Spartak team?"

"I do . . . Why should I know the Spartak team? . . . Why?"

"I think in the tunnel they hug and encourage. You know why they have that name?

"Should I fucking know?"

"There was a gladiator. Rome, before Christ. Led a slave revolt He was Spartacus. Our team is named after him. You should know that."

"Okay, I know that. Did he become king or emperor? Was he the new Tsar?"

"He lost, Konstantin. I think they crucified him."

"Fuck you, a bag of laughs, great company. We do it, with your slave or without him. We go get him."

Anatoly pinched Konstantin's thigh, alerted him. Locked his fingers together and made a stirrup for Konstantin's right foot. Heaved him up and his weight surprised him and the loss of his own strength astonished him. But Konstantin was up and swung his other leg and was astride the top of the fence, and maybe his privates were exposed to the sharp tops of the fence palings, and maybe they were crushed. Konstantin, holding the rifle, had only one hand to steady himself. For a moment he teetered on the fence, his clothing tearing and Anatoly heard the impact as Konstantin went over, bushes breaking his fall.

Konstantin's scream broke the quiet of the garden. Anatoly, gasping from the effort of lifting him, could see nothing of the garden and not much of the back window. Imagined his friend had turned his ankle on landing, or bitched his knee ligaments or twisted his pelvis.

"What happened?"

"I stepped on a rat, didn't see – fuck, it squealed. Nearly shat myself."

"Just go do it."

Anatoly clung to the top of the fence and the wood cut into his hands and he saw Konstantin raise his rifle to the aim position and begin to lumber forward. And he readied himself for when his good friend came back, the smell of cordite cloaking them and their ears deafened, and the job done . . . Saw Konstantin stop and hold the weapon's aim steady, and he held his breath.

"I don't pretend to be honest. Some do, usually the most corrupt. I like a few good things in my life but I was in Damascus, a liaison team with those bastards who are close to the ruling family. They were shit, animals, and I despised them – and despised the war there. Not a pacifist, but hated it, and we were achieving nothing, you understand, nothing . . . What the hell . . ." And his voice had died.

First they heard the rat's squeal. Then they saw a figure on the screen. Then they reacted, together, silently as the console lights went into berserk patterns. The rifle was up and readied.

The Russian grabbed Benedict, heaved him out of his chair, and flung him face down on to the floor and the carpet pile was in his face and he was six feet from the screen. A weight cannoned down on him, pushed the air from his lungs. He realised that Igor, the one they queued up to bad-mouth, the one who had no supporters and no friends, had covered him, was protecting him. He gasped to breathe . . . and Wally was crouched by the chair, used it as cover, and Doug was standing to one side, his hand gun pointing at the floor while he went through the fast cocking proce-dure with a noise that was almost deafening, then went to what the boys called Isosceles Stance.

They had a clear view of him on the screen and he was white-tinted: the body, the clothing, the balaclava, and the rifle he held, and which he did not fire. Benedict knew about the AK-47. Had had his fill of the weapon in Iraq. It was the rifle a ten-year-old kid could master in five, ten, minutes. It did not fire. He was trapped by the Russian's body and waited for the din to explode around them and for the glass to come blasting in through the blind and would see the rifle kick up when it fired, and might feel pain if the aim was low and might feel the Russian jerk aside if it were higher, and might hear the booming crack, like saucepans bashed together, when Doug shot back. Could see by the man's feet, on the uncut grass of the back lawn, that the body of the rat writhed and it could not move but every few seconds it screamed piteously. Beyond the marksman was the fence and a face looking over it. Might have been saying: "*What the fuck's going on, why don't you just fucking shoot?*" Must have been saying that, except that Benedict heard nothing and could not read the lips because the face was covered by a mask. A good and satisfactory answer was given. No shot fired because the assault rifle had malfunctioned. A flurry of movement. The sight of a bullet ejected, flying clear, and the light from the next door back patio caught the shininess of the brass, and the weapon cocked again, aimed again, and a finger squeezing. And failing. And a repeat of the process.

Doug said, quiet and almost calm. "He's screwed up, he has a jam."

"A Klash jamming. Never heard of that."

He could sense the fury now, as precious short seconds were eaten into, and the pristine white figure on the screen made a last attempt to fire. Did the ejection, did the cocking, did the aiming, and then the squeezing ... and no response from his weapon. Would have known that he had used up time and that the rat's cry and the sounds of the weapon parts' motions would have alerted them inside. Might have seen through the lowered blind the fast movements inside, shadow shapes going down. One last time, and the weapon did not fire. The figure lowered the barrel of the rifle and then stood irresolute and there might have been a call from behind him and he turned towards the fence ... and Wally had moved fast, crouching, into the hallway making for the bank of light switches. He threw the lot of them, would not have remembered which worked the patio floodlight.

The back garden lit up. The screen was failing but maintained enough clarity to show the guy's hand come up to shield his eyes from the brilliance of the bulb. He turned, lumbering and staggering towards the fence. An arm reached over it, hands locked and the guy was hauled up.

Benedict watched the screen and Wally switched off the patio light, now plunging the pair into darkness. The fence buckled, swayed and looked ready to collapse. The guy fell, landed on his backside on the grass. Doug remained at Isosceles, legs apart, feet level, his upper body leaning forward, both arms fully extended and both hands locked on the pistol, his concentration intact. He had not fired. The weight on Benedict eased and the Russian slid clear of him. The guy at the fence was up again, the hand from the other side snaked back down to him, and the panel shook some more, and bent some more, and the guy was over. Air flooded back into Benedict's chest.

"Well, fancy that," Wally said.

"I'd not have believed it," Doug said.

"An AK jamming, never heard of it."

Doug said "Seen everything now, but I'll offer this. Won't have been the rifle, will have been the ammunition."

"How long was that?" Wally asked.

"About forty-five seconds my guess . . ." Doug made the pistol safe and slipped it back into the seat of his trousers, wedged it behind his belt.

Benedict turned to the Russian who seemed calm enough and had not spoken. "You fine, you good?"

"Not bad . . . I tell you, it was not the rifle that suffered the mechanism failure. It is superb, the best, it does not malfunction. The only time you cannot shoot is if the ammunition has not been cared for, then there can be expansion from damp and . . ."

Dry laughter, might be one for an archive anecdote, Benedict thought. Sashcord had been confronted with a Russian engineering fuck-up – which saved his life, perhaps – but was not prepared to criticise the factory that produced an icon weapon. Would be a nice story in two decades time if Benedict were still there, hanging by his fingernails but still employed, and doing an after-dinner chat for Sixers, singing for his supper. Seemed to have been an hour of his life, but less than a minute.

Benedict realised that he had ceded the leadership role. A few words muttered between Wally and Doug, and then Doug had gone into the kitchen, had unlocked the back door and appeared on the screen. There was a wheelbarrow on the edge of the patio and leaning against it was a long-handled shovel. Benedict watched. He saw Doug stride across the long grass and he reached the rat . . . difficult to read a rat's expression when it was about to be sent to its Maker with a swing of a heavy shovel, and it had lost the use of its back legs and could not move. It was dispatched. One good clean strike. Benedict wondered if Doug was the sort of soldier, back in his youth, who would have put a severely wounded enemy out of his pain. The fence was tested and the posts had held.

Sashcord lit a cigarette.

When Doug came back into the kitchen, he had gone to the fridge and lifted out a can for each of them. He could not think of anything that should be said, ought to be said. The others took a cue from him. The Russian drank fast, and it was he who broke the mood. Said he was going outside.

Benedict had considered thanking him. Probably ought to have done. Would have been a proper show of manners to have thanked him for draping his body across Benedict's. A little late in the day for an argument and a church clock far away was chiming midnight – and he had not the appetite for argument. Benedict nodded at Wally, and it was unlikely that his opinion mattered because Wally had already opened the door for the Russian . . . and Benedict had the sudden realisation of what had *not* happened. The door was left wide and he could see the path and the car at the kerb beyond it, where Sashcord and Wally were headed. All changed, as a poet had written, changed utterly. Sashcord reached the car and a window came down and the street light showed the PET girl's face and she looked warily at the Russian as he crouched at her window and the rain battered him . . .

What had *not* happened was intervention by the Danes. They had in their car both single-shot and automatic weapons, gas and flash/bang grenades, bulletproof vests and helmets, and they had not come: not alerted, left in ignorance. Which told Benedict something about close protection and that it had been the Russian – who he had verbally attacked in a mood of cold anger – who had tried to do the necessary, cover him, look after him. No doubt a single sentence from Sashcord and the woman nodded, and the window went up and he and Wally returned to the house. Another lesson for Benedict, and one for which he should not have needed a refresher course. "Look after yourself and don't expect the local employed help to put themselves on the line." He would do a succinct report to VX. No panic, no hysteria. Would let them have the job of locating the source of the leak . . . And the future options seemed limited, or sold out. He found he was shaking. More beers called for.

Sashcord asked; "And they came again, and the weapon malfunctioned, and will come again, and again – so what is your answer?"

"Jonas, it's an awful lot of money."

"If it is what we have to pay, then we have to pay it – cannot *not* pay it."

"I didn't think it would be that expensive, really I didn't."

The fault, of course, though both would think it, would not be laid against the cat. Olaf slept between them. Jonas would not have contemplated blaming the cat for the depredation carried out by a solitary mouse. Not even a family, with a nest, but only one of them the electrician had said after his survey of the damage. Several times, before spring had come, the cat had been shut in the caravan and given the chance to sniff out, then cull, any marauding vermin wintering there. The sum quoted for the repair would be in excess of £800. They lived frugally, Jonas and Vera, and it would not have been an embarrassment to pay out such a sum, only that a call for that level of expenditure came from where Jonas dreaded most – "a clear blue sky". He was averse to the unexpected, although his working life fed from incidents coming without warning from such a sky.

Neither had slept, and the presence of the cat, heavy and unwilling to shift, had not helped. Only rarely did Vera feel the necessity of discussing a domestic hurdle with her husband at this time in the morning, still two more of the small hours left before his alarm trilled. If he had not been wide awake already he would, with gentleness, have urged her to turn over, face the wall, try to get to sleep. Difficulties, major and minor, seemed to shriek in his ear for settlement, and this was the crucial night and by the morning he would know how grave were those difficulties.

"It is not a problem, Vera. You call him in the morning and urge him to get the work done, and in the best possible time."

"You would not have thought it, would you?"

"What, Vera, would I not have thought?"

"That amount of damage."

"It is, sadly, what they are known for."

"One little mouse. So ordinary and so nondescript."

"Yes, if you say so, Vera."

"Just one mouse, a little grey creature, and the havoc it can create . . . eight hundred pounds of chaos. So small, so inoffensive, barely a meal that Olaf would have noticed. I have it fixed in my mind, a grey mouse, and quite a wretched and disproportionate nuisance. Night, Jonas, and I hope I haven't woken you too much."

He would not sleep, not now, not after what she had said, and his mind spun in a turmoil.

10

"Thank you, Vera. Thank you indeed . . ."

He had paused on the doorstep.

". . . Very helpful. Most grateful."

There was a bold wind blowing the length of their avenue in Raynes Park and it flapped the branches of the trees, but the rain had lifted and scudded clouds over him. In the hall she had tightened the scarf around his throat. Quite bracing. She had looked surprised that he had stopped to make such a remark, and had said that the sandwiches were the usual ones for a Friday, tuna and mayonnaise spread, and his Braeburn apple, and a filled flask, milk and no sugar.

He had corrected her. "Not my lunch, Vera, but your thought as expressed in the night. The grey mouse. The line will be pursued. So good of you to trigger the thought. The grey mouse, so cogent. Can't stop. See you this evening."

He had hurried away, walking with the brisk stride that indicated clarity was reaching into his thoughts. He had taken the train and could have sworn that a few of the regulars had started to look the length of the platform, wondering where he was, why he was a minute late. Then into London and he had been flicking on his phone and sorting out numbers, and contacts that might now be dead, or dementia victims or might, God willing, still be sharp as pinheads . . . and other numbers.

Had rung Frank, had told her he was delayed. She had said that Toni was already in VX and awaited their conversation. She would have to wait, he had said. Not a matter of negotiation and no apology offered. He had studied a brief messsge copied across to his secure phone and sent to him from a safe house, supposedly but not actually, in a northern suburb of the Danish coastal town of Esbjerg. Had liked the content as much as the style of it. Calm and matter of fact and Jonas always believed brevity to be a virtue. *Jonas Merrick, Have been instructed to brief you and not my team. Survived an inconclusive hit attempt last night. Intruder in back garden of property but seems his AK malfunctioned, and attempt abandoned. Await guidance. Benedict.* He had a photograph and a file on Benedict, knew of him as resourceful and unlikely to panic, liked the sound of him and liked his pedigree, and knew also that much now would depend on the man's ability to 'carry on, keep calm'.

Out of the station, he set off across Lambeth Bridge, felt a queasiness when he looked down and saw that he was far above a tug pulling a line of barges through the arches against a rip tide, froth spilling from the tug's bows, and around the spray was the dark depth of water: looked lifeless, seemed hostile, and probably was both. Was halfway over when he called a man he knew only as Brian, knew him as security officer of the Embassy on Kastelsvaj in Copenhagen, and spoke quietly and hoped he could be heard over the wind's whistle and the shrieks of gulls.

"I am Jonas, Brian. You will have been told of me and the responsibilities now vested in me. The reasons for such peculiar procedures are to do with a leak . . . You were formerly with Two Para. I cannot conceive that you are in any way involved in such acts . . . Enough. You need to take some serious gardening equipment to our friends, for use by Doug and Wally. I am not talking about hand forks and trowels but a couple of heavy spades and a good tough-duty rake, and weedkiller – the spray sort. You might need an overnight bag – also some heavy boots – and you'll spend enough time to get the allotment into shape. Of course you have a garden shed on the premises with that equipment stored and ready to use. Not for local consumption, but you should be on the road as soon as is possible. Good luck, Brian, and I wish you well."

Had then, approaching the end of the bridge and still setting a good pace, called the man who had messaged him.

"Benedict? This is Jonas. Pleased to speak to you . . . We have limited time and I will be to the point. We anticipate that the failed attack will cause those people to reflect, regroup, consider further options. We anticipate also such a process will take up to twenty-four hours, a day and a night. Early tomorrow you will be told the details of your next movement. Your Danish colleagues should be informed of your intentions only at the last moment before departure. It is important for many reasons, Benedict, that you follow this guidance. You will have further experienced support joining you within the next hours from Copenhagen. I hear you ask, with absolute justification, how long before this matter is resolved. I am suggesting that by Sunday evening we will have reached a conclusion but am grateful that you do not quiz me. Also, Benedict, I appreciate that you do not interrogate me as to the personal safety of those you lead, and of the individual you are tasked to protect, and of yourself. You will have my best effort and that is the sole guarantee that I am offering . . . We are all, believe me, playing for high stakes. Thank you."

He rang off, crossed the road and went to his café. Was greeted by staff with cheerful smiles, who seemed to be pleased that he was once again with them and, without him needing to place the order, his Danish was in a bag and his *cappuccino* in a disposable beaker. He walked the few yards to the gate into the gardens. He sipped at his coffee, nibbled at his pastry, and waited for his protector to join him. With no umbrella shield over his head he would long ago have been booted out of Thames House, given a few months grace after the affair of Winston Gunn, then shown the door and his card electronically deleted. The wind blew around the trees that marked the park's boundaries but he was well wrapped against it, a good coat and a fine scarf and a tweed jacket and a sleeveless pullover, his shirt buttoned at the neck and his tie knotted, and his trilby well down over his head, but he shivered. Could not halt the shake of his hand and was disappointed that he slopped his coffee though the plastic lid was secure. Out from a shed came the man, reputedly a veteran, damaged from combat, who was supposed to find a degree of solace from working in the garden. Was that how Jonas Merrick might end his days? The equivalent would be staying at home, talking with his cat, humouring Vera when she was not able to escape to the gallery, and at weekends hitching up the caravan and finding another site to visit, rain or shine . . . His paper filing system in ring binders, would have been shredded, and the memory of his work would likely linger for no longer than the time the medal and the bar stayed in Vera's drawer. He bit at his lip, felt the flesh sag. The man had a rake and used it on the few dead leaves that had materialised since the previous day. He felt a little ashamed of himself for submitting to the fear – kept his vigil and waited.

"I am married, I have a child. Anyone has an interest, anyone's business that I have a wife and a child who is sick? I get posted to Lebanon, I told you, and act as a link between our forces in Damascus and the Hezbollah leaders in Beirut. That is boring, exceptionally boring, until I meet the daughter of an Italian cultural attaché, and I sleep with her and then life is not boring . . . it is what I do, and my work is satisfactory and not in any way remarkable. I come home. I spend time in Moscow and people drop their voices and seem sombre in the corridors of the head-quarter building, and they ask me, and are strangers to me, how is my daughter. I do not know them. Their question does not fortify me, they want only to learn about me and examine me, and make an opinion as to how great is my suffering and therefore am I a GRU officer who is worth cultivating or not worth wasting time with. And I work on analysis of restricted circulation papers of NATO, not secret but not for general release, and I learn about the plan they have for resupply in the event of escalating tension. That is how many Meals-Ready-to-Eat should be stockpiled for a corps of 100,000 men, and I have to take into account the Muslim troops refusing pork and vegan troops refusing meat, and how many condoms they require and how many sanitary towels. I am a master of the requirements of resupply, and I deal in every free moment with the medical needs of our daughter who is a sweet child and not particularly fond of me, adores her mother.

"I am sent to the north, to the Murmansk *oblast*. If you are lucky you have never been there. It is difficult to know whether Murmansk is worse in the summer or in the winter. Twenty-three hours of daylight in summer and twenty-three hours of darkness in winter. I am supposed, and I told you already, to cultivate a Norwegian officer on their frontier patrol group and we think we might recruit him. I told you and I am sure you pass it to the Norwegians, dull and boring people – but you know that. I am there when they have the catastrophe with the aircraft carrier, the *Admiral Kuznetsov* which almost sinks when the dry dock pumps fail – another fucking power failure, and there are many – and they also have a fire, and we are supposed to go about our work with long, sad-face expressions because it is a national disaster, a blow to Russia's dignity. I could not have cared less. What made Murmansk tolerable was that I met a girl from the secretariat of FSB. FSB, in general, are shit people, this girl was the exception. She screws well and is a fantastic diversion, but every two weeks I go back to Moscow and see my wife and my child and the news is always the same, no setback and no improvement. Without the attention of the girl from FSB I would not have lasted in that city – awful place. And I come back and do some more months on analysis, and I see that I have little future, but they want to send me to Copenhagen. I will not be important there, but part of a team. First, with my wife and my daughter, before I transfer, we will go on holiday, all together. May I ask you, Benedict, one question?"

Was Benedict asleep? Almost. "Try me."

"You do not like me."

"Personal feelings are irrelevant."

"My stories do not fascinate you. I tell you very little that you do not already know."

"Your value as an informant is for others to decide."

"Which is a bullshit answer . . . yet, you stand in the line of fire, and Doug and Wally, and you despise me and I am useless to you, and you will protect me. From both an emotional viewpoint and a professional one, I fail you. But you protect me, and I mean nothing to you . . . Why?"

"Because for all of us – and this is the best answer you will get – that is our job."

And Benedict could recall pretty much every second of the three-quarters of a minute that he had been pushed down on to the carpet and Igor's body had covered him, shielded him. They had collected three bullets still in their brass casing from the grass, and Igor had put down his own body in an effort to stop those bullets, had they fired, from hitting Benedict. Not just the Russian who was 'a changed man, changed utterly', but likely it was all of them, and ever more complicated. The Russian went to use the lavatory, and Benedict waited for a call from a man in London who would relay instructions, had that authority . . . and it was not finished, no chance of it being finished.

"There is, I have to tell you, one fuck of an inquest."

"Did you answer for us, Colonel, or did you not?"

"You told them, Colonel, where the truth was, you did?"

"All I said was that the inquest has started, is ramped up, and we do not have too many who are understanding. I said, one fuck of an inquest after two failures. Got me? Need me to repeat that? Two failures."

The car was off the road. Leonid had found a muddy entry to a strip of woodland and they had moved an unfastened farm gate, had gone through, had closed the gate and had disappeared into the shelter of the trees, pines, planted densely. The Colonel had received a trail of secure texts on his phone, but the last had caused the greater aggravation. He was thought to be a rising star in GRU, a man with a future, one who could be relied upon to deliver . . .

His wife was better travelled than him. She had been abroad more often and knew the principal cities in Germany, in France and in Great Britain. It had been an internal marriage with barely a guest present who did not have a position in Military Intelligence, but her rank had plateaued. Enough. She had visited England two years before, had gone on a day excursion to Canterbury, had walked inside the cathedral and had confessed to her husband that she appreciated the beauty and starkness of the interior, what she called its "simple majesty", and the absence of the gold leaf paint that would have smothered the ceilings in any Russian city church.

More important, she had climbed down into the small area where the life of an archbishop had been taken by knights with battle swords who believed they carried out the wishes of their monarch. The deed done in a small chapel, in front of a tiny alter, a place barely large enough for a third of the coach passengers to squeeze into at a time, a single candle burning. She had told Leonid the story and the remark that had triggered the killing, made by the King concerning his obstinate cleric. *What miserable drones and traitors have I nourished and brought up in my household who let their lord be treated with such shameful contempt by a low-born cleric.* A clear enough invitation but – of course – with built in wriggle-room.

It would not have been a direct instruction from the head of state, the President. An indication would have been given, an obscenity mouthed at the mention of another defecting spy, and there were many who fed off the patronage of the "great leader", who would see the taking down of a traitor as a route to advancement towards the inner circle. How it happened, how it always happened, and the order given to their brigadier back in the glasshouse in Moscow, and his order passed down to Leonid. Leonid organising and planning and giving instructions to two veterans, to Konstantin and Anatoly . . . now a cold grin on his face. What went up also went down. Orders from the seat of power filtered fast through the lower layers of command. But an answering message would travel in the opposite direction.

The two had come stumbling out of the woods behind the house. The only piece of goddamn luck was that they had reached the car, had hurled in the rifle and a vehicle had come down the road, fierce headlights sweeping over them, but the weapon was by then out of sight. They had powered away. He'd asked, was entitled to ask before he was told, that it was good, that it had happened, that the mission was done? A jabber of words, curses, stammers, about a weapon jamming or malfunctioning – failing to fire. Tried three times, failed three times. No shot discharged and they had come back when revealed by a garden floodlight. He was driving fast, heading for a rendezvous on a beach where an inflatable would be waiting in shallow water. He had veered away from that route, had sent the code word for "abort" to the liaison officer on board a trawler and likely already feeling sick, and probably already putting out the beer and vodka to celebrate. Then had lodged the steering wheel in the grip of his elbows, had kept an eye on the open road and had hammered a text to the Brigadier. Not too many ways to gloss over it. A weapon failing to fire. A target not taken down. A mission that was well fucked, and enterprise and resources had been piled into it, and a trawler was at sea and a frigate cruised towards a meeting point in international waters. The Brigadier would have called a general. A general would have called a minister. A minister would have spoken briefly to one of the *siloviki* and he would have phoned, whatever the hour, to a chief of staff . . . at dawn, with his breakfast, the king of the day would have received a message that "a low-born cleric" had not been hacked to pieces by loyal men armed with superior heavy battle swords. And an inquest would have started and blame needed apportioning, and down it would tumble with each pair of shoulders it landed on attempting, fast, to shrug it off and send it on to a lower level . . . the level was inside the car. It stopped at the driver's seat.

Leonid said, "I would kill for coffee . . . I did not dump you. I took responsibility. I said in my messasge, and was rewarded with an accusation of incompetence, that it was not possible to take the weapon to a rifle range to try it out. Which was irony and a degree below impertinence . . . not that those bastards would appreciate *irony* . . . I was heard, I think that was a grudging response and my career teeters – understand me? We have a final chance, perhaps. It is a matter of intelligence and if, again, it is reliable. Otherwise we go home, not with a celebration ride in a trawler, not as valued friends on a warship. We will drive in shame across Germany and Poland, then over the frontier into Kaliningrad, and then we will take a rust-bucket flight to Moscow, and we are shit and have no future . . . Perhaps or perhaps not, we have a final opportunity. But it depends on the intelligence."

"It was good before," Anatoly said.

"What happened to the knights, who killed the churchman?" Konstantin asked.

"Their king did not back them. Their church excommunicated them. They were sent for fourteen years to soldier in the Holy Land . . . today, that is fourteen years fighting in that shit place, Syria. Little changes, fuck all is different."

Again, Konstantin's question, "If the intelligence is good, a location, we have a further chance?"

Was answered, dry and remote and perhaps apprehensive of his future. "*If* . . . if it is good. Because it is important, is about the fear that a man must feel if he is prepared to be a traitor, take their money, betray us . . . *If.*"

Darkness spread beyond Alexei's window. Few lights showed and a snow shower dimmed the ones he could see. They were out of Kirov and the heating was turned high in the compartment. To see those few lights he had needed to wipe the glass with his elbow. It might have been the warmth in the compartment that had brought, already, the sweat on his neck and in the pit of his back, or might have been the nervousness that held him . . . He had bought a single journey ticket. It had been queried.

A pleasant enough woman sat in the ticket kiosk on Friday evenings. Perhaps it was a part of her evening, what she would have set her wristwatch on, that this pale-faced young man would come to her every other Friday and would buy a seat in a cheap carriage for the journey to Moscow's Yaroslavskiy station. Quite a pleasant smile from her . . . she might have seen that he wore no wedding ring, might have seen that he always wore decent clothing and was likely to have a respectable job, and might have had a grand-daughter who was unmarried and needed . . . And with the smile, and an acknowledgement of their peculiar relationship, she had pushed towards him the printed ticket, valid for a return to Kirov on the Sunday evening. He might have said to her months before that he always went to Moscow for weekends each time it was possible, so that he could visit his mother, which would further have enhanced his reputation for reliability. A one-way ticket was what he asked for, and a furrow of annoyance crossed her forehead.

A one-way ticket?

His answer, hushed. It was correct, it was one-way.

Had he forgotten that if he changed his mind about abandoning Kirov and came back then he would need a second one-way ticket for the reverse journey, and would lose the discount for the return?

He had not forgotten . . . and the passengers behind him were shuffling and coughing to make him aware of their presence.

She said that if he were not coming back then he had precious little luggage with him . . . was he intending to return by air? Was he prepared to hazard his safety on one of those "cowboy outfits". Herself, she would have to be dragged into a plane. Did he realise how often aircraft were subject to delay, and how the trains maintained their timetables? It had been enough to kick-start a conversation among those queuing behind him. A man said that he would die rather than go to live in Moscow. Another said that Kirov was the finest city in the Federation and that only a lunatic would wish to leave it. A woman at the back chipped in that Moscow was filled with gangsters and rapists and thugs, and that the church worship in Kirov was far superior. An old man said it was sad when a stage of life ended and all that a man had to take away with him was contained in a small handheld bag.

He had raised his voice. "A one-way ticket. Simple. Easy to understand. A one-way ticket and I pay the extra if my plans change. Are we all satisfied?"

The return ticket had been sourly binned. Its cancellation would cause bureaucratic angst to the woman. He was given a new ticket, paid for it in cash. Had walked away and had heard the murmur behind him. Had made an idiot of himself, drawn attention to himself – had not sat in the waiting room but had taken a cold seat on the platform and had waited for the lights of the approaching train.

Had not shouted out, "I need a one-way ticket because I am quitting this shithole place, and this shithole outfit of GRU – thugs and thieves – and am going with a wonderful girl to the far north and will walk with her into Finland, and I will be welcomed by a foreign country and recognised as a true patriot, and I will never look back. So, please, get out of my life and give me a one-way ticket."

Close to the famous statue at Kirov station of a life-size dog sitting beside a suitcase and waiting, Alexei also sat – for the last time – and waited, for the train.

Alexei had taken a window seat. A man had followed him into the carriage and sat beside him and had immediately started to eat strong-smelling gherkins. A woman opposite him tried to catch his eye as if she wanted conversation to while away the twelve-hour journey. So he had turned his attention to the window, and the few lights that showed once the city was behind them, and the building that housed the basic financial workings of the Main Intelligence Directorate, *Glavnoye razvedyvatel'noye upravleniye*, all gone, and the darkness thicker and the snow shower petered out. And the memory stick was stowed inside the heel of his trainer.

Cursed himself for not asking Maggie what his life would be: who would welcome him, what work would he do, where would they live? Cursed himself for not thinking of his mother. He could see nothing through the window but could see, with total clarity, the front door of his mother's apartment. The door that would open when it was hit with the full force of a battering ram, what the FSB would use to break it off its hinges. The apartment would be crowded with the men that he saw each Saturday morning when he came off the train, and saw again each Sunday afternoon when he went back to the station. He was numb at what he had committed himself to. Cursed some more but found no comfort from it. Did not know what he would tell her, the girl that he believed he loved.

"You'll have friendly faces around you, Maggie."

"And they won't show out?"

"Unlikely to," Lucinda said. "It'll be Josh and Nancy."

The evening came on fast in central Moscow. No snow and no sleet, but a brutal gale seemed to find every corridor between buildings and make a charge for them. It would be a quiet evening for Maggie; she planned to snug up in front of an electric fire and take in a bit of a box set, French crime, and have Hector on her lap and warm, and would have prepared his meal and hers, but would not drink. She could hold her liquor, had showed the boys that when on the Ireland posting, but would not want a thickened head, a lapse in her concentration, when she was at the station the following morning peering into the swarm of people coming off the long-distance train.

"Nancy will be on your pavement and Josh across the road. Usual time, same routine. Do not vary it. You will carry your diplomatic passport . . . they will have their Embassy ID. And me. Surprise? Yes, me, actually taking to the streets. Will be with our driver and will have the link to Josh and Nancy. We talked, Maggie, about what was sensible. It is sensible on this weekend that we are mob-handed and I will not tolerate you being manhandled by their thugs. To be frank: we are unlikely to intervene physically. Not a cop-out, just more of the sensible. What would bring us in, regardless of whether they have a full-strength battalion on the ground, is if there seems likely to be any danger to Hector. That is a red line for us. If they involve Hector then we scrum down and go for them. Understood?"

"Yes, understood . . . Am I being selfish?"

"Not particularly. We are all entitled to an emotional itch, get involved when perhaps it would be wiser not to. You? Predictable, placed alongside, at a moment of extreme danger, a young and decent and frightened boy. Don't see him as a traitor but as a fighter and on our side. I always found that the more you scratch the itch the more the bloody thing persists . . . I don't have it yet, the confirmation of your posting to the bomb people, I gather it's at Bicester, St George's Barracks, but I'll have it by the end of the weekend, Monday at the latest. It's a promise, Maggie."

"Accepted."

"Don't really know how it's going to play out – just have to suck it and see. Try and have a good night's sleep, it's always better with a clear head . . . One last thing, Maggie, and I do not have to brief you at this depth, but I fancy you deserve some of my confidences. A very considerable operation is being played out in another

European country. The GRU goons are on the ground and have twice failed to take down a defector from that august outfit. A bomb was spotted and then a rifle jammed. We are hanging on to the boy we have in protective care and are beefing up the guns around him. He's a bolshie little blighter and damn all use to us compared with *Environ*, not in the same league. We are protecting him so that his name and his death, and the details of his assassination, are not plastered all over the front pages of *Izvestiya* and *Kommersant*, don't lead the *Russia-1* bulletin . . . And in the hope that, grim as things seem, this kid and others down the pipeline can know that we protect people, don't throw them under the bus. Enough said. Cannot believe I actually told you all that, but I did . . . Have a good night's sleep."

The heat had long gone from his coffee, and a sparrow ventured close to Jonas's brogues in search of the final crumbs. The man with the rake covered ground that he had already worked over and Jonas was left to wonder how he had been before the malady had struck him. His solitude had been broken by footsteps and he now shared his bench.

The map was finished with, back in the briefcase with the satellite photographs of the island. Also closed away in the case's compartments were the brief reports that a fishing boat registered in the port of Kaliningrad now reported engine difficulties and "limped" towards the Danish port of Esbjerg. Also that a frigate of the Admiral Grigorovich class had sailed under the Storebaelt bridge linking the Danish islands of Zeeland and Funen and was now headed for the Kattegat and Skagerak narrows and using the route into the North Sea. He thought it came on at a pace and his shoulders were bent and rounded as if by the burden of it.

"You all right, Jonas?"

"Quite all right, thank you," Jonas answered testily.

The AssDep DG grinned. "Not going to welsh on me, I hope."

"Not my intention."

And the moment of seriousness. "Can you take the weight of it, Jonas? I think I deserve to know."

Jonas said, "I believe so. Anyway, have to take the weight of it, don't I? And you do, and a whole host of people and some of them we can identify and some we cannot, and they – with us – are all near to being overwhelmed . . . We are confronting a state-sponsored conspiracy. We are talking about a hit team deployed, and about the high-level direction of their assets. A trawler in the area and likely to take off gunmen and their facilitators, and a naval vessel that can presumably rustle up thirty knots and get the kill-squad off the trawler and out into international waters. The way I see it, if we can follow the course of action I predict, then we will have a very worthwhile result . . . and if we don't get such a result then we fail and badly."

"It is about a leak, Jonas."

"About a leak, about finding it and then stopping it. I take that most seriously."

"And you can handle it?"

"I think so, hope so. Can't say more."

The AssDepDG was on his feet. He cuffed Jonas's shoulder as if that were meant to encourage, gave his watery smile and a half wink of solidarity and walked away. And Jonas could picture a medium-sized trawler, the sort he and Vera would have seen if they had taken the caravan down the West Country coastline and – assuming a wet day – walked around the harbours of Penzance or Brixham and looked at the moored fishing craft. Could also picture the frigate, expensive and powerful, capable of launching cruise missiles, with surface-to-air defences and torpedo tubes, crew of 200, and a Ka-27 helicopter stowed on a deck behind the superstructure. which told him that his opponent had put down on to the field a formidable order of battle.

Overawed? Not in the nature of Jonas Merrick. About to throw a towel into the ring? He did not intend to.

He watched the man with the rake, took a little strength from what he saw. Believed himself mentally shell-shocked by the course of events swirling close to him, then dug his fingernails into the palms of his hand, hurt himself, steadied and stood, and started to walk out of the garden. Enough messing, and time slipping, so he lengthened his stride and would go along the north bank of the river and would step up on to Vauxhall Bridge and would cross it, go back to work in the little basement room that awaited him, and where there was a locked safe. He rang Frank. Said he was on his way, apologised for the delay in his appearance.

Felt uneasy crossing the river, the tide rising and the water lapping higher and wind-flecked white spume. Thought it a dangerous place to be and hurried on towards the Sixers' place. Took his phone from his pocket, went through the security coding, hit the keys, still walking.

"Hello . . . yes?"

"Benedict? It is Jonas Merrick again. You have my terms of reference?"

"Clear instructions have been given me."

"I see from the file made available to me, Benedict, that you are experienced in circumstances described as challenging."

A fair description. A mob armed with automatic weapons and cocktails, the Molotov ones, coming in through the front gate as Benedict and his little band were fast exiting from the back. He thought "challenging" portrayed it, and challenging was also being on his stomach, protected by the man he was supposed to look after, and seeing a guy in the garden with a rifle.

"And you, Mr Merrick – or Jonas – who is now calling the shots. Are you experienced in challenging circumstances? I think it fair I ask."

"Hardly. Little bits and pieces. Nothing in your league. I need to know, and without gilding any lilies, are you all holding up?"

"We are, after a fashion, and are expecting a delivery. We are good, my opinion, but only in a very limited timeframe."

From where he stood, Benedict could see through the frosted glass of the front door that a car had parked behind the PET vehicle. A man was taking something out of the boot and it was a moment before Benedict recognised him . . . What he did recognise immediately was the contents of the bag the man lifted clear: hidden but angular and heavy, something of an escalation.

"I am sending you the details, what I require from you. It is a complicated scenario and one that requires a few disparate parts to lock together. Follow it, please, and to the letter, and it remains a closed book to our colleagues at VX and to our Danish friends – except when I say otherwise ... it will play out on that island, very suitable. A honey-trap. Will work well, quiet and near-deserted, no rubberneckers or voyeurs. I believe we have the challenging circumstances in hand. Hope so. Good luck to you and your colleagues, Benedict. It will all work well, I think it will."

Brian, the former paratrooper, lugged his bag through the front door, called out a cheerful greeting well disguised with mock melancholy.

"Christ, you guys still here? Taken out citizenship?"

"Foxtrot ..." Doug said.

"... Oscar," Wally said.

"You boys all right? And our celebrity?"

"Doing well," Doug said.

"Doing very well," Wally said.

"And you had visitors?"

"Their weapon jammed, three times, and they quit, and we watched them on the camera out there," Doug said.

"What was interesting, they were ancient. It's real quality, the camera. They were as old as us, no wonder they fucked up," Wally said.

"I'm to stay with you ... The new powers dishing out the orders have you down as a couple of snowflakes and needing your hands held. I've some good stuff here so if any beggar comes visiting he might get more than a bit of a bargain."

The good stuff came out of the bag. Brian hadn't seen the Russian for three months, not since the hotel on the outskirts of Copenhagen where he had watched over him before they had moved north. Thought him more haggard, thinner in the face, and without the chirpiness, the cockiness. The Russian said nothing, but had sidled behind Doug and Wally.

It was gear picked up in Syria ... easy enough. Had belonged to the Syrian military. Attacked by the Isis crowd, they had chucked down their weapons so as to run faster, and the Special Forces had hit the black flag boys and sent them spinning off to paradise and had taken charge of the firepower. Plenty was stored in UK military armouries, but some was distributed to embassies and went into the personal care of the nominated security officer . . . two assault rifles, six filled magazines, a Makarov PM 9mm pistol with an effective range of fifty metres, and pride of place was the folded body of a Dragunov sniper's rifle, and bullets for it, a killing range of 1300 metres. Each item was passed to Doug. He examined, looked them over with a veteran's eye, and moved them on to Wally, and another fist intruded. The Russian took them in turn but his face lit when he had hold of the Dragunov. His fingers went to the mechanism and he checked that the breech was clear and squeezed the trigger to feel the pressure necessary to fire, and cradled it, then pointed it at the front window and the gap in the curtains and nestled the stock against his shoulder and let his eye find the scope sight, and aimed at the ear of the PET girl in the car, who had her window down, a hand hanging out with a cigarette nearly smoked. Said nothing, gave it back.

Brian would have followed the aim. "Out there, how did they do when the balloon was flying?"

Wally said, "Didn't know anything about it."

Doug said, "And we've not told them."

Benedict was by the door. "No point in it – would confuse them, would screw us. Into the arms of the Human Resources desk warriors. Said nothing . . . We have a new command structure. A certain Jonas Merrick. Don't know who he is and where they've dug him out from. I checked back just now, at Deputy Director level. First time I've ever spoken to him, had it confirmed. Seemed confident in us, in our ability to survive, and we hang out here tonight and then move early, first light, tomorrow. Seemed to know, this Merrick, what he hoped to achieve."

"He said, 'I wish you well' . . . Any chance of a fry-up? A proper one? Ours not to reason why, that sort of shit. Better than sex, isn't it – so the young'uns tell me – combat. Long time since I did either . . . so should be fun."

★   ★   ★

Volkov worked. A bad day and a good day.

The bad part of the day had been worse than bad. The good part of the day carried merely a promise. He took no calls. Cancelled meetings. Had his PA act as a sentry at the gate. The bad day was deep in the night, not asleep but in bed, his wife's soft snores beside him, when he had heard that the attack had failed. How had it failed? The weapon had malfunctioned. Further into the small hours, those in which death was supposed to visit the infirm – which might have been a blessed relief – he had called his general. The general, wisely, had given him the name and number of the relevant minister and the call had woken a man, no doubt exhausted from his performance with his mistress, and he had passed on the news, and the bollocking had been ferocious. Had been lying on his back, waiting for the alarm to bleep, when a man from the *siloviki* had called him. No abuse but a quiet voice, frighteningly calm, had asked him to explain the failure and then had asked if a further chance remained in place: he had said it depended on the matter of intelligence available.

Those who received the intelligence directed from this asset had – as yet – received no further information concerning the possible movements of a target located in the small Danish city of Esbjerg. He must wait, and he accepted that his requirements stretched the ability of the asset, of whom he knew nothing, to maintain personal security: not his concern.

The good day: a mechanism was in place for a lift on the Sunday afternoon at the approach to Yaroslavskiy station. The arrest team was briefed, confident, the prospect of failure was minimal because the target followed such predictable routes and procedures. He would have sufficient men on the ground so that the target's contact would also go into the net, and the best he could hope for was that failure and success would balance each other.

The time crawled for him. Plans made, constantly checked, plans whose execution was outside his direct control. His career teetered.

★   ★   ★

A good swell at sea, two-metre waves, and a rendezvous as the light over the North Sea faded. A difficult manoeuvre but not one that taxed the skills of experienced mariners: the skipper of the *Katerina*, and the navigation officer of an Admiral Grigorovich-class frigate were experienced and skilful.

An inflatable carried the package over the water, launched from the frigate, to be ferried to the trawler. A dangerous job, but the order for the meeting of the vessels and the handover had come from an element, secretive, of the Ministry of Defence. Not for those on board the dinghy, nor for the fishing crew who would take possession of the item and haul a sailor on board forward of the wheelhouse, to know that an AK-47 rifle, and standard 7.62mm ammunition, had failed to fire in a killing attempt the previous evening. It was considered necessary that the weapon taken from the frigate's armoury, wrapped well against a torrent of splashing spray, then transferred, be tested. It was an RPG-7 rocket launcher: the infantryman's dream weapon. Successful, tried, proven ... it was armed by the sailor, a chief petty officer, and fired, and a flash of flame lit the deck area, and 150 metres away a wave erupted in an explosion ... Not enough, so two assault rifles were taken from the canvas bag and both were fired in the vague direction of a cruising gull, and the weapons performance was rated "satisfactory" and the unharmed gull kept to its course. Then a sack of RG-42 fragmentation grenades, burst radius of up to twenty metres, was opened, shown, then closed. The sailor crawled back into the tossed dinghy and bounced back towards his frigate.

A mood of excitement was felt among the trawler's crew, fuelled by the knowledge that they were due to perform important work in the state's service ... within minutes the two vessels were out of sight of each other. They would meet again, the skipper and the navigation officer, within the next thirty hours, unless there was a second, final, "abort" signal. And the sound of the report when the missile detonated was long lost in the wind's howl.

He watched as Toni was shown out of the room. Frank closed the door after her. Jonas thought it a good moment to wear that rather silly expression, which he excelled at producing and which seemed to convey that insults directed at him were probably justified and, anyway, caused minimal offence. He had been called *a second rater*, had been accused of bringing *empty-headed prejudices inside the building*, and of using *slur and innuendo against a very fine and dedicated team*, and he had written the capital letter I on the pad, and now had scratched it out and binned the page. It represented Ideology . . . She was forty years old, had three children and lived with a perpetual nanny crisis, and her husband was an RAF officer stationed in Cyprus. So, Money and Ideology and Compromise and Ego seemed not to fit the team's principals and he had rejected any idea that Denys Montgomery, the caring and careful Monty, would have gone the felon's way and sought to betray his country's institutions.

"The 'island', yes – that's it. The 'island'." He allowed the word to roll off the walls of the small room, then seemed to correct himself and almost – theatrically – to bite his tongue as if he had broken rules. Made it clear that he regretted the moment and hung his head. The only island that Jonas knew was the one out in the Channel due south of Portsmouth and Southampton. He had been to the Isle of Wight with Vera, but not for some years, wretched weather for five continuous days and they had returned on the ferry a day early. He had not been to the Isle of Man, nor to the Scilly islands, and his work had never taken him over the Irish Sea. He delved in the briefcase, given him by Vera thirty-six years before and rather treasured, and under the plastic lunch box and the chocolate bar and the flask was the map of the island.

Jonas seemed to blink as if that were a way of calling back a moment of memory, and smiled to himself at his success and wrote on his notepad *Fano*. The island of Fano, he had learned, was ten miles in length, north to south, and east to west had a width of two miles, was reached by ferry from the harbour at Esbjerg, a twelve-minute journey. It was known as a holiday resort, with the Hamburg and Bremen breadwinners heading into Denmark in droves when the summer came – which it had not. His research told him that the off-season population numbered 2500, and in high season that would rise to 30,000, and two areas on the island were given up to affluent holiday homes. He thought it perfect as a trap, which would be baited with honey, dollops of it. Ferreting in his briefcase he took out a paper clip, than wrote on the top sheet of his pad the additional words *Fano Vesterhavsbad,* and made a neat cross in pencil on the map, on the western shoreline, then wrote *Entrance Road 6,* and tore off the sheet and used the paper clip to attach it to the map. He left his table and put map and paper into the safe, crouched by her ankle to do so and her eyes had not wavered from her screen, and they went on top of the biographical files of each of the Resettlement team, and the communications logs, and he pushed the safe door so that it was almost closed.

"I think that's it then. But I'm afraid I have to be an old sourpuss."

"You haven't cleared me through the system, Mr Merrick, and tomorrow is the weekend."

"I'm afraid so."

"Do weekends matter to you?"

"I want to wrap this business up and get out of all your hair. Feel I have overstayed a welcome – such as it was. Quite understandable. Anyway, time you were shot of me, and I can get something down in writing, take the advice of this pretty expert team, which I am sure it is, and dump the blame where it belongs. Now, my apologies. I have to talk to you, Frank, do some thumbscrew stuff, you know. So, I'll need your presence tomorrow and even Sunday. I hope that is not dreadfully inconvenient."

"Might be a chance for another couple of slices of coffee and walnut, Mr Merrick."

"Might indeed. Something to look forward to."

Quite pretty, fine bones in her face, nice hair, and a minimum of makeup and discreet jewellery, but so short – it appeared to Jonas – of happiness. He realised he had not seen this young woman, who was the drudge of the team, ever smile or laugh. Had won neither when he had feebly joked of needing to do "some thumbscrew stuff". It should have been a task for a young man to chase after, to win her smile and hear her laughter, but the confidential file reported no involvements, only an emptiness in life beyond the main entrance of VX. So much hidden behind the wall of politeness, deference and painstaking loyalty to the detail of her work, and the officers in the team would likely flounder if she were absent from their demands. Inside the building she was anonymous. They walked down their corridor, the safe and the room locked, and up the flight of stairs, and came to the wide atrium and swarms of personnel crossing it, but no one, not a single man or woman, spoke to her. Outside the wind still blew, and the evening was chasing them, but the rain had stopped. It would be the usual Friday evening after a week's work for the masses spilling out, clusters going to pubs, and others in hungry packs making for restaurants, and others scampering for cinemas or concerts or theatres, or going home to parties or merely to share child duties . . . He doubted that Frank had any of those on her evening schedule.

"I look forward to seeing you tomorrow, Frank – and a piece of cake if that's possible."

"Yes, Mr Merrick, I'll see you tomorrow."

He had left himself time to dawdle and still comfortably catch the 17.49 which he did on every working day it was possible – days when he had achieved and learned little, and also those few days when the enormity of a crisis damn near flattened him.

His phone showed a message. The A Branch people would do one more shadow that evening. They were already out on the business and doing their "plots", and their preliminary report – to be updated – stated that only one of the given targets had seemed to use surveillance evasion training on the route home, and on the route to work. Only one . . . not conclusive and could have been best practice – just one, and he read the name, and grimaced.

By the wall of the Archbishop's Palace, he keyed in a number. Heard it ring out. Imagined an old husk of a man, his past far distant from him. Thought the phone would be ringing in a small apartment in a terraced house, and he would be wearing last week's shirt and yesterday's socks, a month of crumpled news-papers beside his chair, and a TV blasting a news channel in his ear because old hacks likened the addiction to having a malarial microbe in the veins. And found time to thank Vera for the prompt.

"Yes – Merrick, that what you said your name was? – yes, I did Bonn for a couple of the more pompous broadsheets in the seventies. And you were given my number? And you want a word from me on grey mice? Not a problem – all a bit ago, but the memory still holds, thank God . . . grey mice was very German. Bonn was stiff with secretaries. Nice enough girls. Probably looking to end up with a well-placed politician or an ambitious civil servant, except very few did. Most were left on the shelf and the majority of the men were married and so it was all a little sad for them. Except those who thought they'd found true love, and a handsome Romeo had walked into their lives, took them seriously, admired their conversation, and shagged the hell out of them. Good restaurants out of town, candles lit, fine wines. No such thing as a free lunch, or an inconsequential shag. Romeo would get around to asking a question or two, particularly if said little grey mouse worked in the Defence Ministry, or anything involving security, and after a question or two it would be – in the comfort of a warm bed and love whispered in her ear – a request to bring out a certain document which she might be able to filch from a safe before the building had shut up shop for the night. The DDR people took the chasing of the grey mice with great seriousness and they trained their Romeos to high levels of sexual skills – so I was told – and women who thought they were past being found attractive discovered their lives had taken on romantic importance. The East Germans had a conveyor belt for these studs and they would have appeared to be mid-European businessmen, frequently travelling, when in fact they were back in Leipzig or Dresden, humping the missus, playing soccer with the kids, then going back to work in the West. The women who fell for it were mostly alone, plain to look at, the ones that nobody notices, and that was why they were known as the grey mice. As a rule, from what came out in court, they were stereotypically dedicated in their espionage, very difficult to track but they were used quite ruthlessly . . . Retirement was not in the game plan . . . were used until they went in the cage. Rather sad, really. Rather pathetic. Do you want chapter and verse?"

"Thank you, no. You've told me what I needed to know."

"Merrick, isn't it, your name? Merrick, listen – it was a dirty business."

"I think I knew that . . . and think I knew that a little grey mouse could be such 'a wretched and disproportionate nuisance'. Thanks for your time, sir. Goodnight."

He rang off, and the flow of commuters hurrying to Waterloo swept him along. Jonas was not one to punch a fist in the air when a truth was revealed. His face was masked, sombre – and he had no reason yet to punch the air because a bigger game would soon be underway with higher stakes than when Olaf chewed a mouse's carcass and swallowed, all except the tail . . . the biggest game Jonas Merrick had ever played and, on the green baize-covered card table, lives would be at issue. He would be in good time for his train . . . He thought of a deserted island with lines of empty, shuttered holiday homes and wide beaches and a free fire zone for the foot soldiers to scrap in.

11

Jonas crouched beside Frank's ankles and put the documents and maps, more detail of the move from the mainland to the island, into the safe. On his phone, walking across the bridge, he had watched a webcam panorama taken from the ferry pier across the harbour from Esbjerg and had been pleased to note a group of seals lying on a sandbar; no doubt they played a Canute act twice daily before being floated off. He was up before his alarm had sounded at home in Raynes Park and had printed off the blown-up satellite views of the holiday homes built amongst the dunes at Vesterhavsbad on the west coast of Fano. Vera, between quartering his sandwich, had looked at the images and expressed distaste, said they had no view other than sand hills, no privacy because the neighbours overlooked them, thought that Olaf would have found the place noisy and frightening. Sandwiches were not usually needed at the weekend, and so the rhythm of fillings was broken and he was again on tuna and mayonnaise. When would he be back? Usual time. Would he be going into London on Sunday morning? A rather rueful response, he would be, but he'd added the rider that he anticipated the business would be concluded, by the end of Sunday. And then? His face had lightened and he had known a rare surge of optimism: then it would be back in the caravan, electricity restored, mice extirpated or slaughtered, and a return to Orford Ness and the remnants of nuclear detonation experiments and research.

Jonas had walked directly to the VX building. He had been greeted almost warmly by Frank at the outer gate. It was possible, also, that the gatekeeper staff and the armed police alongside were slackening their early hostility. Always courteous, however bogus, he had tipped his trilby to them, had laid his change, his keys, and other minor bits of metal into a plastic tray for the screening of his briefcase, raincoat and jacket, had exchanged a meaningless greeting. She had led him inside and they had paused at a coffee dispenser and it had produced *latte* of a sort, and she'd apologised for its quality.

Pretty soon, *they* would be on the move. Might be in a queue for the ferry, might be approaching the harbour, might already be on board. Jonas had seen the ferry on the webcam. It was a stout little craft. Jonas assumed it would sail in pretty much any weather, would get children to their classrooms on the mainland, bring workers over to Esbjerg to their offices or factories. Only a little of him thought he missed out by not being with them. He owned a relationship of sorts with Kev and Leroy, huge in their bulletproof vests, one that was based on their humour and his respect, and he believed he would have liked the company of Doug and Wally, and the file had shown him that Benedict was a man of integrity. Would have been interesting to have been with them, but also would have meant that he abandoned the title given him in S/3/13 – the Eternal Flame, the one who never went out, who stayed in his cubicle while the A Branch watchers kitted up and joshed and went through the last shouted briefings before going out on to their front line, where the trenches and razor wire were the streets of London or Leeds or Leicester. The last time he had seen the ferry on his phone it had been ploughing into a slight swell . . . perhaps would have liked to have been there, and with them, but his business was where he now sat.

"I brought some more of the cake you liked, Mr Merrick."

"That is most kind of you."

"The coffee and walnut."

"Excellent."

"And your spectacles need some attention."

She'd taken them off his face, done it gently and with care . . . His team might now be on the small ferry and approaching the low-set old buildings of Nordby, the island's capital . . . he checked his watch . . . and another team by now would likely be at work.

The relationship between Jonas and Aggie Burns had never been based on affection but he had begged and borrowed a double favour from her and it had been given grudgingly. One of the Tango subjects under high-level surveillance during the week would have the same treatment at the weekend. Also a deep rummage team would by now be edging up the stairs to a small second-floor apartment in a terraced house conversion in the Paddington district of London, or would already be at the door, or might by now have gained clandestine access and begun their work. They were good at what they did, as Aggie Burns, given a quarter of a chance, would tell him . . . He wondered whether Frank used those degrees of tradecraft taught down at the Napoleonic-era Fort Monckton, the Sixers' out of town haunt overlooking the Channel. She would have been on the courses where the students were lectured in the sophistications of both concealment and recognising when and where the rummagers had been . . . Going through her wardrobe and her jars and bottles and her chests of drawers where intimate clothing was folded away, and into her jewellery – if she had any more than she wore every day. And would almost certainly go under floor-boards and behind ventilation grilles. Might find something of significance and might not. Jonas would have said that the work of a DRT was as much a violation of an individual as a strip search of a passenger believed to be a drugs mule arriving at a UK airport. Something rather horrid – something that hardly affected him. How long did they have? Would have all day because Jonas intended to spend the whole of Saturday in the basement room, and she would be there too. His spectacles, lenses pristine, were put back onto his face: slightly intimate and he flinched.

There would have been something, someone, in her life that had shaped her personality, was sure of it . . . it was rare that a deep rummage team entered an apartment, a living space, and failed to find one item at least that justified their visit . . . and then the papers and the books and the clothes would go back on the shelves and tables and in the drawers and cupboards, and carpets put back in place, and it would be as if they had never been there. Jonas would be in debt to Aggie Burns which peeved him.

"You're very quiet, Mr Merrick."

He smiled. "Yes, good of you to notice. Had a little indigestion in the night but it's wearing off. Just thinking through my sign-off report, then I'm out of your hair. You've been very kind to me, and I'm grateful. I expect it will all be a bit of a whimper rather than a bang, which in my experience is how matters normally wind down."

Two women worked the street, each with a bag that carried flyers advertising a concert to be performed by a youth orchestra at a school hall in the small town of Varde, north of Esbjerg. It promised to be a celebration of rare talent, and the two women emphasised that the principals were exceptional.

Smartly dressed, and well wrapped against the cold, they were willing to linger and discuss the concert, the music that would be played, the city in Poland from which the performers were drawn. Many from that street had already left home for. But they found enough householders with whom to talk, and some of those might have been surprised that the two women had time to be on the doorstep and engage in accented Danish conversation . . . not fluent but almost so.

The women were from the Russian Embassy, in Copenhagen. They performed the daily duties of interpreters and were used to accompanying the Ambassador, the Deputy Ambassador, or those senior people of FSB or SVR or GRU, anyone of status who needed confidentiality. They had been pressed into service in the early hours of the morning, had been in the print room in the basement of the Embassy while a staffer had designed the flyer had run off 150 copies, then had been packed into an embassy car and had been driven at speed across central Denmark. About the oldest trick in the book, and one that had been useful in the past . . . Where they lingered longest, dragging out a conversation, was where they had a view of the bungalow, with a vehicle with privacy windows parked in front. When they had started on the street, the younger woman had, with an apparent sales flair, approached the vehicle and had tapped on the window and had been rewarded with a man's sullen face, a bored woman beside him, and a canvas bag by their feet, and a fast impression that neither of them gave a fuck for classical music, next week or any week, in Varde or anywhere else. More satisfaction followed when the front door of the bungalow opened and a column of men emerged, carrying bags and plastic sacks which they dumped into the body of the car on the forecourt – and they had gone on talking about the artistry of one particular juvenile clarinettist.

The message that the occupants of the target bungalow were about to move was flagged back to the Embassy. From there it would go direct to the glasshouse building in central Moscow, classified as *Immediate* and *Secret*.

Not much to carry out, but Benedict was relieved they were going out on their feet, not in wooden boxes.

Nothing heavy, except for the load that Brian had brought them. The next heaviest would have been the screen and the console and the sensors and the folded cables from the warning system looped around the garden. Not that it would be needed if the plan given him by Merrick's quiet, calm voice from the UK was followed to the letter.

The car was loaded. Decisions were slipping away from Benedict, like a transfer of power. He had the civil service grading, had the rank and had a first class honours degree from Oxford and he doubted that Brian or Doug or Wally had had much educa-tion after their sixteenth birthdays: they led and he followed. They said what went into the boot and what would be stuffed down by their feet. Brian to drive, Benedict beside him. Behind would be Sashcord sandwiched between the two muscle men. Brian's car would be left parked up around a corner, and one of the kids in the consulate attached to the UK mission would collect it. Benedict realised that a new horizon beckoned for all of them. He supposed that the sweet whiff of gun oil would have lifted their spirits. They were all livelier and he had noticed that the Russian now bonded better with them. Began to see a different man . . . He was not asked whether he wanted to take a last look around the house, was not asked which route they would take.

And another sea change. Wally had told Brian. *Sashcord* had knelt at the window of the PET car and had apologised, done it with grace.

Brian had the map out and had laid it on the car's roof. Could have sworn it . . . Bloody hell . . . Jette was out of the car and Benedict might have seen she and Igor exchange looks. Did not think that keeping Igor safe necessitated eye contact. Embarrassment put on the back burner and now a low priority. Going to the island and moving to another safe house, and leaving a trail, that was the big priority. Benedict had seen the two women working the street, and saw the flyer inside the PET car advertising a concert . . . They pulled out.

Same routine as before, the PET team in the lead and then letting Brian come past them while they blocked oncoming traffic. They swung on to the fast road and left behind them the cemetery where old enemies kept each other company and a small middle-class suburban estate which had briefly become a hot spot in a cold war, left comfortable, conventional lives behind as if they had never infiltrated the territory. Now the PET car was behind them: there had been some talk with Nils and Jette about keeping the matter close, not involving the men and women who liked to cry foul and reach for the file that carried the Risk Assessment and Mission Statement, and it had been agreed that a drive was in order, an antidote to their cabin fever . . . Benedict would have sworn that the message had been clear between his Russian and the Danish minder, but he understood little of such moods. It was accepted, the journey and the relocation, and all against any better judgement that Benedict might bring to the party.

They drove through the dock area of Esbjerg. A few statues, some decent traditional buildings, a glass and concrete shopping mall, and old military fortifications that had narrow gun slits facing the harbour. They slowed and the PET team were close behind them as they joined the queue of traffic for the ferry.

"The island, anyone, what sort of place?" Brian asked.

Benedict said, "It's a sandspit. A big one. It will be on the move a bit and it will shift some more after a major storm. It has dunes that are held in place by that sort of rough grass, has massive beaches that are favourites throughout Europe for windsurfers. A bit of pine forest. Two villages only, the one this ferry goes to, and down in the south there is another. In the summer it is overrun with pretty tacky tourism, and also has – but does not boast it – the highest per capita scale of both murder and drug addiction. They get rid of their visitors, primarily Germans who find it cheaper than their own North Sea islands, in the autumn and then the place is left with a population living off the money they have made from the visitors, and the state workers – teachers, medical staff, the usual. They are, history says, a contrary crowd, always have been, and only reluctantly does central government's writ run. There used to be a strong tradition of seafaring. They built the boats that sailed south to Europe, navigated the North Sea, went to St Petersburg through the Baltic . . . Enough?"

Wally said, "And what do we actually need to know?"

Benedict winced, gazed out of his window, saw the few vehicles coming off the ferry . . . Nils had bought the tickets and passed them through to Brian. "Need to know? Interesting question. Tactically I would not be able to offer an informed opinion. You need to know that the island is severely under-populated. The chance of collateral casualties is therefore lessened. It's a good place for big boys' games. You won't have an audience and they won't be selling places in the better hospitality boxes. Chances are that you will do your stuff, good or bad or indifferent, without an audience . . . More to the point, none of this is down to me, there's short shrift given to my opinion . . ."

The car nudged forward, bounced on the slipway and then the ferry's ramp and they went onboard. No rain but a wind blowing, and spray splashing the windscreen. Benedict wondered what *Sashcord* thought, and why he was now so quiet.

*   *   *

A message from the Brigadier came up on Leonid's phone. Not a man that Leonid liked. A man who Leonid feared. He would answer to Volkov, would face a charge of dereliction of duty if he oversaw further failure, and would be rewarded with further privilege if he was responsible – at this late hour in the mission's history – with success.

It was flagged as raw intelligence: There was an island across from the harbour of Esbjerg. A ferry linked the island to the mainland. On the open coast of the island were holiday homes. The target would move to the sixth block of the resort of Vesterhavsbad ... There was information about the location of a trawler dinghy and the one point on the island where it could get close to the shore and where that limited stretch of beach was located, and when it would happen. More would follow.

Did fear of failure drive Leonid, or the desire to be rewarded? Time to learn about the island, what was there, and how they would push forward. Where the killing zone would be.

"They actually saw them, that right?"

Konstantin answered him. "That's what the Colonel had. I saw his screen."

"He does not tell us much – fuck all of zero."

"We had people in the street when they were pulling out. Saw them. It's what the Colonel was told."

Anatoly asked, "What sort of people?"

"Just said they were old people."

The Colonel had gone into the wood to piss. Anatoly and Konstantin were the low life, told only what they needed to know, and then only when it was convenient to tell them.

"What does 'old people' mean?"

"People like us. Veterans, same as me and you. Three were seen coming out, and two had grey hair, and one was bald. The target wasn't seen."

"Like us then?"

"Like us. Need the money. Have no family that wants them. Guns for hire."

"You know what . . .?"

Anatoly interrupted him. "They'll be very like us. They won't love the guy and we don't hate the guy. But we need bread to eat and so do they."

"And beer to drink, and they need the same . . . what beer do they drink? Same shit as us? And they dream the same?"

"They dream, Konstantin, of owning a bar, or having a kiosk, or being housekeeper in a *dacha* down outside Lazarevskoye or Vityazevo, Black Sea. Maybe they have places where they want to land a soft billet. They'll think the same as us."

"Will they stand in front of the guy, the traitor?"

"I don't know? How can I know?"

"Will they take a bullet for him?" Konstantin's fist punched the open palm of his other hand: like the bullshit was over and this was business, what mattered.

"Maybe they will and maybe they won't." A shrug from Anatoly, and how the hell could he know?

"And give a bullet, take us down – so the target survives?"

"Why not, why wouldn't they?"

"Not arguing, Anatoly. If they are like us then they will have done time killing. They'd have been in Iraq and in Afghan, and they'll have seen serious shit. Won't be sentimental guys if they're like us – we're not. We are paid to do the job, will do it as best we can. And them, paid, and want to move on to new work . . . But they have a problem."

"What is their problem that we don't have?"

"They are not as good as us. No fucking way. Not as good, no."

They were laughing, like two old drunks coming out of a closing bar. And they wiped their smiles when their colonel returned, still zipping his flies . . . Nothing to do except wait till dark, and then take a ferry boat ride.

"So, let us get on with it," Jonas grimaced.

"Should I sit opposite you?"

"Whatever for?"

"So you can better read me, Mr Merrick."

"Pretty much for the form book, Frank, just ticking the last boxes."

"And once you've disposed of your thumbscrew, Mr Merrick, then lunch and we might sample the cake."

She stayed where she was and switched off her laptop. It was a talent possessed by Jonas, a useful one in his trade, that he was able to recognise small shifts of mood and body language. He did not attend interrogations in police stations but they were always filmed and he liked to watch them in the peace of his own cubicle. He thought she toughened as for a moment her face took on a steeliness before she surprised him.

"Can I say something, Mr Merrick?"

"Of course you can, Frank. Whatever . . ."

"It is about what I believe and what I don't believe."

"Please."

"A little game I've been playing. Just me. The others in the Resettlement team see you as a rather dim intruder, sent here to embarrass . . . What I believe is that you have an outstanding record in Counter-Intelligence or Counter-Terrorism, whichever – I also believe that you adopt an impression of self-denigration, selling yourself short. I do not believe that you are either stupid or naive . . . anyway, let's get stuck in."

Which would have taken some guts. Direct and businesslike. He had never regarded her as flaky, but his opinion of her had risen: brave to have done that, told him she had seen through his public style which seemed to have been swallowed by her superiors. For a moment Jonas was silenced, then grimaced – she was entitled to her opinion, but he made a little gesture to pretend that what she had stated was inappropriate. He said something about the need to push on so that they could get the main body of work done before lunch time. He started with her childhood.

Crisp answers, no waffle . . . father walked out when she was two years old, and her mother had died when she was nine, and she had been taken in by a childless uncle and aunt, Rex and Prudence, both retired. An independent day school in south Oxfordshire, and most of what she had been left from her mother's estate had gone into the fees. Rex had been in defence and intelligence and had done time in the Gulf.

Took it chronologically. Further education and recruitment, and she talked easily and her tone was conversational and he rarely interrupted her ... decent and expected school grades, and a place at Canterbury. No particular hobbies, no sport, and a 2.1 in Ancient History. Her joining the VX crowd was helped on its way by her uncle and his long-standing friendship with an SIS manager. Arrived aged twenty-four, but not as an officer.

A vague outline of life as a junior Sixer ... Been there thirteen years and so had missed the "sexed-up dossier" inquest, had worked in Accounts and in Personnel, had done a two-year stint in Buenos Aires. Had come back to Russia Desk and was under the guidance of Denys Montgomery. He had been promoted and had brought her with him.

Jonas allowed her to talk. Was she sleeping with Montgomery? Not asked. Had gone with him as the principal theorist in the Resettlement team. Her role: pretty much to anticipate disasters, catastrophes and steer a course around them. Her job satisfaction: not great, but acceptable.

And the inevitable stock-in-trade questions as used in Positive Vetting. Recreation? A bit of amateur dramatics but years ago. Lovers, partners, best chums? Not really, time didn't allow for it, and the team relied on her – which was an abbreviation for saying that she was indispensable, and Jonas reflected that she had positioned herself, with no little skill, into a role where she could "talent scout" at will. He thought her intelligent and driven. And ... she glanced at her watch, pinched her cheeks, made a gesture that meant greater forces were at work than she could control, and was abject in apology.

"Sorry, Mr Merrick, something that I did not say."

"Which is?"

"Well, it's Saturday and I did not expect to be working and . . ."

"And you have a commitment?"

"The dentist actually. Quite difficult for me to fix appointments. I really am sorry."

"I hope it's nothing serious. Me, I'm terribly squeamish at the mention of dental demands."

"I should have said."

"You go to the dentist, and I'll content myself outside. Not a problem. That wretched rain seems to have moved on. I'd like to sit in the sunshine, have a good coat, gulp some air – and, Frank, I'll be rooting for you."

Straightforward. She would scamper off and head for the bridge and then the bus from Pimlico, and he would be on the phone, double damn fast, calling Aggie Burns, reporting the movement and they might have time for a tail and might have to pull back the deep rummage team working her apartment. They went out of the building. He said where he would be, on the walkway alongside the river, with a view of the two bridges, Vauxhall and Lambeth, and of Tate Britain and the Millbank tower.

"I'll be here, Frank, no worry. And I hope after the ordeal you will still be able to enjoy the cake."

"Yes . . . yes, I hope so too."

The Line Manager, at home in the Surrey conurbation of Thames Ditton, rang Denys Montgomery.

"Just warning you, Denys, the word I have is that the little toad is going to call for the disbandment of the present Resettlement team. Thought you should know."

Montgomery abandoned his train display and called Barker.

"I know you've not long left with us but just wanted to say that we're likely to split and fragment, and by the time you finish, God knows where we'll all be. What I hear, that's the verdict of our snooper."

Barker, watching TV sport from the southern hemisphere, dialled Toni.

"Hope it's not too bad a time and the kids aren't driving you insane – when's your husband going to take a break from bombing Syria and get back to you? Thought you should know that the little beggar from Five will recommend that the team is taken apart and that's the price levelled at us for the Hun's incompetence. Thank Christ I won't be around, but I hope you do well. Such a shame, I thought we were rather good."

Toni called Symonds who answered irritably and was due on court for the Sixers' tennis squad.

"Bit of bad news. The team's for the chop. What that shite will recommend and unlikely our lords and masters – who have been utterly supine – will stand in the way of it. I'm wondering where you'll end up . . . anyway, regards to your mother."

Symonds, spitting anger, called Chiswell.

"That fucker from Five, he's going to break up the team, it's what I hear. Scatter us to the winds. Just wanted to say, Chis, that if you're on your way somewhere interesting I'd be grateful to go with you. Frank? . . . No idea where she fits in. Don't know, don't care. But you'll think of me, Chis – hope you will. What I called the 'fucker from Five', did we under-estimate him? Well don't bloody ring off on me, *Mister* Chiswell, arsehole top order." He put the phone down and lectured the mirror. "So, obviously, a slight rap on the knuckles for our German friends, and we get chopped. Maybe I'm the only one cares what happens to Frank. Or is this just a bigger game than anyone deigned to tell me?"

"I suppose I'm actually rather selfish," Maggie said.

"Selfish, yes, could be." Lucinda's answer.

They walked across the main hallway of the Embassy. The interior dripped prestige and status from the decoration to the images of former glories . . . all that stuff about "punching above our weight". By the door and the security gear – the X-rays and metal detectors and card checkers – Josh and Nancy waited, dressed down. Jeans and leather jackets and beanies and dirty ankle boots. And the Ambassador emerged from a side door, flanked by a PA and a First Secretary. A lip curled. He would have seen Lucinda, the station chief, and seen her two minders. Not usual for the Ambassador to be in the building on a Saturday morning. Would have seen Maggie, the white powder brushed on her cheeks to give her the impoverished and hungry look, and a drab coat over a long lustreless skirt and boots that were scraped where the fake leather had failed, and pushing an old buggy. Would have known of Maggie who half the men in the building quite fancied, would have known of her job in the Military Attaché's office and of her moonlighting with Lucinda's people. His lip curled because the station crowd were not answerable to him but to the people in that revolting building on the south of the Thames. They caused trouble, did nothing to enhance the ability of the Embassy to achieve successes, big or small. Their activities led to expulsions and further chills in relationships. And they were gathered in the main hallway, blatant and brazen.

"Morning, Lucinda."

"Morning, Ambassador. Spot of snow in the air I fancy."

He would have thought that a covert job was in the process of kicking off, and Maggie recognised the expression on his face, the lips narrowing, the distaste. "Not going to give me grief, I hope."

"Who knows? Never can tell."

"And I would not want little Hector involved in any hooliganism."

"He'll be a very happy little chap," Lucinda answered him.

The diplomat and his people hurried away, had that brisk walk which seemed to indicate purpose and business. He was described to lowly Maggie by the station chief as "that right pillock". For the Ambassador, "grief" would be a summons to the Foreign Ministry and a lecture on the damage of "illegal activities" and Lucinda being expelled along with others from the Culture and Economy sections, and Maggie having to be hoiked from Lubyanka custody, and Hector, and a lead story on the TV news, and some half-wit guy looking like a rabbit in headlights with bruised eyes and a split lip and staring into a lens for a mug shot . . . Josh and Nancy were guaranteed to treat Maggie as if she were a kid sister, and Hector was gurgling and he was being tickled under his chin. They would use a back exit from the compound and would synchronise it with the Ambassador's departure through the main gates when attention would be concentrated on him, and his escort, and the trailing FSB motors.

Maggie said, "I asked you about being selfish. Ditching the boy, scrubbing a promise I should never have made. Liked him, really did. Frightened and vulnerable. Don't feel good about it. And selfish because I want back into the Army. What do you say? Selfish?"

"I say 'bravo'. Bravo and twice over. Time to hit the street, and remember we are right there with you, today and tomorrow. You know what they say to aristocrats' boys about actresses? 'Take her to bed but not to the altar.' What we say, 'Do a bit of comfort stuff, but don't get friendly with an asset.' Selfish, no, Maggie, not you."

They headed out and the buggy's wheels whined, needed oil. Would split before they emerged on to the pavement, and would meet again at the forecourt of the wholesale flower market, the Tsvety ot Machelyuks. Josh and Nancy would be behind Maggie, and Lucinda way back but able to see them . . . The guys she had worked with in the Province, the bloody good guys, would have said, "So, what can possibly go wrong?" and would chuckle. She pushed the buggy past the policeman and gave him a slow sad smile.

During the whole train journey, Alexei would speak to another passenger only if he needed to climb over a pair of legs in order to reach the aisle, go to the toilet. Would not have tolerated a stranger attempting to talk to him. Where was he from? What did he do? Why was he returning to the capital? Refused to engage in conversation. He kept his head down through the long night hours as the train ran sweetly across the great Russian plain.

Not many stops, few passengers leaving, and few joining.

They had pulled into Nizhny Novgorod. Half the journey done, and the compartment darkened. There was snoring, some hacking coughs and some people were interminably on their phones, and a few still filling their mouths with smelly spiced food. Alexei thought he recognised a man from the return journey a couple of weeks before. Had walked in front of him along the pavement and into the station: had seemed well presented, dressed in a casual style but of good quality, and then Alexei had lost sight of him because of the greater concern for his tail and for Maggie . . . The man wore a heavy coat, an artist's hat with a brim, but what stood out was a tartan wool scarf, with squares of orange and green. The man sat almost opposite Alexei. His arrival was the cue for another attempt by Alexei's neighbours to strike up conversation, but they were put down, almost with brutality. The man had closed his eyes, stretched out his legs so that his feet nestled close to Alexei's and had said, barely audibly, that he was tired, needed to rest, had nothing of interest to communicate, and nothing of interest to learn. A lesson to Alexei in how to counter the demands of strangers that stories might be exchanged in order to pass away the night hours. What he should have done on these journeys, and had not. Alexei wondered why such a man, with good clothes, and a fine leather laptop bag, travelled in the third-class seats.

The train had passed Vladimir, was in the last ninety minutes of the twelve-hour journey. Alexei had dozed, but had not slept. Around him was the stale smell of other passengers – wind, belches, sweat, old socks. Always when he came back to Moscow he was tired from lack of sleep on the train and often at his mother's apartment he would sleep all afternoon which annoyed her. There was snow on the track. Alexei noticed that the man who had boarded at Nizhny Novgorod slept deeply, breathing regular, face calm, a child's innocence on his features . . . not so Alexei.

Alexei's bag was wedged between his feet and one of the man's shoes rested on it. Which reminded Alexei that everything of value to him was in the bag, and that nothing else mattered. He needed to stiffen himself, be resolute and blitz out the growing fear. He locked on the image of Maggie's face, her grin and the gold of her hair . . . and he did not know whether *they* would be waiting for him at the terminus, would take him before he even saw her.

The train carried him closer to Moscow, and his fear grew, and he could not escape it, and the source of that fear was the memory stick in the heel of his trainer. He saw Maggie's face, clung to it, and imagined the wire of a fence and the collapse of a door and his mother's shrieks of terror. The man slept well, and Alexei's breathing came faster.

*   *   *

"You want to know why I came, the reason I came?"

They were off the ferry. A brief stop in a parking area close to a shed of parked bicycles, and the sea flapping the pier, and seals resting on a sandbar, and spring sunshine on their coats, and the decision that the PET pair would lead.

Igor said, "My father-in-law, he has a small apartment in Sochi, that is the Black Sea. You have heard of Sochi, it is the principal resort. There are modest apartments and there are modest hotels and there are modest campsites, and they are for the ordinary people. I am only a major in GRU and therefore I am ordinary . . . but there are also superior apartments and superior hotels and superior campsites with luxury facilities, and I am only a major in GRU and therefore am not eligible for superior privileges. You understand me?"

Benedict thought it was because the firearms were evident. Not displayed, but visible. God forbid the end result might be an accidental discharge in broad daylight. The weapons were tucked down by their boots and the barrels up by Wally's knee and Doug's, and there was a pistol now between Benedict's and Igor's hips, as if it were available but not yet claimed. If they had been blocked or driven into, or come under fire the Russian would have had his fist on it, would have cocked it, would have fired it . . . They had driven past more seals and then had been beyond Nordby and had turned inland, had seen a sign that indicated the location of the police station and the fire service, and a school, and the village, with its little houses with thatched roofs, and narrow streets, gave way to stunted woodland. The winter was lifting and the first daffodils were out, but the wind had a cold cut to it and the trees were without leaf. Now, late, the guy tried to justify himself.

"I was there with my wife. I was to be posted to Copenhagen, so we took a holiday. That is my wife and my daughter and myself, and we stayed in my father-in-law's apartment. It had a view of a gas station from the front window and a sewage farm from the side window and a furniture factory from the back window. That is because he – my wife's father – was also not a superior person. But, there is a pleasant beach in Sochi and beyond the main city there are smaller and more attractive stretches of sand. I drove to one of them and we had our picnic prepared. It was to be a happy day because my daughter showed sign of improvement in her health. I may have sinned, but I tried to be a good parent, and tried, not hard enough, to be a good husband. We found this beach. Plastic on it and paper and wipes and bottles and cans. Many people there and at the edge, where there was a small headland, was a single strand of barbed wire, and a notice that said entry was forbidden. I look and beyond the wire is a beach without litter and clean sand and sea that is blue and clean . . . and I am a major in GRU, and I step over the wire and am carrying the picnic bag, and am holding my daughter's hand, help her over, and my wife is hesitant but I tell her to come."

Only when they had come off the ferry, had Nils and Jette been given an address: the name of a house that was in the sixth sector off a service road to the south of Vesterhavsbad. They drove past cafés and fast-food chains, and the shops that would sell holiday clothing and boards and balls and screens for the beach, and bars, all shuttered. Tennis courts with no nets up, all-weather soccer pitches without posts. A place of ghosts, and a few, very few, pensioners struggling against the wind's force. The PET pair stopped. Jette came to them. Did they want to see the beach first, then find the house? She spoke brusquely, like she was indifferent, would rather be back in Copenhagen, and her look at Igor was brief. Benedict said he'd like to have a look at the beach, and the sea. They drove on. Igor continued his story . . . no one in the car gave a damn for his tale of grievance . . . but he was determined to be heard.

"We are around the headland, we are beyond the sight of the ordinary people who are on a dirty beach, and we see perfection and I put down the rug on which we will sit and the picnic bag, and my wife is not happy and is tense, and says it is a private place. I say it is a good place . . . and I take my daughter to the sea and to paddle. We are in the water, up to her knees, and she is beginning to lighten her mood and the happiness is starting to return to her face and the illness is at that moment in the back seat, and . . . I hear the shriek, my name, my wife's voice. There are two goons standing over her. They wear black, the shit that have shaven heads, tattoos on their arms, the crap that do security. They are lecturing my wife. I am walking back and my daughter has caught the atmosphere and has started to cry. I can see that beyond my wife and the two men is a villa raised from the beach and a patio. There are loungers on the patio. Two people on the patio, a man with a stomach and a woman who should not display herself in a bikini. The men, their goons, wear face masks so that their identity is hidden. On the patio they are laughing . . . I wonder if the man is *siloviki*, or near to it, or thinks he should be elevated to such heights. I tell the goons that I am a major in GRU and that I and my wife and my daughter will have our picnic here, and they tell me that I am nothing, and that I should fuck the hell out, and my wife now is in tears, and my daughter is screaming. What to do? I have the picnic bag and I have the rug and I hitch my daughter on my hip, and my wife cries all the way back to the strand of wire and the sign that says entry is forbidden, and no one who is there amongst the mess and filth of the ordinary people's beach catches my eye. They know their place . . . We went back that night to Moscow. That is the modern Russia. It was a lecture in our country's habits – a lesson well taught. I came to Copenhagen and knew when the time was ready that I would walk out on them. You understand?"

They were on a hardcore road. Either side were comfortable houses, four or five bedrooms, detached, with plate-glass windows for the view: the steep banks of sand dunes, tufts of grass and a horizon of sky and cloud.

Benedict thought it a place without soul, and the houses would each have cost a million euro and the PET car led them on to a paved forecourt.

Doug asked him, "This the one? We have a deal for it?"

Benedict answered, "I wasn't told, Merrick didn't say. Wouldn't have thought so. Just, sort of, stopping by and using the facilities."

Wally said, "For what you said, what it was needed for, I think it's good."

They scampered for the rear door and Benedict heard Wally say to Doug, "So that's what this song and dance is all about. Got himself booted off a beach. Pride hurt, self-esteem clocked. And all this born out of it – makes you want to fucking weep."

And heard Doug's response: "Ours not to reason why."

"Because we are so ordinary."

And both laughed softly, but had a tight hold of their weapons.

And laughed some more.

Wally said to his friend, "You reckon we were watched on to the ferry?"

Doug said to his friend, "Watched off the ferry, watched all the way here?"

"I thought that was the idea."

"The game we're signed up to play."

"Reckon you might find something to say to the guy who thought this up, this game?"

A credit card in the lock did the business.

They went inside, and Brian had put away in his bag the jemmy he had used to open the back door, and they smelled the must and the damp of the winter weeks stored in the building.

An almost pleasant afternoon in London and Jonas had taken possession of a bench and had a good view of the river.

He and Vera liked to take a jigsaw puzzle when they were on a caravan break. Always best, they would agree, to put the big effort, maximum concentration, into getting the burden of the puzzle sorted. They liked landscape jigsaws, usually 500 pieces, always worked on the outside together, and then would leave it and simply put in the filling at leisure, a piece at a time. Always seemed easy once the limits of the puzzle were in place – which it was. And the centre would come together fast.

He had twice tugged at the brim of his trilby to prevent the wind from carrying it off and dumping it in the river, so dark and hostile. An alien place, and was surprised because when he walked to work each morning, he hardly spared a glance between Waterloo and Thames House at what was below him. Funny, the way a mood swung. More important than the mood and the river's flow as the tide turned was the fitting of the last pieces.

Growing easier by the minute.

He could have thought himself rewarded by the brittle sunshine that, almost, warmed his face, but he was glad that he wore gloves, and a scarf, and his raincoat, which protected him from the bluster of the wind. A gull hovered over him, showed him no respect . . . safe to assume the contact had been made.

One of the last pieces to drop in place. His phone rang.

"Hello, sir . . . well, I've agreed to call you because I was told there was a degree of anonymity involved here. But was told to speak freely. I was the secretary of that amateur dramatic society. Secretary and treasurer and chair of the steering committee, and sold tickets and stood in as prompter, and cleaned up the hall once the punters had left. Of course I remember her. We knew her as Frannie . . . Pretty quiet, a shy sort of girl, not long out of university. Had a Whitehall job but she never talked about it. Made some of us wonder if it were hush-hush. Quite lonely and I suppose we were near her digs, or bedsit or whatever, and she needed a hobby. We never had much for her. I mean, she didn't act but could have done some walk-ons. Never pushed for the chance to get the greasepaint on. She helped with costumes, and posters, did the coffee and cake tables on performance nights. I can't say she made friends, only that she had that ability to sense where the heavy lifting was going to be and would help there . . . then the change. One of our mainstays called it the Damascene conversion. Altered her. The live theatre, sir – I'm calling you "sir" because I wasn't given your name – has an extraordinary effect on people. Not just those in the heat of the spotlights but also all the foot soldiers, what I call them, who are around the fringes. She had no boyfriend – and no girlfriend – was wrapped and private in herself and . . . It was all instant, that chemistry thing that the stage does rather well. He was Peter, can't remember the last name . . . might have been Pieter. You see the difference. Not English. Anyway, we thought he was Serbian, certainly central

Europe. Took some minor parts, really threw himself at us, and at her. Brought Frannie out of herself, and they were inseparable. What one of our stage managers said, if we'd done *Romeo and Juliet*, and he'd taken Romeo's role, then she'd have been a shoe-in for the Capulet girl and it would have been quite steamy on stage. I'm not proud, but it gave us all a bit of a laugh. She lost some photos once, fell out of her bag and then on the floor and under a table, till found. They were well thumbed by one of our more nosy ladies. A love nest in a Hebridean croft. Malt whisky and log fires, beach walks and hair blown about and cheeks flushed. Getting the picture, and I think shagging like rabbits in a warm burrow, and a going-away party. Had to get to Australia for a sick mum, and due back soon. Never seen again. He'd have deflowered the little virgin, we reckoned, and no one else in our gang had even been close. She started to come less often, and he was never mentioned, seemed to be off the radar. And she had a new address, down near Paddington station, and life had moved on but she still turned up when we needed extra hands. About November last year, middle of the month, and we were doing *An Inspector Calls*. Don't tell me how boring that is, with cobwebs hanging off it, but it was a schools exam textbook and that would marry seats and bums, and she was doing front of house. A bunch of flowers arrived. A big enough bunch, ridiculous, and God alone knows what it cost. *To Frannie with love, P xxx* and a mobile number: not much escapes us. Her chin fell so low that it slapped her boobs and she blushed pillar box. I saw her make a call just as the audience were pitching up, then she gathered up the bouquet, lovely it was, and was outside and waving down a taxi and off she went into the night. Haven't seen her since. Have called but she doesn't ring back . . . Did it work out for them? I do hope so. She was a sad person and deserved a bit of luck. The one big love of her life, we all said . . . I talk too much, don't I? Not in any trouble is she . . .?"

He did not like to lie.

Jonas Merrick had no qualms about deceit where his work was directly concerned but did not care to tell untruths merely to massage anxieties. He took the other alternative if he was not to lie. *Not in any trouble is she . . .?* And rang off. The phone went into his briefcase and when he was back in Thames House he would hand it in and it would be disposed of, wiped, its numbers and memory erased, untraceable. He looked at the water, saw its surge and thought it had a grim dreariness in spite of the filtered sunshine playing on it.

She came back.

He might have seen himself as a ferret. Bright little eyes, awesome teeth, and scurrying down a hole, pattering along tunnels, and flushing out the rabbits so that they scampered for their lives towards the daylight . . .

"Hello again, Mr Merrick."

"Good to see you, Frank, and I hope it was not too awful."

"Not bad – and you are all right?"

"Good, thank you. Very pleasant sitting here, watching the world go by."

The ferret drove the rabbits towards the warren's exit points, where the nets were pegged out.

"So, before we get back to work, let's go and treat ourselves, Mr Merrick, to cake."

12

They walked back together and towards the VX building. After what had seemed an age of rain and cold, enough to have floated old Noah's craft, it was pleasant to have the brittle sunshine lancing on to their faces.

Jonas assumed himself a fairly typical male approaching old age, his middle years past and peeled off like a snake's skin . . . But what did he know of women? Know enough to make a judgement?

It might have been because the low sun was full into his face, but Jonas stumbled when the toecap of his right shoe clipped the edge of an uneven pavement slab and he might have toppled and would instinctively have reached out to find support, and her hand caught him. He was steadied . . . Not a word said. He did not thank her, she did not query as to whether he was all right. Frank had taken hold of elbow, had paused mid-stride, long enough to ascertain that he was not ill, then they had moved on and they walked at a leisurely place.

Might not have answered the question himself. Might have waited until he reached home and had hung up his coat and put his trilby on the hook, and unfastened the clasp holding the chain their linked his briefcase to his wrist. Might have walked into the kitchen and asked Vera. What did he know of women?

Her hand stayed at his elbow. Jonas seldom talked if he had little that was appropriate to speak of. He believed that Frank was also content to hold her silence. They would have seemed to passersby like father and daughter.

What did he know of women, their moods and motivations and incentives and pleasures and hates and loves? Vera would barely have raised her head from whatever task involved her in the kitchen and he would have stood in the doorway, a puzzled look on his face and in a rare and rather self-conscious way he would have posed the question, and added a second. "Do I know anything of women?" Vera would have thought it a quite fatuous question. "Nothing."

He could not ascertain whether her hand on his arm was a gesture of charity, of mild friendship, or whether she sought further to manipulate him.

The book had been dropped on his desk in the cubicle of S/3/13, by the AssDepDG. A grim remark about the need to further Jonas's learning. The book's title was taken from a keynote lecture – one of those bullet points that a seminar director would have had up on a screen better to hold the attention of an audience – *Shoot the Women First*. There had been a throwaway aside from the AssDepDG about Jonas being careful not to bandy the book and its cover where any of the more feisty young goddesses of the A BranchWatchers would see it . . . "Will confirm all their worst fears of you being a dinosaur rooted in a claypit of stereotype and prejudice" . . . The kernel of the book had been that the female target was more likely to have bitten deeper into the meat of necessary ideology, would be more committed to the guerrilla cause, to the espionage credo. It had arisen in Germany, had been adopted as a theme by Interpol and circulated throughout Europe to those likely to lead storm squads. It was passed on as general knowledge that a terror cell would best be hit at dawn, five in the morning, and the chance was greatest that the guys would be pissed out of their minds, or stoned to hell, and that the girls would be quickest reaching for the AKs, loaded and on automatic.

They walked in step. Gulls bawled at them, cyclists swept past, and the first of the joggers leaving work at VX, from a Saturday shift, went by, and the wind seemed to clip the water and threw up diamonds, but the moments of beauty were lost again in dark and deep water . . . Jonas would have said that there was almost a moment of frustration when he held the last piece of a jigsaw puzzle and his hand hovered over the picture. Vera always made certain that it was Jonas who provided that last touch. At times he felt a degree of reluctance to slip the piece into place and so end the game, disrobe the mystery.

He broke the silence.

"I should have said this to you before, Frank, and my apologies for leaving it so late. The way I want to play this is that I go home this evening and I'll take a note on the text of my final analysis, and then ask you to come in tomorrow and I'll need an hour or so of your time, not more. I hope that is not too inconvenient . . ."

"I can manage that, Mr Merrick."

"The broad conclusion, but it will need a bit of spit and polish, will be that the leak was from outside. However . . . always an *however* – I've made a recommendation, just the one. It has already been flown past your senior people and there seems no overwhelming objection. It will lead to a disbandment. The current Resettlement team will be allocated to other duties. That does not imply any level of guilt, any degree of negligence, but a fresh broom is required, my humble opinion . . . For you, Frank, I would suggest a complete change of scene. I don't like the way – and I've eyes in my head – that crowd walk all over you, nor do I enjoy witnessing that degree of bullying. You're better than they allowed you to be, my opinion after our brief acquaintance. I have a friend in Work and Pensions, sounds dull but in fact is rather rewarding, and I'd like you to meet her tomorrow once we've killed the beast, put the report in order, and she works most Sundays to get ahead of her emails. We'll talk about it in the morning."

He'd smiled. She had nodded, noncommittal. They had walked on, her hand still on his elbow. Past the pub and the petrol station and the small supermarket, and on along the Albert Embankment.

"You know, Frank, what I am already looking forward to?"

"What is that, Mr Merrick?"

"Looking forward to my cake."

He thought her smile forced, and could not assess whether she believed the act he stuck with. Did not know to what extent his apparent pedestrianism alerted her antennae to the dangers she faced. She took her hand from his elbow. They were coming within sight of the VX entrance and the police and the gatekeeper. She would sign him in, they would go back down to the basement bunker. They would each eat a slice of cake off a cardboard plate and use plastic forks, and he would clear from the safe what he needed to take home but would leave the maps of the island in place. And then she would see him out of the building, and she would stand beside an armed police officer as Jonas thanked her for cake, and on a strap around the policeman's neck would be an assault rifle, his finger always within half an inch of the trigger. Would he shoot her if it was deemed necessary? Shoot her first? She wore her dignity well, smart, competent, loyal, and seemed to carry no threat . . . He would start his journey home . . . In his mind, Jonas put the last piece of the puzzle in its place and felt only a little elation and a rather great tiredness.

Benedict accepted that his control was ceded. His first experience of the stripping of responsibility was when a big Chinook, double engines, and its twin rotors kicking up a dust storm in the darkness that had damn near choked the lot of them, and his little multi-national band had been grabbed by coalition troops, probably American. Behind them, an Iraqi mob was in full voice and had his makeshift headquarters well alight. He remembered seeking out an officer and making a suggestion, and had been curtly told to take a seat, fasten the waist strap and shut his face. There had been gunship birds overhead. Where had they been earlier? Where, when they were needed and authority should have been restored and the building saved . . . had not gotten around to asking. The military rescue party had seemed more interested in saving some of the female staff of Benedict's pint-sized mission. He learned fast, then and now.

They were inside a holiday home, and the sunlight pierced the window blinds. Would have been a good time for a long beach walk, which was Benedict being stupid, and Benedict regretting that no one came calling to ask for his opinion. Both cars were parked outside at the front. He heard eddies of the conversation as the rest of them huddled.

A jerked thumb, in a plastic glove, from Brian towards Benedict. "He goes with the pull-out, and you, Igor, and Jette – and me, more's the shame."

Cigarettes being passed around by Jette. All of them wore gloves from the PET vehicle.

A nod of agreement from Doug. "I buy into it. Nils and Wally and I remain in place – for the fun time."

And a lighter from the Danish boy.

Accepted by Jette. "Would have enjoyed staying, but . . . it is high risk."

And Brian's hand deep in his pocket and a briar produced.

From Wally, "They won't show up before dark. We'll have done the walk around by then, know where we want to be."

And matches lit.

Doug, scratching at his thinning hair, "You know who he is, the guy calling it?"

They were in the living-room filling it with the pipe's smoke and the cigarettes' fumes. When they had checked the house, Benedict had noted a prominent No Smoking sign in each room, in German and Danish.

From Brian, "No idea, never heard of him. He has a map and a satellite picture and thinks we'll do well. How we'll do well is in our court. First time ever I am not second-guessed by a desk warrior."

Benedict noted that both of his muscle boys had lit up as soon as offered. Wally and Doug had not smoked once during the whole exercise, not even on the dash out of Hamburg, and not in the aftermath of the malfunctioning rifle. He supposed the matter now ramped to a different level . . .

Benedict looked around. Comfortable rattan chairs, rugs on tiled floors, displays of shells on shelves along with books and photos. There would have been a party the night before the owners had left in the previous autumn because on a sideboard was a stack of almost, not quite, empty spirits bottles . . . he could imagine one of the family being unwilling to pour away good alcohol and ditch the empties. Beyond the smoke-filled living area were the bedrooms – beds stripped – and bathrooms and a well-fitted kitchen that boasted the best modern appliances, and the tea towels were dried out, rigid. Quite a decent place . . . insurance might cover the damage might not, and Benedict doubted that the predictable events of the night could be classified as an Act of God. No ashtray so they used a breakfast bowl from the kitchen.

Wally said, "Good way, only way, best way."

And the Russian interjected, as if the thought – since it was about him, only him – that a contribution was necessary. "I have to tell you, the people they will have sent will have reckoned they are an elite. They will have said that it was not their fault that the bomb, the Hamburg attack, failed. Not their fault that they failed again when they came over the fence and the blame goes to the weapon. Perhaps they did not clean it properly, perhaps the ammunition had deteriorated, but not their fault. Never their fault . . . Maybe when this fails they will not have the chance to explain how they were not to blame, again."

And a dry smile played on his face, and the message was clear . . . They entered a killing game, waited for its starting whistle and had enough to do between them to pass away the hours. The weapons were checked and checked again. And Brian had the sensors and the cables and the console in his bag, would take responsibility for them.

Benedict had a smattering of Danish, enough for a newspaper or a radio bulletin. He heard Jette's query to Nils: was he all right with what was asked, and a frown of concern on her face. His answer was a shrug, and a grin. She persisted. He was comfortable.

When Benedict returned to the UK, went up north and found his family again near to Loch Linnhe, he might break the stricture of the Service and actually tell his wife something of where he had been and what he had seen and who had been alongside. First thing he would say is that, as hours, minutes, dribbled away before a confrontation that seemed inevitable, little was said. They were all spare with words . . . and it slotted into his own big moment of life when the mob might have caught him and those he tried to protect, and a belated rescue, and being hurried into a briefing officer's canvas tent and being asked to tell his story. Done in a staccato and economical way, as if outsiders had no place there.

A good question had been asked. Who was Merrick? He could recall the rather halting voice, competing with the cries of gulls and the noise of traffic, and thought he had heard a church clock strike. Had sensed a nervousness in the voice as if the man was bent under a weight of the bloody responsibility, same as Benedict. Thought also he was told the bare minimum, and that he would have to accept that. Thought also that *if*, always that damned *if*, it worked, happened, then a huge statement was made, and the implications would run riot.

He was spare. Sat himself down.

Close to where he sat was a table and Brian had fetched a saucer and used it to leave his pipe on. Quite a pleasant scent, reminding Benedict of a grandfather and childhood. The house reeked of the damp and the cold of the winter and wrestled for supremacy with the smell of tobacco.

Wally did the weapons, the final check. Had the rifles out on a rug on the floor, and involved Igor. All rather childish, Benedict thought. Benedict did not do firearms. They were supposed to have shooting practice down at Fort Monckton, and it had been compulsory to take part: would have failed to get out of probation if he had refused. He remembered that some of the intake pretended to be indifferent about holding a lethal pistol in their hand, and some had seemed genuinely terrified, and others had declaimed – too loud – that they would never be able to take a human life, not even in the protection of themselves or colleagues: a few had said that if the time came they would fire in anger, hope to kill, and not give a damn . . . None were like Wally and Doug and Brian who seemed to find a simple pleasure in having a weapon close by, and about stripping down the mechanism. Igor and Jette were sitting on a rug, both cross-legged, and the Russian talked the Danish girl through the engineering qualities of the Dragunov snipers' rifle, and they had disappeared the two of them, into a bubble.

He was not part of it. Did not wish to be, and it was not expected of him. Benedict took his phone out. Sent a message. *In place Benedict.*

Imagined it coming up on a phone screen. Tried to imagine the man reading it. Saw the view over a shoulder, and saw the river and the gulls, and the man would be quite elderly – from his voice – and not physically dynamic from his hesitations when speaking. Would likely be bowed by the burdens he carried but would be wearing a thick coat in the cold of the London air. Benedict's phone told him that the weather around VX was dry, cold, that a penetrating wind blew. He pictured the heavy coat the man wore, and a stout hat would be rammed down on his head.

In truth, knew nothing. But had laid faith in this man. Had given his life into his hands.

Wished he smoked . . . the weapons had been stripped, were put back together. The magazines had been emptied and were now refilled. Igor and Jette had edged aside a corner of the blind and took turns in peering into the telescopic sight, and she uttered little cooing gasps of admiration at the quality of the optics. It was Brian who told Benedict what was needed from him.

To build a man, his given task. Not told how, and not told why, and not told where it should be placed. He liked it, enjoyed that rare autonomy. There was a low table in the kitchen which he brought out. He stepped over the couple admiring the rifle, proven killing range of 1000 yards, and carried a pair of upright chairs from the master bedroom. Went to the porch area inside the front door and took a rainproof coat and a hat that would have been there for use when the heavens opened over the North Sea in mid-summer. He stood at his full height in a bedroom and unscrewed a lamp shade, useful because it was quite narrow. Enough to start with.

The message sent to the Esbjerg harbour authority from the trawler, the *Katerina*, sailing from the Russian port of Kaliningrad, the enclave on the southern side of the Baltic Sea, listed "engine trouble" as a reason for slowing to a crawl. Her position as reported by the skipper and which also figured on Danish radar, put her some twenty-five nautical miles from Esbjerg, to the north, and off the virtually unpopulated Jutland beach area of Henne Strand.

Engine trouble, as if that were a surprise. The reason for slow progress would have amused the harbour staff, had any bothered to note it – a Russian trawler delayed by a malfunction and likely sailing under the power of a Russian-built engine. It was far enough to the north of the navigation lanes used by the resupply boats going out to the North Sea rigs and wind farms and would prove no obstruction, no danger to regular shipping. Accepted that the Russian trawler fleet was cheapskate and floundering on its last legs for want of investment. If the *Katerina* stayed clear of the lanes and did not fish in European water then none of the staff at Esbjerg control need show a scintilla of interest. None did.

Except that there were parts of that fleet, sailing from Kaliningrad, that had split loyalties. Interests were divided. Most times they took orders only from their skipper and he from the trawler's owners. Sometimes, not often, the route and its timetable were dictated by men and women sitting in the command bunkers in the port of Baltiysk, home of Russia's fleet of warships operating in Baltic waters. A further indication of such dual loyalties was the installation of a four-stroke diesel-powered Yamaha engine, of the highest specifications, built in Japan and fitted in a Netherlands port. The possibility of such an engine giving grief – if correctly maintained – was ranked as remote. The only fishing done from her, as the afternoon merged with the evening, was by the trawler's mess cook and he used feathers on hooks, tied by himself, to attract mackerel on to his line.

In the failing light, and bobbing as the swell came up, the *Katerina* waited for a radio signal that would send her – and the dinghy stowed on board, and the launcher for rocket-propelled grenades – close in to the north-east corner of the island of Fano . . . Always helpful on such voyages when the weather turned and the wind grew in intensity because then the "poppling" of the sea would distort radar signatures. They waited, idled and rocked.

*   *   *

A small man, with naturally smooth facial skin and a balding head and never without his rimmed spectacles, Volkov's appearance was deceptive. A regime such as the one he served would always have need of a man who had earned the title of the Wolf, who had collected that title on the back of work done under his orders in the cells of the Lubyanka, and in the gaol favoured by the GRU hierarchy for those stepping beyond lines laid down, and enforced. He did not take his work home . . . That night he would be out late in central Moscow. A private room at a restaurant in the Arbat quarter was booked for the celebration, or commiseration, party to send a general into retirement: no great hardship as the general had enjoyed many years of preparation for it, lining bank accounts that would see him beyond old age. Later, Volkov would enjoy a meal at the home of a friend of his wife, an artist – talented and sensible in that he painted only attractive landscapes. His phone would be on and texts would reach him. He would sip orange or apple juice with the old military men and would stand apart from the scheming and dealing, but would be there and seen to be there. Such was the fear he created that few confidences would be offered him, and serious drinking and serious indiscretions would only start when he had left. With his wife he would enjoy the artist's hospitality, and he might indulge her and buy her a picture, a watercolour of a tundra view. At neither event would his professional work intrude. He had become skilled at being able to anticipate the slight heave of his phone, to glance and absorb a message and hardly seem to have taken his eye off the individual he spoke to . . . He was satisfied with his preparations.

His family had little idea of the work carried out in the interrogation cells in his name, and of the broken lives he was responsible for, of the pain inflicted. He had heard of a man who had lived into his late eighties who had been a Lubyanka killer in the time of Stalin's rule, and who had needed a bottle of proof vodka a day to get through the numbers of back-of-the-skull single-shot executions he performed – hundreds, maybe thousands – and when he had finally packed it in, hand too shaky even to ensure a point blank hit, his family had believed him to be a clerk with the state rail administration. With the artist and his wife, he would seem charming, humble, and interested. It would be inconceivable that a man so obviously pleasant and intelligent could destroy a career and a livelihood by lifting a phone, giving an order. He expected to hear very soon that a target had reached the railway terminus, travelling from the east, and would be told the results of the surveillance, and would also hear that an arrest squad was in place for the following day. Always good when arrests were made and the video tape messages reached him and he would see the fear spreading on the face of a target as the "boys" closed around him . . . He would also hear of three men in place on an island to the west of the Danish mainland, and a heavy weapon delivered to them and the final preparations for a last-gasp assault. Would be sipping at his juice and nibbling at fruit at the dinner table, and about to go home, when the phone would flicker to life and a result would be given him . . . No more he could do. Success on the two counts would enhance his begrudged reputation. Failure might well topple him. He did not know what else he could do, on those two counts, to better his planning.

Lucinda was the first to get back to the Embassy.

She carried a plastic bag loaded with vegetables from a street kiosk, a usual cover.

She had been too far back from the contact to know how their meeting had played out: the asset *Environ*, and the rookie girl.

Getting so bloody tired of it . . . The police guard at the gate had recognised her – should have done, had all the principals' photographs on a board in the back of their cabin – and had smiled and touched his cap and she had passed him, no acknowledgement. Realised her rudeness. Most times would not have given a flying fuck for an ill-mannered ignoring of a Russian low-ranking cop. Did that morning and had turned on her heel, taken five steps back, had smiled and thanked him, then had gone through the gate.

Always that sense of relief when she came through the gate, past the UK security, on to Embassy territory. Not that she could be touched . . . not that Maggie could be, beyond the discomfort of a few hours in a drab interview room while her immunity was sorted out, and Hector would be fine, well looked after. All right for them, not for the asset.

The train had been late arriving. Had encountered a points problem, a few hundred metres, literally, short of Yaroslavskiy station. Had been there two hours. Meeting a late-running train had put a strain on all of them, had screwed their operational techniques. She had been in the east quarter of the city, not smart and not where the shops were and not where she would normally have gone for coffee, and had had to loiter. Josh and Nancy had faced the same difficulty. They would have been up and down between the wholesale flower place and the steps of the Metro station for the Krasnosel'skaya stop, but not able to get far away as their task was to keep Maggie and her buggy in view . . . and the kid had done well. Not possible for Lucinda to stride ahead and get alongside the girl and reassure her that she was not abandoned, and that the train was late, held up, delayed, wrong sort of snow, wrong sort of leaves, points failure, and it was a Saturday and who in the maintenance section gave a damn – fact of bloody life. She had started to feel vulnerable. Had begun to imagine that she stood out, that her presence fitted no pattern, and then had seen the goon guys. Interesting, and another matter that was pikestaff plain, bloody obvious. The goon guys would have been FSB, were also screwed because a train was late and they had time to kill and even the privacy windows or their vehicle had come down, elbows out and fags lit. She did not think she had shown out, nor that Josh and Nancy had, and Maggie had twice been into the station and out of sight and would have checked the board to see if a new arrival time was displayed, and the goons had not moved. Why would they have? Not that interested in Maggie and Hector, and not recognising Josh and Nancy, and not briefed to keep a weather eye for herself. Waiting for *Environ* . . . as they all bloody were. And she had been needing to pee, had eventually begged in a clothes shop, and been ushered to facilities in the rear, had come back. Had seen Maggie on a bench in the square in front of the station, doing a newspaper puzzle, Russian of course. And the goons hadn't moved and Josh and Nancy were at the window of the pawn shop on Konsomolskaya Square and almost opposite the station entrance.

She had seen him, the asset.

Pale-faced, hesitant, looking around him. One face among many as an impatient stampede carried the frustrated passengers out of the terminus. Josh and Nancy on the move, and Maggie coming towards her, and the boy looking around him another time: poor little sod, scared witless. Could have reflected that he'd need God's help to unfasten him from the grip of Lucinda's talons. And she might rot in hell as a reward for professional effort . . . The boy had started out across the traffic lanes. Might get lifted now, and Maggie. Felt her stomach screw tight.

Wondered if, maybe, it was time for another station chief, one whose ambition was not yet blunted . . . She had a future, sort of. There was a Portugese sea captain. He flogged a tramper back and forth across the Atlantic, Lobito to Porto de Santos. Back and forth between the Angolan port and the Brazilian harbour. She had done time there, Angola, for the Service and then had come home and then had taken the Moscow posting. She would ditch her husband and fly out to the sea captain and make a beach-side life when he chucked his Master's ticket. He might or might not have waited for her while she dithered. Might or might not have put her ahead of a pretty girl, half Lucinda's age, waiting in Brazil. Had a picture of him by her bed in the service apartment at the Embassy. It was only a sort of a future – and now her enthusiasm and her professionalism and her tank supply of will to win took over her mind. She saw Maggie take her time and neatly fold and put away her newspaper, and a pencil went into her bag, and she wiped Hector's face with a tissue and binned it.

The boy came past the goons' van and a parked car with four, five guys in it. The boy stared straight ahead, made no eye contact with them . . . Lucinda, in her working life alongside assets, had never let one go, had kept them working. Had lost some but had retired none. She relied now on Maggie taking the sensible line, and was confident because being sensible was the route into

Ordnance, IED clearance, lunatic but what the girl wanted. Fantastic kid, that Hector. On cue, he threw something out of the buggy which landed almost at *Environ*'s feet. Lucinda reckoned they'd have thirty seconds to transfer the memory stick . . . and the goons had moved off, the van and the car, and the lift would be for another day. No more than half a minute.

She was pleased that she had stopped and been polite to the cop at the gate. She'd go back to her den and take a shower, and stand and gaze at the wild old beggar who took cargo across from Africa to Latin America, and she'd not be writing out her resignation that day, that week. The sight of Maggie with the asset had revitalised her appetite for the trade, reinforced her bloody hunger for it. Had to hope the girl had stayed tough, remained sensible.

Pushing the buggie, Maggie sang softly.

Hector had done well – better than well, had done brilliantly – and now he was hungry. She had not factored in a late train arrival and she had given him an apple to chew at, not successfully. What had been good was the way he had tossed his soft bear out of the buggy, had dumped it at Alexei's feet. Smiled for the policeman on the Embassy gate, gave him a little wink and won a grin back, and was inside. Hector was grizzling.

She had seen the surveillance team pull out. They would have noted Alexei's arrival in the crowds streaming from the station, and then had coughed their vehicle engines into action and had left. Always did the heavier surveillance on the way out, the Sunday journey. He had reached her, his bag tight in his right hand, and his left hand in his coat pocket. They had never touched, let alone kissed, had never sat together let alone slept in each other's arms. Would not have minded it, and thought him up for it, but . . . They had been close and he had opened his left hand, eased apart deli-cate fingers and the memory stick had fallen beside the bear. Hector's best toy. A Christmas present from the wife of the Military Attaché. The stick had disappeared into her hand, then into her bag, and the bear was reunited with Hector and the little fellow shouted pleasure . . . thirty seconds and starting to count.

"Do we go, go now?"

"No."

"Go when?"

"We don't go."

"Did you not travel there, and . . .?"

"I did."

". . . and looked?"

"Was close to the wire."

"But you say we do not go."

"We don't."

"Why not, go?"

"We get shot if we do."

"Many go through."

"I was there, you were not . . . I am not prepared to be shot, and for Hector to be shot."

"And me?"

"I imagine that . . ."

"What do you imagine?"

"I imagine you continue doing what you do."

"And tomorrow I am arrested."

"I don't know."

"You saw them, watching me, you did . . .?"

She shrugged, looked away.

". . . You saw them?"

Hung her head, and lied. "I'm sorry, truly . . . I don't know what I saw."

Maggie stood. She gave the sort of smile a girl gives to a pleasant and helpful stranger as gratitude for a courtesy. Hardly moving her lips she murmured, "I see you tomorrow, Alexei, and the usual procedure. I promise this . . . We value you, will look after you, Alexei, take your security very seriously."

She was gone and had not turned to witness how he absorbed the final lie. Had done her newly learned tradecraft, had twice switched trains on the Metro, and had gone into a department store and had used both lifts and a staircase, and had come back to the Embassy.

She took the memory stick to the outer door of the Six suite, did not wait for Lucinda to come to collect it, gave it to Josh who waited with Nancy.

He said, "Well done, Maggie, like a proper trooper. All good?"

"What else? Said we took his safety very seriously . . . Don't we?"

"That's the party line," Nancy said. "Best to keep spieling it."

She took Hector back to her apartment. Needed to change out of the Russian clothing and wash the makeup from her face, and maybe clean the dirt from her mind.

Jonas paused for a moment on the pavement, and half-turned, made eye contact with her, and waved. She stood in the stiff wind and it ruffled her hair and her arms were folded across her chest. She was between the policeman and the gatekeeper, and he could not have read her mind.

He headed away. The sun was lower and would soon be dropping behind the Tate building. He felt an emptiness because, truth to tell, he rather missed that hand, reassuring, at his elbow, and the cuff on his wrist seemed to chafe and that was an irritation. He took out his phone and called that old friend now hamstrung with mobility problems and seeing out the start of the dusk in his home in the Province.

"You asking me about women, Jonas? How the feck would I know about women? Just a detective sergeant from the Branch – what do I know of their women, the Provie bitches? Smarter than the guys, that good enough for a start? More dedicated to whatever cause they've hitched on to. You have one in your sights, Jonas, and she's messing your brain? Cannot distance yourself from your preconceptions about gentleness, having a homemaker role, giving comfort . . . All shit, Jonas. The women would take an eyeline on the ceiling in the interview suite, might find a spider hanging off a cobweb. Would not give it up, would hold that focus. Ask all the questions I have in front of me, get no answers. Can be bodies on the pavement and blood in the gutter, can be that the wee girl's done the come-on bit and lured a victim to a killing zone, but don't expect remorse. You'll not get shame . . . That's what I'm saying. My experience and I cannot offer you more . . . Defiant, and they'll use the fair sex crap to advantage, to derail you. It's what I'm saying, and it's what I learned. Don't get yourself manipulated . . . Heh, Jonas, your time of life, what in heaven's name are you doing asking questions of me? Why aren't your feet up and the telly in front of you? It'll be the death of you, Jonas and don't say I didn't tell you . . . When you're dead, remember what I told you."

He heard a croaking laugh and rang off, and walked some more and made another call. He said how he thought the next day would play out on either side of the river and repeated the gist of the retired detective's remarks.

The AssDepDG's response. "Don't quote me or the sisterhood will make garters from my guts. The *jihadi* girls, what we've seen of them, are harder than carpet tacks. Sounds good . . . And at the other end?"

"We'll see, won't we . . . know what they say about the best-laid plans and all going down the pan once in contact with the opposition . . . Must be moving, Vera's doing chops tonight . . . yes, have to wait and see."

The three of them walked separately on to the ferry, were swallowed amongst a mass of local people returning home after a day's work in Esbjerg.

They relied now on intelligence received, had no reason to doubt it. No eye contact and they stayed apart and climbed the ladder to the area where there were seats and a coffee machine. The intelligence had twice been good, was their eyes and their ears. They would have seemed to any who noticed them to be three middle-aged hikers, dressed for cold weather.

The light was failing, the skies clear, and it was reasonable to predict there would be a light frost on the island during the night and a moon would soon be showing.

Between them was a canvas grip bag, held by Leonid, and two rucksacks, each loaded with a folded-down AK rifle. The ferry had a slight motion in the swell that came from the north and rounded the island's headland. Once they were out in mid-channel it was possible to see the extent of the harbour behind them. Travel to the West from Russia, moving far beyond the Federation's frontiers, irritated Leonid because he could not banish his envy of the obvious wealth of the societies he visited. He had overseen the killings of old Chechen warlords in France and Germany. The attack in a French city had been in the city of Lyon, in Germany the hits had been in Munich and in Cologne. The restaurants and the bars and the shops had all seemed to drip affluence. He recognised that there were areas of Moscow that were no-go to him, and only welcomed men and women with bulging bank accounts. What was different in the west of Europe was that the humbly-dressed were using fine shops – irritating and annoying.

A strip of lights ahead showed him how close they were to the pier head.

The two women driving back to their embassy in Copenhagen would have known little of the fruits of their work. A house identified, the movement confirmed. They had performed their final task of making the crossing, twelve minutes of it, had gone to a café and wolfed down a mug of coffee each, had hurried back to make the reverse journey, and had been able to report that no security seemed in place.

For Leonid and his two men there was little chance to reconnoitre, minimal opportunity to stake out ground ... and they knew also that the hours ahead provided the last opportunity that would be given them. The ferry juddered to a halt and he thought that Konstantin might have toppled but a young Dane courteously stopped his fall. The ramp went down.

They were swept forward with the returning islanders and a line of cars waited to collect some and others hurried towards the big sheds where cycles had been stored during the day. Leonid led them north, away from the main lie of the island. At first they took a road towards a new development of houses all darkened, and then on ahead to a complex of buildings and accommodation blocks which Leonid's phone identified as a residential school for navigation. Leonid chose a path beyond the building's overhead lights and they were soon slithering on mud and splashing in pools but they pressed on and could hear the ripple of waves on a sandy shore. He had told them once, and told them again. It was a stretch of sand not more than a hundred metres in length.

"On the whole length of this island, because of the strips of shallow sand, this is the only place that a dinghy can reach us. When they come from the *Katerina* they must find this particular stretch of beach. Other than the main pier where the ferry comes, this is the only place it can get to – it is why we come here. It will be three hours at least until they think it is dark enough and quiet enough to bring the trawler closer to shore and then to launch the dinghy with the heavy gear. This is where we come to and we will be told at what hour."

He could not see their faces. He did not know whether their eyes mocked him, whether they thought him an officer and an arsehole, whether they had respect for him or merely took the money. He could have said with certainty that failure to succeed with this last-chance attack would mark the end of their Vympel veteran careers – and his own.

With his phone as his guide, he led them back to the main track. The three of them blundered forward, Anatoly skirting a puddle deep enough to go over his boots and falling into a ditch, and an owl took off in a panic flight. Konstantin had sworn at him for his noise and clumsiness, and they persevered – and seemed to come to a place of ghosts. The moon was effortlessly rising and it carried a shimmer of light. Leonid could make out the great dark, angular shapes around him. He had been told that this was a place where the three of them could lie up, could wait and fritter time. He heard a rustling, coming closer, and flinched and grabbed at Konstantin's arm, and the Vympel man had murmured in his ear that only a grandmother would be scared by the wind blowing an empty plastic bag. It had been a flak battery, the biggest flak battery in the whole of Denmark, the biggest in that sector of the Atlantic Wall, where the batteries of anti-aircraft guns attempted to intercept the allied flyers coming from Britain and into northern

Germany. Their bodies threw limp shadows on the concrete walls. Leonid had been in Syria and the Isis bastards had edged forward under cover of darkness and tried to infiltrate their camps, and with him there were older soldiers who had fought at the end of the Afghan adventure: what he had seen and what he had been told had frightened him enough to destabilise his resolve . . . No fucking lie, Leonid would not have gone into one of those subterranean black holes where young German troops waited almost eighty years before. Had never been frightened of insects and could imagine the wafting hold on his skin of cobwebs that might strangle him, and the crawling movement of disturbed spiders – and shivered.

When the dinghy came, Konstantin and Anatoly would go forward. Not Leonid. How far? Four kilometres. Was there a road and a bus? Was there a path and a light other than from the moon? He said nothing, sensed his control slipping – and wondered how many other reputations, beyond his, rested on the ability of these two cretins – once fine fighting men but not today and not yesterday – to navigate through the darkness across country . . . He sat down and leaned against a concrete wall, and waited for the message on his phone. He marvelled as they reverted to type, had their own phones out to check where they'd be heading, and talking animatedly about a new infantry boot that had come, surplus stock, on the market and could be bought online from a warehouse in Krivoy Rog. He depended on them, as did many.

Jonas, approaching Waterloo station, found himself swept along by football supporters celebrating their team's victory. Blue shirts, cheerful and rowdy. Up the steps and into the wide concourse, and their chants were amplified under the high roof.

Jonas hoped for a victory the following day but his celebration would be neither cheerful nor rowdy . . . He had not taken alcohol after either the capture and disarming of Winston Gunn nor after the arrest of Cameron Jilkes. He never went down to the Oak, or any of the bars near the Five building after a successful lift. Chance was good that his input had been knitted into the analysis needed to justify a suspect's detention. Spirits would be high and there would be relief, but Jonas would have been off and hurrying for his train home. He supposed that he deserved the title of "miserable old git" or "proper saddo" and the usual refrain that he imagined accompanied the denigration of "God, and he must be a penance to live with". In spite of the limited knowledge of the medal and its bar that Vera kept shut away in her drawer, opinions on him had not changed in S/3/13 in Thames House. He had to rummage in a pocket for his ticket because his season was for five days a week and he had bought it that morning with poor grace . . . Some of the supporters, flushed with their triumph, would be on Jonas's train but he doubted they would trouble him. As with any other day, going home on the 5.49, he would be huddled in a seat, his coat collar up and hiding much of his face, and his scarf masking his mouth and his trilby shading his eyes, and in spite of the chain fastened to his wrist he could still hold tight to the briefcase Vera had bought him all those years ago. He hoped for victory overnight and then again in the morning – what the young people in A Branch would call a "double whammy".

Jonas followed the fortunes of no football team, barely absorbed the cricket scores, could walk briskly but never ran. Sport, its excesses of emotion, failed to move him. If, in the next twenty-four hours, the whammy worked twice over, then it would be savoured briefly, then pushed aside. The supporters who had shoved their way on to the train with Jonas had the names of players emblazoned on their shirts . . . Jonas's players, on whom he relied, were Doug and Wally and Brian, who would be a most useful addition, and Benedict, and what was interesting to him was that so much rested with them and he knew so little about them. He would never meet them. His thoughts drifted.

It would be good to be home. Good to have the chops, grilled, and boiled potatoes and greens and the thick gravy that Vera did so well, and they would sit together in the evening, and one of them would have Olaf on a lap, and she would tell him that the work had been done on the caravan's cabling. They'd have a guide book out and would discuss the trip, not confirmed but heavily pencilled for Monday, to Orford Ness . . . His concentration might slide if she spoke about the mouse, the little grey mouse, and the cat's gobbling of it, and the reports that had been posted to his phone from the surveillance team assigned to the Tango. Might see her for a moment in his mind and take in the cool and under-stated elegance, and her ability to blend, and the tragedy of it . . . only briefly and he would return to the guide book. He would read further about Cobra Mist, the code name for the system 441A of "over the horizon" backscatter radar, a project earmarked as Top Secret, and he'd enjoy reflecting on the burdens heaped into the in-tray of the hapless security officer of the day. Vera would lapse into a study of what she'd hope to see, lapwing and redshank and wigeon, rising and shrieking when the dreaded harrier overflew them. And . . . he would go to bed, and would wait.

He dozed, often did on the way home, but instinct woke him when the train slowed on the approach to Raynes Park. Good to doze now; he doubted he would sleep that night.

13

Jonas sat quietly, sphinx-like, in his chair.

The cat was on his lap and Vera had gone to bed.

Some evenings when he was up and alone he had the radio on, occasionally watched TV. He reflected, palms of his hands together in the prayer posture and his chin resting on his fingertips. The silence was barely broken by Olaf's regular throated purr and by a rare car going the length of the avenue. He sipped from a mug, careful in his movements not to disturb the cat. Vera had made him cocoa before going up, and had laced it with a swig of whisky from the bottle on the dresser ... He had wondered if he would spill something of the potential of the events that *might* be played out that night at a beach resort on the western coast of Denmark, off season, but had decided against confiding. She could not have altered events and therefore he had reckoned it unfair to share the burden with her. More importantly, she had recognised, clear as a harvest moon, that a crisis welled inside him, which was why he was left to himself and given the drink, fortified. It had been a long week since Olaf, now regularly flexing his claws into Jonas's trousers, had killed the mouse. And would be for others – one man in particular.

Jonas had no idea of that man's name. Could not picture him, but understood that he too would be buckling under the strain of events – fickle and awkward, always the character of them ... events.

Imagined him, but with a blanked face. Probably younger than himself, and probably with far greater seniority, and most probably with a larger personal burden than the load Jonas himself suffered. Not that he felt sympathy for the man but he acknowledged that for the two of them the night would be long and the outcome uncertain . . . The difference? His opponent had failed twice to destroy a target. Sharks would be circling him. He liked that image . . . the one where blood seeped into the water. A third failure and the feeding frenzy might well kick in. And for Jonas? Different, but . . . if it failed, if he lost his man, lost those good fellows, Doug and Wally, then the razor teeth would be closing on him and his dismissal would follow double damn quick.

Another sip from the cooling cocoa and the slug of whisky that bolstered it, and for neither of them could responsibility be adequately offloaded. One of them, by the time the night ended and Sunday morning dawned, would be in the water and – mildly put – vulnerable. Responsibility for anything important, as Jonas had learned, was rarely shared. To an extent he was the man who reported to the AssDepDG but there were deft sidesteps involved and no paper trail that compromised his senior man. The same in the ministries and palace buildings and opulent apartments within sight of the Kremlin's onion towers? Of course. On neither side would men of stature want to know the detail of engagement . . . The cat's claws, working steadily and with obvious pleasure, penetrated his trousers and caught in the flesh of his thighs. He wondered if the man, Jonas regarded him – and smiled to himself – as the Friend, had involved senior personalities in the nuts and bolts of the project. Most unlikely. For neither of them could the matter have gone well if tactics were determined by a committee.

And he reflected, sitting in the kitchen which doubled as a snug, that the politicians were uninformed about the actions taking place that night on the far shores of the North Sea. Not informed and not wanting to be. Already the control, which the politically elected classes valued so highly, was far from their hands. Jonas doubted that any of the Permanent Under Secretaries who stalked Whitehall were briefed, nor would wish to have been. If, *if*, horrible damned word, it ended as the youngsters of the A Branch sharing space with him in S/3/13, would have called a cluster-fuck, then either Jonas or his newfound Friend, would discover true loneliness . . . probably the way he preferred it, and so would this other faceless, nameless man.

And both of them – each no doubt with a phone close at hand – depended on the *pongos*. There was a small army of men, variously aged, who spoke by phone to Jonas, and he valued their advice. Some had experience of the real world of combat situations from the perspective of senior non-commissioned officer rank, others had been officers. The *pongos* were the Poor Bloody Infantry, were Doug and Wally, and Brian – and the likelihood was that his Friend would have similar men to move around the board – the foot soldiers. His own feeling, Jonas's, he would not have had it another way.

He eyed the phone. It would ping, the screen would light up, he would be told. And, at about that time, give or take five minutes, another phone in another place would tinkle or wriggle and deliver the message. No hurrying it . . . He saw no reason to break his normal rhythms of an evening. He stood and the cat was turfed off his lap without ceremony and scowled at him – and the big beast would have made a most valued foot soldier – and went to the kitchen door and opened it, allowed Olaf to step outside and circle the small grass patch and sniff at the beds, and do what was necessary – and thought again of Olaf crunching through the skull of the mouse, and saw briefly the face of the young woman, but that was for later, was not immediate. He put down food for the cat and filled a bowl with milk, and looked around him. The evening was cold and the wind sang among the road's TV aerials. He switched off the light and went across the hall, more lights doused as he went, and began to climb the stairs.

He went to bed. Others, on his instructions, were now going to work. The responsibility, heaviest in the last hours before action, slowed his step but he could reflect that matters would have changed for the better or for the worse by the time that he came down the stairs in the morning, past the watercolour of the Old Harry Rocks on the Dorset coast, close to the caravan site where their honeymoon had been spent, and crossed the hall and went again to open the kitchen door for Olaf's convenience. There would be a similar ritual for his Friend, both of them isolated, waiting for news of how their men had fared, and the clock below him struck a late hour and the best "best laid plans" launched.

It was an old trick and one that usually worked well.

The skipper of the trawler, the *Katerina*, had loitered just to the starboard side of the incoming channel to the Esbjerg harbour and had been rewarded by the approach and then the passing of an oil rig supply vessel.

The dinghy had been launched. Three men aboard, and one awkward-shaped object that was well wrapped in waterproof canvas and tightly zipped and strapped, and with it went the grenades an RPG-7 launcher would fire.

The trawler had come in close with protestations to the Harbour Master's office of continuing engine "difficulties" but had also pronounced themselves hopeful that the fault was now identified, could now be made good. In spite of the swell and the fierce currents that rounded the northern headland of Fano island, it was still useful to have the bulk of the supply ship on the harbour radar screens when the dinghy came into the gap between island and mainland. Could have done without the bulk of the 3000-ton vessel but was pleased to use it.

For the three-man crew of the dinghy, there was exhilaration at the tension their small mission created. Better than fishing the drab waters of the Baltic, better than having the nets trail behind them in the sea around the Heligoland rock. They showed no lights, kept only a few metres from the turbulence thrown by the propellers of the supply ship, and had the chart that would guide them towards the calmer waters of Esbjerg before they would switch hard to starboard and make the short run to the beach where they would be met. They had no idea, nor had the remainder of the crew left behind on the *Katerina*, as to the target that would be attacked on the island later that night: but it was a choice target, certain, because all of them had seen the test firing of the RPG-7 and its grenade . . . And afterwards they would return to the small beach nominated for the rendezvous, would take three more men, fellow countrymen, on board, would open the throttle of the dinghy engines and would travel like the wind that plastered spray over them – but that was afterwards.

Volkov had managed to slip away early from the retirement party, would not be missed. His rank and position in GRU, and the power of his authority, were liable to make even more senior men uneasy in his presence. Deals, scams, profits were better discussed far from his hearing, not left as hostages to fortune if he was aware of them. He had left and not a man in the room would have claimed to have enjoyed his company, nor valued him as a colleague. He had collected his wife. They had shared a taxi to the artist's home. That pause between courses. Soup taken, meat being fetched from the kitchen, and his wife had risen half out of her chair to help the hostess with the pork, done in the *buzhenina* style, with garlic and thyme, and . . . He held her arm, stopped her. Their host had gone to get more wine or beer, or to pee . . .

He murmured in her ear. "We leave as soon as decent after the meal."

"But, we should . . ."

"Maintain politeness, maintain manners, of course. We go, after the meal."

"But coffee? Liqueurs?"

"Straight after the meal.

"And . . .?"

"And pack a bag."

"Each of us, a bag?"

"One bag, all of us."

"For how long, for how many days, nights?"

"One day, one night, and anything that is precious to you."

The artist was back. His wife was released, went off to the kitchen. Volkov, the Brigadier and the man given the jobs that the regime wanted completed but also to be smothered in deniability, reverted to charm. Neither his host or hostess would be given cause to wonder what stress dug deep in his belly, but his wife was quiet, had little to say. Minutes slid away, but no message flashed up on his phone's screen.

The dinghy came in, seemed to ride the waves and then juddered as it scraped the sand.

The beam of a pencil torch guided it. When they hit the beach a bigger torch was switched on and caught the faces of Anatoly and Konstantin, and of Leonid, and there were grunts that the light be cut. It was a bad moment in what had been pitch-black darkness to have their faces illuminated, left them feeling as if they had been stripped bare. A seaman reached out from the dinghy's front end and Anatoly waded in to the surf. An arm swung, the bag was thrown.

A yell from Anatoly to the bastard to watch what he did, and the bag had smacked the old Vympel guy in the stomach but his hands closed on it. Konstantin called that he was ready. The grenades came. Konstantin swore. The bag with the grenades hit and bent two fingers on his left hand.

Leonid called from behind them, "This point, four hours. Here."

A shout from the dinghy that the pick-up point and its timing were understood. And like an afterthought, "And you understand that we cannot wait, hang about while you old men scratch your bums. We have to go. This is a bad place and . . ."

Konstantin answered, "Go play with yourselves, we have work to do."

The hissed voice of the crewman, "Do your work well – and, look after yourselves."

The dinghy pulled away. The veterans – still "boys" in their own minds – waved their colonel away from them, like he was just a goddamn officer obstructing, interfering and . . . They crouched and split the bags between them. Already decided that Anatoly would take the RPG-7 with one grenade unarmed, and a rifle and three magazines, and Konstantin would have the remaining grenades in his rucksack and another rifle and another three magazines. Perhaps it was also the moment that their colonel understood the fragility of his own role. Perhaps it was the moment that he came to terms with his own inability to stay with them on the fast trek across the width of the island, and then their stampede back. He would return to that ghost camp, where the flak guns had been, and would settle himself down in the lee of a bunker's walls, and would smoke and think and dream, and would listen for the sound of distant explosions, carried on a sharp wind, and would wait some more, then would come again to this place on the beach. He held out his hand and both of them ignored it.

"Good luck, guys."

"Don't fucking patronise us."

And a further response, "If what we need is luck, then we're fucked."

Anatoly tugged Konstantin's coat. They were gone. Left their colonel behind, had no more use for him.

Anatoly to lead, the launcher up high on his shoulder, and his free hand carrying a torch. Another pocket of light behind Anatoly as Konstantin used his phone to trace their route. It started as a good path, might have been used by any of the school parties that came to the battery place in high summer to camp there. Other than their own faint lights, they were in a cocoon, and all around them was darkness. Not silence . . . Sounds came from the wind, from their grunted breathing, from the squelch of their feet when the path merged into bog, and then they hit the treeline, conifers densely planted and they both ducked down but the branches laced against their faces and upper bodies. The sound of the blundering advance frightened an owl and it clattered away and Konstantin called forward that the bird had so frightened him he'd thought he'd wet himself. Anatoly's response was that a heavier branch had near pulled the launcher off his shoulder and that his nose was bleeding from the impact of the weapon's stock. Kept going, and swapped stuff about whether their boots were good enough, or if the ones they had seen in the advertisement, surplus stock, might have been better and talked some more about the women they had once known and did not know any more, and about the hope of the small farms, side by side, where they would breed pigs, chickens and have a bar up the road for the evenings . . . They were through the trees and their wheezing seemed louder.

They broke from the treeline, out onto open ground and smooth grass.

And both also might have thought: "Why in a shit place, in the middle of fuck-all nowhere, is there smooth grass, like a lawn, like a place a general has?" A sensible question, worth asking, and there were faint lights in the distance. It had been, Konstantin could have said, a triumph of navigation to have come within sight of a holiday place and to have crossed a wilderness without a track, but that remark would not have explained the cut grass that was heaven beneath their feet. Still confused until Anatoly's shrill oath and his disappearance, and he had vanished and then had risen, like a fucking wolf from a den, but covered in sand, and . . . Konstantin said they were on a golf course. Neither played golf, knew anything about golf, cared a kopeck for golf, except that the course was marked on the map on the phone screen. Ahead were street lights, not many, and the silhouettes of the roofs of houses with chimneys, and a couple of apartment blocks.

"You good, Anatoly?"

"When am I not good?"

"I am hungry, and I am thirsty and I cannot remember the taste of a woman."

"I tell you, Konstantin, all that I remember is when this fucking launcher hammers into my shoulder, and when the flame rips out past my back. Right now that is the taste of what I look for, because I remember it."

They ducked behind a concrete wall. A small van dawdled along the road, its headlights would have hit the wall and bounced back. Like old times . . . Behind the lines and in the face of danger where the odds dictated that only Vympel trained troops could be sent – a mission none but Vympel boys could be trusted with – the breath sighed in their throats and their legs ached and their eyes strained, and the road was quiet again but for a solitary dog, thin and wary, that scampered across the road ahead of them. They could smell, faint on the wind, the scent of the seaweed thrown up by a storm and dumped on a beach. Anatoly said that Konstantin should mark the place where they had crossed the road, and himself he would still have the blast of the launcher in his ears when the grenade was speared out and his eyes would be screwed by the brilliance of the flame. Konstantin's job was to memorise where they crossed the road, and where they went on to the golf course, and where they had found a route through the trees – and where the beach was, where the dinghy would be.

They would have been shadows hurrying past the steel shutters of a row of closed stores, shapes drifting along a pavement by the faded signs for ice creams and karaoke and booze. And amongst the first of the sectors of empty holiday homes, a few showed dulled lights. They were on a road, sand scattered on tarmac. Signs around them claimed that the ground around each property was *Privat*. Darkness engulfed them. Anatoly said that he had to rest because his goddamn chest was killing him. Konstantin said he too needed to rest and that his feet hurt.

Konstantin caught Anatoly's arm, pulled at it. "What am I?"

"Fucking useless, what else?"

"Not useless, brilliant. Look ahead."

"What am I looking at?

"Follow my arm."

Anatoly on his knees, behind the large plastic rubbish bins roped to a post in front of a holiday home, looked down the length of Konstantin's arm, like it was a rifle barrel and squinted through the open sights . . . and saw, 300 metres ahead of them, thin light filtering from one house, either from a thick blind not correctly lowered or a gap in curtains. The light reflected brightly from a car's bonnet and from a second vehicle's roof.

"I have it."

"What am I?"

"A good man . . . What do you want? A whore to massage your back, your ego? You are fucking incredible . . . A rest, then we get close. Circle it, do it, get the shite out."

Their palms hit, like that was the moment of triumph.

Both were sagged in the depth of the darkness, and nothing moved and only the wind kept them company. But in front of them was their target. Time to rest, then circle and plot the line of attack, then shoot. They huddled beside each other, and made the momentous decision that they would have a fag, keep it in cupped hands, pass it between them, smoke one last cigarette . . . and think of the adjacent farms and the rewards on offer, and the praise, and the respect that would be showered on them. A flash of the flame and the sucking in of the fumes, and the weight of the launcher biting on Anatoly's shoulder.

One word only on Benedict's screen. *Quit.*

Non-negotiable.

Palms thumped together, backs slapped, murmurs wished good fortune . . . Brian led. Out through the kitchen door, inner door closed and no light on. Then Jette and close behind was the Russian. Last out was Benedict. Closed the door after him, turned the key in the lock and threw it: the owners had left it neatly and conveniently on a prominent hook, but Benedict doubted that it would be needed any more, not by anyone. All down on to their haunches. Brian had made good preparations, might have won some admiration from Sashcord. He had gone through with each of them everything they carried and had made damn certain that nothing in their pockets could rattle or clink and there was a bowl on a table in the living area which they had filled with their loose change.

Benedict did not know where, outside and on a black dark night, Doug and Wally and Nils had taken a vantage point; they had the image intensifier optics and the magnification on the sight of the Dragunov marksman's rifle. His gang had been poised, coiled, waiting, and were gone, quick, scuttering like crabs. Out of the back, into a cleft where two dunes came together and there was bramble and coarse grass that grew tightly in the shifting sand, and then wriggling up a defile. It would have been the route that kids took each summer, the short cut to the beach. There was a moment when Benedict slowed, then stopped, had his face near the Russian's boots, had a chance to look behind him for a final glimpse of the house. A dark outline of the roof and a chimney stack, and a garage at the side which was an add-on construction using the foundations of German fortifications, and a picture window around the corner from the kitchen door, and light spilling out in thin zebra stripes on to a patch of grass where the washing frame stood. He could not see inside the room where the only light had been left on. Would have liked to see his own handiwork. Could hear the radio that was tuned to a jazz station. Was disappointed that he could not pause, slide back and get close to the window and lie on his stomach and peer in, try to find one place where the blind slats allowed him to see the living area, and find his man and the shadow shape he had created . . . thought he had done it well.

What he wanted to see was a low table with a chair balanced on it. Over the chair's back was draped the coat that he had found in the porch, would have set the purchaser back four or five hundred euros. Wedged on to the coat collar was the lamp shade. He supposed it was the lamp shade he most wanted to get a sighting of because it was important and carried weight for all of them. They had all signed it and the Russian had drawn the eyes and the nose and a mouth and had scribbled a heavy Stalin moustache. It had been a good prediction that the building was set for a blasting and that the model man would be demolished – fire and detonation and explosives – and the place would disintegrate into a charred mess with grenades or whatever they would use, and the lamp shade would lose its shape and identity. On top of it he had placed the hat. They had left on one side light in the room and that was enough, Benedict believed, to make a good outline. Jette's hand came back and, without ceremony, Benedict had his collar grabbed and he was dragged forward and then they were crawling again, Brian hissing that they must "keep your bloody arses down". Benedict realised that in their small group he was the only one who carried no weapon. Brian had a rifle and the grenade sack and a pistol. Jette had her own issue. Benedict was not sure when, but there must have come a time, when the room was fugging with fag smoke, that Sashcord had managed to place his hands on one of Brian's rifles and that would have made him feel good.

They crawled the last yards then had reached sight of the beach.

The moon was up, had not noticed it before. It illuminated the higher beach where the tide had gone out, leaving a sheen of silver. He would like to have stopped and just gazed at the enormity of the sands.

Jette held one of his arms and the Russian had a grip on the other, and they hurried him forward. They stayed in the loose sand at the bottom of the hillocks where the grass and the bramble had taken hold. On the line that Brian took for them they threw no shadows that mattered.

How far to go? Had asked it before. Had Benedict asked again there would likely have been a snapped reply from Brian, not rude but just annoyed because it wasted breath. "Same as I told you, that's how far to go." Or, "Same as last time I told you", and a rasp of irritation from Brian ... who Benedict liked, who Benedict thought special. Not that he would ever tell anyone, not a chance of it, but Benedict thought Brian would damn near have given his right arm, or his right ... and had volunteered not to be with Doug and Wally, and with Nils, to have the chance to look through the weapon sights and hold a zero.

At first they were slow because of the softness of the sand. A couple of times birds screamed away from them. How far, if he had asked? Eight or nine kilometres if he had been answered. They had started to veer off the tumbling sand at the bottom of the dunes and were now on the beach where it was hard under their feet, and their pace quickened.

His phone pinged, he drew it out of his pocket. The screen was lit. Wanted to pause, draw breath, assimilate the message, but no chance was given him. He snatched at the words. *They're knackered, resting up before the charge, and have an RPG and extras Keep safe.* He remembered his Iraq times and a phrase used by the young officers and old NCOs when they set an ambush and spoke of creating a "kill zone" ... And the moon rose and showed more of the beach, limitless, ahead of them.

Benedict was in a relay run and had passed a baton ... was chivvied along, all of them faster and fitter than himself so he was a sort of burden to them, but each time he sagged, arms reached back for him and he was tugged. Benedict realised he was a passenger.

Jonas did not sleep, Vera did. His mind roved.

It was not usual for Jonas Merrick – beyond retirement age but still cuffed to the Service – to ponder on the faces of those whom his work involved. Tonight he saw them all: some in sepia photographs, portraits, and some in the mug shots that had been taken by official snappers and would most likely only surface if a picture were needed to accompany a criminal conviction or a death notice, and one in a candid image taken with the power of a long-distance zoomed lens. He believed it would be finished in the course of the next few hours and once the business was done he would discard this indulgence of lying in his bed, dressed in his flannel pyjamas, and staying closer to all of them than to his wife of close to four decades ... This lot he barely knew, and many he had never met, but he let them run past him as in a kaleidoscope. Why? Because of the damned power that he held in his clenched hands, and because their futures depended on matters he had set in hand.

And with the photographs was also a postcard in gaudy colours, showing a wide beach lit by sunshine, unimpeded by cloud. A perfect image of the "clear blue sky" out of which would come, without warning, one of those wretched and unwanted *events* that so stymied the most perfect of preparations. Young girls in apologies for bikinis walked on the sand and were overlooked by a windsurfer towed by a jeep, and kiddies made sandcastles, and others had taken pint-sized nets to pools left by the retreating tide and scavenged there, and clusters of lads were eyeing talent and chucking the empties of their six-packs over their shoulders. Saw all that, and wondered how it was on that beach in darkness lifted only fractionally by moonlight. Saw also the men he had moved into place, little people on a chessboard and some would survive and some would not. And policy would be served, and they propped up a corner of a bar and the empties were stacked around them and the ashtray overflowed, and he realised that he could not distinguish the words spoken because they might have used UK regional accents and might have chattered in the Slav dialects of the Russian landmass. And saw Benedict who he hoped was safe unless an "event" intervened, and saw Igor. Had forgotten the man's last name. Had only the photograph of him from the hotel front steps and the scratches on his face, and the cockiness of his expression, and Jonas peeled that away and recognised the gaunt and nervy reality of a defector, and little trust, and approaching like a fast train in a tunnel was the truth moment . . . and saw her.

All of the little courtesies – kindness or attempts at manipulation? Not sure. A clean scrubbed skin, and a hair style that was without fuss, and understated lipstick. Jonas liked to walk on clifftops when they had the caravan down on the coast and he would leave Vera behind and she'd be managing their evening meal and keeping Olaf company. He would walk and the wind would blow hard on his face and almost cleanse him from his work.

She – he had been told – had chosen to be the wallflower in the 'amdram group', until the Serb had pitched up, and they had been on an idyll on an Hebridean island, and she'd have walked, the wind playing with her hair and her clothes pressed tight to her body and her skin scoured by rain. She would have been, then, a full beauty and all the dreariness of a little grey mouse would have been scraped off her . . . Imagined it would have been the one time, a few weeks may be, of anything similar to real happiness. The days when she'd have climbed out of bed in the mornings before taking the bus towards VX and would have relished daybreak and the chance to look forward to a meeting with him, with Pieter, in the evening . . . Except that riding shotgun with both of them would have been the need to exercise full tradecraft.

He said it loud, "Such a damn shame."

Olaf stirred at the bottom of the bed between their ankles. And Vera hoisted herself up on an elbow.

"What's the matter, Jonas, what are you mumbling about?"

He answered her, "Nothing is the matter. It never is. Nothing."

Still staring at the ceiling, he tried to wipe the faces from his mind, but again and again he was passed the cardboard plate with the piece of cake.

Jonas said, "Don't mean to disturb you but better said before I forget – just that I won't be needing a lunch box when I go in the morning. Quite confident that it'll be wrapped pretty soon, won't drag on."

And could not read those eyes when he made his thanks for the cake . . . and there would have been others for whom he had no faces, no names, no situations, but who also would depend, short or long term, on how the morning played out . . .

His mother would have prevented it if she had known but she was asleep in her chair. Alexei washed up the supper dishes.

Not a special meal but one dominated by his confession.

A small piece of meat each, and potato, and boiled greens, and then a pastry with a fruit filling, and a beer for him and water for her.

He had thought it necessary to offload his burden. Had imagined she would be devastated.

He had gone to her radio, old but reliable and encased in a wood frame, and had turned it on loud, and that station on a Saturday late evening was guaranteed to air a full concert orchestra performance by one of the great Russian composers. She had brought the main dish, as always going short herself with her portion of meat. He had sat and faced the window, confronted with pinnacles of tower blocks festooned in light, and she had faced the wall on which a wooden crucifix was the sole ornament. He had taken a first mouthful. Tears had welled, his voice had cracked. He had leaned forward, spoken softly and she inclined towards him to hear him better . . . The men of FSB might already have been inside her apartment, laid audio bugs when she was at work cleaning hotel rooms, and he'd not make it easier for them.

"Much that you should know, Mama. Too long I have kept a

secret from you. I think tomorrow I am to be arrested. I believe I will be held when I am returning to Yaroslavskiy for the train to Kirov. I have to imagine that matters will be hard for me after my arrest. You know the time of my train, and if – it is not certain but I believe it most likely – if I am held by FSB, within a very short time they will be here and they will break in and they will search our home, Mama. Will search it and will destroy it and will threaten you, try to intimidate you . . . I had considered if it were best that you knew nothing and were an innocent. I thought you should know what I have done. It will be bad for me and hard. It will be, I am certain, worse than anything I can imagine and harder, but I feel I must have your support. I had thought that I would attempt today to go over the frontier and into Finland, and that an accomplice would guide me. She has declared to me this morning that it is too dangerous for her, and her baby, and for me, to go over the fence. She could take a plane and go home, but she does not believe me capable of getting out alone . . . and if I had succeeded then I would have abandoned you, Mama, exposed you to their anger because you would be the mother of a traitor. My crime is the most serious. They would believe it more heinous than taking another's life. It is the form of treason that has made me a 'scum' man. I am a spy for the intelligence agencies of the British. Everything that crosses my desk, I put on memory sticks and deliver to my British handlers. I am met each time I come out of the station and on my way back here to see you, Mama, and we do what they call a brush contact, and that is when I deliver the stick to them. On it are details of cash transfers made to banks throughout the world, anywhere that GRU has illegals, those working without diplomatic protection. And from the information I give them the British and their friends are able to identify agents of the Russian Federation. They say I am very good at what I do, they say also that it is unlikely they would – at this stage – help me to defect to their country. I have to tell you, Mama, that we have been followed towards the station each Sunday that I am returning to Kirov. The main person who handles me – and you do not need to know her name – identified the FSB people doing the surveillance on me. She no longer comes because she is too important to risk arrest, then deportation. They send a girl who is a clerk and she has a small baby, one year old and a few months. Mama, I love that girl . . . I cannot say what she feels for me. It does not matter what she feels because I am not leaving here. I am telling you that I think it happens tomorrow that they take me. It is right that I should have told you."

And while he had talked they both had eaten. When he finished, and the cymbals of the orchestra crashed around them, and his plate was clean, he leaned across the table and kissed his mother's forehead. He thought her features serene.

"Have you hurt them?"

"I think so."

"Hurt the regime of the man too afraid to give up power?"

"I believe so."

"He is like the boss character in a mafia story, and if he tries to retire from power it is regarded as weakness. If he is weak then his enemies are strong. They will kill him . . . He will fear that he will swing on a rope from a lamp post beside the river once he has lost power so he must cling to it. And you, Alexei, you have hurt him?"

"Have hurt his agencies."

"And I bless you, cannot say more. In the cupboard, you know what I have there."

He left the table, went to the cupboard, knelt and retrieved the bottle, a third full, of Puschkin Red Orange Vodka Liqueur. It was her favourite alcohol. He and she toasted each other with it at Christmas, and it was not touched between. Alexei swilled out his beer glass and emptied his mother's water into the sink. He poured two measures, generous . . . He had looked into his mother's face and she had returned his gaze, unwavering, and they whacked their glasses together, then drained them.

They had listened to the music, and she had slept.

He had listened to her gentle and contented snore, then had gone to the kitchen area to start washing up the dishes and utensils from their meal.

*   *   *

In a near destitute hamlet, where a line of dwellings – all needing maintenance – was hemmed in by night-time darkness and wall of trees, a woman could not sleep.

She listened. Under a heap of blankets and with the cold settled around her, she heard the singing of the wind in the tops of the pine trees, and the squeals when their branches rubbed against each other, and the call of a fox. What Galina listened for she did not hear.

The chance that she would have heard a single rifle shot was slim. The chance of hearing a burst of firing from one or more assault weapons, at that distance, was marginal. It was possible – because the wind was from the west, the direction of the fenced border – that she might be alerted by the sound of the sirens that would be activated on the wire if a fugitive tried to scale the mesh and the barbs. More likely, there would have been the noise of the border guards' vehicles accelerating on the track past the turning to this remote row of houses . . . If she had not heard gunfire or alarms, she would most certainly have heard them return and in the open back of one of the jeeps would have been the bodies.

From what she had seen and knew of the girl, Galina did not think she would have surrendered when challenged by the warning shouts or first overhead shots from the guards. Would have run, would have kept going, would have had her child tucked tight against her stomach, would have been dragging her boy along with her, would have jumped for the wire, would have been killed there. She heard nothing except the sounds of the buffeting wind. That same wind, when it blew from the west and the Finnish tundra, scoured the grass around a grave and slapped aside wild flowers and shrieked among old headstones and was funnelled down a narrow path and whipped the bramble growth, and beat on to the back of her own home and rattled the corrugated roofing.

She thought the girl had listened to her.

Thought also that a small victory, all she believed herself capable of achieving, might be possible – and doubted she would ever know of it.

Galina was an academic by training, had a good and analytical mind, and lay on her back and listened, and reflected that defeats she would know of but victories only rarely could be cherished . . . and said a prayer for the girl, out loud, but heard only the wind in response.

Maggie slept. Had the peace of an angel, had Hector wrapped in her arms.

And held a sheet of crumpled paper.

Wore a skimpy nightdress which had been a birthday present from her mother, and no guy had had a decent handle on the skin beneath it since the civil servant in the car . . . Could remember the conversation, but sometimes clarity lapsed. *"My wife doesn't understand . . .""Understand what?"". . . my needs." "Really. Jeez, you poor old thing:"* But had a reason to be grateful to him, which was Hector whom she held close. Would have been good, perhaps, to have that nightdress pulled high by young Alexci, but never an opportunity unless she had taken that huge step and walked out on the job given her by Lucinda and her ambitions in the military. Lucky really that she had met that wild woman in the village of sad old people up by the frontier and been taken to a grave and lectured on the marksmanship of the border troops. The daftness had been whittled out of her: had always had a soft spot for daftness but thought it was gone, and his long and delicate fingers would not have a chance of exploration. The truth was in her own fingers, written in Lucinda's handwriting on a sheet of paper and pushed under her door at past midnight.

One last go for you and we see what happens. You will not be alone and we will be mob-handed whatever plays out. Last time you'll be on the plot, of course. And – whatever – you are on a flight out at the start of the week and it'll be "cam cream" and fatigues and straight in to the recruit section to learn bomb fiddling. All fixed. Best, Lucinda.

Which was why she slept well. There might be one evening when her grandfather could lecture her on the "shit gobbler" he'd driven through the bad bits of Aden with what they'd pumped out of the Para latrines, and from her dad who had done a couple of

Gulfs and a bit of Afghan and some Bosnia, before she went to the new depot – and one day she might meet up again with the guys she'd driven in the Province. All wild and what she hoped to be when she knew about explosives and making them safe . . . but that was all for the morning, and thinking about then.

She held Hector, slept deep. If she had not owned that luxury she would have tossed, turned, woken him, with nightmares of goons spilling from their vehicles, in balaclavas, charging at Alexei, and at herself and the buggy.

The phone screen lit.

Benedict's stride was broken as he dragged it from his pocket again and slowed, needed to steady himself, and was rocking as the wind came in off the sea and the wide beach, and his eyes were crusted from sand and spray.

Brian had one of those stubborn running styles so beloved by old people: would have been one of them in shorts and a singlet who needed to shove their fitness down everyone's throat, would do it until he dropped. The moons' light showed him edging away. Closer to Benedict were Jette and Igor. How close? Pretty close, very close, and their hands might have been together, their fingers locked. Gaps opened, widened between them. It was the exhaustion that wrecked him and his fingers were clumsier than he could remember, and the phone slipped from his hand. Was on the beach, face down, and he could not see the lit screen. He dropped to his knees, scrabbled for it. Thought he had it, realised it was a shell, threw it. The moon seemed to highlight it and reflect off it. Benedict snatched for the light and a length of thin plastic crunched in his hand. He had started to weep, then found it. Read the message. Still on his hands and knees and taking in the content of the message.

Brian had him, had looped a hand into Benedict's armpit.

"Come on, sir, not the time to throw a wobbly."

"I just wanted to say . . ."

"To say you were tired. We're all tired. All dead on our feet. Nearly there. Best not to try to talk, Benedict, best to keep trying to run."

He dropped the phone in his pocket.

"Nearly there. Make the effort."

He was propelled forward. Assumed they all thought him pathetic and letting down colleagues, and wanted to report on his message, but the words were stuck in his throat.

They had made huge distance down the beach but Benedict could no longer measure how far or in how many minutes he had come. Could not recall any time that his legs had been heavier, and his breath came in big gasps . . . then back into soft sand. He tripped, stumbled and barked his shins and had careered into a navigation buoy that must have broken free of its anchorage and been swept high up on to the sand. He collapsed against plastic bags where collected rubbish broke his fall. Without ceremony, he was heaved to his feet, led off the beach.

Up a concrete ramp and on to sand that spilled over the end of a road and past the formidable outline of a bunker, and the light filtered on to a road ahead.

He was manhandled as if he were dead weight and of no further use, and felt no loss, merely a sense of relief . . . and realised that a career had wound its course.

Realised that he did not care how it ended, what would become of him and what he would tell his wife when he reached her in Scotland, the next evening or the one after. And thought himself no longer big enough, strong enough, to play the game.

Did none of them want to know what his phone had told him? Not asked. Off to the left-hand side and up a short driveway of crushed stone. In front of them was a low house and because he no longer exercised control or authority, his opinion was not sought as to its suitability for the third safe house, supposed, of the day. Around to the back and the tinkle of broken glass as Brian put the shoulder stock of his rifle through a pane of the kitchen door window. Perhaps could not be bothered to do a discreet entry. Lights inside winked at them. They seemed – Brian and Sashcord and Jette – to take pleasure in seeing which of them could find and disable the alarm system first. It was done. The lights were killed . . . They gathered in the living area and sat on the floor and the wind hit the roof and sang. No lights on . . . did they want to know what his phone message had said, back there on the beach? He had not been asked.

"I had a message, Doug again. 'They're up and closing. We are about to kick off.' That was my message."

Brian opened two windows, let in the night. They listened, all of them. Heard the persistent wind and a distant ripple of waves breaking, and sometimes the gulls yelled. And they kept on listening, and then the cocking of weapons, and then more listening – and he wondered who the casualties would be and who would count them out.

Shift change. Past midnight. An upper room in a guest house that usually bulged with Chinese tourists but in these times the management were grateful to have a room taken by a man and a woman who brought only a camera, a tripod and binoculars.

The street, narrow and having known better times, separated an all-night supermarket and a fire station. Opposite their window was a fast-food outlet of no interest to the watchers, the A Branch crowd answering to Aggie Burns, which anyway was closed. There were tarts doing poor business at the north end of the street, near to the Paddington rail terminus. The pair in place had been watching a particular front door since around six that evening, had seen the Tango go in. The pair taking over from them would see out the rest of the night and into the morning, but would clock off when the Tango left, apparently going to work that Sunday morning.

A replacement asked, "What's new, anything new?"

"In place" handed over the log. "As you can see, went in. Saw her there, third floor, then the curtains went across but can see movements. She's not been out. Bob's up at the end of the street, the blue van, and all he does is moan how bloody cold he is. The front is locked down and we're all in place in the event she does a bolt. There's a fire escape at the back which is a possible exit route but Daff and Tommy have that covered. She might go for it, as a bolt."

"Has cause to."

"Nice looking, not that I'm making a judgement. But nice looking – won't matter where she's going."

"That's what I heard, about to be lifted . . . and I also heard that it's that old beggar, Merrick, the Eternal Flame, that's running the show. Do you reckon they know, that sense, if they're going to be lifted and still go after a long night's sleep or does it come as a God Almighty shock? Who knows . . . Anyway, guys, safe home."

So, sandwich wrappers and coffee mugs went into the rubbish bag and the new team was told that the toilet flush chain was faulty so had to be used carefully, and the old team left after one more glance at the darkened window across the street.

The circle of the property was completed.

In front of them was the pull-off from the track where two vehicles were parked.

Anatoly knelt, the launcher on his shoulder, and the aim was towards the big plate-glass windows beside the main door. Music played inside and from their position the figure was easy to see.

Konstantin crouched beside him and had taken from his rucksack two more of the grenades for the launcher, and also had an assault rifle hooked across his back. Neither could see the others in the house but they might have been in low chairs and might have been on the floor . . . The women who had been the spotters back in Esbjerg had identified two cars and had memorised enough of the registrations to match what they could see now. Had been able to work out that there were three bedrooms and none had the curtains drawn or blinds lowered, and all were darkened, and the only light falling was in the main room.

"You happy?" Konstantin's growl.

"As happy as I'll ever be." Anatoly had regained the rhythm of his breathing and the rest time had been necessary.

They had been professional, thorough, and had done the circuit slowly, using the low leopard crawl that their instructors had taught them half their lives ago. Would not have managed it

without a sagging collapse by the rubbish bins for their lungs to fill
again and strength to return – and would need their strength, all
of it.

"We hit and we're gone."

"Hit hard, Anatoly, and hit again and hit again, and maybe
shoot some, then gone."

"No time for a victory lap."

"No need for it, not when we're sure."

"You know what that music is?"

"Only that it is shit. Hit like we did those Chechen bastards."

Anatoly the weight on his knee, held steady. What he remembered was that at this range, around fifty metres, the RPG had a
hit probability of 98% and he aimed at the guy inside the room
where that shit music played which meant they could not hear any
voices. He would be firing over open sights . . . and Konstantin
had the two spare grenades ready beside him. It was the way they
had been together in the Chechen times. In the mountains of the
Argun Canyon and at Nokhchi-Keloy and each time the Vympel
boys had needed to put down walls of fire to keep the savages
back, and had launched enough grenades to leave the barrel
scorched, too hot to be close to. The best weapon, everyone said it
was. It had armour-piercing capability, could penetrate the protective screen on the hull of a main battle tank and then a molten
metal lump would be inside and flying free. If the RPG had not
saved them and the guys in their section then that Vympel team
would not have survived.

Nothing else for Konstantin to say, nor Anatoly. The warhead
and sustainer motor were screwed on to the booster charge. A
squeeze on the trigger would ignite the strip powder charge on the
grenade, eject it from the launcher at an initial speed of 180 metres
a second . . . so, less than a third of a second from firing to impact.
They knew all of the statistics of the weapon, and trusted it.

Konstantin squeezed, both of them braced and readied for the
shock moment, and Konstantin squeezed some more. He had the
target over the open sight, knew the man was a traitor and a scum
bit and had betrayed his country. Seemed to see him holding a

beer, with a fag in his mouth and listening to the shit music, and thinking he was clear and safe and . . . squeezed some more. And was deafened, and almost blinded by the light of the flame thrust, and could in a blink of his eye follow the flight of the grenade, point blank range, and it hammered into the plate glass and exploded. Hanging about? No fucking way.

Like a good team, as good as they had ever been, and Konstantin had done the screwing and armed the next grenade and slotted it, and another squeeze. It jerked on his shoulder, bruised it, and aiming was always difficult with the kick of the beast, and squeezed harder and again there was the impact and the noise and smoke, dirt, dust, and the first spreading flames.

"One more time."

"Doing it."

Konstantin armed and loaded the third grenade. He had his rifle firmly against his shoulder. The grenade was fired and went, orange flame trailing, into the window space. Perhaps one of the projectile's hardened metal cores had sliced through an internal wall and careered into a fuel container that powered the cooker, but there was now an explosion and more vivid rising flames. Konstantin had memories of the bad battle days when they had survived, narrowly, and when the Chechen bastards had been closing on a farm complex where the Vympel section was sheltering, had come so close that there had been moments when Konstantin had fired his Kalashnikov pretty much from the hip, used automatic as the setting and not the single shots that gave hope of accuracy. He sprayed bullets the width of the living area and smoke rose high and the flames licked up, and it was Anatoly who had the bad moment . . . worse than bad, and his breath seemed sparse and he was almost suffocating for the lack of it, and the shock bit deep.

"Stop, Konstantin. Stop. Look."

His colleague didn't stop, not until the magazine was exhausted, and then was slapping a spare on and was about to raise the barrel when Anatoly gripped his arm.

"Look, fuck you, look."

"What, what am I looking at?"

"Looking at what is there."

Konstantin peered into the mess of debris, the battered shape of a holiday living-room now well alight and saw a table, and a toppled chair on it, and saw a long coat draped on the chair. Felt that moment of collapsing excitement. Saw the table folding and the chair falling off it and the coat was gone and the movement seemed to throw up a hat that rose, could have been a metre, then was subsumed in the fire.

There should have been people there. Should have been bodies on the tiled floor and casualties crawling from one centre of fire to another, looking in desperation for a door, any form of escape. Should at that distance, accounting for the damage to their ears from the launcher's firing, have heard screams. The music had stopped, burned out. They saw the fire climbing and the room engulfed and flames reaching into the other rooms, and they heard the cracking of glass and the collapse of roof timbers.

"Get the hell out."

"Yes, and fast."

"It was a trap."

"We bought into it."

They were on the track that linked the houses and would have been silhouetted against the fire, now, raging, and heard a scrape as a weapon was armed, and another, and heard a third – three sides of them, boxing them – and the two tried to run and their legs seemed leaden.

"Did you hear something, dear?"

"I heard nothing."

"Are you listening, Jonas, for something?"

"Yes, but not anything that should worry you."

"An anxiety that cannot be shared?"

"Cannot be."

A church clock had started a brief chime, a minute or so after their own downstairs, and Jonas was startled to hear it. Might have been the one at Malden or the one at Merton. Faint strikes carried on a brisk wind that rattled the window.

"It will be good, Jonas, when we get down to Orford and take that ferry to the Ness."

"Yes."

"It's what you want?"

"I want it quite badly. Want to be where it is safe. Where there are only ghosts to chase around after us. Where all those people were – scientists and engineers and chemists and physicists, and some poor devil who was driven to near distraction, the security officer – and all their work was done which they would have thought of life-saving importance. And time has passed, and their buildings are monuments to a defence system that was never called upon. Just great monuments to the futility of an age. I think most of them would have thought their work vital, at the cusp of the nation's efforts towards survival, and now it means nothing. That, Vera, is where I want to be and to talk a bit with those ghosts and . . ."

"You'll be on your own. I'll be watching the birds. Stop it, Jonas, and try to sleep."

"It would be a blessing. The trouble is that too many people at this hour are very much awake, have to be."

"Quiet, Jonas, please, or you'll wake the cat . . . Is it bad out there, wherever that is?"

"It is, yes, quite bad. Quite uncertain and quite dangerous."

He glanced again at his phone and its darkened screen, and did not yet know how bad and how uncertain, how dangerous.

14

Jonas was almost asleep, but not quite. Wished he were asleep, but his mind rampaged.

He lay on his back, in his warm pyjamas, and reflected that he had sent men to work and their job description would demand they were as much in the cross hairs of risk as he was safe, comfortable and close to his wife. Beside him his phone neither bleeped nor wriggled and the screen stayed dark. He might as well have put firearms, lethal weapons, into the hands of the men he had never met, Doug and Wally, and himself. He had never held a rifle or a pistol, been shown how to load it, have stood for a pistol shot or lain down to aim through a rifle sights, had not – not ever – pressed the trigger and felt the impact of the recoil. His own weapon was different. Where he had now put the two veterans . . . and he had not seen the results, close up and personal, of the wounds caused by gunshots . . . and involved a defence of a form, self-explained, of legality.

"Just doing my job." Good enough?

There were, a cast-iron fact, plenty of boys, and a few girls, sleeping – or trying to – in the cots of the high security cells on closely monitored landings who were there because Jonas Merrick had just been doing his job. No sympathy, no pained resignation, no apologies, as he had lined up the analysis, hunched like a squat toad over his screen, that had been deemed enough of a closed book to warrant letting loose an arrest team.

Liked her, of course he did. Liked her, and actually rather admired her. Wondered how well she slept and supposed that she had given her teeth a good brush before going to bed and had erased all taste of coffee and walnut cake from her mouth, and there would be a chair in her bedroom where her day clothes were neatly left, some for the morning and some for the wash basket . . . not that it mattered.

"Nothing personal, Frank – sorry, that is over-familiar and not appropriate – nothing personal, Miss." Would not say that.

"I want you to know, that I get no pleasure from this aspect of my work." And not say.

"Just doing my job, Miss, and I don't make judgement." Not a chance he would say that . . . did not have to say anything.

Did not have to be there. "Being a bit of a rubbernecker, and I hope you'll excuse me for that."

Except that he would be there . . . and the night crawled. Nothing on his phone.

What else, lying on his back, Jonas had to imagine, was himself going down the road and all his neighbours at their front gates, and him doffing his trilby, and straightening his back so that his raincoat hung better, and having the briefcase cuffed by a chain to his wrist, and him saying, "Hello, everybody, I'm that miserable old sod, Merrick, from number 29, and dear Vera, who you all like and sympathise with, is my wife. What do I do? Just a job of work. I keep you safe, and I do my damnedest to lock people away. Don't think twice about it. It is what I am paid for . . . On the staff, tax deducted at source, and no fancy schemes, and a very fair pension waiting when I care to draw it. Am a Counter-Intelligence officer – yes, me, old miserable Merrick, who you never get a smile out of . . . And today, if you are interested, I am going to throw the book at a very pleasant lady, who buys me quite delicious cake. Except that after today she won't be going home, won't be ordering another couple of slices of *gateaux*, won't be coming in on the bus from Paddington. Tell you the truth, I am fond of her and have only known her five days, and respect her intelligence and don't pass judgement on her conduct. When this long bloody night is over, she will be dressing with care – always does – nothing fancy, and by the end of today it will all be behind her. No more home, no more wardrobe, and the bus pass will not be used again, and the card that she swipes to get through the security barriers at work will be invalid, and she will

face a cesspit full of condemnation. And I will have been responsible. Swallowed all that, have you, guys? Why I am not sleeping
well tonight, waiting for the damn morning to start. And I have men
on my authorisation, all linked to this lady, who are in harm's way,
and they will take lives or will lose their own . . . That, gentlemen, is
who I am, your neighbour. Just a job of work, and today there will
be an end of sorts to a parcel of the current workload . . . I don't
have to be there, do not need to partake in that bit where the target's
face goes into shock, and the numbness sets in, and the imprisonment starts and the humiliation. Don't have to. Except that is the
narcotic . . . Anyway, have a nice day."

The church clock struck again, was not sure if it were the
Malden one or the one in Merton. He thought of the boys a bit,
thought of her more, tried to estimate the collateral, what would
land on his doormat.

Konstantin and Anatoly had the light of a blazing holiday home
behind them and had darkness in front but had heard the clear
scrape of three weapons being armed, ahead of them and to their
right, and to their left.

The shout that did not come would have told them, in any
language but clear, that they should surrender. Chuck down their
weapons, let them clatter on the hard track, then a further shout
that they should lock their hands on their heads. The next demand
would be that they kneel, then lie on their stomachs. No voices,
only the crackle of burning and parts of the house's roof falling in
and the wind fanning and whistling.

After the shouts and their obedience, black-dressed figures,
wearing balaclavas and carrying stubby weapons, would come
sprinting towards them. Tough hands would dive into their clothing
and fingers poke into each big orifice, arse and mouth, and pinions
going on their wrists, and maybe a kick or two, and maybe a slap,
but not too much that was worse than a boot or a fist . . . It was
Denmark, fucking Denmark, not their own country, and the guys
with the armed weapons would not be Vympel boys. But there were
no shouts and no figures came sprinting towards them.

"What do we fucking do?"

"Run, down the track, weave."

"We don't get taken."

"Do not get taken."

"Ready to go."

"Faster than the fucking wind."

Konstantin sucked breath into his lungs. He gave his friend, Anatoly, who had bad breath and whose feet always stank and who he loved more than any woman, a jab in the side of his solar plexus. It was intended to shock, jolt him forward. It could have been Konstantin's intention that his best friend went first and would take the initial fire, but if so it would have been the instinct for self-preservation more than intention. Not that it mattered whether he had intended that Anatoly should draw the first bullets and give him the chance to start, get speed into his legs and be crouched down and ducking, weaving, going for shadow and a storm ditch that was further up the track. Not that it mattered because the blow – seemed to be from a sledgehammer, one with a three-kilo head on it – whacked against his hip. Did not hear the crack of the shot, nor hear his own gasp as the breath fled his lungs. Konstantin was spun and fell on his back and it would have been a reflex to try and kick some movement into his legs – the start of an attempt to survive – but they were unresponsive. Then a cacophony of firing.

He saw that Anatoly had gone rigid. Did not run. Stayed with him. Anatoly who was his best friend, only friend, and who he had belted so that fire would be drawn and he would have a better chance to get clear, had kept a faith. The launcher, no grenade, was thrown down. The rifle was unhooked from the shoulder strap, a crash as it was armed . . . He saw Anatoly holding his weapon low, level with the bulge of his belly, and was letting go clips of fire on automatic, but random and without a target.

Konstantin heard his own voice, a croak. "Fuck you, silly bastard, run."

"Would not have run in Chechnya, not left you."

"Run, save . . ."

"They cut your balls off there, fill your mouth, then cut your head off."

"Just run."

Another single aimed shot came from the darkness, over to the right side of the burning house, smoke billowing and hiding the moon. Konstantin saw that Anatoly still had his rifle and still fired, but this time the barrel was aimed up into the night sky as if reaching to the hidden moon and then his knees failed him and he sank down, then slowly jack-knifed at the waist. His friend, the man he might well have sacrificed to save himself, collapsed and the rifle was still tight in his hands and his finger on the trigger, but the magazine was emptied and the bullets used and Anatoly went down. A sort of truth came to Konstantin. They had three times come to take vengeance on a spy. The President had said that a spy was a dog, and a "dog dies a dog's death." The words were well reported. Except that it was not the spy who died but Anatoly and Konstantin could see that half of his head was missing.

He tried to crawl. Had no movement in his legs. Realised his rifle was no longer in his hand. Did not hear the shout for him to throw away his weapon, did not see wary men coming forward, hunched and ready to fire. No shadow shapes crouched over him and felt for his pulse and worked at his trousers to free them from the wound leading internally to his shattered pelvis. He needed attention, needed to hear an ambulance's siren. Heard nothing and saw nothing.

Doug thought Wally had the better angle. Not a matter for Nils. Personal between Doug and Wally, and the man crawling had the grace and energy of a butterfly with a wing missing and had obscene injuries.

They had been in the car, Wally at the wheel, when they had been about to drive out through the main security entrance to the Hamburg police headquarters, would have caught the full force of the bomb stowed in a Mercedes. Not their fault a young police officer had recognised that the make of vehicle and the registration were out of kilter. And they would have been in the living-room of the first safe house, in the Esbjerg suburb, when the white figure on the screen from the image intensifier camera had pitched up with an assault rifle. Not their fault that his weapon had chosen to malfunction. Double times over, Wally and Doug could have been sharing, like it was hot-bedding, the same slab in the morgue.

He would not have accused himself of gratuitous violence. There was always a lecturer shoved up in front of the private military contractors who would tell them of the evils of anger and the need to control any vindictiveness, and always to play by the rules of the game . . . Where, laid down? Fuck only knew.

No need for them to have a discussion. Did not require four copies of the paperwork and the confirmation of a sub-committee. Had heard it from Benedict, what was required. Where had Benedict had his spine stiffened? On his phone from what he described as a rather hesitant voice who had seemed to be at the edge of his personal experience, and who had talked about a requirement to settle matters so that they would not reappear, be repeated, but might just get put to bed. Time to move it on.

One shot. If Wally had used the Dragunov, then the side of the laddie's head would have more than filled the scope, or the logo on the tracksuit top of a gasoline company, would have been as big as the scope could take. A head shot or a heart shot? Not important to Doug. Wally fired.

The guy might have moved three metres in total, was well screwed and was going nowhere but had been alive. The scenario, as explained to Benedict, did not allow for that. Sometimes, pulling the pisser and joshing with him, Doug would rubbish the best that Wally managed and get to remind him that he had never known the delights of travelling down Route Irish on the way into the Green Zone, and having the famous "arse-pucker factor" near to going off the dial. Doug would not acknowledge that Wally's time in the bandit country of the Province was much worse than taking the dog out on a Sunday afternoon stroll . . . but they would have been together on the slab, twice over, and not a pretty sight.

Wally went for the chest. Seemed to jolt the target, knock him a foot, and there was a last flap of an arm, and that about concluded the entertainment.

Well, neither Doug nor Wally, nor Nils, were about to stand on ceremony and give a respectful salute. They were outside the military family. Most likely the two guys on the track were former serving people but now were guns for hire. Or had been. Pretty much like themselves . . . Nils was not one of them and had turned up with them on the guarantee of anonymity, and the chances were good that he could lie and deceive sufficiently to deter investigators. Wally was up and running, and Doug went after him and felt that bloody rheumatism in his hip and also his knee, which hurt when the cold got into the joints, but went fast enough to catch Wally. Two bodies, both stone cold dead, and a final head shot not necessary. The cadavers were tapped down and phones hooked out, wallets left because they were shown to contain no state sponsor identification, and the spare magazines and the grenade supplies. No photographs taken, not necessary . . . Last thing, Doug had his own rifle and an arm out to take Wally's and he scooted back towards the fire and threw them high into the depths of the flames. Job done. The Dane joined them.

"You fit, boys?"

"Good and fit," Wally told him.

"Fit as I'll ever be," Doug answered.

They managed to run together, arm in arm and in step, back into the lea of the burning building. The front seats in both cars were draped in fine plastic sheeting which they slithered onto. Engines starting well, like it was synchronised, and they pulled away and down the track, the Dane leading and showing when to do the full swerve and miss the two bodies. Doug heard the sound of a gunfire rattle and knew it would be from the scorched ammunition of the dumped rifles. Enough light from occasional street lamps and the moon, and Doug drove fast, and did not use the headlights. Foot down and surging away from a deserted community, and a glow in the night sky behind them but diminishing. A lonely cat crossing the road alarmed by the sound of the engines and doubling away. They passed signs to a bed and breakfast, darkened, and a petrol station and a bungalow supposedly used by the police, and then burned the tyres and went hard right and were driving south on the island's only through road.

Doug said, "I reckon we did well, what was asked of us."

"Did it well, Doug, and to the letter, and made some grief, but I'm thinking that's just a part of the great scene."

Standing on the top of the concrete shape, once the base housing an anti-aircraft gun, Leonid could see the distant light.

He had poor hearing, ever since his service in the forward echelons of the Syrian deployment, and the hammer of artillery and close support bombing, but his eyesight was unimpaired. He had strained to hear the impact of the RPG-7 grenades being fired, and maybe the clatter of rifle shots, but his effort was not rewarded. What was without doubt was the scale of the explosion and the fire that gutted a building across on the west side of the narrow sandspit holiday island. The blaze made a good show.

When he had first noted it, Leonid – alone and cold and cut off from any flow of information – had made a single unseen gesture.

Surrounded by darkness that seemed hardly affected by the thin moonlight, he had first slapped a clenched fist into the palm of a hand, then had raised the fist and had punched high above his head . . . He believed, almost, that a cavalcade of praise would call at his door: flowers, champagne, medals, embossed invitation cards from the principals among the *siloviki*, and there could even be, *perhaps*, an invitation to an inner area of the Kremlin palace, and a firm handshake and a nod of the head that showed him that note had been taken of his dedication.

The fire burned well. The platform where the flak guns had been set gave probably the best viewpoint on the island from extreme east to the western coastline. The amount of light spitting up into the sky showed him the attack had been pressed home and he could not believe that any living soul could emerge. They would now be on the move. Leonid could not have managed the overland trek, part striding and part jogging, to get to the target area and back. The boys would have the guts and the sinew for it . . . what they were fucking paid for. He could not speak to them, could not call and hear them gasping and wheezing, as they came towards the rendezvous point because it had been agreed that telephone silence should be maintained. That traffic now, in the wake of the attack and the fire, would be the same as leaving a calling card with GRU fingerprints, or scratching their names on a car door.

It would hurt not to have the confirmation of success, but he would wait.

Leonid craved coffee, and needed food, but later, before dawn, he and the boys would be transferred from the trawler to the naval vessel and there he would have coffee, be toasted with vodka, would have secure communications, would have a fast ride back to the safety of the Baltiysk naval base.

He sat on the cold concrete and had an owl for company, and some bats flew low around him. He might have heard the first sirens.

Immaterial, because his boys would be well clear. He waited . . . might even hug them when they made it to the beach.

Benedict sat, alone and cross-legged, on the floor, in complete darkness.

The Danish girl and his Russian had slipped away, had gone off down the corridor. He would have heard them if they had used the bed and assumed they satisfied themselves on the floor of whichever room they had chosen. He did not make judgements . . . had heard Sashcord mutter a further half-hearted apology that seemed to hold no sincerity, had heard a snort from her as if water under the bridge was rarely measured . . . He kept away from judgements because he rarely gave himself the importance of sitting up on a bench and dispensing morality. Benedict's long-held view was that he understood nothing of the mind of a woman who would take a turn with the defector, ignore his history. And not important . . . Benedict mentally shrugged.

There was a rifle close to him. The Russian had taken his weapon with him when he had gone down the corridor, and Jette had taken hers, and he'd supposed they'd stack them carefully before getting on with the matters in hand. Brian was outside, armed up, festooned with kit. One AK-47 had been left for him . . . An old hack had once been wheeled out for the enlightenment of the new recruits into the Service and had talked about Vietnam and being embedded with Yank special forces and stuck up high on the summit of a hill, surrounded by razor wire coils and claymore mines, and further down the hill had been ARVN local troops. The hack had been asked to help on the main machine gun if the Cong came in under darkness and the locals were overwhelmed. Had been offered an M-16 rifle and allocated a fire slot hole in the sandbag wall, and had declined, declined three times until a spaced-out lieutenant had said to him, "So what are you going to do, Mister ArseFace? When they come and swamp us, you going to stand on the parapet and wave your passport and yell, *Don't shoot me, chaps, because I'm a British non-combatant?*" The rifle was within arm's reach, but he was not sure how to arm it, not sure where the safety was, was not sure how much pressure the trigger needed. And waited . . . and thought briefly about his family, and wondered if he were missed, if it would be awkward when he went home, if they did well enough without him.

He waited for the sound of the vehicles.

Heard nothing but the wind in the roof, blustering off the chimney stack, and sand coming off the top of the dune and spattering on the front window. They could, the Danish girl and his defector, as far as Benedict was concerned, screw each other right down and through the floorboards.

He reflected . . . what it would have taken in terms of personal resolve to walk out of his own embassy that morning back in November, get in his car and drive out of the city and reach that hotel, then park the car like it was any other day and look out for old Griff to show up, all fussy and talking too much. A total change, a reinvention. Becoming a new man and all of the past irrelevant and rejected. Big step, huge step, so probably it was a poor attitude to rustle up criticism of the guy. Benedict was part of the Resettlement team, and their job was to handle the guys that came over, made the big step from which there was little chance of turning back. Did anyone outside the confines of the Service understand what it would be like to defect, and what the hell it would be like to wake up the next morning and assess the enormity . . .? No one was his friend, and he would never belong, would always be under threat.

He waited.

Wondered how Mr Merrick passed the night hours.

Wondered how it was for Doug and Wally, and Nils.

Wondered also how it was for the big white shape of the guy who had been on the overgrown back grass of the safe house and who had the rifle, trying to fire the damn thing, and the second guy beyond the fence who was helping him back over. Wondered . . .

He heard a crunch of glass. Benedict reached for the rifle, did not know why and did not know what to do with it.

Brian came close to him, reassuring, sweaty, stinking of the beach and the sea.

"Can't tell you a whole lot."

"A little bit would be good for a start."

"A whole lot and a little bit is that there is an almighty blaze up the beach. Too far for detail."

"Which tells you?"

"Didn't we get to talk about a tethered goat?"

"Except that the 'tethered goat' is inside and shagging the Viking girl."

"I reckon they bought the tethered goat, came looking for your Sashcord. The wind is wrong and the distance too great for me to hear what's happened there. All I have is a major fire. But I don't have the casualties."

"Paint me a picture."

"Cannot see it any other way. *They* came looking for the target. *We* had it staked out. *They* hit first. *We* responded. Cannot see any other way . . . and the guy in London?"

"The guy in London put this concept together. Imagine it, Brian. Look at the scale of it. We are stamping on their feet and how. Hammering them . . . How did that get past all the queasy folks? Should there not have been weeks of consultation, risk assessment, check it out with State, run a wargame programme, endless. How did he manage to get it through?"

"Only one way."

"Which is?"

"Keep it tight, so that it stays inside the smallest circle. Bet your last dollar, Benedict, that very, *very* few at *apparatchik* level had even a whisper of this. Bet your last shirt that no politician has put his stamp on it. That is a class act . . . and it stays deniable."

"And there is blood in the gutter?"

"Likely to be, substantial blood. I would like, Benedict, to offer advice. Don't want to sound preachy. It's kindly meant. Don't ask what happened. There is a big picture and it will all get coloured in. The people who run this show will have a bag full of crayons and they'll make a good story out of it. It is not a matter of why prisoners were *not* taken. Not a question of why they were *not* left at the side of the road with a sign pinned on them saying 'Return to Grizdubovoy Street, Number 3 – with love'. Doesn't happen that way. It will have been a rough business and what happened up there is not going to be your concern, and not mine. Are you welcoming that advice, Benedict?"

"I think so."

His agreement died. The couple came back down the corridor. He was tightening his belt and she seemed to be tucking her blouse into her trousers, and both making a meal of it because they were clutching their weapons. The Russian asked if there was news and Brian said there was not, only that a big fire burned up the coast. Jette asked if they were likely to be here long, and Brian said that he did not think so, that they would be well out by dawn – like they had never been in the house, and only a smashed window to show for someone's visit – and on to the first of the Sunday morning ferries off the island.

"And me, then?" asked Sashcord.

Benedict said, "It's being sorted out today, where you're going and when – don't ask me more, just don't."

★   ★   ★

Alexei slept. His bag was beside the cot bed he used when he came to his mother's apartment at weekends. He would take his bag with him when he left. Would have changed into clean clothing would have stuffed extra socks and underpants into his anorak pocket for use if taken into custody. Would have his mother's photograph in his wallet, and only a little money. Almost all of the cash that he had withdrawn from the bank he would leave with her.

It was a good sleep and mercifully dreamless.

So right, his decision. He could not have abandoned her, and she would not forget him. He had imagined that she would be one of the old women who came each Friday to the visitor gate at the Lefortovo gaol and harangued the guards, gave them shit and eventually won their visiting rights. When he was put on the train and sent far to the north and the west, towards the city of Perm, the hub for the gulag camps, he believed that she would come, make that great journey – hours in cold carriages or ones that were stinking hot in summer – to take advantage of a single hour's visit in a year. He valued his decision not to press Maggie to take him to the fence and to try to climb the razor wire, and to have Hector, screaming, handed between them, and all around them the howl of the sirens they had set off, and hear the jeeps, and the cocking of the weapons . . . Alexei had heard that a trooper in the Border Guard was rewarded with extra cash if he showed his diligence to duty and shot to kill. And the regret that he would never get to touch her, Maggie, would not have that chance.

Now he slept, would face in the morning what the regime threw at him.

Maggie did not know how she would be.

Knew that her diplomatic status was cast-iron, valid even for a bottle-washer clerk who typed for the Military Attaché, and was an errand girl for the Six people. Could not have said that any restraint would remain in her 8 stones, 5 feet and 5 inch body, if a hand were laid on Hector's buggy. Might fight, kick, scream, bite.

Might use her fingernails and go for the eyes, or direct her knee hard into . . . God help the bastard who touched Hector's buggy.

Her child slept well, she did not. They'd not take her without a fight. Maggie expected that, in the morning, when they were lining up to go their separate ways out of the Embassy's compound and off to the meet-up point, she'd get a Force 8 lecture from the station chief. It would be about staying calm. "You do not resist in any way, Maggie, and we are very close to you and we'll have a body camera on you. You are not alone. Your situation and *Environ*'s are quite different. We are talking chalk and cheese . . . I don't want to cause upset, Maggie, but you have to realise that he is an agent, an asset. Someone who works voluntarily for us and is fully cognisant of the risks he takes. Very easy, Maggie, for a handler to get sympathetic to the plight, potential, of the people we use . . . You know what? Nothing we can do if he goes off on a different tack and has been spending his morning chattering away to the FSB's Counter-Espionage Ivans, and he might be thinking that ingratiates him, makes him a hero, wipes out the sins of the past . . . Be a sillier boy than I take him for if he did believe that. We owe him nothing, he owes us nothing. We will be very close . . . What I am saying is that there may be some bad minutes, even a few hours, but time flies fast and we'll do the best for you." Something along those lines.

The cars came. Headlights flashed briefly. A single blast of a horn.

Benedict led them out, Sashcord and the girl trailing him. Last was Brian. All bent low and running. Lights came on in the cars as the doors were heaved open.

Ordinary faces, not stressed faces, not those of men who had taken lives. If a trap had been sprung, and that had been the plan, then the killings would have been done in cold blood. And hardly a one-way road because the fatalities would have been the men who had failed to set off the car bomb in a parked Mercedes, and who had failed to blast through French windows. Two gangs of creatures able to take and to give. Three guys in the cars and all smoking, which might have been the only sign they gave that anything beyond the ordinary had happened. She took the seat beside Nils, and not a backward glance as Sashcord and Brian piled in after her and on to the rear bench seat. And the door was slammed shut and the engine hacked again into life. Benedict went behind Doug and Wally, barely acknowledged. The two vehicles skidded as they swung on wet grass and then they were back on the road.

"I have to report back."

"Of course you do," growled the front passenger, Wally.

"Don't need chapter and verse, just the bare stuff."

"We did as we were asked." Doug dragged on his cigarette and spilled out smoke.

"All that we were asked, just that," and Wally hacked a cough.

"And all clean?"

"No eye witnesses and no trails left. You can spin it however you want to . . . The two of them came and they are both now on a fast ride to Hades or Heaven. End of story."

Nothing more to say.

They went towards the village, Sonderbo, at the southern end of the island. Drove through it, past a big church that seemed out of scale, would have been a sign of the place's importance in a previous age, and down a narrow street between low-set cottages with thatched roofs, a chocolate-box sight, lit by occasional lights, and the moon was now wrapped tight in a mist.

Benedict typed his text.

They bought into the story of the tethered goat and it ended badly for the building and for them, and they are not able to tell the tale. You are free to spin.

He gazed at the message, hesitated . . . Could remember how it had been in the car when the warning was shouted and they had done the breakneck reverse and the speed over the lawn to get them out and away. And could remember the stumbling chaos of the big guy on the grass, jerking at his weapon that had malfunctioned . . . Hesitated, gazed at his version of the epitaph of what had happened. The lead car braked hard at the end of a track. There was a wall of mist ahead and leading into it was a narrow pier.

"You stay here, Benedict. Don't move."

Doug out first, then Wally, and Brian from the lead car. Brian carried an armful of plastic, what Nils had sat on, then came to Benedict's vehicle and snatched up all the plastic from the two front seats and marched it towards a rubbish bin. He saw that Doug and Wally, not shy, had gone on to the pier and had started to strip off. Not bashful, the whole damn lot. Anoraks and sweaters and shirts and vests, and then socks and trainers and then trousers and underpants. A little of the moonlight shone on their backsides, and they hopped off down the length of the pier. He saw, beyond a reed bed, a thin sliver of water, and then the mist thickened and he lost sight of them both, but heard the splash when they jumped, and imagined them. Two "good old boys" as the phrase went, standing up to their waists in water and rubbing themselves down, scrubbing at their skin with their hands, and sluicing the water over their heads, and perhaps Brian had tossed them a bar of soap, and celebrating with a skinny dip the success of a job well done.

They came out of the water and up on to the pier and dripped a trail of water behind them. Brian had the back of the car open and their bags out, and Jette had tossed a towel through her window for them to share. Benedict saw that Doug had a bit of a paunch and saw that Wally had thin scarecrow legs and each towelled his body hard and then began to dig in the bags. Underwear, clean shirts and sweaters, and trousers hitched up high and zipped and buttoned and belted, and socks and shoes, and more fags lit ... Brian had the armful of plastic and used clothing and pressed the load down in the rubbish bin. Probably used, Benedict thought, the cigarette lighter's fuel to start the fire, and the blaze ripped upwards and smoke bounced back down off the mist ceiling. He rather admired the professionalism which took DNA and gunshot residue out of any investigative equation. Brian used sterilised wipes over the seats of the car, and the wheel and pretty much everything that the guys might have touched, and Nils did the front of the PET car, and the wipes went into the fire ... No lights came on behind them and no curtains were drawn, no front doors unbolted and opened, no shouted questions thrown at them. The operation, and Benedict acknowledged it, oozed a degree of class, and a bucketload of desirable deniability . . . He gazed at the message he had made. And sent it.

Jonas scrabbled with his fingers across the bedside table.

The phone screen was lit.

He read. It was that ghastly hour of the night when death came calling. He switched on his bedside light, found his spectacles and sat up in bed and pressed in the code that would pass the message to the AssDepDG . . . And put the phone back on the table and felt a degree of emptiness because there was nothing significant he could contribute before the coming day dawned, and thought of her, seemed to see her.

He stared at the ceiling, then at the walls, of their bedroom, in a mock-Tudor style 1930s home in the ordinariness of Raynes Park, and glanced over the pictures, three watercolours that Vera had accumulated from the gallery where she worked, and the old wardrobe that was too large for the room but had been one of their first married purchases and where his clothes were hung or folded on the right side, and her dresses and skirts on the left side, and the chair on which his clothes were draped and the other chair where her own clothes were more tidily piled; and on to the dresser where the top drawer held her most intimate clothing and also the items she prized, a medal and a bar to it, and the hooks on the back of the door where their dressing-gowns hung. Olaf, from the bottom of the bed, gazed at him, annoyed at the disturbance. It was his command and control bunker, his communications centre, where he received news that lives had been stolen, and imagined that blue lights rotated on a track and that occasional sirens were heard in the darkness and bodies grew cold and blood congealed, and that an escape route was in use.

"Is everything all right, dear?"

"I think so, but it's just work."

"Was it something satisfactory."

"I believe so, but it's only a part of the whole, and the rest will be finished – I hope – this morning. Try to get back to sleep, dear."

Jonas turned off the light. The darkness settled around him again. The attack on a location on the west side of an island off the coast of the Jutland region of Denmark, and the deaths of two men provided provenance of guilt, which rather saddened him . . . should not have done, but did. But that was a matter to be dealt with in the morning and would be straightforward, without undue fuss, and with a modicum of dignity. He closed his eyes.

"Come here, Trace, get a gulp of this."

"You want breakfast or not want breakfast?"

"It'll wait. Get an eyeful of what she's dishing up."

George, from A Branch, sat on a hard chair and had the camera on a tripod, and had binoculars up to his eyes and peered out through the gap between the curtains of the guest house's darkened upper-floor room. Tracey came and stood behind him. The breakfast preparation she had left behind her in the ensuite, was ham rolls for each of them, with a taste of chilli and twenty-four hours past the binning date, and lukewarm tea from a thermos. But the shift was nearly through.

"George, you are a lucky old sod."

"Why – and I wouldn't have a clue – is she putting on that sort of show? Curtains wide open, light on behind her. Into the living-room with her towel wrapped around her and an arm loaded with clothes, and putting on a show. Who for? The street? Anyone having a gawp? Us? Has to be us, doesn't it?"

"Not arguing."

His camera shutter clattered. Perhaps George thought it would be a useful entry for the Christmas collection, what they put up on the screen at the party when everyone's hair was down Tracey crouched behind him and gazed over his shoulder. They watched. The towel was dropped. A rather good-looking woman, well kept and well looked after, and the underwear was pulled up and fastened, and then a neat white blouse was buttoned at the cuffs and up to the throat, and there she stopped and seemed to peer outside as if an answer was to be found there. Good legs, George would have thought, and a figure to be envied would have been Tracey's reaction. No woman who was not an exhibitionist would stand, back-lit, stark naked, close to a window and then begin to dress and take her time ... If not an exhibitionist, then a woman who sent a message. Sent it to them? Had to be them. They were always briefed with a résumé on the supposed character of the target they would be watching, in the hope they would not be surprised and caught out. And the woman reached behind her and took a skirt from a hanger and stepped into it, and wriggled her hips and fastened it at the waist.

"Has to be us."

"This time in the morning it will be only us watching. No one else and the street quiet as a graveyard. Did it for us – sending what message?"

George said, quietly, "The message is that the developments of the day are predictable. That we are here, close surveillance in place ... and add to that the dressing, very sober outfit and no jewellery. No makeup. Look behind her and the room is as tidy as if it's in for a competition. Can't see the bedroom but I'd give odds that it's stripped, and all left folded on the mattress. Like she knows she's going somewhere and that her appearance won't matter. Somewhere not that pleasant. There you go. Picked up the towel and off she goes to the bathroom, and the heating will be off. One of those people, thankfully not many of them, that no one ever knew, that no one can read."

And she returned to the living-room, smoothed her hair, and shrugged into a coat, and Tracey called their control and broadcast that the Tango was about to move. The woman came to the window and pulled the curtains closed. The light in the room was switched off.

The front door opened and she was a shadow on the step and dawn had barely broken.

George muttered, "I'm thinking what Winston said."

She stepped out on to the pavement and the shutter went again.

"What did Winston say?"

"Eighty plus years ago, about Russia – well, she's a Russian asset, right? – suppose it's relevant. 'A riddle wrapped in a mystery inside an enigma'. That's her . . ."

A back view of her going down the street towards the hospital where she'd get the bus that Sunday morning into work and never looked around her, only straight ahead.

"What I said, one of those people that no one can read."

The beach was alive with the rippling of the surf.

"We cannot wait, have to go."

The waves broke around the dinghy and lurched it higher on the sand.

"I have an instruction, Colonel. I have waited all the time I am permitted, cannot stay longer."

Leonid broke his self-imposed regulation. Took out his phone, went to the contact list, highlighted Anatoly's name. He thought it a sufficient emergency to set aside protocol and ignore the requirement for phone silence. He heard it ring out: the anger was boiling in him and the riposte. "Where the fuck are you? We are waiting. How long will you be?" Waited.

"We have to go. I have authority to demand it."

He was not a civilian fishing hand off a trawler, but would have had the rank of chief petty officer in the regular navy, would have been shoved off his state-of-the-art frigate, Admiral Grigorovich class, put on to the rust-bucket fishing boat and was responsible for taking the dinghy into the shore, setting it down on this one short strip of sand where a craft could get close to shore.

"Colonel, we go."

His arm was taken and he was jerked into the shrinking surf. There was a pistol in a shoulder holster and Leonid had little doubt that if push became shove he would be facing the barrel and hearing the safety slid off or would be belted with it and stunned if he refused to obey the instruction. Boots soaked and the hems of his trousers. He stepped on board, then his shoulder was pushed down and he sagged on to a cross board. The craft was heaved off the sand and, for a moment, it hesitated then it launched, bucking from side to side as the man swung his leg lazily over the side and took a place close to Leonid. The second sailor on board whipped the engine to full power.

Still his phone rang out, still it went unanswered. He cut the call . . . He could not remember another day in his life, the whole of it, when he had felt that sense of anguish. He left two men behind. Not friends, not colleagues, not soulmates, but men who were under his nominal command. They went out to sea at speed. Enveloped in fog and mist and soon losing sight of the shore. Left them, his Vympel veterans, in whatever state, unknown circumstances, and himself had cut and run . . . and sensed the scale of catastrophe.

Jonas slept in. And Vera.

He might not have woken if the cat, frustrated at not having been fed, had not walked over him and tapped his shoulder. It had been a dead sleep. He had glanced at the clock beside the bed, the had jack knifed up and swung himself clear. He could not remember when he had last slept through an alarm. He would have missed his intended train into London. He showered, shaved without care, dressed fast, yesterday's shirt, snatched socks out of a drawer, and would not have the time to buff his brogues. Definitely no chance of breakfast.

He hurried down the stairs. Took an apple from the bowl on the dining-room table and pocketed it. Scooped food from a tin for the cat and opened the kitchen door. Quite a pleasant day, already a hint of sunshine but the wind was sharp. He called upstairs, sharply, ungraciously, to let Vera know he was leaving and that the back door was open. A quick glance into his briefcase and he fastened the clasp on his wrist, but had checked the file – thin, little substance to it, with Frank's name scrawled in his dreadful handwriting, and almost winced. And a message stored on his phone: of men already dead and his shadow outlined over them. He unlocked the front door, settled his trilby on his head, gulped the morning air, and heard her question from the top of the stairs.

"Back late this morning, early this afternoon, and then we're off?"

"That is my intention. Please, have everything ready."

"And you'll behave yourself, not get up to mischief."

He thought momentarily of Frank and the deceit he would play on her, and her innocence of the way the day would play out.

"No chance of that. It's not a mischief matter."

And he was gone, scurrying down the front path, past the caravan on the hardstanding that had replaced most of their front garden, and one of his shoelaces was loose, and as best he could he started to hurry along the pavement towards the station.

15

"Yes, can do that, Mr Merrick," Kev said.

"Have to square it with the boss so there's cover while we're off up the road. Not a problem," Leroy said.

He liked them. Jonas had long enjoyed the company of the two cops who always shared the same shift, toted H&K weapons, seemed to flinch at the idea of exams and promotion boards and advancement, were happy enough to stand outside Thames House – all weathers, all hours – and do guard duty. He found their openness and friendship enervating, and twice before had used them when help was required.

"What sort of time, Mr Merrick?"

He was a little vague, gave them a half-hour window mid-morning and a little bit more about powers of engagement and conditions of arrest, and there would be Branch behind them, but they would be the first to engage.

"Are we expecting a bit of rough stuff, Mr Merrick?"

Jonas snorted amusement at the idea that a prisoner would take them on, and he shook his head. The first time that morning that he had managed a token attempt at a smile. They were festooned with enough gear to confront pretty much any challenge thrown at them – assault weapons, handguns, tasers, gas grenades and the flash-and-bangs, plastic hand restraints and extending batons, and their belts seemed to creak under the weight of the hardware they carried.

"And the Person of Interest, Mr Merrick?"

"Will be walking with me, hopefully deep in conversation. A fast controlled lift and then to the side door where Special Branch will be waiting. Should be quite simple, and ready for it as we come off the bridge."

A nod of agreement. Already their eyes were off Jonas and had started to rove over pedestrians and cyclists and joggers and motorists who were passing the front of Thames House. He thought that Kev and Leroy would have been a few years younger than the other stalwarts figuring in his mind that morning, Doug and Wally. All of a breed . . . Would like to meet up with them, the other two, if a chance ever materialised but it was the nature of the work that the chance of a quiet drink in a quiet corner of a quiet bar – him on sparkling water and them on lager – was unlikely.

No chance of *cappuccino* or a Danish on a Sunday morning, the café was closed, nor any chance of sitting on a bench in the gardens, and the man with the past who came and raked scarce leaves would likely have Sunday off. He went inside, flashed his pass at a security pad, paused long enough for the biometric stuff, facial recognition, to identify him, grant him access: not that Jonas in his private and dinosaur world understood too much of the technology that now seemed essential. A roll of the eyes from Security because Jonas was in frequent need of help – where to put his damn feet for the machine to work, pass him through. Just a curt nod to the desk . . . There would probably be a slight huddle of heads after he had headed into the atrium and discussion as to what grim-faced Jonas Merrick was doing in at work on a Sunday morning. Was excitement to be predicted? He took a lift to the third floor, took a corridor to the south side, walked along it to Room 13. Had expected to find the work area deserted.

"Morning, Mr Merrick." He barely knew the man. George dressed and spoke in the style of a Borough Market stallholder. A team leader, said to be versatile in disguise, and had the reputation of speaking more than might be necessary.

"Hello, Mr Merrick, didn't expect you'd be in." Knew her better. Tracey, a minor legend, attached to A4 Branch for a dozen years and was good enough to be used for lecturing newcomers on tactics, techniques. She would not have liked Jonas because all the time he'd known her he had never acknowledged her status inside the walls of S/3/13. A trace of a sneer in her voice.

He barely nodded, could be rude when his mind was elsewhere.

Unlocked his door. Opened up his fiercely protected cubicle. Went inside and heaved off his coat and hung it behind the door, and his hat, and as a reflex straightened his tie. A different key required for the lock on his cabinet, opened it, then pulled open the bottom drawer. Underneath two pairs of socks, two pairs of underpants, a clean shirt and a miniature spongebag, was a pair of handcuffs. He had not had them out of the drawer for two years. A rap came on the frosted glass of his door.

He might have called for George to enter and might not. Might have asked him what he wanted and might not. Did not matter what he might have done because George was inside the cubicle, leaning over Jonas to drop the photograph on his desk.

"Thought you might enjoy having a squint at this, Mr Merrick." And was gone.

Jonas stared at the picture. Blown up. In focus. He saw the lines of her body and the dark mass and the angles and the bulges, and recognised the calmness on her face, and her hair hung loose on her shoulders, and saw that his first ideas of innocence were on shifting sand. He stared at her and reckoned she dirtied him.

Beyond his door, George's voice bayed out, "A bit of a statement, Mr Merrick, wouldn't you say?"

He did not answer. He fed the picture into the shredder, then groped into the open drawer and removed the handcuffs, let them tinkle as he slid them into a pocket of his tweed jacket Reached again and took the small key attached to the length of pink ribbon provided by Vera a couple of years before: not that she had known why he wanted it. He tested the key on the handcuffs lock, was satisfied, then slipped the ribbon over his head and let the key hang by his tie, almost hidden. He sat in his chair. Could have been on the move by now. Blinked, then closed his eyes. Had lost the urge to hurry . . . Felt old and tired, and bent by the weight of it, and considered that maybe he played beyond the limits of his abilities, of his emotions.

★   ★   ★

The news came to Volkov. A cold clear morning and the weather pleasantly bright over the centre of the capital city. He had been fobbed off by reports of glitches in the communications necessary to punch him through to the frigate under power in the western expanses of the North Sea. It had come finally and he had recoiled. Two men dead. No indication of a target individual touched. A trap sprung. He had believed himself most adequate for the planning and execution of the killing, had not thought that a more senior officer needed to be involved, would have argued against it. Had dictated that the two Vympel veterans be allocated to the task with a colonel to control localised detail. Nothing in his planning had called for the "statement of murder" as used on the traitor Litvinenko, Polonium-210, or for the traitor Skripal, Novichok. What he had asked for was the most simple killing methods of all, a car bomb first, automatic gunfire second, a grenade launcher for the third and the support of a naval vessel far outside territorial waters. Each time, climbing the ladder of resources, he had demanded more. His wife had phoned him twice, where she would have the single packed bag beside the front door of their apartment, but he had not taken her calls. Only a skeleton staff were at work in the office around him but word would already be abroad that a great man in the organisation had failed in an assigned task.

Doug had barely needed to touch the car's brakes. At the approach of the PET car in front of them, the red and white striped barrier had swung up to the vertical, and armed guards doing the Sunday morning sentry roster had turned away as if they were unwilling to be witnesses to the entry into the Aalborg base of the Royal Danish Air Force. They were directed to an annex off the officers' mess, were met there, were "quarantined", isolated with a coffee machine but no food and were told that an RAF flight was on its way from the UK – and that Brian would get a lift back to Copenhagen in the PET car.

It was a talent of Wally, and likely the same with Doug, that he could shut out the images of the night, those of fire and bodies, of blood and devastation. He'd heard people say, those who had done combat, that the reckoning came later. After the entry into civilian life, when supposed normality ruled, the black dog days would come calling. He had a couple of magazines in his bag and tossed one of them at Doug. Benedict was fielding texts, and the spin was in the air and a story concocted and it had nothing to do with either of them, not Wally and not Doug. The Russian was quiet as if, now, he had a realisation of what had happened in the last week and how much had been put into play to save his life and that any thought of going back, flying east for two and a half hours, was well dunked. He was sitting close to the Danish girl, like both of them knew that no future existed but the short term had been good . . . and Brian slept. Which was another skill.

If Wally had been asked what he thought of his importance in the operation – which he was not – then he would have said, "Same as always, what the little guys are called up for and when the smelly stuff needs sorting, what we always do. And nothing works without us little people." Would never be asked.

The report had traction and was climbing. It would travel from the office of the Brigadier, of Volkov, the man given difficult areas to master – and who had presided over a failure on an industrial scale. It went from his office in the glasshouse building of GRU to the *dacha* of a major general and appeared on a phone screen on a kitchen table where this officer of substance took a late breakfast after a carousing evening to celebrate the birthday of his youngest daughter. Many of influence and wealth had partied with him, and his home was not yet tidied of debris, and he did not know with whom his daughter was now asleep, and his own wife snored loudly in their bedroom, and the *dacha* was a tip, . . . He read the message, added to it, then sent it on, and hurled the phone against a wall and saw it split open and fracture.

News of killings in the western area of Jutland, Denmark, wherever the fuck that was, was relayed to a member of the illustrious corps of *siloviki*. The news was passed on. On that Sunday morning, it fell to a little known member of staff, young and ambitious and not wishing to be a carrier of bad news, to enter inner sanctums to which, for important news, he had access. He was allowed two minutes in the presence of a man not yet fully dressed, and gave him the bare detail of the events in a far European corner. No oath, no obscenity, but a cold biting together of teeth and a narrowing of lips, and a moment of extreme irritation – and a reputation for competence once owned by an underling was shredded.

Benedict broke it, how it was to be played.

"There was apparently, last night, a fight involving extreme violence between two factions of Russian organised crime groups. They are St Petersburg based, smaller groups trying to muscle into the wealth of the Tambov crowd, and the rewards from amphetamine products are big. They would have been buying supplies in Denmark from laboratories there, but two groups fell out and each would have thought themselves short-changed by the other. The men involved are hoods, criminals. There would have been some sort of meeting utilising the empty houses on the deserted tourist island of Fano. The disagreement was unresolved. There are at least two fatalities. The weapons used went as far as an RPG-7 grenade launcher, and automatic rifles. The government of Denmark will be seriously annoyed that Russian-based gangs are prepared to use their country as a sewer of violence. It is believed that small craft came into Danish coastal waters in the night, in the aftermath of this violence, and took off survivors from the confrontation. That is what is being released by the Danish interior ministry . . . Quite neat, don't you think?"

With the city around the great glass building came awake, Volkov took a phone call from his wife.

She told him that she had been near frantic with worry because he had declined to speak to her before, said that the bag was packed as she had been told and was by the front door and she only waited for him to tell her when she was to leave in the family car and where she would come to meet him, except that . . . Volkov began with a perfunctory apology which carried no sincerity. She started out again that she needed to know where they would meet and was ready to leave, and their daughter, and should have had more explanation, and that all was well with her except that . . . He held the phone away from his ear and stared out through the window of the building. It had been constructed on the site of an old airfield, a big site, and one with good parking provided for the officers and staff of GRU working there. He could see their second car, a compact, usually used by his wife to drive to the school where she taught, for local shopping and occasionally by him when he went to his workplace at weekends and did not need to impress. She was persistent, annoyed, and it showed, and her impatience grew . . . except that she could see from their domestic security system that men waited by a car in the forecourt of the block and stamped their feet on the frost-covered ground, and talked among themselves and smoked, and sometimes spoke into their sleeves. What was she to do?

It would go badly for him, he realised it. From his window he looked down on to the parking area reserved for officers of his rank. A Sunday morning and only his car was there. More men waited close to it and across the route through the empty parking bays were vehicles with their engines idling. He would not reach the Leningradsky station for the train to St Petersburg, and most certainly he would not make the connection with the fast and luxury service to Finland. His privilege crawled away from him as if it were a rat and he was sinking. He told his wife, no explanation, that she should unpack the bag. He knew that the two men sent to Germany, then Denmark, with reputations for competence, were dead, that a plan of assassination had been out-manoeuvred, that opponents pissed on his weakness and denounced the tackiness of a gangland feud fought out by sadists, brutes, psychopaths, which could not be denied. He hoped that a fraction of his disgrace might be mitigated by a successful Counter-Espionage arrest, had only that to cling to.

At the far end of the long runway at the Aalborg base, an RAF Hercules transporter turned to start the long taxi back. Doug heard it from Brian. Too good to think it had come just for them, all the way from Brize. Delusions of bloody grandeur as Brian had put it to him. Was on its way back from a base up inside the Norwegian sector of the Arctic Circle and was loaded with marines who'd been catching the last of the winter snow up there.

Fond farewells from the Russian, Igor who was *Sashcord* but not for more than a few hours, and from the Danish girl from the PET intelligence division, who did a cuddle and a kiss and seemed to get a little closer than was decent. He might have said that he'd see her "sometime" and she might have asked when "sometime" might be and where . . . and Benedict murmured about "ships that passed in the night" rarely getting to see each other again.

Short and rather embarrassed hugs from Brian for the two guys. Doug reckoned that the man from the Embassy security had had two great days in his life, not easily forgotten, but not to be spoken of. Brian asked him what his plans were and Doug said that he'd a terraced house in Swindon and the guttering was playing merry hell and he'd have to be up and fix it next week – and Brian said that he should be most careful because ladders were so dangerous: neither laughed. Wally had shrugged like there was nothing much important beckoning him. Nils had shaken their hands. No passports, no formalities, no crap that would obstruct them – and no officer on the base wanting to be contaminated by contact.

Benedict wore a jacket and had smoothed his hair and had changed into a clean shirt. Not Doug and Wally who smelt as strongly as when they had come out of the water after their scrub down. They walked from the annex and towards a truck that would take them out to the aircraft where they'd have the pleasure of the company of 100 bawling marines for the ride home.

And Wally said, "Not sure whether I like it or not, but I reckon we're a couple of fossils and they won't see the likes of us again. Won't want to know us."

"Until the next time comes around, old cocker, and they'll come digging for us then. Because we stuck it on the opposition, like it was Route Irish, like it was the Bandit Country, and how."

*   *   *

Out of the mist, coming slowly, was the naval frigate. Leonid prepared himself. There was a fair swell and he was drenched with spray as the dinghy bounced off the crests of waves. He could see that a flimsy ladder snaked down from the warship's deck. He crouched. The one who had the shoulder holster and who did not bother to wear a life jacket grinned – no humour – and smiled and shook his head, Leonid was not to be awarded the fast ride back to the Kaliningrad enclave in the prestige naval vessel. He would be going in the trawler, flogging its way through the weather . . . Was ranked a failure, and could remember . . . officers had come back from London having failed to put down the traitor, Skripal, and had to endure the ignominy of lying through their teeth on TV in the pathetically small chance of being believed as tourists who had gone to visit a British cathedral, but it had snowed an inch and they had not managed it. He, Leonid – also a colonel – would be as disgraced. And the attempt on Navalny had failed. Trails had been left after the killing of a political enemy in Berlin, and another trail in northern France after a stabbing. Leonid had not expected he would be found wanting, would be joining a shamed queue of *failed* men. The naval man climbed the ladder nimbly, did not look down nor give any form of farewell to Leonid. When they left the shelter of the frigate's hull they were tossed and shaken and he was powered a few hundred metres through the mist until the outline of the trawler, kicking and rolling, was clear. He would have to jump, and laconic faces would watch him and might reach out to grab his flailing arms.

"I like what I'm hearing, Jonas."

It was a knack of the AssDèpDG that he could intercept those he wished to speak with in quiet corners on the way to the elevators.

"So far so good, but only so far."

"I'll put it more bluntly. We have *them* by the short ones and the curlies. I would not wish to be the Kremlin's ratting terrier this morning, likely to be kicked from one end of those awful gold-ceilinged corridors to the other . . . And the beauty of it is that their room to refute this delightful rumour, as circulating in the blessed media, is so limited. Cannot say that these men were heroes, first-class chaps, not thugs at all, but perfectly loyal citizens sent out on a mission of murder and mayhem, and proven incapable of delivering the goods. Have to take it on the chin which will make them decently grumpy, and is a rare experience . . . And another thing, Jonas, while I am dishing out plaudits, we have done the Sixers an almighty favour. Sticks in the craw but . . . a massive favour. After Litvinenko and Skripal we were grovelling, could not protect those who put their lives in our hands. Failed them, and others. Any asset now looks each day at the TV in whatever dark hole he exists in and waits to see if another 'enemy' has been taken down while supposedly enjoying our hospitality and might conclude that we are not worth the candle. They have to think that, at the end of their usefulness or at a time when a domestic net is closing, they can quit and be welcomed and live out their time with us, not be in fear of every shadow looming behind them. Well done, Jonas, and now you'll be wrapping it all up."

"Hopefully, yes."

"This young woman, what's she like?"

He did not answer, would not have trusted himself. Might have confused a driven man, might have stuttered in the description. Could have snapped, "None of your damn business." Shrugged, said he had to get on.

But the AssDepDG persisted. "It's a feather for us, Jonas, what you've done . . . The end result is that a new resettlement crowd is being put in place, so I'm told. Montgomery will disappear on a lecture tour, evils of the Bolshie empire, anywhere that's far away. Chiswell is being offered Kabul as second man, and Symonds will be shipped out to Paraguay, Barker is retiring. The woman, Toni, is going to Nicosia so will be near her husband, RAF Akrotiri, which will suit neither and God help the pair of them . . . and then there is the lady. Not gone soft on her, I hope – sorry, meant as a joke, Jonas – and putting her in Work and Pensions and it can be a pleasant deception for the little while it is needed. You'll bring her back over Lambeth, won't you? I'll look out for you . . . When is it you'll be hooking up the caravan again?"

"This afternoon, I hope."

"You coming over, I'll enjoy the sight of it."

Jonas left him. The AssDepDG would probably turn out on a New Year's Day, frost on the ground and hounds baying outside the pub, and rather relish the thought of blood, and a hunting down of vermin. Would have thought of her, of Frank, as vermin. As many would. Just a job, wasn't it?

She had Hector well wrapped and with him was his favourite bear that he held tight as best as fingers in mittens could manage.

Maggie could not turn around and rake the pavement and look for them. Took it on trust they were in position. Behind her and across the street from her should have been Lucinda along with Josh and Nancy, and some of the others who did Embassy protection and had been pressganged. Always busy on a Sunday morning because the Moscow people used that time for meeting, for shopping, for window gazing, for running . . . which made it hard for Maggie to see far ahead or across the street.

The set routine was that she walked from the Metro station, going slowly, taking each opportunity to stop and fuss with Hector's clothes. The timing was down to the minute. She came up the flight of steps from the Metro, into the daylight, and he would pass that point a couple of minutes later, and would catch her, then Hector's charade would be played out as they approached the Yaroslavskiy terminus. Much to say, not much time to say it.

Saw it from the corner of an eye, could not mistake it. The van with dark privacy front windows edged past her along the street, and enough Moscow people would have recognised the purpose of such a vehicle, with such windows, and dawdling, and no motorists hammered a horn in protest and no pedestrian turned to gasp. It came to a stop in a parking bay where a large official sign demanded that no one enter the space. Felt two emotions. A twist of fear and a quickening of her breathing, and a surge of defiance: apprehension and a stubborn streak had a hold on her.

What she had to say had been drilled into her by Lucinda, crammed into the minutes before, separate routes, they had left the compound.

He passed her. All choreographed. Short of the forecourt of the station was a small arcade of shops, mostly clothes and he would pause there. Hector would be prompted to do his stuff. Probably she screwed up at that moment, him coming by her, and she was not supposed to gaze at him, but Maggie failed to help herself and stared those few seconds longer than was natural or necessary. He had not glanced sideways at her but carried on walking, and she thought his stride was remarkable and steady. Remarkable because the van was parked ahead of him and he could not have failed to see it pull in there, and would have seen it when he was behind Maggie and coming closer to her . . . and now there were more of them. Another van and a car, both level with Maggie and her buggy. She did the trick that Lucinda had taught her.

Most of what Maggie knew about the mystery world of trade-craft was from Lucinda. Lucinda said it was nothing special, simpler than the instructors told it, but they needed to portray something sinister and something right only for an elite or they were out on their necks and without employment. They would, wouldn't they, talk up the mystery bit. Lucinda said it was only common sense, and that Hector had mastered most of it, the little gem.

About stopping and looking around. Maggie took her phone out of her pocket. Anyone who was not immediately alongside her and watching carefully would not have been able to ascertain that the phone was not switched on. She seemed to take a call. Paused and her face broke into a broad smile. She seemed to talk and her mouth moved, but said nothing. And she could stop, because people usually stopped and looked around and would listen and chatter alternately, as Maggie did. Played the part well and seemed oblivious to all and everything around her and saw plenty. Saw at least three men loitering on the far side of the street, making little pretence of window shopping, and wore suits and anoraks and their hair was cut close to their heads. Saw a man ahead of her who had no obvious reason to stand and watch the people coming closer to him ... Saw a man who was well dressed and wore a distinctive Homburg hat, and saw a windowcleaner with a short ladder on his shoulder and a bucket slopping water. Saw a mother with twins, and a trio of students with ring folders under their arms, and saw a drunk who was already pestering. Saw so many people along with the goons ... and could make out behind her, just, the head of Lucinda, station chief, and Nancy and Josh who were on the street's far side, and somewhere unrecognised were the people roped in from Embassy security. The two character traits kicked in harder, and the fear was losing ground and the defiance was edging forward, and her jaw jutted. She pushed Hector toward the arcade and had so much to say.

A man walked past Alexei, wore the hat that he remembered and a tartan scarf and carried an expensive leather laptop case, and goons were edging closer and a van and a car dawdled in the street and in front of him another van was parked up and had a front window barely lowered and cigarette smoke spilled from the gap. He saw her. She was talking animatedly on her phone, looking around her, and he checked his wristwatch and calculated how long he needed to get through the barrier checks – if he were free to – and ... saw the goons again.

Such a pleasant morning. Spring coming soon to Moscow. A biting cold wind but the first tepid sunshine and not long until the blossom spilled on the trees, and flowers broke out from the frozen ground, not that he believed he would see it. Doubted the residents of the interrogation block and the holding cells had a sense of spring's arrival ... He had left his mother an hour and ten minutes earlier and nothing of moment was said and she had hugged him tighter than for many years, and put a kiss on his cheek and he had realised that his tears, not hers, made her face wet. Nothing more about the politics of his life, and the deceit he had woven, and what he now faced: confirmation of the immediate future with the vans and the car and the men walking. It seemed pointless and yet they went through the play-act of the tradecraft, a "brush contact". Did it the same as every week and seemed that neither of them had the wit to change the routine.

She came close, was almost beside him and then – slight but noticeable – jerked at the handle of the buggy, flicked it sideways and sharply, and anger seemed to cloud the child's face and his temper soared and the bear was thrown out and fell to the pavement. He crouched. At that level, Hector's eyeline and Maggie's knees, Alexei could see the wheels of the van that was parked farther along the street, close to the station, and also the second van and a car that seemed to have stopped level with a kiosk selling newspapers. Saw that men on the far pavement were poised, looking for breaks in the traffic to cross. He picked up the bear, and his hand shook.

She said, "Just listen to me because there is not long . . ."

Staring up into the fullness of her face, the chin he had never touched and the mouth he had never kissed, Alexei lifted the bear towards the child.

". . . Hear me out, Alexei. What you have to remember is that we do not, not ever, forget you. We always remember you and will do everything in our power to win your freedom. We will be waiting for you. However dark the future, you must never lose sight of our friendship for you. The less you can say about us, about the personalities that you have met, the better it will be for all of us. Try to fob off the questioners. Behind the scenes, however awful things seem, our people will be working night and day in your interests. That is what I have to tell you, Alexei. Never forget that your friends care for you and regard you as a true colleague."

He put the bear in Hector's hand. The child cooed at him, recognising him, and she was tucking it under the blanket.

"We will work for your freedom, all the time, every day. And that day will come. You will be on a flight out of this country, the prison will be behind you. Always these matters end in a swap, it's the way it is. We will get you out and you will fly to Britain and a new life will be arranged for you and we have people who are sympathetic with resettlement and the resources are generous. Hold firm, Alexei."

He stood, and she straightened, and the bear's head was outside the blanket and Hector watched him.

"I'll walk with you."

"You do not have to."

"I will walk close to you. We do not forget a friend."

"It has been valuable what I did?"

"Really valuable, most appreciated," she said. "I promise it, we do not forget a trusted friend. Stay strong."

He was ahead of her when they started to walk, level with the buggy's front wheels, and twice Hector put out an arm, tugged at Alexei's trousers. He held that dream in his head: he was coming down aircraft steps and she was at the bottom, on the apron, and a small boy, dressed for school, came bounding up the steps towards him and had his arms out and jumped and was clasped by Alexei. He saw that the men were crossing the road, jogging, and one had his arm out to hold the traffic, and the back door of the parked van was opening as if those inside needed to see out, get their bearings, ready themselves.

And thought of his mother and of the door to her apartment caving in.

Thought of the picture she kept there, framed in old silver, and it lay on the carpet and the glass was cracked and the picture disfigured.

Remembered the silken words of the woman in the hotel room in a lousy corner of the lousy city of Limassol. Recalled the desks in the office block in Kirov, and the woman with the useful strands of hair trapped on her sweater. His breathing came harder . . . If she had not been beside him, guiding him, he might have turned tail, spun and started out into the traffic and run and dodged and swerved. Gone where? No idea where he might have headed. But she was there and he did not. In front of him crowds headed towards the station terminus and he saw their bobbing heads and hats, and the brightness of a scarf, and looked back at Hector and tears choked in his throat.

*　　*　　*

It played out in slow motion.

Lucinda, by fortune, had a fine view down the length of the pavement.

She had seen the brush contact, done well enough, not brilliant but . . . Had seen the parked van and the idling van and the saloon car. Had seen the traffic part to allow three men to sprint and side-step across the wide traffic lanes.

She was experienced, reckoned to be capable or she would not have landed the prestige appointment of station chief in the Russian capital. She would have expected, from that vantage position – if she stayed – to end up in an upper office suite at Ceaucescu Towers and have a picture window overlooking the Thames. She realised that the experience of old postings, and the capabilities supposedly given scope in recruitment of assets and managing her teams, and staying utterly calm when others might wilt, barely covered this moment on the approach leading into Komsomolskaya plaza and the station. The van's back doors had opened.

Remembered, because they all did in that trade, the grand words of a bodyguard who had undergone probably twenty years of coherent and tough training and was supposed to protect a President, a man designated as leader of the free world, and the principal was down on the pavement with pistol bullets in him and the guy had stood dumbfounded, unresponsive and had shouted, "Christ, it's actually happening". They played through the sort of situation that was spread out in front of her on courses down at Fort Monckton, or would gather in Army barracks and do their wargames, would try to familiarise themselves with the reality of a prized asset going into the enemy's net. She was a voyeur . . . Josh and Nancy had caught the message and were halfway across the street. Lucinda could see *Environ*; more important, she could see Maggie and the buggy two or three paces behind him, and she winced.

The goons were closing in, and the second van was stationary and the back door was opening. Doors snapping wide on the saloon car.

She knew a little of the girl she had plundered from the office of the Military Attaché, knew where she had been, and had helped to sort out where she was going. Would have signed off any CV that referred to a streak of determination – which gave Lucinda that flash of nightmare. In half a minute or less, Alexei – who was a useful agent but not of the highest importance – would be taken. Truth to tell, might not be a top man in the traitor stakes, but was the only intelligence source, deep inside an area of the GRU bureaucracy, that Lucinda possessed. They didn't grow on bloody trees. The only bloody one they had, and the Yanks were impressed when *Environ*'s details, what came off his memory sticks, were dropped on their table. Important and within seconds of being lost.

And her girl stayed close to him. The nightmare could be about to get a screening. Crossing the road fast, spilling from the backs of two vans, snapping out of the saloon car. Hands reaching up to tug down balaclavas. Saw a fucking cameraman, pocket-sized video job in his hand, climb down from the parked van. The nightmare was as to how her girl would react. Come out kicking? Go for the shins, or maybe plant her knee in a goon's crotch. And bite? And scratch, and reckon the sharpness of her fingernails would rip a balaclava on the first slash and get to the skin by the second. Or do that "kiss" from a Scots bar rumpus and use her dainty little forehead under her crop of uncombed golden hair and smack one of them across the bridge of his nose. And, if she did, if she let loose her full retaliatory armoury, then there would be batons out, whacking her, and the kid would be screaming and there would be blood, and a whole amount of nightmare.

Lucinda was uncertain as to how much the girl could see as the net circled them. There would be that moment when the Gold Commander, whatever he called himself on a lift in downtown Moscow, had given the authorisation for the arrest.

He knew. *Environ* knew. The boy had frozen, and they were yards from him.

A bad thought, not one for Lucinda to take pride in, not one that she'd tell the old skipper who did the Angola to Brazil freighter route if they ever were back again and doing pillow talk. Lucinda wondered whether the girl had done all the promises correctly and credibly. Important that the bullshit came out with apparent sincerity, had a ring of confidence, so that the poor beggar was sustained when times were hard, and the least said was the better for Lucinda and her tribe. She would not have wanted to be stuck in a primitive gulag camp, eking out the days and waiting for her "friends" in distant London to be arranging a swap and losing sleep themselves for every day, week, month, that she spent behind the perimeter wire. Lucinda had seen the brush done and the bear on the pavement and him crouched and her bent, and had assumed that the party line had been delivered.

Big men all of them, and a few paces behind and out in the middle of the traffic was the cameraman, and he'd have a shake to his pictures which would add authenticity. She saw that Josh and Nancy had stopped on the line in the middle of the traffic and looked uncertain and had reason to be. What next? Hardly knew what would have been a half-decent answer because no possible way could they intervene if Maggie went in the bag – and God alone knew what to do if Hector was half out of the restraints in his buggy and bawling with fury. Easy to pack the street with watchers. Difficult to tell the watchers how they should respond. All the men were running. Big bastards.

Closing fast and hard – and a miracle moment. Could have been called a true cluster-fuck moment. Something was unveiled in front of Lucinda that was not true, not possible.

Some of the men went past Maggie and her buggy and kept on going and passed *Environ* and hit a guy in front of him. And some were coming towards *Environ* but charged at a man a dozen paces ahead of him. And more of them were coming out of the traffic and reached the pavement and the line they'd taken put them that same distance of a *dozen steps* to the front. Lucinda had a good enough view.

It was one of the style of hats that arty people were supposed to have worn in the Bloomsbury days, or *Rive Gauche* would-be painters, and making a statement that was rare in that city

– Moscow – in those days – Putin's. The hat flew high, wobbled and then dropped into the gutter. She saw the vivid colours of his scarf as it was dragged away from his neck and chucked aside, orange the most prominent. At least four of them had a grip on his clothing and there was another of the frozen snapshot images when he stood and they scrabbled around him and he looked back up the pavement and might have seen *Environ* and might have seen Maggie and the buggy, and then he took a blow to his kidneys. Quite a proud face, and Lucinda had a quirk of memory, recognised something but did not know what . . . They were moving him and went past her boy and he had the sense to duck out of their path and they formed a wedge going down the street towards the cavern of the open doors at the back of a van. They bumped, no intention, into Maggie and toppled the buggy. Lucinda waited, gasped, hoped it was not the trigger for the red mist moment, but the boy reacted faster. Seemed that the goon had neither noticed the buggy nor realised he'd flattened it. Alexei, *Environ*, was beside her and straightened it and there was a moment when they touched but it went unseen except by the station chief. Now the sirens were going, and the man was handcuffed and was being levered inside the van, and the goons were running for open doors, and the cameraman. All over, finished and gone.

Lucinda reflected on how many Sunday afternoons there had been since the surveillance was identified and she had stepped back and roped in the kid and the kid's child. Still scratching in her head for the memory of the man's face as he had been lifted.

And they were close and there were words between them. Lucinda did not lip read. Had an idea . . . "There's always a later train."

She said, "Yes, a train that's quite a bit later." It was what she, Lucinda would have said, and would have answered.

Both turned and went toward the Metro entrance and they passed Lucinda, and the boy looked ashen and the girl pole-axed, but Hector recognised her and waved his bear . . . Josh and Nancy were with her and the sirens had faded and traffic flowed and people hurried on.

Lucinda said, "I don't know who he is and it's irritating the hell out of me."

She was told he was a poet and published an underground magazine which lampooned the man in charge – the Tsar in his bunker. Enough, of course, of a reason to be lifted off the street. She said where they would be going, but not quickly, and added, "Want to know something that I currently consider important?"

And Josh and Nancy would be told whether they wanted to know or not.

"She'll be going home in the next forty-eight hours, and well out of this shit heap. Going back to do something honest, something clean and wholesome. She will be lying on her pretty little stomach and clearing minefields and defusing roadside IEDs, and well shot of this dirty, mucky bit, and peddling lies . . . Fuck me, I cannot believe what we saw."

And they were laughing, all of them, near hysterical and they started walking and looking for a bar.

He stepped out on to the bridge.

Jonas could think of no predictable reason why, after this Sunday morning journey, he would need to use it again. Quite an attractive bridge.

Vera had asked him the previous evening where, in general terms, he might be going the next day and he'd said that he'd cross Lambeth Bridge, then go into Thames House, then go along the north embankment, and would walk over Vauxhall Bridge. Do a bit of business and then go back towards his office and retrace his steps on Lambeth Bridge . . . and conversation had been thin and she had opened her tablet, and done research for their Suffolk trip. No further questions, nothing about the *why* and the *who with*, but she had traced out his route.

At the far end of Vauxhall Bridge was the Sixers building. Its inhabitants believed themselves superior in pretty much any discipline to those at the Fivers' place: himself, he would be rated as a cretin, an under-achiever, a "little man" . . . The bridge, Vera had told him was a little more than 100 years old and had been built at an exorbitant cost, £175,000. Joggers passed him, and cyclists, and some swore at him for blocking their way, and women negotiated around him with large baby carriers, and the road was busy with buses and cars and vans. A stiff wind tried to lift his trilby off his head but he clung to it.

More useful information about the bridge he had no reason to think he would need. It was Grade II listed, 250 metres long, had five spans and a steel and granite system of deck arches, and was wearing well. A gull flew alongside him as if he offered a better chance of a food handout than the more athletic users, but he told it, a black back, that he was only in London briefly and was not that day carrying his lunch with him, and no morsel would be flipped its way. The bridge, painted pink with orange highlights, had an old-fashioned and substantial balustrade and Jonas could see that the tide was high, incoming, but about to turn. The sky was bright and the wind sharp, but the flow of the river seemed dark and deep and hostile, and the image was sufficient to terminate his conversation with the bird, and he looked ahead and quickened his step, and wondered if she watched him coming and thought he knew why she had posed in that way in her living-room with the curtains drawn back

16

The Six people remembered him at the screening checks.

He knew the procedures. Coins and keys, including the one attached to the bright pink ribbon, and a fountain pen, all went into the tray, and he unlocked the cuff on his wrist and that and the link chain and the briefcase went on to the moving belt and was gobbled into the X-ray system. Jonas went through the metal detector arch and was verified by his eyes, and his Five identification was looked at as if it had the importance of a lottery ticket and, almost an afterthought, the pair of handcuffs, folded, given a quizzical glance. He was cleared through, and pocketed his possessions, and the key with the ribbon stayed with the handcuffs he had brought from his own office. It would be the last time that he entered this top-dog kennel . . . and the policeman nodded to him and he noted that there were another pair loitering behind the gatekeeper's desk. All seemed to have enough weaponry for an outbreak of major hostilities. Not that it would come to that. All planned and intended to be a calm ending and one with dignity. Seemed to fit into place and then he was waved through after the pat-down, and he saw her.

Felt a shiver of shame as he looked at her.

Was not sure if, from what he had seen in George's photograph, he would have recognised the woman standing with her feet a little apart and arms folded across her chest, and her hair pinned up as normal, and a crisp white blouse and a severe suit, but no makeup and no jewellery. Embarrassed because he acknowledged that his gaze had lingered a second or three longer than was necessary when the photograph had been dropped on his desk, before he had picked it up as if it could infect him and had fed it to his shredder . . . Jonas realised that Frank had made a statement by standing, almost posing, by the open window, back-lit, would have stayed there long enough for the focus on the camera to be adjusted to the finest detail. But could not say whether she would have expected him to be shown the image, whether a print would be run off with the intention of showing it to him.

"Good morning, Frank."

"Morning to you, Mr Merrick. Was wondering where you were, not that it was a difficulty. Problem with the trains?"

"Don't often, just slept in a bit. Hope I have not inconvenienced you?"

"Not in any way."

"Thank you."

She had a crisp, cool voice and played politeness and a modicum of concern, and he wondered if his deceit was in any way successful, or if she had read him, had stripped out the lies, and then would . . . No idea what she might do. He had been moderately concerned that she'd try to leave her building by the rear fire escape and take a rucksack of personal gear and run. Run to where? To the Embassy, to the trade delegation, to one of those front Friendship societies, or to an airport, or any harbour where a continental ferry was waiting to sail. But she had not, instead had posed for her photograph to be taken and would have known that men would ogle the image and would remember her: and anyone who had liked her would have been saddened to have rubbernecked the image. Jonas's voice had a slight stutter to it, which was not entirely fabricated. The police watched her closely, did not look at Jonas.

He followed her. Thought the game of innocence was beginning to bore him but must play it out for a short time longer, and then . . . off to Waterloo, on a train, up his road and the caravan doors open because Vera would have packed, and the cat already in its travelling cage. Taking the caravan out, only the second time that year, and all the electrics working, and then his expert manoeuvre into their road, and off.

She opened the safe and extracted the map that showed an island across a wild, dark sea, and another that showed a suburban street adjacent to a large cemetery, with woodland marked on it that ran up to rear gardens. The biographies of her colleagues came out, and of the men who had maintained a watch on a defector, on *Sashcord*, which was an irritating and stupid name for a man with a price, a high one, on his life. A moment for last rights . . . Jonas went to few funerals but had the opinion that most of the obsequies had as little match with truths as his performance now.

He dictated. A half-page would do nicely. The slight weight of the key hanging from the ribbon had separated from his tie . . . Clear for her to see . . . Sometimes he hesitated in mid-sentence and she prompted him and he would agree to her suggestion. It annoyed him and she would have seen it but neither referred to it nor gave any indication she had noticed it . . . All exonerated of blame, and she was at the end, like an afterthought, and it was his suggestion that she might take a secondment in Work and Pensions, where valuable reporting could be done on benefit claimants straying into territory watched over by both the Fivers and the Sixers, and with a recommendation for a salary upgrade. He was uncertain if anything dictated was believed. She made no comment. He read it back, said he was satisfied, asked for it to be sent to the Line Manager, and tried to smile affably.

"Won't take long, and then you're free of me for the rest of the weekend. I really appreciate your cooperation. And, I hope you'll enjoy the new life."

The wheels of a Hercules transport aircraft, the familiar and reliable C-130, smacked down on the long Brize Norton runway, and the engines did the reverse roar and it slowed and turned and started to taxi. A company of "booties" clapped the pilot for bringing them safely down and whooped and cheered. Not the small group of outsiders stowed at the tail, their feet hampered by a mountain of kitbags, skis and sledges, and weapons. There would be, that night, a monumental drinking binge in pubs in Portsmouth and Plymouth, but not for this small flotsam gang.

They were bussed to a terminal, and split there. They were studiously ignored by RAF police and by Customs. The marines would get a going-over, not that much could be bought in Arctic Norway, but the defector and Benedict and the muscle were gestured towards side doors, and a girl waited for them and handed out travel warrants for taxis to take them to Didcot or Swindon stations, and onwards, except for the Russian. A man and a woman, not a glimmer of a smile between them, waited for him. Benedict was for Heathrow and a flight to Scotland and a bus into the Highlands, and Doug was for Swindon and his ladder and his guttering, and Wally was vague, but Doug told him, hopefully, he'd see him around, and Wally nodded.

Volkov had cleared his desk. Security had stood watch over his safe and prevented its emptying, so he had only taken a photograph of his wife and daughter and a pen his wife had given him last Christmas, and his spare spectacles, the gear he used in the glass-house gym, and the suit for wearing at "must attend" receptions. No staff to see him go, no avenue of applause, and by the morning his name would be off his door and a new occupant at his desk. He had hit the phone when the news had reached him that an intellectual had been taken into custody and would face charges of sedition for the denigration in print of the president. He had pleaded his loyalty to those who now cooled on praising his efficiency. To some purpose . . . He was to be posted to the city of Voronezh, only 500 klicks from the capital, not that his mood made irony welcome . . . At some time the opportunity would arise for the train journey to Finland or the flight to Vienna, but not yet.

He represented failure and had no way of learning the name of the man who had pitched him there.

The bed had belonged to his maternal grandparents. His mother had been born on that bed, and so had he. It had old dark wood panels at their heads and at their feet and they creaked as the bed heaved but it was the sound of the mattress, shrill and loaded with old springs, that serenaded them. Years since he had done it, and then it had been with local girls from the block and fast, behind the walls where the communal bins were kept, sometimes rats for company and sometimes smaller children sniggering. Had never stripped off, been stripped, and lain on his mother's bed.

They had come back to the apartment. A look of surprise from his mother who might have recognised Maggie vaguely from the grocer store, or might not. The buggy had been wheeled in. There would have been immediate understanding from her. He had not had to head into a multitude of explanations, had just gone to a cupboard in the living-room, had opened it and it had been overflowing with games and books and wooden bricks and tin trucks. He had placed them by his mother's feet. Had taken Maggie's hand, not a word said, and they had gone through the door into the bedroom, where the door did not close properly. Their clothes were a mess on the floor. And Alexei wore his socks, his best pair, that would have done him well in the Lefortovo and might have lasted through to the autumn and the winter in one of the gulag camps.

Maggie, who showed him how and what he should do, was not prepared to waste his time, her time. She'd said it was safe. Not love, but a basic form of affection. Nothing about spending a life together, what he had believed was possible, nothing of tenderness and a part of each of them prepared to suffer together. Him in her and plunging, and her moving like time was sliding, and he wondered if the bed had made that much noise when his mother had been conceived, and whether the springs had squealed in the same way when his father had been with his mother, and a vodka bottle likely already sunk and maybe being sick on the carpet afterwards because of the exertion. He cried out. Saw on her face a look of triumph and held her as tight as his fingers were capable of and did not know if it mattered to her.

Wondered if it were gratitude for the memory sticks that he brought her.

Wondered if it was the reaction to seeing the men charge and bracing herself and clinging to the handle of the buggy and them sweeping on past – and he had almost wet himself. Could have cheered them because they went for someone else not him. She might have felt that fear. Wondered if it were farewell but doubted she would admit it.

Wondered if she would ever tell a small boy, named after a Greek god, a warrior, about him. And . . . what to say, nothing to say. And . . . what to do, more to do. Trying to extend each moment and fearful he would forget, not remember her and be bereft.

He said, "When they came past us, and did not take us, what did you feel?"

A little gasp and breathless. "I thanked God it was not us."

"Felt nothing for him, the man they took?"

"Nothing. His problem. Relief. Will I ever think of him again, who they took instead of us? No. Just us. We are little people. If we do not just think of ourselves then we are crushed . . . Do it, Alexei, for us. Go hard, Alexei, for us."

His breath came in sobs and he bit at the skin of her neck and the sweat swam between them, and the door was open, and with them was the radio music in the block and the sound of the crowd at the football stadium.

"I tell you one thing, Alexei."

"Tell it me."

"I would not have had it otherwise, not . . ."

He cried again, one last time. She groaned and he did not think it pretence and they sagged, were spent. Her fingers loosened her hold on him, and the muscles in her arms slackened, and he did not bite her skin again. And he could hear his mother chuckling and the child squealing with pleasure. A bell rang. A thin and reedy shout for attention. A shuffle of feet, and the sound of a lock turning. Alexei had imagined that door, now opened by his mother, would have been hit with a sledgehammer, hard enough to take it off from the jamb and spit it into the narrow hallway. They would have swarmed in over the worn square of carpet . . . He supposed it should not have happened, her and him. Thought in her language they would have been bracketed as an asset and a handler. Soft voices, his mother and a woman's and he recognised the accent and the English attempt at vernacular Russian.

They lay on the bed, only their fingers touching, and he knew it had ended.

"Come on you two. Time to shift yourselves."

Lucinda stood at the door.

"For fuck's sake, Maggie, let's have you. He has a train to catch."

The child's games were on the floor. Hard for her to recall when her own daughter had been that age and where they had been in the Foreign Service and which nanny would have ruled the roost, and likely most Sunday afternoons she would have been working and her husband bitching that they had no life . . . was probably right but that was before an accommodation.

She had left Josh and Nancy in a park across the street from the apartment block and it had been poor procedure on her part to have come here: would have shrugged if challenged, would have said it seemed necessary. If he had been lifted, were in custody and not here with his arse in the air, then Lucinda would have hustled back to the Embassy and into the Service section, past the armoured doors and the specialist security, and would have gone into the "change everything" mode. Change the codes, change the methods of operating, change the names used by personnel, change the rendezvous points and the places where there might be a dead letter box and change the brush contact locations and the clothes worn and the recognised items carried, and then hammered messages to London. They did not expect that a guy who went into the Lefortovo, lifted off the street, would stay silent long – not against the shouting and the threats and the first signs of acute violence. Might attempt to portray himself as just handing over chickenshit information. It would have been a scramble to safeguard the remnants of the operation. But the agent was not being beaten nor facing truth drugs, but was shagging little Maggie, and her a willing co-conspirator. Made Lucinda yearn for her skipper.

"For fuck's sake, Maggie, get your knickers back on."

The little boy played cheerfully, seemed not to notice her. Alexei's mother, face lined with struggle and skinny from poverty, wore a wider smile than Lucinda could have managed ... Lucinda's daughter was seventeen years old and she thought her a minx weighed down with entitlement and rude and having affection only for her father: did not seem to know, or care, who paid the bloody bills.

Had seen the men spilling from the vans and the car, and the ones coming across the traffic lanes and had wanted to yell out a warning and had felt that surge of anguish, welling up, and then the anti-climax of the whole damn century as far as she was concerned. Gone for someone else ... had felt weakness in her legs and realised that Nancy – posh little thing – was clinging to Josh in relief.

Maggie emerged first, knelt on the floor and was helping Hector with the bricks. She'd a bite on her neck that would need a scarf in the morning. Lucinda was tired and fed up with the game she played, and wondered if anyone had bothered to pick up that attractive tartan scarf off the pavement and the hat, or whether they were still there with people stepping around them.

The boy was dressed. No time to mess about with small talk. Not too many trains did the long haul to Kirov on a Sunday, and he'd need to be at his desk at whatever God-awful hour GRU clerks were required on duty.

Lucinda said, in Russian, with that emphasis in her voice which meant that she'd not expect argument nor contradiction, "Bit of a false alarm for us, Alexei. Happens in our world. Need luck but always have to deserve luck. That makes us clean. No more talk about bugging out, Alexei. You are safe. Your circulation of material is very limited. We disguise the source if posting to foreign customers, the Americans mainly. But the Israelis and the Italians have sung your praises. When you come back in two weeks Alexei, you will have a new contact because Maggie is taking a little bit of leave. There will be a brush outside the station. It will be fine. So, we had a scare and the scare is behind us, and that is where we are. Is your mother aware of ... of anything?"

A nod, she was.

"I might call by again," and smiled. An anonymous block in an anonymous estate could be useful as a stash, as a place to put a fugitive off the street.

Not now, but later, she would grill Maggie, on the end of her drive far to the north, to beyond the pretty town of Vyborg and up close to the Finland border, about a village, and about a woman living there who tended a grave. Name of Galina today, but a code name would be allocated her within twenty-four hours and the real name buried and forgotten. Graves, Lucinda's experience, were always good currency for bringing people on board. The dead, if put there by the state and buried in Mother Russia's earth, tended to spawn bitterness, made the grieving folk possible to recruit. Not all about colonels and brigadiers and men with strutting self-importance – as much about the small people and the location was good for both a stash and a bed where few of the security teams would come looking. Would have been disappointed to have passed up such a promising recruitment opportunity.

"Right, let's go back where we belong."

Alexei's mother, Lucinda and Maggie settled on the carpet and started to stow the bricks and toys back in their boxes, and a couple of soft animals went with them, and for the child that too was all part of the game. A satisfactory afternoon following an extraordinarily good morning. Lucinda said a formal goodbye to the mother but not to Alexei, actually had no eye contact and had nothing especial to say . . . best that way because agents, her experience, if given too great a length of rope would always want to start hammering on about getting off the treadmill. Best to avoid the chance of it being demanded. The boy was of no use unless at his desk, fielding invoices, making foreign currency exchanges, paying for airline tickets, refurbishing the bank accounts of "illegals".

Hector, the little star, was strapped in and they left, closing the door after them. Between them they carried the buggy down the flights of stairs. At the bottom they parted and Lucinda went right, would get a tram and bus and then a Metro, and Maggie would go

straight for a Metro, and Josh and Nancy would see them leave
and then peel off and take their own route . . . Poor girl, it would
seem dull for her when she was down in the dirt and dealing with
miniature circuit boards and built-in booby traps. And had a sense
that a door on the day was closing but not fully.

They walked on the south side of the river towards the Archbishop's
Palace. Jonas and Frank would have seemed a conventional couple,
to the runners and riders who competed for their space. He had
shaved poorly and there was a nick of blood on the collar of his
day-old shirt, and his tie was not quite straight, and his coat was
buttoned against the wind and he kept a firm grip on his briefcase
– and she was elegant in a way that an absence of ornament often
highlighted, and seemed clean, almost scrubbed. The same image
as before, a daughter taking her father out for a walk and then
packing him off, duty done, on the Underground to wherever he
lived. Conventional . . . except that the Counter-Intelligence
officer had planned to disorganise the thought processes of his
Tango as far as possible so that the impact of arrest would be
greatest.

A good plan, one that seldom failed to deliver. *Except* that the
target had already thrown his ideas askew by posing naked in front
of a surveillance camera. *Except* that she had come out with no
makeup and no jewellery as if knowing they would not be important by the end of the day. *Except* that he believed she might play
with his intentions, have read them.

He said, "I'm hoping to get away after lunchtime, just a sandwich for me, want to be up on the Suffolk coast. Chance there for
a spot of contemporary archaeology, pottering around some old
war ruins, but also looking at the wild life. Any plans, Frank, for
this afternoon?"

"I don't think so, Mr Merrick, nothing particular."

"Not a big person for weekends myself. But spring is coming
and it's a good chance to pull the caravan down there, and our cat
comes with us. Best time of year, before the hordes are let loose.
Quiet and good prices. And then back to proper work after a

couple of days in lieu. It has all been a rather interesting experience, but I confess to having been somewhat out of my depth."

"I hope we've made you welcome."

"Don't get that cake, not the coffee and walnut, where I am. I've been very well looked after."

"You'll not see much bird life, Mr Merrick, if things don't improve."

He looked out over the Thames. Indeed, if these were the weather conditions at Orford Ness then spying harriers and whatever else Vera wanted to see would likely fail. The mist came in quickly, seemed to settle on to the water. The wind blew sharply on his face, lifted his hat and ruffled her hair. He wondered to where it had fled, that bright start to the day.

He said, attempting a smile, "Anyway, we'll worry about that when it happens. I have to say, Frank – not too familiar, I hope – that this position at Work and Pensions may seem rather downmarket in comparison with what you are used to handling. I don't regard it as taking you off the coalface. It will enable you to be very close to a myriad of files that will really help our efforts and those of your colleagues. Sorting out winter fuel payments sounds mundane but it gets your knees under the table, and when things have settled a little I would hope you go back to VX but with an enhanced position, as an officer. And not before time."

He walked a little faster. Had too many doubts that nothing of what he sought to achieve was likely. Could not get that image from his mind, the picture dumped on his desk. She was more aloof and more distanced. Would have one more crack at it. Try another lie.

"When we're over at Work and Pensions, you'll be meeting their HR people, and the team leader is excellent, switched on, and has long been an ally – know what I mean? – of our people. Most sympathetic . . . Being there will give you access to the case histories of scores of the parents of these wretched potential *jihadis*, and then it's snaking trails that lead from the old people to the new generations. I tell you, very sincerely, Frank, that the urban guerrilla problem, inside our country, is not yet muzzled. For you, for your career, it is rather a good opportunity, my opinion."

And he thought that he spouted nonsense – what the AssDepDG would have called "poppycock" and what Aggie Burns would have described as "Grade Alpha One rubbish", and what he himself would have labelled as "drivel" . . . And all a lie because he had no idea of the name of the team leader of Human Resources in Work and Pensions who dealt with Winter Fuel allowances, and doubted that anyone there would be allowed within a mile of sensitive websites.

"Yes, Frank, well the fog has certainly come down with a vengeance. Don't think it was on the forecast . . . could be quite a tricky drive up to the coast unless it lifts."

And he realised that he babbled. To have done the lift inside the Sixers' place, or even at the front gate would have been a pleasing, though gratuitous, insult to that Service. Better if it were done with discretion and off their territory, hence the nonsense that he coughed up in the hope of relaxing her, making the job easier.

Jonas could no longer see across the river but he noted the outline of a tug in mid-stream, towing the shadowy shapes of half a dozen well-laden barges, and a church clock boomed out the hour but the chime was muffled. The damp settled on his face and the wind massaged it and he had to squeeze his fingers together and find something deep in his pocket for them to hold, or he would have shivered. What his fingers found was the pair of hand-cuffs retrieved from his cubicle drawer.

She matched his step and Lambeth Bridge loomed ahead of them. The key on the ribbon, damn thing, bounced on his tie. A similar bridge to the description that Vera had given him of the Vauxhall Bridge: Lambeth was 250 metres over five spans, 160 years old, painted red and Grade II listed, but it had come in a fair bit cheaper than its neighbour and was on the site of a Victorian horse ferry, all just bloody irrelevant. She walked straight-backed, head erect. There was little about her that he did not admire. The tug and its barges had gone under the central span and the tide was high but might just have turned, and gulls merged with the fog, but still shouted.

She said softly, "Excuse me, Mr Merrick, but I feel you are rather patronising me."

He pretended not to hear, thought that best, and a significant part of his day had unravelled. He shook, did not know whether she had noted his reaction.

They climbed the steps to the bridge.

Rare for the DepDG to be seen on a Sunday morning.

"A bit like gathering to watch the hounds at the kill."

"It's been a good show. Old Merrick has justified our faith."

"Not that we're going to see much of the blood sports."

"Bloody awful, and came out of nowhere."

He stood beside the AssDepDG and they had a vantage point on the fourth floor, but bugger all of a view, as both had complained.

"The man has come in around whom this whole business roamed."

"The Six folk called him *Sashcord*, bloody silly name, but not here for long. Within a couple of days he's off to South Africa. Probably get funded to start a chicken farm. Good riddance, utterly useless and squandering the budget."

"Not entirely, because Merrick managed to pull off a very decent one, and they will be chewing carpet tacks in Kremlinland – and all deniable."

"His big parade, pity the weather's against him – but we'll see him at halfway."

They were on the bridge, going up the incline.

Enough of the kid gloves act. "In a hole," they said, "stop digging". He reverted to type, not pleasant.

"Something you should know, Frank . . ."

"What's that, Mr Merrick?" Quiet, composed.

"The island off the coast, a few minutes on a ferry from Esbjerg. Fano."

"Yes, you had a map of it." Gave no sign that the enormity of what had happened had yet settled on her shoulders, but looked briefly down into the water. A tourist boat went under them, going upstream, fighting the turned tide and almost empty, and from its picture windows the few passengers would barely have seen either shore of the river.

"Going back to the start of the week. Last Sunday an attempt was made on the life of a defector, codename Sashcord, using a car bomb that would have killed him had it been detonated and also the protection travelling with him."

"Yes."

"Obviously a security leak, and the reason someone as inadequate as myself was shipped in . . . Sashcord was moved, along with his minders, to the outskirts of Esbjerg. That location was also leaked, and a further attempt was made to kill him, and the British personnel with him would have been collateral. It is the appropriate word but one which I rather detest. On that occasion a gun jammed. I don't know much about firearms, Frank, but I suppose they jam as often as office printers do. A further failure, and we now accept that we are dealing with a state player, a department with resources and the determination to see matters through."

"Yes, would seem like that, Mr Merrick."

"They were moved again. Pretty straightforward. We shipped Sashcord and his team across on the ferry to the island. We had a location for them to go to and that was written down. I expect you saw it, Frank. You should have seen the piece of paper because it was clipped to the map and put in the safe in the certain knowledge that you would see it. There was a house that we used in Section 6 of the development of prestige holiday homes on the North Sea coast. Actually, a rather smart house, probably going to sell at well in excess of a million euros, but that's only money and money rarely intrudes into matters of political necessity. With me, Frank?"

"I think so, thank you."

"We wrote off the house. Easy for us to do that as we did not own it, had no rights to be in it. The expression was used, Frank, of 'tethered goat'. It means that we had marked out a bait that a predator would be drawn to. It is how in Raj days the *sahib* could be guaranteed an easy shot at a hungry and careless tiger, and he'd have something to boast about at the Club, and a rug in front of the fire. Not going too fast for you am I, Frank?"

Said easily, as if humouring an old man, "Very easy to understand, Mr Merrick."

"Too kind. Vera often says I waffle and am difficult to follow . . . anyway. We did the obvious and shipped the target out, on all-fours, crawling into the darkness and down to the beach and then he had to run like hell. Shift himself and a team leader who you know, young Benedict, and the chappie from Embassy security and a Danish officer from the PET organisation, and a dummy was dressed up and one light left on and jazz music playing. All pretty old-fashioned stuff, but it delivered the goods. Interesting, yes?"

"Fascinating, Mr Merrick." Her head stayed up and her back was straight and she gave no sign of being cudgelled by what he told her, and looked straight ahead.

"I imagined you'd be interested, and even more interested in the end product. The hit men arrived long after their target had been removed from the house. There was a stake-out. Marksmen covered the house which was empty but noisy. An RPG-7 launcher was fired and rifle fire on automatic, and the house caught fire. The hit men would have been euphoric. After two failures they had carried out their mission. They would have been confident that the intelligence provided them was accurate, utterly trustworthy and supplied by an asset of proven value. I am sad to say, Frank – and I take no pleasure in gratuitous violence – they were both shot dead. Left as corpses at the scene. A long way from the intended ending as planned by the state sponsor."

"Is that right?"

There was an edge in Jonas's voice, something brutal. "We have taken it further, of course. Had a little story put out that the dead were caught up in a *mafia* feud, St Petersburg thugs arguing over the Scandinavian amphetamine market. Which has credence, par for the course. The state sponsor is humiliated amongst the few who know the reality, and an asset is left exposed . . . quite a price paid . . ."

Just clearing the first span, not yet halfway.

"You ready, mate?" Kevin asked.

"And willing and able," Leroy answered.

"Those other jerks, they show up?"

"They're there."

The two armed policemen stepped out and crossed a pair of traffic lanes, and motorists gave them a wide berth, and they had rifles across their chests and readied for whatever – and behind them against the kerb in front of Thames House was a parked mini bus. Three plainclothes Special Branch detectives had stepped out and fags were lit and feet stamped, and all of them peered up at the bridge and saw only a low wall of mist.

"Can't see a bloody thing . . . Reckon we're wasting our time?"

"Don't give up, not if Mr Merrick's in on the act."

Jonas kept talking had expected by now that her cheeks would have flushed, her eyes drooped and her shoulders slumped. It was not necessary, but he did it because her refusal to be shaken annoyed him, and the fact that he thought she had laughed in his face by posing at the window of her flat for the surveillance camera. He was confused and knew no other course.

"Always a favourite one, amateur dramatics. That's what I'm told. Place for lonely hearts. Far from home, strange city, short of company, get a good welcome. They must have targeted you, Frank, and then realised that you were there for the taking. They run the rule over so many people and spend all day and every day following and learning and assessing. Had a line into you and might have thought it their lucky day . . . Cannot say that I know why an attractive and very pleasant woman such as yourself, and intelligent, would have gone short of affection and friendship. He walks into your life. Treats you in a way you have not known before. It would have been as happy a few weeks, or was it months, as you had known. You would have walked tall, believed yourself someone on whom the sun shone, would have had a swagger in your step and been a changed person in that 'amdram' group . . . And it provided substantial amusement, as you can imagine. How you fell for it I cannot quite imagine as I would have thought that every security lecture you had attended would have warned you off. But . . . but . . ."

They were over the second span of the bridge. Still, Jonas could not see the far end nor the south-facing facade of Thames House. He assumed that she would have read him adequately on about the second day of escorting him, certainly by the time that she had first bought the cake and might then have realised the threat she faced.

". . . but you chose to ignore the message of those lectures. He was, tough to swallow, a trained stud. Quite vile of me to say that, but it's a truth. The tradecraft that he had learned at whatever espionage college he had attended, was in productive shagging, and doing it well – Vera would give me a good kicking for using that language to you, Frank – and then he went away. Surprise, surprise, because he has to go home and see the wife and the kids, and maybe buy a new car, and perhaps take them off for a Black Sea holiday, and could have been running another lonely lady in Paris or Rome, anyway in a security or defence ministry somewhere. They will have put you away on a shelf and filed your details, and you were into Resettlement. Did they get you out of limbo for Skripal? Probably not because he lived so openly and you'd not have been needed. But along came another one, and he'd left a Copenhagen apartment and his Embassy desk, was GRU, and had done a runner. The thought was that this was several notches above the level of acceptable to them, and the traitor needed taking down, needed to pay a high price. And you were so perfectly positioned and going to make it very easy for them to carry out a successful hit."

His voice died. Had said almost all that he wanted to. Accepted that he did not need to be there, and that only the predictable urge to see the matter to a conclusion had brought him into London that morning. Could have been flogging at a snail's pace through the fog up the A12, around the Colchester bypass. Could have been with Vera, and with Olaf, who had provided the clarity, and left this wrap-up stage to the detectives. He supposed it a bit of a malarial microbe, something lodged in him that he was unlikely to rid himself of. Actually, he felt ashamed.

And a couple more had taken up position on the south side of the bridge, had come up off the Albert Embankment. They had similar weaponry, and restraints slung on belts and hooks.

The lad said, "I can only just see them, Lizzie. Sod of a day and started so well. About halfway. Can't see what they're at."

The girl said, "All looks, what I can make out, pretty innocent. A bit of a duff call-out. What are we expecting to happen?"

"What they say . . . 'Just in case' . . . They've stopped in the middle."

"Perhaps the old bugger needs a rest."

Both chuckled. Both knew an arrest of significance was minutes away. Both would have said that being pushed out from guard duty at the VX building was always welcome. Both could only see two shadowy figures who seemed to have stopped in their tracks.

"Which gets us to the business of what happened at the hotel up in Aarhus, you and Sashcord. I'm just going through the salient points, Frank, which I suppose exemplifies what a tedious little man I am, always needing to tie the loose ends. Having a breather are we? Not a bad idea."

They had reached the high point of the bridge, above the third span. There had just been a foghorn blast as an empty pleasure-craft had come downstream and had passed underneath them and had spat out two small walls of froth. She had stopped, rested her backside against the balustrade. A bus went by and a couple of cars, and a cyclist loomed out of the fog, and a family with small children passed them and a little clutch of tourists, Japanese or Chinese, gave them not a glance and seemed annoyed they could get no picture of Westminster. They stayed, the two of them, cocooned by the mist, as if it put them in a small, self-contained bubble. He stood awkwardly, facing out over the river and now a tug approached, towing barges loaded with gravel.

"Cannot say, Frank, that I am charitable. Never have been. You and Sashcord were put together. Maybe he misread what was on offer, thought you were a part of the emoluments. Maybe you reckoned it good tactics to get close to him and learn a bit more. He may have misread you ... God knows, Frank, but in such matters I am rather out of my depth. Whatever happened, which of you made the mistake, it ended up with you sporting a bit of an eye and with him well scraped on the face, and a determination on your part to go to the limits of your ability to see him dead. I think you were a captive of your handler's wishes, and they would have given you one once the Romeo lad had moved on, but I think your dedication to see Sashcord killed was over and above the levels of compromise ... And my difficulty is that you were prepared to facilitate your colleague, Benedict, going up in a pile of debris and those very brave men who are Doug and Wally who you had flown over with. The scale of your anger meant that you were prepared to ensure others were slaughtered. Sorry, but it does not speak well for you. I suppose that once you are on a treadmill it is difficult to jump off – anyway that is for others to decide."

He had waited until an articulated lorry, low-gear and noisy, passed them to work one side of the opened cuffs on to his wrist, beside the fastening for his link chain. Closed it, and checked the other cuff was open, ready for use. He looked down the length of the bridge as it sloped away towards Thames House. There was a small traffic island at the far end and he caught a glimpse of Kevin and Leroy, and he turned his head and hoped it was casual and there were two more figures at the other end. Nearly done.

"Do you think, Frank, that we should get a little farther on, conclude our walk?" .

She did not answer him and he could not read her, but he thought she settled more of her weight on the barrier she leaned against.

*   *   *

"You've got them?" A little party hosted by the AssDepDG had gathered. He stood at the corridor window in front of the door to S/3/13, and had an elevated view of the bridge, but could see only half of it, the fog was too dense.

"Yes, a good view." The Director's chief woman, Hazel, Liaison with the London police, had called in Special Branch who would actually finger the traitor's collar.

"Have to say it, but this is a rather famous day for our lot, and a rather ignominious one for them over the river." Would have been unusual for the DepDG not to play the rivalry card. Almost boisterous while waiting for Merrick and the Sixer woman to come across the bridge, exit the fog wall. Too early for drinks, just, and they would come when she was taken away.

"He's remarkable, old Jonas, grim as sin, but still a deliverer." Grating praise from Aggie Burns.

"What's she doing?"

"Not sure."

"Why doesn't he chivvy her along?"

"Is she actually on the wall or just against it?" Aggie Burns queried and her forehead had knitted and she peered at the bridge.

"He should get her moving." From Hazel.

"I don't like it," said the DepDG.

And from the AssDepDG, the man who carried the banner for Jonas Merrick, "For fuck's sake, Jonas, what are you doing?"

Jonas held the opened handcuff in his pocket. Frank had heaved herself up to settle more of her weight on the balustrade above the central span of Lambeth Bridge. Her feet were no longer on the pavement. At either side of her body, her hands steadied her.

He smiled, not much warmth, and the pretence was pretty much played out.

A deadened look, the brightness taken from her eyes. What did he expect? Pretty obvious. A sort of backward flip, what gymnasts were supposed to do, and her head would go down and her legs would go up, and she'd be gone. It was something as flimsy as a plastic bag that swept towards the span and showed Jonas the power of the tide as it approached the arch below her. Not enough of an expert, but he thought the bag would be carried at four or five miles an hour. What did he want as an outcome? Would be the same as he always wanted: to deliver an accused person before the courts, into the presence of justice. Guilt or innocence was for others to determine. He did not seek to play God, was no more than a messenger, an errand boy. He had the open cuff ready, was poised.

He looked over her shoulder, peered into the wall of fog and towards the outline of the Tate Britain and the Millbank tower.

"What's that, Frank? What in heaven's name is it? There . . ."

He seemed about to lift his hand from his pocket to point. He caught her off guard and the image of the doddering old fool was bought. She looked where his eyeline led her.

His hand went fast, and his body twisted, and the wrist with the briefcase chain was swivelled so as not to obstruct him. Had the cuff on her wrist, snapped it shut and squeezed so that it tightened a fraction above her wristwatch, and might have hurt her. She looked hard at him. Her lips went thin, and her eyes sparked anger and her chin jutted. She was up on the balustrade, her legs dangling, but he had a hold on her. The traffic was erratic behind him and cars, vans, and a bus coughed out fumes, but there were no walkers at that moment on that section of the bridge, the highest point.

Jonas said, "It's not anything personal, Frank. Not my job, not what I am paid for. You might guess my feelings about a person prepared to satisfy whatever inner debt she might feel by pushing Benedict and Wally and Doug into the line of fire. But that disgust does not cloud my actions. I do not like you nor do I loathe you. Have enjoyed your company but . . . I think it better if we can get a bit of a move on now, finish our little walk."

He thought she braced herself: not expected and not as Jonas intended. She leaned back and wriggled her backside further towards the edge of the balustrade. A river boat headed under the arch and he saw people looking up, confused shaking their heads but inside the plate-glass windows of the viewing cabin. He gave a tug, was not rewarded.

"I think it better if we don't mess around, Frank. You're an adult person and I am sure you would have weighed the risks attached to espionage, the betrayal of your country. In the MICE bit which you've heard me flog to death, you would have started out as Compromise after the supposed love affair, and then you moved into Ego and that would have been stronger. None in your group would have appreciated the arrogance and the contempt you felt for them. They rarely survive, the spies. The best of them died on assignment: Sorge hanged in Tokyo, Cohen hanged in Damascus, Amiri hanged in Tehran, Penkovsky and Polyakov shot in the basement of the Lubyanka, and Philby dumped in a braindead isolation in Moscow which might have been worse than a noose or a bullet, and Blake. The common factor for all of them? They were despised by their one-time handlers. Shall we wrap the show up? Just walk with me, and I'll be grateful because I can then get off home and pull the caravan up our street and be on my way. Not thinking well of you and not thinking badly of you. Chin up, Frank."

He felt a surge of her strength, and his arm stretched out and his muscles had to flex, and he thought she might have slipped backwards and he reached to hang on to her coat and drag her off the wall and back on to the pavement.

"Steady, Frank. I've a hold of you and let's not mess about. We need some dignity, always best. Walk tall and straight, best advice I can give, and don't let them see your fear. So, come on off there."

It had come late, the realisation. He took the strain . . . She was half his age, might have run in the evenings or done circuits of Regents Park, or used a gym . . . it would have been better if he had not taken hold of her coat. His feet slipped on the pavement. Too old and too tired to fight her. He recognised the stubbornness that had brought them out on to the bridge and his own stupidity. She had a leg over the balustrade and used it to heave herself away and drag him with her . . . and looked into her face. Did she mouth something? Might have, might not have. Could not hear her, saw the movement of her lips. Something about "collateral" and might have been something about "if you hadn't poked your ugly wretched little nose in". She did the big heave.

The water was dark and churned against the edges of the pillars on either side of the central span. Would have been many metres deep and he could see nothing beyond the skim of its surface. Tried to loosen his hold on her coat and she held tight to him and tried to wedge his legs against the wrought-iron shapes of the balustrade – and failed. Her second leg was over and he could not lose her weight and their faces were close and he saw, was damned certain of it, that same pleasure at her mouth as when he had complimented her on a choice of cake, bloody coffee and bloody almonds, and almost laughing at him.

They fell, linked together.

The water rushed, soared, to meet them.

17

Jonas made a last attempt to catch at something, anything, on the bridge but was too far gone in his fall and his fingers caught only the cold air.

She hit the water first. Not a sound from her as they fell. Nor from him. Too busy trying to catch at something. He could not see her face as she went into the water, and did with a certain grace. She went in with her legs together and one arm against her body and the other raised as it dragged him after her. One moment there where he could see her, and the next gone, and him following.

He had not felt such a dose of fear as his splayed feet hit the surface water above her disappearing head. No fear when he'd dismantled the detonator from the trigger switch in the vest worn by Winston Gunn, nor when he had made the decision to hand-cuff himself to Cameron Jilkes and known he would unleash a fury and aggression. Just a fraction of time but the sensation was clear: he was sixty-four years old and had not before known real fear.

And went under. And darkness closed. And he gasped . . . would have wanted to keep his airwaves closed, seal off his mouth and his nose, preserve what he had in his lungs, and could not help himself . . . eyes firmly closed and his arm being tugged down and deeper, and the cold smacking into him. The gasp was involuntary, a reflex, and the Thames water would have flooded into his throat. It was the first stage of the process of drowning and he might have sensed it but could not in those seconds process it. She had gone into the water smoothly and with purpose, but Jonas went in ugly, flailing with his free arm and thrashing and did not know whether his eyes were open or closed . . . and plenty more that he did not know. Did not know that the time when the body was at its greatest risk of death was when it hit the water surface, had gone under, and the following three minutes when the cold shock response would be to gasp, for its heart rate to increase, and its breathing rate to surge. An old cliché that very few could speak of with authority, that a drowning man sees his life pass by in his mind. Would have been within the limited seconds of that span. Jonas Merrick had the experience.

Saw Vera, and the cat.

Saw the medal and the ribbon that went with it, and the bar, buried in Vera's knicker drawer.

Saw the cubicle in the corner of S/3/13, and his chair and his desk and his filing cabinet, open and showing his indexed sheets of paper and card.

Saw the faces in the room, Aggie Burns' people, and a token of respect and no affection.

Saw the caravan parked on the concrete in front of the house, in Raynes Park.

Which was probably all that mattered in his life . . . not seeing more because he was – involuntarily – heaving with his chest and trying to cough out the water gathering and settling in his lungs but an impossible task as his mouth was open and more water was flowing in. Nothing of his parents, nor of his childhood, and nothing that reflected his education and his courtship and marriage except that the briefcase she had given him was now filled with water and was pulling him down, as did his heavy shoes, as did . . . Jonas Merrick had never learned to swim. His hat had gone as he fell;, and his spectacles as he sank.

He went down deeper.

Who needed to swim? Might have said, if it had arisen in conversation, "If the good Lord had given us fins then . . ." Did not know how to swim so the panic was greater but was soon replaced. A sense of the hopelessness of where he was, and his heart hurting as it hammered in his chest, and life starting to ebb.

Much else that Jonas did not know. And no one there to tell him. His arm was dragged lower and he seemed to float, and the cold and the darkness and the weight of his clothing were close around him, and . . . he was pushed.

Pushed upwards.

Hands were at his chest and his hip and pushed him. He thought he might have kicked. Jonas had no comprehension of the urges towards survival. Did not know, in the many areas of ignorance now swirling around him, that would-be suicides, those choosing to go into the water, would make a decision – a bit late – to fight the inevitable, to grapple with it and struggle, seek to destroy it. Render the inevitable invalid. Did not know that rescue teams told stories of family members in the water scrabbling to get above spouses or children. He tried to push the hands away from him but could not and the handcuff joined them and dictated that he would fail. Again he was pushed, again he kicked and must have hit because his arm was wrenched cruelly at the shoulder, but the link held.

Had a sensation of light growing around him and the darkness shifting to a fading grey. A great black shape surged past his head and the motion funnelled a water flow against his body and disrupted his balance and then he felt the hands again. He was rocking and sinking and then rising again. He broke the surface.

Was close to a propeller screw that churned the water. Could see only the uniform pale greyness of the mist and was thrown up on to the crest of waves that blocked any view of the bank, north or south.

He was coughing, retching, spluttering. And the water lodged in his lungs refused to move, and the air from inches above the water could not be dragged down. His body shook as he heaved to clear himself, get the filth out of his body. She came up beside him. A sodden little face with plastered urchin hair. He could not swim. He would sink again, go under. He understood that they had drifted some metres from the bridge piers . . . and something extraordinary. She had a hold of him, her arms under his shoulders and she was on her back and kicked some more, and dragged him. What lifesavers did. How they brought people back to safety. He would have been a lumpen weight. He realised that she had taken her bearings before starting this impromptu act of rescue. The current helped her. He could not. Could barely cough, could not lose more than dribbles of water from the sides of his mouth, and she coughed and choked with him.

Between the race of the waves and the wash from the tug, Jonas saw haphazard shapes appear on the bridge but was too exhausted to shout.

He realised then that the handcuff meant they were joined, could not be separated and that if he sank again and drowned, was submerged and left to float away, she would go with him. He could not understand how she had gone into the water off the bridge and now tried to live. Understood damn all . . . A line of boats was moored on a quay that protruded from the embankment. And did not understand where her strength came from. She took him to the far side of the outer boat, and grappled for a hanging rope. He went under again, but was lifted up, and coughed some more.

She slapped his face. Used the hand that was cuffed to his, and her other hand held the sodden length of trailing rope. Slapped him hard enough to hurt him, and he coughed more and spilled more water.

"Where is it?"

A small but fierce voice. Had never heard her speak in such a tone. A demand.

"Where is it, the fucking key?"

And Jonas did not understand, and her voice hissed in his ear . . . So tired and weak in every limb and needing sleep, and more heaving in his chest and her voice drilling at him.

"Where is the fucking key to the cuff? Is that it?"

Her nails scraped against the skin on his chin, then on to his throat, and then the ribbon was snatched.

*   *   *

The AssDepDG, from his prime point by the window, had kicked off with the inevitable, "Oh, my God – oh, God."

And from the DepDG, "I cannot believe what I am seeing."

And from Aggie Burns: "This looks like the biggest load of piss poor planning I've ever seen. Heads will go down for this. He's handcuffed to her and she wants to top herself. Should never have been permitted to happen, bloody obvious statement."

From Hazel, only the sound of subdued sobbing.

Their faces were pressed against the explosive-proof glass. A decent view had been enjoyed before the clear sight of old Merrick, miserable Merrick, the Eternal Flame who "never went out", was dragged by his suspect over the balustrade above the midpoint of the Thames, and they had not seen him again. What they could see was Kev and Leroy, rifles bouncing on their chests, lumbering forward, and detectives behind them, and more coming from the far end emerging from the fog. A helplessness at the window and no intervention possible.

Jonas had the loose rope tangled around his free arm.

"It is this key, yes?"

She tried to break the ribbon but could not. Bit at it, to no result.

She lost patience.

The ribbon was loosened. Her free hand found a way into each of his trouser pockets, had roughly driven her fingers down and had brought out a handkerchief and small change and tossed them away. Had gone to his hip pockets and had found only his rail ticket and it had floated off into the dark. Again he had gone under, but briefly and he had bobbed up again and been greeted with another snarled obscenity. Searched his sports jacket that hung so heavy on him, retrieving and dumping his wallet that carried his ID, foldaway map of London, and his spectacle case. And God alone knew where his spectacles were, on what part of the river bed they had sunk into the mud. Lost a pen that Vera had given him the Christmas before last into the pockets of his raincoat, and she had difficulty with the zip on a sealed pocket and spat some more anger at him in her frustration. And found a key, ripped it from the pocket.

But it was his house key, back door and front door. He had not the energy nor ability to wrestle her for it. It bounced against the hull of the boat that had the trailing rope and slid down into the water. And would have seen that none of those keys would have matched, and she looked again for the ribbon at his neck, twisted around his tie, and found it. Sharp satisfaction briefly crossed her face. She had the ribbon in her hand, heaved it over his head and was near to strangling him. The ribbon had come from Vera's work box. Vera had never known, when he had asked for a length of it, what it was required for. Had given him pink ribbon. She gazed into his face, and flicked an eyebrow and he realised that he knew nothing of her.

It took some manoeuvring but she managed to keep him close and reliant on the rope and to get the key into the lock on his wrist. She turned it and the handcuff flapped off her wrist. A moment of hesitation and an afterthought: the key? She held the ribbon in between them. He wondered, that moment, if she would drop it, let it sink, but did not. Reached down beneath the water and groped around him and found a pocket in his raincoat and shoved ribbon and key inside.

She said, "You hold on to the rope."

He nodded, could not speak, and his throat was raw and ribbed with pain.

"Intended to drown you, and me. Both of us."

Could not answer, could not shrug, was not capable of reaction.

"Could not help myself. Changed my mind, woman's privilege, know what I mean." Had control, mocked him. "Didn't want to. Not die. Nor will I be going in the cage."

And the water fell on her face and his hair was flat and her cheeks pale and puckered.

"They'll be here very soon. They come from the north side of the Waterloo bridge. The lifeboat people. They'll find you. Just hang on."

She trod water and wound the rope around his stomach, did it a couple of times.

"Some of our people bought into you, I didn't. Some were naive, not me. Not sure why I hung around so long. Too big a decision to bug out, in spite of the alarums. I'm glad I saved you."

His body took the weight and the rope went taut and he sank some inches, had the level of it a hand's span below his chin.

"What you said, nothing personal. Remember me."

He would.

"If you ever get to eat that cake again, coffee, and walnut, remember me."

Did not answer her.

"I had a good run, rather enjoyed it, walked all over them. Goodbye, Mr Merrick."

What to say? Nothing to say . . . she seemed to laugh at him. Both his hands were firm on the rope and he started to spin slowly, turning in the water. Her eyes had regained their brightness and the pale puckered lips, bloodless, were opened and she might have grinned and for a moment she was close to him and he was turning and he faced the hull of the boat and dark, rusted metalwork and the lumps where the rivets had gone in. That maddening smile that seemed to condescend and he was turning, and between the two boats he could see a strip of the fog that was unmoving below the sky and he heard a splash and felt a ripple that washed against his chin and he could not stop it and dared not free either hand – and wanted to live. The spin on the rope took him further around and he faced an emptiness and beyond it was the second hull, that of the other boat, and the two hammered together, lurched against the old tyres and the fenders.

He was glad, small mercy, that he had not seen her go. Did not know, never would know, why she had struggled and fought him and had saved his life and hers, and brought him to this – perhaps – point of safety, then had left him. Would have been there one moment, and then the smile wiped and the humour gone, and him irrelevant in however long her life had to run. Would have slid away and only a small kick to get herself down and go deep and then . . . She was the past.

He tried to shout but his voice died in his throat. Jonas could not estimate how long he could continue to hold the rope nor how long it would be before the winding of it, twice, around his waist began to slip. He would not have surfaced without her, would not have reached this point, among the boats parked up against the pier beside the wall of the palace at Lambeth if it had not been for her. He understood so little. What she had said to him was fading in his mind.

Could barely recall her voice.

He looked at the water that slopped between the two hulls and thought that he remembered her face, and blinked and tried to recreate it, but failed. His voice was little more than a hoarse whisper and the sounds of the water and the banging together of the hulls killed any shouts he tried to make.

Jonas wondered – hanging on to the rope and turning those slow circles each of which loosened its hold around his waist – how much longer he could stay above the water line, how many minutes before cold and exhaustion finished him. His mind had deadened and he supposed that he relied, if he were to live, on the same characteristics as his cat would have, or the same misplaced sense of survival that a mouse depended on when scampering across a caravan floor . . . Needed a target for concentration and did not know where he found it, and a sort of madness was pinching at him. He saw the pillars of the pagodas where explosives had been tested, and heard a foghorn blasting, and gulls, and heard more sirens. Wanted to be there, in the shelter of the Ness constructions and dream of them. But to dream he must sleep. If he slept he would die.

The lifeboat – a Mark 11, E-07, with the name of *Hurley Burly* – had started to search. Its massive diesel engine power, capable of generating 435 horsepower and taking her at 35 knots, was almost cut and the four crew raked the river surface for signs of bobbing heads. Their eyes were well trained to piercing the river fogs and mists but as yet they had not seen the two persons reported to have fallen from the bridge, one taking the other. The coxswain understood that he spoke to the Security Service, that his explanation had been routed to Thames House, just upstream.

"All we can do is look for them. Doesn't matter who they are, they get the same degree of attention . . . the water is cold, the shock of going into it, particularly for the older male, will be considerable. I would not expect death from hypothermia before half an hour in the water, though whether they have drowned in that time is a different concern. If they are alive, on the surface and as yet not found, they will be weak, have no voice, and in this tide they have next to no chance of reaching a beach and there are sheer-sided walls. We are tasked to search for an hour and a half, after that assume the worst . . . We are always asked when bodies will turn up – could be very soon and could be weeks away. And where – almost anywhere and the tide plays a big part . . . But we are still looking, and will continue to. Now, if you will excuse me."

They quartered the river, and had begun to work the south side, along the Albert Embankment, close to the tied-up craft, surplus to winter requirements, of Lambeth pier.

"Christmas come early. He's here, and looks alive."

Jonas vaguely heard the voice.

"I'll have to go over the side to fetch him."

There was a droning sound close by but he would have assumed it to be the effect of water saturation in his ears, not the noise of the engines of *Hurley Burly* ticking over. Water slopped over his face.

"Just getting a rope hitched up, sir, then we'll be coming to get you."

He thought he understood but was no longer certain whether it was a dream. Not a nightmare because he no longer felt the cold, and his mind had numbed and his hands seemed to be moulded around the rope, and he had coughed a bit but the choking was past. He was worried because his briefcase, held to his wrist by the link chain, might have suffered irreparable damage and was uncertain if it would ever dry out. He had one certainty, the bollocking . . . He could see the front of the lifeboat and it blocked most of the gap between the two craft, and a man was poised to slide off it into the water, and was now clipping a rope to a harness. A woman was behind him and gave him a smile and a little wave as if he had merely stepped into a ditch and gone down to his waist, had not been dragged off the balustrade over the central span of Lambeth Bridge. The clarity was returning, and an apprehension of the bollocking he was due. He could make out two more figures on board. All four of them were huge in rubber suits and their heads were encased in crash helmets. To him, they seemed cheerful, which fitted with Jonas's diktat about dramas and crises . . . and he heard some more, the woman to the man with the rope.

"Go easy on him, likely he's delirious and won't know his arse from his elbow."

More water splashed against him. He wanted more than anything to sleep, thought that way he might avoid the full fury of the bollocking, and would have nodded off if he had been able to free his fingers from the rope, but he had lost all sensation in his hands. The grotesque figure, white helmet, bright yellow suit and red life jacket, went off the craft and paddled towards Jonas.

"Well done, sir, have you out in a jiffy."

Such a tone of friendship, but was never going to be the source of the full frontal bollocking . . . He was gripped and held tight, and felt himself lifted higher and the water streamed from his raincoat and his jacket.

"Could you let go for me, sir? There's a good chap. I've a hold on you so you can let go of that rope."

Except that he could not, which was when it became rougher for him. The face inside the helmet maintained a tolerant smile. The woman was now in the water and had reached down behind him and lifted him at the waist. Force needed. Between the two of them they prised his hands off the hanging rope. Had to do it finger by finger, and he struggled and they made cooing sounds of reassurance but he could see both their foreheads knitted with annoyance. And when one hand had been freed she took it and he seemed to sag down and almost went under and they had to heave him up again and a rope went under his armpits.

"You're all right with us, sir. The problem, it's over now."

It was a confined space and they had to lever their way back between the two hulls and then he was hoisted up and more hands grabbed him and he felt himself dragged over the front end of their boat. Not that it hurt, not that he could feel.

Had the words in his throat but could not get them out, "Frank's out there. Don't know where she is. Have to find Frank."

Heard his voice but they did not. And the spray came up and the boat turned tight, and the engines kicked in. He could see the ceiling of mist as he lay on his back, the woman crouched over him and starting to free his tie and rip open the buttons on his shirt, and he tilted his head a little and could make out their boots and the rescue gear, and saw his hat. How extraordinary, Jonas thought. Might be delirious, as they had predicted, but recognised his hat and tried to point to it and gargled sounds came from his throat, and they were close to a pier. He saw blue lights and a couple in the green of ambulance uniforms, and police, and more of the yellow-clad monsters. The woman had about undressed him but had trouble with the laces of his brogues because he always double-knotted them. She used a penknife. Had his trousers off and his pants, and cold air floated on his privates and then blankets covered him, and his coat was off and his jacket and his shirt, and the penknife was pressed to duty again for his tie, and more blankets smothered him.

He needed to tell them about Frank but no one seemed to want to listen. His memory flickered back and he had the words again. *I had a good run, rather enjoyed it. Walked all over them. Goodbye, Mr Merrick.* Wanted to tell the crowd around him . . . and felt himself slump, and would have slept then had it not been for the knowledge of that bollocking in the pipeline.

"Right, sir, let's get you off for a check-up."

He was lifted into an ambulance.

And heard the lifeboat woman say to the lifeboat man, "That handcuff on his wrist, and a briefcase chained to him. What have we got here? God alone knows. And rabbiting on about Frank – who's Frank? Wasn't it a man and a woman that went in? Odd . . . Better get out and look for her. I suppose he just forgot, but you'd have thought he could have said 'thank you'."

The doors closed and the ambulance pulled away.

He could not see out of the darkened windows. He did not know which bridge they crossed. Waterloo or Westminster or Lambeth, and which street they went down. Might have been the one he walked over twice a day, five days a week, and perhaps they went by the back of the Palace, and near to Morton's Tower, or close to the Special Operations Executive memorial, or the new-filled flowerbeds beside the embankment wall.

And felt the feeling seeping back to his legs and his voice seemed to surge in his throat and he shouted and kicked.

"I want out of here. I'm fine. I want out."

And he was kicking with his bare legs and the blankets fell off him, and the ambulance woman tried to restrain him and made a poor job of it.

"I've places to go and things to do," he yelled.

About an hour later . . .

Word had spread.

Monty had hit his phone. "Extraordinary business this morning. That funny little chap, seems he was walking Frank over Lambeth Bridge, taking her to be arrested by Special Branch. Claimed she was our leak. Had handcuffed her, except that she goes off the bridge, mid-stream, tries to top herself and drown him. I'd never have believed it, not about Frank."

Chiswell phoned Symonds. "Personally, never liked her. Reckoned she was over-rated. Quite dull really, without ambition. Can't have been very good at her trade of treachery if that little toad was able to identify her. But that's not the rub. The toad has shafted me and I'm being posted to Kabul, fucking Kabul, that graveyard of ambitions. Frank, anyway, won't be missed ... I heard she took him with her, into the drink, and a bit of luck they sank together, and stayed down ... fucking Kabul."

Symonds called Barker. "Who was that guy? Waltzed on to our territory, allowed in by the God Almighty clones up on the top floor, and we were never told his status. Made an industry of it, talking himself down, little rat. And Frank, butter not melting in her bloody mouth, always watching and listening and always in the background and never contributing ... Personally I rated her as a deceitful little cow. Suppose I should have shouted it ... Anyway, the rat's recommendation for me is Asuncion. I mean, where the hell is that? What sort of tennnis am I going to get there? What use my bloody good Russian in bloody Paraguay? We are all on the floor and bleeding because of him, because of her."

Barker called Toni. "I'm well out of it. Can't wait for the clock or the sherry decanter, and be with the darts team and get the arrows working ... Have to say this but I was suspicious of her way back. She never cut it with me ... Bit of a drama queen, going into the Thames with the pompous Five arsehole attached by handcuffs. Which was style, admitted, but she won't be missed, not by me."

Toni called Monty. "Frankly I'm speechless. They want me on the same island as my bloody spouse. God, the thought of it, and three kids to cart off with me. She was a vindictive bitch if that result is anyting to do with her, and not half as good at her job as she reckoned she was ... The little chap, can't make up my mind whether he was just the useful idiot or was pure poison. Have to think about that ... Anyway at least it wasn't skinny dipping, but I wouldn't want to be wild swimming in the Thames, not this week. Bigger trouble is that rumour has it that we pulled off rather a good one last night and that he – idiot or poison – had a hand with it. Don't know how good."

A little more than two hours later ...

He would have classified his future as uncertain, his prospects as bleak. Not that Leonid was capable of much coherent thought.

He had been given, with some reluctance, a bunk below decks, hot and stinking from the trawlerman who had vacated it. He had been sick in it. He was now on deck.

They seemed to drop down hard and then clatter in the sumps of the swell, then be lifted up and tossed on to the white-capped crests and lurch there before falling again. He had a rope tied around his waist and the other end was fastened to a ring on the side of the wheelhouse. Now he had been sick on deck, but into the wind and the mess had come back and splattered his face and his body. The rope gave him room, just, to lean over the side of the boat and heave some more. Somewhere ahead was a frigate of the Admiral Grigorovitch class, and the navy would have had a cabin where a respected guest could have been accommodated, and it would have enabled him to endure a smoother ride as it powered back into the Baltic and towards the base at Baltysk. But Leonid was not respected, was a casualty, sailing home on a bucking, tossing trawler, and there would be other casualties, which was some consolation.

He could, between the spasms in his empty guts and the bile in his throat, reflect on the future. Might be a bodyguard to a junior gang leader, or a wannabe entrepreneur who would like the status of having him on a payroll, but costing little, and taking the bastards' wives shopping . . . or drive a taxi which enough did who had failed to fulfil expectations, do nights, get the drunks. The consolation was that his superior, Volkov, would face a greater fall from power. And he could reflect how it was that a proven intelligence asset had led him . . . well, almost, but had led his guns . . . into a trap for which a high price was paid, higher for them, and high for those in the capital who winced under the weight of criticism . . . and wondered who it was who had flattened him – and was sick again.

And later that evening . . .

The AssDepDG said to the DepDG, "I'd say very frankly that it is as if it came gift-wrapped. He discharged himself, and I had Harry drive him home. Not his greatest return from the fray.

Wearing a hospital gown and all his clothing in a plastic bag, and Harry says he was then lined up for a God Almighty bollocking – started when he was still on the step. A seriously frightening one, Harry said. Looked quite shame-faced at the end of it. Anyway, the medics gave him a clean bill of health and he needs a good sleep and a couple of days off. He's going to Suffolk tomorrow and Harry will drive him and tow the caravan . . . Why I said it was 'gift-wrapped' was that the Sixers' girl did us all a favour. I'd call it a substantial favour. They searched all the rest of the morning for her which was 'rescue', then went to 'recovery' for the afternoon and kept going for a bit after dusk. Not a sign. A body can travel for miles and we may not get another sight of her for weeks. Drowned cadavers and where they'll finally beach is an inexact science. A favour, I think so. Hardly want her in the Old Bailey, or at Southwark Crown Court. Youngish woman, an English rose, signs of possible rape and none of the officers checking it out and total failure of Duty of Care . . . And then you have the Danish end where we've spun an attractive fantasy web which she could have rather damaged. It is satisfactory that she's off the radar . . . No, don't mind if I do, another one would be most welcome . . . I confess, I didn't think I'd see the old beggar again but he was in fighting form with the medics. Harry says the missus was quite savage with him, started when she found the handcuff among his possessions. My experience, Vera can be deceptively flinty . . . I think I'd better have some water with that measure . . . Anyway, I'll see him tomorrow and check up on him."

And a morning later . . .

There were slippery steps to negotiate, weed and seawater lapping over them, Jonas looked frail, but felt strong, determined.

And he shook away Vera's helping hand. Negotiated the short climb himself.

Had been brought home. The clothes he'd worn when taken into the hospital for the check had been fast dried in the Thames House laundry room, supervised personally by the AssDepDG, and he had been dressed in them when he had arrived home. Had looked a scarecrow. His wife had known only that he had "had an accident" at work, not that he had survived a damned close-run thing in the dark, deep Thames, but had guessed from the smell of him that his life had been on the line. Then the cuff had shown up. His parting quip that morning that "no mischief" was involved in the day had been shredded. The bollocking was predictable, intense, and only completed when she had lain beside him on their marital bed and had wept on his chest ... but that was yesterday. Harry had arrived early and brought the AssDepDG down to Raynes Park.

They came off the jetty. The brightness of the previous day, after the fog had cleared, had gone. It was overcast, cold, and rain threatened. He felt uplifted. He wore his "second work outfit" few differences from the clothing he had dressed in to go out to meet that young woman, to see Frank and take her across the bridge and into custody. A folly ... Similar jacket and a Tattersall check shirt and a similar tie, and trousers that had a better crease and his older pair of brogues – and his spare spectacles, broken but repaired after a fashion – and the usual raincoat and the hat, that had been retrieved and looked much the worse for the dunking. Vera might have thought it looked ridiculous, but had not commented. Harry had rolled his eyebrows at the sight of it, and the AssDepDG had openly laughed. They were met by a warden. He gazed away into the distance and absorbed the size of the pagodas and their symmetric beauty. Vera ignored them, already had her binoculars to her eyes.

With the caravan hooked up and Jonas fussing in the passenger seat, and Vera behind him and Olaf caged on its floor as it bumped along behind them, their day had started. First to the Heathrow complex. All prepared for them and the two cars and the caravan in parking spaces coned off at the airport police yard. Vera would go to a canteen. Jonas would travel with Harry and his mentor, and they were met with the necessary passes and were taken "airside" and had an armed police escort and doors swung open for them. The boards showed that a flight from Moscow had landed.

The AssDepDG told him quietly, "It's on the periphery of what you did by preventing that killing and slapping them back, those hooligans back there. Because of it an agent is – not very happily, but happily enough for our purposes – back at his desk and will continue to feed us sweet mouthfuls, useful stuff. And this little soul was his contact, job completed and coming home. She wants as I am told, the safe life and the predictable one of defusing bombs and clearing minefields. It's the world you were moving in, Jonas."

A girl came into the long straight corridor, almost at the back of the passenger surge, and pushed a buggy. She looked tired, distracted, had bobbed gold hair, wore slashed jeans and a heavy sweater and an anorak, and there was an obvious bite mark on her throat. In the buggy, sleeping, was a small child – perhaps eighteen months old – and little of his face showed under a pile of blankets but his hands clutched a small soft bear, grasped it closely. She passed within a yard of Jonas and he managed a smile, first of the day, which she ignored. And, also the first of the day, he had chuckled, felt a sense of purpose . . . He was told there was another flight they should meet, and see a passenger who was in transit.

They split. Vera would walk with the warden and they would head towards the flooded lagoons where the different species of ducks and waders gathered and over which the harriers flew. He would walk alone. Mutterings from him that he was good and strong and did not need company. He went towards the great edifices of earlier global wars, and the ones that had been constructed, at whatever cost was required, in the days of a Cold War that seemed not to have thawed in more than half a century. His stride lengthened. He went past rusted signs warning of Hazardous Materials and demanding No Entry, and where pits had been scooped out by diggers and filled with rusted debris. Saw the concrete posts that had once held secure chain-link fencing and would have been topped with barbed wire. And noted a little hut that seemed ideal as an office for that hapless security officer. Loved it, and felt a belonging.

Jonas did not do foreign holidays nor did he travel to conferences on the continent where cooperation was discussed. He knew the bowels of the airport only from the videos sent him of the initial interrogations of Irish and *jihadi* fighters done in featureless rooms, and from the CCTV images of Russian "diplomats' passing through. They passed endless crocodile columns of people in gaudy clothing who wanted to emphasise they were on holiday. They came to an area that dealt with long haul flights, a place where the travelator no longer moved and where stewardesses waited at the entry to the aircraft. The AssDepDG spoke softly in Jonas's ear. 'As you very well know, he was called Sashcord, was a major in GRU and pretty useless to us which was why he hadn't been shipped to a safe billet in UK and we were working on where to offload him. You, Jonas, made him useful. He brought precious little information with him, but it was your intervention that gave him a purpose. Using him as what was described as a 'tethered goat' gave us a very substantial reward. There will be inquiries, inquests, investigations, two a penny of them, in the ministries and agencies over there. Prominent officials will be on their way to what used to be a salt mines destination, will have been tipped off the gravy train they had gotten used to. They hate being caught out and ... the beauty of it, Jonas, there is not a scintilla of a chance they will know your name, have a file on you, be able by any stretch of imagination to target you. His destination is South Africa, pretty cheap there, and we'll set him up with a small-holding, Orange Free State. Won't cost more than pocket money and then he's on his own ... I think that'll be him. He owes much to you, Jonas."

Led by a pair of detectives, off the airport detail, quite a good-looking young man and dressed casually, but not expensively, and the budget would already have kicked in. Slacks and sneakers, a quiet pastel shirt and a windcheater and carrying an anonymous, tell-nothing, sports bag. He paused for a moment and peered into the face of Jonas. Would have seen an old guy with bags under his eyes and a wan pale face and wearing spectacles that were held together by adhesive tape, and a silly shapeless hat was perched on his head and must have shrunk because it could not slot far down over his scalp. Eye contact. The detectives nudged him forward and the stewardesses were smiling and he was smirking. Only one blemish, but Jonas had noted it – a healed scar running very faintly down the man's right cheek. Barely visible, but in spite of him being reduced to his out-of-date lenses, he had noted it. And thought of her, and imagined those plain nails scratching his flesh.

Enough of the sightseeing, and they left the terminal and were driven to the police park. And told finally, with a droll smile, that the chaps who had done the heavy lifting in the early hours of the night, done the mucky bit, done it well, were back home – one of them was in Swindon and by now expected to be up a ladder and repairing his guttering, and the other would likely be sleeping off a damaging hangover from a long night in his local. Enough? Enough. His hand was shaken by the AssDepDG who would go back into London, and Harry had again settled behind the wheel and they had started out for the coast . . . All little people, and him.

Half of the Ness, where Vera had gone, was wet and green. And much of it was flooded and the birds there had found a paradise.

Where Jonas went was shingle and flat, scoured by a wind that came sharp off the North Sea, and littered with abandoned concrete buildings, and the only conventional brightness was from the tower of a white lighthouse. He saw a solitary wild deer and a huddled pair of hares sheltering behind a long-abandoned petrol pump, but none of the curlew and whimbrel and greenshank that would excite his wife. Where he walked, the earliest boffins had developed crude bomb aiming and the development of machine gun sights for aircraft. Then scientists had started to breach the problems around the concept of radar . . . not really his interest. He wanted to see the MAD buildings, to wander amongst the massive, ungainly constructions that had enabled the policy of Mutual Assured Destruction to be adopted.

Around the time of Jonas Merrick's birth, this would have been the most security-sensitive base in the kingdom, and the prime target for the foreign agencies. Would have been where a security officer wore a perpetual frown of anxiety, and paced the same tracks between the shingle, and been desperately concerned that the enemy was within, had beaten him. The same fear then that Jonas knew now, knew most working days.

The pagodas loomed in front of him. Inside their hugely reinforced concrete walls, the atomic weapons' detonation systems had been tested. They rode up above angular concrete bases, and the pagoda roofs were supported on more than a dozen pillars, all strangely beautiful. Jonas should have shivered because of the cold and the force of the wind. Reflected that a security officer in his dotage, long retired, would have said, "It was all right on my watch". Reflected also that an engineer might have said, "We had to do this work, it was necessary". And a scientist might have claimed, "I'm sure it was important what we did, vital for our safety". And all around Jonas were ruins, and their decay seemed to mock the security officer, the engineers, the scientists – and they laughed at Jonas.

Had believed briefly what he did was important, was necessary, and heard the words of a country vicar. One of those weekends when they'd gone away with the caravan to Dorset, and Vera had wanted – no idea why – to attend Sunday morning service in the village church. Barely a dozen parishioners spaced out among the pews. The text had been from the book of Daniel, had dealt with the famed monarch, Nebuchadnezzar. Had not expected to be either entertained or interested, but Jonas's attention had been rapt. Recalled verbatim the vicar's soft-spoken address ... The king had claimed, *Is not this great Babylon, that I have built for a royal dwelling by my mighty power and for the honour of my majesty? A voice "fell from Heaven", The kingdom has departed from you! Your dwelling shall be with the beasts of the field. They shall make you eat grass like oxen ... know that the Most High rules in the kingdom of men, and gives it to whomever He chooses.* A pretty large-scale put-down for Nebuchadnezzar as told in Daniel, 4.30–32, and he'd built the Babylon marvel. Was likely the only biblical text Jonas could recall at will, and why it was important for him to worship here, learn modesty. The single deer watched him and the two hares still sheltered and the wind bit into him.

His phone stayed silent. It had survived the water, had dried out, worked, but did not ring. He had been promised he would be told. What did he expect? That a body would have been found down by Southwark or as far towards the estuary as Wapping, or snagged at Rotherhithe? Easy to recognise because neither the crabs nor the eels had had a chance to chew her features? Not a chance.

Could remember the face that had entranced him. And heard the last words spoken to him. *Good run ... enjoyed ... walked all over ... Goodbye, Mr Merrick.* Had a better memory of them each time, would not, not ever, forget them. Imagined, a heap of clothes dumped among bushes. A dark grey jacket and trousers, a white blouse, perhaps a pair of low-heeled shoes, barely hidden, near a tower block or in a small playpark. And imagined ... a woman coming out first thing that morning and the street lights barely off and having left a loaded drying frame out in a yard except that half the lines had been raided and only a little pile of discarded pegs to show it.

He stood, bowed his head, pondered, was in a place where men's and women's efforts had once seemed supremely important, and where their efforts were now mocked. Jonas reckoned all of it, and what he had achieved, would be remembered only by the widows ... He slapped his hands together and startled the hares, and looked a last time at the pagodas, the follies of MAD days, and felt as if he had cleansed himself from any delusions ... Was not important, nor was anything he did. And walked away from the site, abandoned it to the company of the ghosts. They'd not find her, seemed clear to him. He reached the jetty. Vera was waiting, said she had been too cold to stay longer. He started for the steps. Sure that he was ready to go?

"Yes, thank you, seen enough. Finished there and cleared it from the system ... what I want to do now, Vera, is go and look for that place where the red-legged spider-hunting wasp might be seen. That sort of predator. I'd like to be where there's a chance of spotting one. Get to know it, be up close ... No, I don't need help."

Jonas went down the steps, had a rusty iron rail to hold. Stepped gingerly on the seaweed. Forgot about the lives he had entered, and altered, put them beyond recall.

She called after him, "I don't suppose it's all finished, your stupid damned games?"

"Never can tell ... come on, the wasp won't wait around for us. And Olaf will be wanting his tea. Always have to be alert for them, for the predators. They'll keep coming, keep on coming."

Turn the page for an exclusive look at Gerald Seymour's thrilling next instalment in the Jonas Merrick series

IN
AT
THE
KILL

HODDER &
STOUGHTON

PROLOGUE

He edged forward and with each step his breath came faster.

Every time Pablo moved closer he increased the risk that their dogs would see him, hear him, smell him.

But he had to go closer because Nikko had demanded detail. The questions he must answer were specific. He could not even see the building yet but was aware of the drone of machinery and of the arrival of more vehicles.

He was there because of his kid brother. Pablo was middle-aged, near to his 45th birthday. He was married – happily, he thought – and was the father of three children, two boys and a girl. Neither his wife nor children knew where he was at that moment in the dwindling afternoon light, nor would they benefit in any way from what he was doing. This was all about his kid brother who would be locked in the crowded cages of the prisoners awaiting trial or investigation in the La Modelo gaol in Bogotá. Each time Pablo thought of his kid brother, 22 years old, an after-thought or accident by his parents, and the reputation of violence and bestiality in the prison of 11,000 inmates, his resolve was strengthened. He edged forward, pushing away undergrowth. Thorns cut his face and hands, and sometimes he scuffed dead leaves and foliage. He was careful to avoid fallen branches where the sap had long gone – they would be brittle, would crack easily, noisily.

His home was four rooms, a bath behind a curtain off the kitchen, and a living area where the TV was. He and his wife shared one bedroom and his children slept in the other, which was an increasing area of difficulty as they grew older and more sensitive about their own sex. At the back was a brick shed for the toilet with a drop under the seat, and beside the shed was a lock-up garage. Pablo parked his vehicle at the front of his one-storey home, built of concrete blocks with a roof of corrugated iron. In the garage, protected by a padlock, he stored the tins of paint that he tried to sell six days a week at his stall in the town's market. The ability to feed and clothe his family depended on the amount of paint that he sold. He could have made a better living if it had not been necessary to pay a sum each month to the enforcers of a 'prominent person' in the town, and also to contribute to the wages of the local municipal office, and sometimes to the police.

Now, his pick-up – 16 years old and with 110,000 klicks on the clock after at least two modifications of the gauge – was parked on the verge of a main road, four kilometres out of the town of Leticia. Pablo had walked, and then crawled, and his trousers were filthy from the mud and his fingers bled, and insects swarmed around him, searching for the softness of his ears and his eyelids and his nose, but he did not swat them away or clap them between the palms of his hands.

The river was a meld of reds and browns, and was constantly changing in texture. It was raining. When the rain came down from low leaden clouds, the river rose quickly, and the mosquitoes multiplied: he had been brought up to exercise self-control and had been lectured at home, in school, in church, that it was wrong to blaspheme. The mosquitoes were feeding off him now, and when he hissed at them some took advantage and flew into his mouth and found his tonsils and went behind his yellowed teeth and he had to stop himself spluttering.

It was the dogs he feared most. The engineers had brought them and the older, fiercer ones were kept hungry and were tied to running wires, but there were also the family dogs and puppies that some of the men, were fond of. Pablo knew about the dogs from the many times he had edged close to where the work was taking place on this bank of the upper reaches of the Amazon river. The only times in his life that he had been close to messing his trousers had been when he was close to the big shelter that had been built and where a generator throbbed and where the dogs barked, sometimes in a frenzy and sometimes out of boredom. Men patrolled the perimeter of the site, where the cleared ground met the wall of the jungle. They carried automatic weapons and he presumed them to be veterans from the war with the guerrillas: they had faces as hard as those of their guard dogs. Pablo had not been in the military, had never owned a firearm. Here, away from the town, a shot would not be heard, and a body could be quickly lost: a shallow pit would suffice or a splash in the river and a brief feeding opportunity for catfish and piranha.

He had seen the strange craft grow over the period of seven weeks that he had been coming to this place and each time he came he was more terrified. After pillars had been sunk and the steel frame erected, a roof had been built to cover the first stages of the craft's construction. Day after day, and usually long into the night, the generator moaned and cried, and the welders had fastened the fierce lights, and hammers had belted at the joints, and twice a week Pablo had taken up his position and had observed.

It was a huge project, building the craft – would have cost more money than he could imagine – here in the dense jungle beside the river, and with skills that he could barely comprehend. He did not know where it would sail to, how far, and through what dangers if it were not assembled with every rivet, nut, bolt and sealant secured, and an engine inside that must not fail, and the risk – so great – of the men in it drowning ... But he did know what its cargo would be, the white powder that ruled with such violence, and brought such rewards. Pablo had felt quite safe at the start but it was different now as the long length of the hull had become recognisable and more men had come to the site by the slipway that a bulldozer had fashioned. More armed men and more dogs and all of them hungrier. Last week a portable crane had lifted the diesel engine into place. The fuel tanks were already there and the previous evening they had been filled and Pablo had estimated that the tanks had each been capable of carrying 20,000 litres. A small, squat tower sat on top of the craft and he had seen two men who disappeared into the hatch more often than the others – and he assumed they would sail with it when it was launched and went down the river towards the open ocean. It frightened Pablo, now that it had taken the shape of a boat that could travel underwater, just to look at it, and he tried to imagine how far away was its destination. When they had tested the engine at the back it had raced, chucking out fumes, acrid and black.

Pick-ups arrived in convoy, came along the track to the building inside which the craft had been built. Pablo thought the cargo was stored here because those who held the guns had become more menacing and the dogs took a cue from them. There was a bedlam of noise. Pablo needed to be closer, needed to see better. And fear became almost terror. He knew, as would anyone who lived in that town on the Colombian frontier where the state's boundary was marked by the winding path of the Amazon river, what fate would be handed out to him if he went too close. But he moved forward, ... and the mosquitoes attacked his face in waves, and the thorn bushes were dense and caught at his clothing and he had to unpick himself each time and not let the material rip. He had to get closer if he were to assess the quantity of the cargo, its weight and its packaging. And he was there because of his kid brother.

The boy was an idiot. He had none of the disciplines taught to Pablo by his parents. He had been spoiled, protected from the reality of humble life, and had repaid his parents with shame and anguish. The last few years of the family's life had been made a misery by the choices of the little bastard. It was not good enough for him to make a living through hard graft. He wanted affluence, and fast. He started work as a junior in the lower ranks of a cartel that functioned in the capital. The kid had been a courier and had ridden his scooter into a chicane set up by the paramilitary police. Had been arrested, and been relieved of ten kilos of pure uncut cocaine powder. Had gone into the communal cell at La Modelo, and Pablo winced at the thought of what might happen there to his kid brother. He had been spotted by an agent of what they called the Administration who would have been trawling through new prisoners to identify some who might be useful. He had gabbled out to the agent where his parents eked out their last years: irrelevant . . . Had spoken of an elder brother who lived in that useless backwater of a town, Leticia: a chord struck, interest piqued. A military helicopter had flown the agent from Bogotá and had landed him in the compound of the community hospital. He had sat astride the pillion of a Honda bike and been driven away into the night to a lock-up garage at the back of Pablo's bungalow. Not a negotiation, not a matter of haggling as it would have been over the price of paint.

'Quite simple, my friend. Easy for you to understand what I have to offer,' Pablo had been told. A cigarette had hung from the side of the man's mouth. He spoke with a calm American drawl and seemed unconcerned at the matters he spoke of. 'Your little brother is in a bad place, my friend, and I would not like to contemplate his future until he has aged, lost his looks, and the passage between his cheeks is no longer tight. Luckily, for him and for you, I happened across him. It is possible that – for very specific information – I might find the time to intervene on his behalf and see to it that he gets a gentle ride, and is soon at liberty. That's one side of the coin. The reverse of the coin is that I do not have the information that is important to me and I do not have the time to get the kid a better outcome. You are with me? Not too difficult to understand?'

'What do I have to do? What information?'

The smoke from Nikko's cigarette kept the insects at bay. Pablo had had to strain to hear him, he spoke so quietly. 'The information I need is exact and particular. I don't want shit. Fuck with me, Pablo, and the kid has a hard time of it. Cooperate with me, it is possible that he might one day see the light of day. I don't do charity, Pablo. I do deals, and I rely on honesty in return. Your kid brother would wish you to comprehend the terms of what I offer. You are following me?'

'What must I bring you?'

He had been told. He had been given contact codes. He had been handed a mobile phone that was programmed to transmit only text messages and with only one number loaded. A last drag on his cigarette. He had been shown a photograph of what he was told was a similar craft to the one about to be built on the river bank downstream from the town. The cigarette was thrown away, then stamped on. 'You do not deliver, I do not deliver. Understand, I could intervene in mid-build, any day I want, and could catch a crowd of little guys, but I'm hankering after bigger cats. They're not here, they're way down river, far from here. So ... This is good, my friend, because I want to know when the big splash happens in the river and you want your kid brother to get clear of that gaol. My word is my bond ... Keep thinking of the boy and where he is. Been a pleasure to meet you.'

A quarter of an hour later Pablo had heard a helicopter go low over the town, almost above his home, and veer away into the night. He had been told the next morning that a woman in the San Rafael hospital was enduring a difficult birth and had been airlifted to a larger medical unit, and people seemed satisfied with that reason for an army Huey flight coming in during darkness. He had looked outside his garage before setting up his stall in the market and had found the crushed cigarette, half smoked, a Marlboro Light. A week later he had started his regular vigils on the river bank and reported on the phone given him ... and each time he was there, and the fear began to merge with terror, he would try to imagine what his kid brother, the idiot, might be going through.

The rain was torrential and the cloud ceiling seemed barely above the caps of the trees. In front of him, mostly masked, the work had intensified. More noise, more clamour, more shouting. He thought it must have been a tractor that had dragged the shape out from under the protection of the roof. Next came a torrent of men carrying packages the size of the sacks used for cement, but he could not see clearly, not enough to satisfy him that he had fulfilled his obligation to the American who called himself Nikko. Had to perform the duty or the kid would remain in the cage at La Modelo, where old men would want to penetrate him. He went even closer. It was about family blood and family responsibility, and he moved closer still. He crawled on his stomach, prising creepers and low branches aside, and tried not to curse the insects hovering around his face, or the thorns snatching at his clothes.

He saw the tankers' pipes had been detached, the fuelling finished, and the trucks reversing away. All done as a military operation. Ladders against the hull and men on different rungs, taking the packages and dropping them down through the hatch: he saw the way that the men buckled under their weight and realised that several tonnes of cargo were being loaded. He recognised faces. One from the bank where he lodged money every week, precious little of it. One from the police, traffic section – a joke in Leticia because there were so few vehicles – who had gained a good discount from him for paint, avocado colour, to decorate his home. And another stallholder who had ordered three tins of magnolia for freshening the interior of a parochial hall. He needed to go closer because the mosquitoes had bitten around his eyes and they were swollen and his vision was poorer. It had rained each day of the last nine, and each night, and was worse than he could remember.

A small branch snapped under the weight of his right hand as he pressed down to lever himself closer. He had almost reached the line where the foliage finished and the cleared space started.

He had not noticed the branch until his weight rested on it. It made a sharp crack. Would have been a half-centimetre in diameter ... he might have eased from his path, just that evening, a hundred branches of that size. This one had broken. He froze, and thought he was rewarded with luck. The knots in his shoulders loosened. The loading continued, the armed men strutted in front of him, laughing and smoking, and the tractor had been driven off to the far side and he saw two men in dark boilersuits being hugged and kissed: he assumed them to be the crew and knew it was very near the time that the beast, all gleaming metal, went down into the water. He would see it engulfed by a wave of mud-brown water, would watch it go out into the river, would send his message to the man, from the Administration, would turn around and head back the way he had come.

He heard a little high-pitched squeal and a snort of breath. He decided he would say that he had drunk too much beer – the Costeña label – and had fallen asleep on his porch and the mosquitoes had found him. That's what he would say to the other stallholders in the morning to explain the state of his face. The squealing was in his ears, and warm breath was panting on his face. He thought it was a rat. Only the black caimans of the crocodile family could keep the number of rats along the river bank under some sort of control. He lashed out at the creature. It screamed, and he felt teeth fasten on his hand, needle sharp, and he could not free them. A moment of agony coursed through him, and the craft was moving down towards the waterline and torches were following its progress . . . He had struck a puppy. Its mother came fast. The bitch was snarling, and heading for Pablo, and the dogs on the wires took up the frenzy, and the men with guns turned away from watching the hull, moving on tree trunk rollers, towards the dark expanse of the water.

The bitch found him and only then did the puppy loosen its teeth from his hand, and more dogs came, and torches. The craft went into the water and a rippling wave surged across the width of the river. He had the phone out, and tried to read the screen and to hit the right keys. Just needed the one word. *Launched*. Should try to add something about his brother, and the validity of the deal struck, but the bitch had a hold of his shoulder and was dragging him towards the cleared ground. He thought he had pressed Send, did not know if he had, and lost his grip on the phone. A torch shone in his face and alongside the beam he would see the short barrel of a rifle, and more men came running. The bitch was pulled off him and kicks began to land on his head and shoulders.

A voice called out, "That you, Pablo? What the fuck are you here for?"

Another voice. "A spy. What else? A fucking spy."

He was lifted, sagged, then stood. He was punched and then clubbed across his head with a rifle. More men came. Perhaps they were distracted, perhaps the major moment was behind them, the launch into the river; perhaps it was surprise at finding him there – Pablo, the poor cretin who sold cheap paint off a stall in the market each day. Perhaps it was confusion based on his

sodden appearance and his puffed and damaged face. Perhaps . . .
There would not be another moment, that he knew. He turned in
a quick swivel movement, stamped his feet and lifted his knees,
and tried to charge away back into the undergrowth. The dogs
came with him. He thought they did not shoot because of the
dogs. He was stumbling, slipping; they were jumping clear of the
branches and the vines, and birds scattered above them. The
torches from behind showed him the way towards the river and
the ground dropped. It was a game for the dogs. The shouting of
the men dinned in his ears. If they had hold of him they would
interrogate him, torture him. After they had tortured him, and
gained the name of Nikko from the Administration, they would
kill him. After they had killed him they would go to his home, the
bungalow where his wife and children were, and they would burn
it and then set light to the garage where he stored his paint. He
heard a blundering pursuit, had only a few more metres to fight
through before he came to the sodden bank and could slither into
the water.

There was much that Pablo did not know.

That a minimum sum of one million American dollars had
been budgeted for the building of the craft.

That the total weight of the cargo was four tonnes.

That the street value of the cargo, pure cocaine powder, would
be in excess of 300 million euros, a currency he had never seen
nor heard of.

That the craft was starting its journey to the mouth of the
Amazon river that was 2980 kilometres away, and then would
attempt to cross an ocean and sail another 6000 kilometres.

Knew only of the deal done with Nikko and the presence of a
stamped-out cigarette to prove they had met. He loathed the
drugs, detested the agony they made in his life, hated them for
where they had put his kid brother.

He slid into the water. The dogs gathered on the bank and their
barking was raucous behind him. Away to his right he could see
the outline of the craft, a shadow on the deep brown murkiness of
the water, and could hear the engine engage and smell the foul

belch of the diesel fumes. And he went under. He kicked and struggled and panicked and floundered, and imagined the circling piranha and catfish, and thought a black caiman would soon find him and they could grow to five metres in length and had wicked jaws. The rain spattered on the water around him. He could barely see, and for the last time – and with a prayer in his mind – he went under.

The craft passed, and the river swirled hard against him and he saw the name of Maria Bernarda painted on the hull. Then Pablo's consciousness failed and the last sensation he was aware of was the churn of a propeller driven by a modern 350 horsepower diesel engine. He sank, gulping river water into his lungs, and no longer had the prayer in his mind or the image of his brother.

I

The wind was in his face. There were not many mornings, as Jonas Merrick maintained his schedule and crossed the bridge over the Thames, that the damn wind was not blowing. One more morning when his raincoat was plastered against his back and he needed to have a firm hold on his trilby.

He was shovelled along by the gusts and felt uncertain on his feet. Out on the mid-way spans of Lambeth Bridge the memories came hard and bad. Truth to tell, an expression that his wife, Vera, liked to use, his recall of the matter of the bridge and his fall into the water, his near-death experience and his ultimate rescue, was never to be erased from his consciousness. Jonas had been 'loaned' by his employer, the Security Service, to its rival and senior organisation, the Secret Intelligence Service – as welcome as a cuckoo in a songbird's nest – to root out a traitor in their building, a leaker to the hostile Russian agencies. He had succeeded, had identified the miscreant, and in a foolish moment of vanity had dispelled his image of boring naivety, and had handcuffed the guilty party to his own wrist as they approached a discreet welcoming party of detectives from the Branch. Totally unexpectedly, she had seemed to face a death wish who had plunged over the bridge balustrade, and taken him too, throwing him down into the cold, dark, strong and hideous current. All more than a year ago and still as fresh as the previous hour.

It was his habit to walk from Waterloo station along the embankment beside the wall of the Archbishop's Palace and then turn sharp right and, using the bridge pavement, face his destination. The bleak, grey stonework of Thames House was where he would end up each weekday morning, and in the late afternoon,

punctually enough to set a wristwatch by, he would reverse the
trek and stride out for the station and the crowded commuter link
to his home. He did not have to walk. He could have taken a bus
over Westminster Bridge and walked past the House of Commons,
or he could have taken a taxi each way. He walked because he
always had done and prayed God that he always would. Protection
was now offered only on random days. If that Friday had been
chosen, by now the first part of his escort would have peeled off.
Sometimes they were in uniform, sometimes obviously armed,
sometimes drifting along behind him in 'civvie' dress. He
approached the high point of the bridge, and always quickened
his stride to reach it. Could not really help himself, same every
morning and afternoon, every crossing. He would look away from
the pavement, from the traffic lanes and from the safety of the
parapet and balustrade, and would peer down at the water. Often
he would lose sight of oncoming pedestrians and bump into them
or get in their way. Sometimes he was cursed, sometimes snarled
at: he never apologised. Jonas Merrick never apologised for
anything or to anyone.

He gazed down at the water. The wind buffeted him. He held
tight to the handle of his faded and water-damaged briefcase that
was linked by a fine chain to a handcuff bracelet on his right wrist.
He wore the same coat that he had worn that weekend morning
and the same brogues, and the lifeboat team had fished out the
same hat which had lost a little of its shape, and he had on the
same jacket and the same trousers. Vera would turn up her nose at
them, complain they still stank but had not binned them. On his
right wrist, close to the bracelet, was the white scar where the
police-issue handcuff fastening him to that woman – called herself
Frank, had a lowly rank, but total access – had dragged away a
ring of skin when they had gone down together into the river.
Then must have had a second thought about dying in the cause of
a faraway motherland. Might have reckoned, with icy water
swamping her, that Czar Vladdy's regime was only worth living
for, not dying for. Had changed her mind, and had heaved him
up, fastened him to a rope dangling from a moored barge, and

had made her farewells. Always saw her face, quite calm, and to
hear her voice – 'I had a good run, enjoyed it, walked all over
them. Goodbye, Mr Merrick.' Had rather liked her, had rather
admired her, and all his own fault anyway for wanting the vanity
bit of planting cuffs on their wrist and leading her towards the
cage.

It never seemed good, the water flowing beneath the arches of
the bridge. Cruel, mysterious. That morning a little tug boat was
pulling a line of barges weighed down low by a load of gravel. He
shivered, had cause to, and kept going.

He saw Kev and Leroy coming towards him. Nobody barged
into them. Nobody swore at them, was sarcastic, complained if
they got in the way. Both had H&Ks in their hands and Glocks in
holsters bouncing on their thighs, and gas and flash-bang grenades
hooked to their belts, and both were huge in vests that were
supposed to be proof against low-velocity bullets. Always, if they
were on shift, they came a little across the bridge to meet him and
then walk behind him as he completed his journey. There would
be light conversation: the weather usually did the business. Some
2000 men and women, from a kaleidoscope of races and ethnic
origins, worked in Thames House, and none was brought by
escort to the bridge's median point and then handed over to the
care of other guns . . . only Jonas Merrick.

He had been parked in a backwater. Little was expected from
him, and he would be out of harm's way.

Her body had never been found upriver or down towards the
estuary. Not all bodies were recovered but the Thames gave up, in
time, most of those who had gone in and drowned in the foul
water. It was possible that she, 'Frank something', had survived.
Possible, but not probable. But a difficulty *if* she had made it out
of the river. Quite a big difficulty. A difficulty that would have put
Jonas Merrick's life in the cross hairs. Two men from Czar Vladdy's
'elite' GRU assassination team, on a mission into Denmark to take
down a defector had, with Jonas the puppetmaster pulling the
strings, been killed by British 'irregulars'. He always let a sneer
play at the sides of his mouth when the word 'elite' was used,

thought it exaggerated and seldom an adequate description of incompetence . . . but dead, they were. That pretty young woman with the gold hair and the starched blouses would have known that he, old Jonas and past his retirement age, had done the necessary, been the facilitator.

Pack the job in? A flat refusal.

Move house, go into hiding? Not considered.

Close protection? For a few days, then withdrawn. But he was seen off the train some mornings and into work, and back again in time for the 1739. That, with a poor grace, he accepted.

Kev and Leroy watched him carefully. Both had seen him go into the water, both had thought him lost. Both would have blamed themselves without having cause to.

"Morning, Mr Merrick."

No familiarity. A curt response. Jonas seldom showed warmth. "Morning."

Kev suggested there could be a shower before midday, and Leroy believed it would get brighter in the west, and the wind was expected to drop.

"Have a good day, Mr Merrick."

"Will try . . ."

Actually, he rather enjoyed the backwater into which he had been dunked. He went for his coffee and pastry in the café by the side door of Thames House. The backwater into which he had been put was crime. Jonas was off counter-terror, withdrawn from counter-espionage, and concerned himself now with OCGs. The *Organised Crime Groups* had swallowed his interest. That morning he wolfed down his Danish, gulped his coffee, and hurried to his desk because a tasty little business was coming to a completion. Enjoyable, most certainly.

Jonas took a lift to the third floor, walked along the south-facing corridor, went into Room 12. The surveillance people had the room and he was left with a cubicle in a corner, a locked door and frosted glass to screen him. Facing him were a rogues' gallery and a large-scale map that showed land masses at the extreme west and extreme east and otherwise was ocean, but he ignored those. On the wall in front of his work surface, above his computer screens, was a soft-focus blow-up that showed a youngish man – slept-in jeans with worn knees, a crumpled T-shirt, a light-weight windcheater, a gaunt and pale face with a week's growth of beard and tousled hair – who leaned against the door jamb of a corner shop. Seemed to be a busted wreck of a young man, all ambition gone, and maybe waiting for his next dose of brown, or some smack. Jonas took off his raincoat and hung it on the hook below the one holding his trilby, detached his briefcase from his wrist, and took out his lunch box and a thermos for later. He switched on his computer and sat while it ground through its wake-up.

Jonas looked up, smiled as if to a friend, said softly. "Morning, Kenny, hope you slept well, had a good night."

Low sunshine blistered on to his face.

He blinked to clear his eyes and coughed to free up his throat, then sharply shook his head as if to rid himself of his mind's confusion.

Where was he? Why was he there? Most important, who was he?

It was a ritual that needed doing every morning, and was better performed alone. He could hear her in the kitchen, bare feet slith-ering, and a kettle starting to scream. Started to find answers – and who was she? More blinking and more coughing and more shaking his head and the answers came and the boxes were ticked. He arched his back, yawned. He heard cupboards opening and closing, then the clatter of mugs being set down. Did he want milk? She had a prim voice, tutored with the help of a language school but her idioms were flawless and she owned that confident – arrogant – gait of the Dutch, and he was long down the road from merely liking her. Yes, milk but no sugar.

Where? Easy. In a renovated cottage, once part of a cattle barn, on the outskirts of a village on the Atlantic shore. Rented it – one bedroom, a good living space with a kitchen at the back, a bath-room, and a patio with views across the harbour and then the expanse of the sea. The place was Camariñas and the outlook was over the *Costa da Morte*, and he hoped that the cottage brought him only to within touching distance of death, but no closer.

She carried two mugs from the kitchen.

Why? Always important in his circumstances to wake and get those damned questions answered, not to slip head over heels before he was alert. He was there because of his work. The work was in the main city of the region, Corunna ... Never did count the tourist trap of Santiago as the principal place with its hotels that fleeced visitors who had come on pilgrimage or to gawp at old churches. Corunna was almost 50 miles away and he did the round trip three or four times a week. He was an investment advisor. A grand title. Here, he was called an *asesor de inversiones registrado* – important to be 'registered' which gave a ring of honesty to what he did. In uncertain times, where pitfalls were littered to trip up the ignorant, he took savings and placed them where they were safe and could be relied upon. Had been there just over three years and had put together a respectable portfolio of clients, mostly with small sums, some who had believed in him sufficiently to place larger amounts that they needed to safeguard from the scandalous greed of the tax authorities, and a very few who needed the full washing machine treatment.

He pushed himself up and his shoulders were high against the bedhead. She wore nothing. None of her own clothing, nor any of his, not even a towel. She walked towards him and held the mugs firmly and did not slop any of the coffee, and did not have to step over or around any discarded underwear thrown off in a hurry. Not that sort of an occasion. All rather orderly. Everything folded neatly. His were in a stack on a hardback chair by the window, his shoes placed together on the floor. Hers were on the lower chair and lying on the cushions. Done slowly. She had started to strip off in that way, carefully, no shyness, and he had followed her example. There would have been in Corunna or Santiago plenty of celibate monks who knew what it was to have purposefully tied a knot in it: this was the first time since he had come to live in the Galicia region that he had shared the bed, old and with ferociously noisy springs, with a girl, with a woman, with a friend or with a lover, and both of them stone sober. 'They', his crowd, were advised against 'relationships'. They were warned of complications. Top of that list would be speaking, half awake, of a dream or a nightmare and then having to offer an explanation, or of the pillow talk when queries were dripped in an ear while fingers played on the lower stomach. 'Better not to,' the psychologists urged, 'better to just go and take a cold shower, alone.' No regrets and he thought her brilliant. Brilliant and important. He took the coffee mug. She sat beside him, made no effort to cover herself with the rumpled sheet.

Who? The time of maximum danger was on waking. The 'where' and the 'why' could be fudged, not the 'who'. Had to have in place who he was that day . . . bad times ahead if the legends became knotted, twisted. Seriously bad times if he were living the identity that he had cast off before travelling on the slow ferry across the Biscay and docking at Santander, or the one he had perfected before that, and worse than bad times if he slipped back into the times when he knew his own name and so did everyone else who knew him, at school and at work, and his parents – and his wife, and his son and daughter. Had to scrub them out. She was looking hard at him. He felt the coffee slurping over the mug's rim and was sprinkling across his stomach, and more of it glistening on the pendant that hung on a chain around his neck. He was 29 – which was a constant in all of the legends – and was unmarried and not tied down, and she'd said that she was two years older and had no ties, no complications . . . Not a one-night stand, not an occasion on which lifestyle journalists laid down behavioural rules. He thought there was a possibility that it was a relationship with legs – needed one, and thought he deserved one – and that it could go places when the matter was closed down, curtained off, and he had moved on. When he had ditched the legends and the deceits, had handed in his card, had cut the links. Big stuff for him to think of and the coffee had scalded his stomach. His work would likely be done by the end of the coming week, and then it would be time for a fast exit. He pulled a face, grimaced.

"You all right? I have that effect on you, that you tremble?"

A limp smile. "I'm good. Fine. You know, waking, getting bearings. And another dull day lining itself up . . . The coffee, thanks."

He was beyond allotted time anyway, and should have been withdrawn months earlier, had been almost ready to leave with all the attendant complications left hanging. A quiet voice had come through on his phone, with a tinniness that meant it played through the scrambler connection, so quiet that he had to strain to listen with the mobile clamped to his ear. He thought it an old man's voice, and he had been told that he was staying in place, not a request – just told. And work had started to fidget for his attention and only for a few more minutes could its demands be delayed, which was a bastard. Reasonable to assume his long-time control officer had been by-passed and was now outside the inner loop of the new regime handling him. He grimaced, like that was a nervous tick when he lied. And the week, he predicted, would come fast, always did at the end, would stampede, be hard to keep abreast of: with the lies came danger.

"Promise?"

"Very good – and thinking you very special."

She laughed, more of a chuckle, and used her hand to wipe the coffee off his stomach. Then kissed him lightly. "And I am happy that you said it, Kenny."

Like a well manufactured cobweb, fine lines stretched out across an ocean, across a continent and half the length of a country. At the heart of the web, in the cubicle inside a work area designated as 3/S/12, devouring information and coordinating action, an elderly man played the part of a spider.